Jumpback

Terry Hayman

Fiero Publishing

For my wife and kids, who teach me each day about character
and courage.

Contents

The wound

2003

A TRANS AM DRIVES in through the open bay door of the auto chop shop and growls to a stop just short of the two mid-size goons thudding their fists into my big brother, Kenny.

Those guys look up, distracted. So do the two bigger goons holding me from behind. I use their temporary distraction to yank myself free, but the Latino goon, a guy with a goatee and spider tattoos, grabs the back of my pants. Then the other one, a bald, thick-necked white monster of a man, flat hands me on the back of my head before he grabs me by the collar of my sweatshirt and pulls me up to his snarling face.

I'm gasping. Burning up with the heat and struggle. It's blazing hot outside. Worse in here.

At seventeen years old, I'm almost six feet, with great cardio from all the running I do on the track team at Lindbergh High School, just south of Seattle. But none of that helped when I showed up here to beg Kenny to leave this street gang and come home. Even less when the gangsters jeered, threw rags and empty oil cans at me, then started slapping and kicking me back and forth between them. Finally, two of them started beating up Kenny while Goatee Guy and Flat Hand trapped my arms to make me watch.

Stupid to come here. I shouldn't have come. Had to come.

The Trans Am's motor cuts. Its door opens, and everyone turns to look. I see who climbs out and swear under my breath.

Cutter.

It's not my name for him. They actually call him that. Kenny pointed him out to me once as someone to stay away from, and I've never forgotten because, like Kenny and my big sis, Kansas, I don't forget anything. The Traine family memory—an endless set of full boxcars.

But I'd never forget Cutter anyway because he's like some kind of nightmare king rat. He's mid-twenties but shorter than I was before I hit my growth spurt. A raggedy mustache and long, greasy black hair pulled back in a ponytail are the nicest things about him. He's so emaciated that I'm pretty sure he's hooked on the same crack as Kenny. Or he could be a meth addict. I read that methamphetamine has a longer half-life but is harder on the body long term, destroying your teeth and gums, giving you skin infections and acne, lung and liver damage. Cutter's got at least the acne and bad teeth.

And all of that somehow adds to his scary power. I feel it when he sees me and grins. Then he flicks his index finger, and Goatee Guy to my left runs and hits the button to close the bay door.

The door rattles down, shutting out the afternoon light. Everything becomes a surreal orangey-yellow from the caged bulbs overhead.

"Bring him closer," Cutter says to Flat Hand, the guy who still has the collar of my sweatshirt bunched up in his fist.

Flat Hand lets go of the front collar of my sweatshirt and grabs the back of it instead, then makes me stumble toward Cutter before Cutter redirects him with that index finger toward Kenny. The thugs who were beating Kenny have now hoisted him up by his arms and seated him on a metal chair, holding him upright. They're by a concrete wall lined with waist-high cabinets and shelves loaded with greasy tools and car parts in battered cardboard boxes. Kenny's normally long, strong face is all bloody, and his eyes are staring and blinking like he's only half there. I can smell his blood and vomit as the sleeve-tattoo guy brings me to a halt a few feet away.

I register that the only reason they've hauled Kenny up off the floor is because Cutter is here. Which means, I think, this is about to get *really* bad. Kenny's eyes are glazed. He's breathing roughly through his bloody nose and mouth, but I'm not sure he can see or hear anything that's going on right now. His brain might be swelling for all I know.

I fight back the panic that rises in my throat.

All those other times I managed to pull Kenny out of bad places? They were just flukes. What was I *thinking?* I've made things a hundred times worse by coming here.

I jump when Cutter suddenly snickers right beside me. Probably on some kind of signal, Flat Hand turns me to face Cutter himself and pushes me down so I'm on my knees. Cutter is about six inches taller than me now. This close, my nose isn't far from his armpits. He's all rank and sour, like I imagine a rat would smell. And his acne, on his drawn, older face, makes his skin look all greasy and crumpled.

He grins his rotten-toothed smile at me like he knows exactly how his appearance affects people. "So you're getting to be a bit of a fucking problem," he says.

"Me?" I blurt.

"Talking with your brother, making him think he's got somewhere else to go."

"But—"

His bony hand is so fast it takes a second to register that he just slapped me. Then it stings like my skin's on fire, and I can taste blood in my mouth.

"See it's that lack of respect you got for me, for all of us," Cutter says. "It infects your brother a little every time you see him. Like a virus."

I open my mouth to speak, remember the slap, and freeze.

Cutter waits a second, staring at my stupid, open-mouthed face. "What do you want to say? Go ahead."

Speaking in a voice that, even to my ear, sounds like a sniveling five-year-old, I say, "I just want him to come home."

Cutter doesn't slap me or laugh. Instead he gets serious. "Problem is, kid, your big brother's way in debt to us. Bone deep. Which is a problem when an organization is trying to grow, you know? So we gave him a chance to work it off. Making deliveries, bringing in some friends, and pledging his *loyalty* to us. You see how going home with you would fuck that up?"

Before I can speak, he holds up a hand.

"Unless *you* want to take over his debt."

That stops me cold, and I can feel my eyes go wide as my brain explodes with the possibilities—hope and terror and trying to figure out how I can contact my parents because they're in Idaho right now, or maybe Indiana, and they're both horrible at keeping their cell phones charged because they like doing business with their franchisees face to face, but maybe... "I could... If you give me a day or two. How much...?"

Cutter's upper lip rises in a kind of sneer that's twenty times worse because his gums are all mottled and pulled high above yellow teeth. He shakes his head. "You don't get it, kid. His debt's not just money anymore. He went way past that. He owes us his soul. We own him and ain't never gonna give him up. Unless..."—he raises his eyebrows and voice like he's explaining to me a magical one-time offer—"you want to trade us *your* soul, *your* loyalty. Join the Demon Monks as a junior soldier, and maybe we can let your big brother just go home like you want. What do you say?"

My mouth has dropped open again. I can feel ice racing through my arms and legs, my chest, neck, head, mouth. That's why I can't talk, right? Just that. I'm frozen. I should talk. I can't talk. My jaw is quivering. How can I be such a coward? Kenny saved *me* lots of times when I was younger. He's my *brother*. He's... But if I...

Cutter breaks out in a hissing and grabs me by both my ears, shaking my head back and forth. "Time's up, kid. No way we're letting your brother go for a pansy smartass has to think that long."

He throws me aside and turns to my brother. "Heyyyy, Kentucky!" he calls.

And this is where my insides go from ice to a kind of churning panic. Kentucky. Only Mom and Dad call him that—Kentucky like the state, where they conceived him. Our big sister is named Kansas. I'm named Jackson, as in Jackson, Mississippi. It was like our parents named us that to remind us we were born somewhere other than here, so we had to stick together. Especially since our parents are almost never around, always traveling. But then Kansas left for college, Kenny's manic depression started taking over, and he turned to street drugs from these assholes...

"Kentuhhh-cky," Cutter coos again, like he owns him.

Like he can do anything he wants to him.

Almost like he's read my thoughts, Cutter nudges me and grins with his tongue between his pitted teeth. "Nice you got your baby bro' out to watch this, Kentucky. He had a chance to get you free but took a pass, so it's good he gets to see what he made me do."

"No," I beg under my breath.

Cutter backhands me this time, again so fast I don't see it coming. I almost tumble sideways off my knees, except that Flat Hand won't let me go down. He holds me up and shakes me, an unspoken command to keep watching.

Cutter turns back to Kenny and pulls a knife from a scabbard hooked onto the back waistband of his jeans. It's not huge, maybe four inches, but comes to a nasty point. And when he spins it around his right hand, it's clear he knows how to use it. *Cutter.* Of course.

I whimper, too scared to open my mouth.

Kenny, though, hasn't responded to any of this, even though his eyes are still open. His head has sagged forward and he's blinking. Trying to focus?

Pass out, I hear myself wishing at him. *Lose consciousness.*

Cutter steps forward, brings Kenny's useless, sprawling knees together, and straddles them so he sits on Kenny's thighs like a perversely ugly girlfriend. Once upon a time, Kenny looked like a square-jawed, All-American quarterback, six foot two, blond, strong. He could have just thrown Cutter off him.

But now he's almost as skinny as me and loose-limbed, a shell of what he was. Easy to beat up. Easy to sit on. It makes me wonder what it is that Cutter sees in him that makes Cutter need to destroy him like this. Or maybe it's not even about him. Maybe it's about everybody in the gang and me and the world. Cutter has to teach them all that the king rat with the knife *must be obeyed.*

"Grab his hair," Cutter says. "Hold his face up."

The scarier of the two men holding Kenny—the guy is white, clean-shaven, but has dead, light gray eyes with a ragged scar under the right one—stabs his tough-looking fingers into the top of Kenny's dirty, blond mane. He jerks Kenny's face up so my brother's blinking eyes and cheeks covered in blood reflect the yellow glow of the overheads.

"Hold him still now," Cutter murmurs as he brings up the knife and presses the tip into Kenny's face.

Kenny grunts and cries out as Cutter slowly and carefully carves a D on Kenny's right cheek. When he's finished, he starts into the M on Kenny's left cheek, and Kenny finally starts to scream...and scream louder.

My muscles go silly. I want to drop down and hug the concrete, but Flat Hand won't let me. The collar he holds me up by is so twisted around my neck and under my arms now that I'm thinking I might pass out from the restricted blood flow. I wish I had.

Kenny screams the whole way through the M, and I can hardly read the letters through all the blood. His face is just a carved up, gory mess.

Still, when Cutter finally slides off him and uses Kenny's pants to clean his knife, I find enough guts to cry out, "He needs a hospital!"

Like a little kid. I feel my hot face running with tears and snot and can't help it.

Cutter just laughs at me, letting the rest of the goons laugh.

"Oh, don't worry, kid," Cutter says. "We're not going to let him die. 'Specially now he's branded. Only question is whether we let *you* go home now you seen all this."

"I haven't seen anything," I blurt, hating myself the moment it slips out.

"'Cause you know, Kentucky here has this freaky, crazy memory, right? Remembers everything he reads and sees? You like that, too? A little freak with the memory?"

"No! No. I don't remember. I haven't seen..." I sniff, then try to huff out all the snot from my nose like I'm scared I can't breathe. It's partly true, but it's also to gross out Cutter, distract him so he'll forget what he just asked me. Because of course, I *am* a little freak with the memory. My memory's even better than Kenny's. I know this address. I could recite everything I've seen in this chop shop, including the Trans Am license plate, the top license plate stacked near the stripped cars, the eye color and identifying marks of every gang member here, every article of clothing they're wearing, and everything Cutter is saying to me now.

"But you still might just run home and call the police on us, hunh?"

"I won't!" My mouth is dry with terror. Of course that's what I was going to do! So what happens now? Think! I've read *The*

Godfather. I've seen Scorsese movies. But I can't think. My brain's locked up.

Cutter squats down so he's right in my face. "Real simple, kid. You call the police—and we'll be watching you. We'll know. You call the cops and I kill your brother. Slow and painful. Like this was nothing. You get it?"

I jerk my chin down. Of course. Of course that's what they'd do. Of course.

"Say it."

"Yeah. Yes."

"The whole thing."

I reel it off: "'Real simple, kid. You call the police—and we'll be watching you. We'll know. You call the cops and I kill your brother. Slow and...'" I catch myself and cover it by sobbing and trying to blow out my snot to the floor again.

Cutter jumps back and up, close enough to be disgusted this time. He points to the scary guy with the dead gray eyes who's still holding Kenny's hair. Then Cutter looks at me.

Dead Eyes obviously understands, because he drops his grip on Kenny's hair and walks over to me. He waits for Flat Hand to release me, then kicks me so hard in my chest it sends me tumbling across the concrete floor. The pain in my chest is like someone's carving me up from the inside, but my peripheral vision still registers Cutter directing the other three gangsters to load Kenny into the back of the Trans Am, roll up the bay door, and gather up any other stuff they've left lying about.

They're leaving.

I'm never getting out of here.

Dead Eyes is at me again, kicking and punching me again and again so that I can't actually see or hear the Trans Am and the other guys leave. I'm in a world of pain and fear, sure my bones are breaking, my brain's hemorrhaging.

I'm going to die.

I'm going to die.

...

It stops.

My body's a tight, pulsating clot of pain. But what scares me, what makes my testicles shrivel and try to crawl back up inside me, is how everything's dark. Have I gone blind? Did he kick out my sight?

I try to blink and find I can't, and that's a relief. Maybe my eyes are just too swollen to open. Or maybe it's psychosomatic paralysis because my body is totally clenched in a kind of death throe.

At least my ears still work, because I hear a raspy voice beside one of them. I assume it's Dead Eyes.

"Like the boss said, you ever come back here, you ever go looking for your brother, he'll die and I'll kill you."

Then he's gone.

I lie clenched up and blind for what seems like hours before I can move again. My sense of time is all messed up, but I can feel the eyes of Cutter and Dead Eyes on me somehow. And maybe everyone—every classmate who ever reasoned I had to be damaged like my brother, every adult who ever tested my memory and found it freakish—they're all watching me now to see if I'll follow directions for once, like a good little boy, or screw it up, blab, and get my brother and me killed.

Because I failed. Because I couldn't figure out how to get Kenny away from them fast enough, then couldn't step up when Cutter offered to take me instead of him.

I want a do-over, I sob silently at the universe. Let me save Kenny somehow. Let me fix things. Whatever it costs.

And I swear I hear the universe answer back, *Be careful what you wish for.*

1

A face from the past

2021

THEY ALL HATE YOU, Jackson. All your students.

They do not, or they wouldn't have stuck with the course.

You're messing up.

I'm doing fine.

They're laughing at you.

No, I'm *laughing at* you.

I was teaching my first-ever class of students at the University of Washington, fourteen days before the winter quarter exams, and I was handling the mental chatter of my social anxiety and PTSD pretty well today.

True, at this moment I was finding it hard to turn back from my PowerPoint review of COVID-related drug use and suicide to actually face my students again, but I *would.* My studies, my carefully-controlled lifestyle, my self-prescribed desensitization —teaching this class!—were paying off.

I cleared my throat nervously, tried to ignore the sweat dripping under my armpits and around my nose under my COVID mask, and turned.

My class of forty-one upper year students was still there. I knew all their names, class habits, and even where they'd sat on each day of the year, which wasn't as amazing as it sounds since most claimed a favorite seat and COVID guidelines dictated a certain spread across the lower third of the hundred-plus stadium seats.

They were good kids, mixed backgrounds but all smart, here to learn about phobias, anxiety, and panic attacks from someone who was a published expert in the area. That was me. It was why the university had recruited me so soon after I'd obtained my psychology license in Chicago. And the challenge of speaking each week in front of a group of students was why I'd agreed to uproot my private practice and come back to Seattle.

Very bold. Knew my stuff. I could do this. I smiled, opened my mouth, and—

Danger! There is danger here!

I froze.

My heartrate sped up.

I looked down, took a deep breath, but my heart didn't slow.

Okay, apply reason. I didn't know what in my environment had caused this, but I knew it could be almost anything. Something in the room, the way a student was sitting or looking at me. If it triggered the PTSD paranoia that conflated social judgement and physical harm, my amygdala would shoot panic signals at my hypothalamus and...

It didn't matter! Right now, this close to the end of my time with these students, I owed them my best self.

So I pictured my terror loop speeding up into nonsense chatter, high and comical, then made it swirl and get sucked away as I focused on my body, breathed deeply, and recommitted again to my in-the-moment, calm life.

Got it?

Yes.

I raised my head.

"All right!" I called out, to the obvious relief of my waiting students. "Apply what you've learned. We've got someone with an intense, always-there fear of embarrassment, humiliation, rejection. Social anxiety. Has COVID made it worse or better?"

Hands shot up around the class.

I nodded, still breathing deeply, slowing my heart. These *were* good kids. That was the reality. I was grateful for their patience with me.

"Shawna?"

The robust redhead followed her alarming habit of tugging at her mask so she could lick her lips as she prepared to speak. "They obviously like it," she said and let her mask settle back in place. "Because they're supposed to stay home and limit how many people they see, right? Isn't that what someone with social anxiety wants?"

"Good reasoning," I said. "Very possible. Someone else. Carlos? *¿Qué opinas?*"

"Yeah." The short, intense boy looked over at Shawna. He didn't touch his mask before he spoke. "But now they got even more worries when they meet someone. Even an Amazon delivery guy. COVID. Or people crazy from being locked up. Or QAnoners."

"And money!" called out another boy, Mikael. Bigger. African American. Arbiter of all things revolutionary yet deeply compassionate.

That encouraged others to join in. "Changing government!" "Lockdowns!" "Beatdowns!" "Cops!" "Sports shutting down again!"

I let the shouting go on for a minute or two, knowing this was one small way for them to blow off exam jitters and fears about finances, relationships, the environment, and COVID. It was amazing, really, how well they all coped.

"All right!" I said. "But are all these fears and anxieties cumulative? Can they join with a preexisting anxious state? Or are they a separate phenomenon with a different treatment? How would you go about..."

I blinked.

For some reason, my eyes had risen to the shadowed upper back rows of the class where students never sat and...

Someone sat there.

A new student. No, not a student. A man in his...forties?

He sat slumped low in his chair with his face half covered by his long, dirty brown hair, his scraggly beard pressed into his chest. No mask. He wore a battered, patched-up tan military jacket over layers of stained, filthy tee-shirts and a pair of patched-up jeans, like he'd been sleeping outdoors.

How had he slipped in? Was he homeless? Seattle's relatively temperate climate attracted scores of homeless, particularly after how hard winter had hit the rest of the country this year. They were everywhere.

But then he became aware I was looking at him and raised his head. I felt myself go cold and dry mouthed as I looked into his dead, light-gray eyes, a scar under the right one. I knew him. It was the man who'd held Kenny up by the hair when Cutter had carved him. Dead Eyes. The man who'd then beaten me half to death and whispered the threats in my ears that made me abandon my brother.

"Professor?"

The unfamiliar female voice dragged my eyes further to the right, a few rows down, and I saw that, impossibly, another unfamiliar body had slipped in. But I could barely focus on her, other than to notice she was older than my regular students, vaguely Middle Eastern, beautiful even with her mask on, but...

A sudden sound near the classroom's entry door jerked my gaze that direction, and I saw Dead Eyes slipping out.

Focus found.

"That's all we're doing for today!" I barked out. I flicked off and disconnected my laptop, shoved it into my leather satchel, whose strap I slung over my shoulder and neck, and turned back to the class. "Read the last chapter of the text. Last two classes we review for the exam. Mikael, please wait around and close the lights and lock the door on the way out."

Then I sprinted up the steps between the first and second columns of stadium seats, ignoring the muttering and looks of my students, avoiding the gaze of the beautiful mystery woman who'd called on me, even as I crazily imagined I could smell a waft of her perfume on the way up the stairs. Maybe her soap. Maybe just my imagination.

I lunged out the door at the top and looked around wildly. Thought I saw a pair of dirty jeans and the back flap of an army shirt duck around a corner down the hall.

"Hey!" I called and ripped off my mask, stuffed it in my pocket. "Wait!"

I needed to know why he'd come. It couldn't have been to punish me. Not after all these years. I'd never talked! It had killed me all through the months of my parents searching for Kenny, and the later news that suggested he was dead. I'd said nothing.

So I continued my pursuit again, driven by my guilt and my anger. Because what was Dead Eyes *doing* here? Did he have some kind of guilty conscience after all these years? He should have! Did he want to tell me how Kenny died? How it was his fault? Not my fault. His fault. All their faults.

"Hey!"

I reached the corner, screeched to a halt, and peered carefully around it, suddenly scared. Because what if someone *thought* I'd talked? What if they'd been biding their time all these years until I'd come back to Seattle and someone had seen me. Had reported me.

Then I had to tell them I never talked. Right?

Danger!

Yeah? No shit. And more if I just wait around for...whatever.

There was a new short stretch of empty hallway, then an intersection. I swallowed dryly, clutching my satchel to my side. I had no idea which way the different halls went, where the stairs were, where they came out. This was Bagley Hall, where administration had only moved my class a week ago. Not where I usually taught. I'd never explored this part of it.

Listening for all I was worth, I thought I heard feet thudding down stairs somewhere ahead to the right. And behind me? I ran for the sound ahead of me and tore recklessly around the corner, but there was nothing there. All these halls were deserted, like most of the campus seemed deserted much of the time. A frigging COVID ghost town.

I backtracked. Ran down a different hallway. Found some stairs. Ran down them to a door leading outside.

When I oh-so-carefully slipped outside, Dead Eyes, if he'd ever even come out this way, was gone.

Shit.

And it was raining.

I swayed back and forth, clutching my satchel hard against me, my heart pounding. My jaw and fingers trembled violently. A part of me worked through Dead Eyes' actions and concluded that whatever had brought him to my class, it wasn't to actually interact with me or he'd have done so.

But it *felt* like he'd interacted. Because now all the panic and guilt that came from losing Kenny and running from my own shadow for over a decade were wracking my body.

My stomach tightened. My skin crawled with a nameless terror.

The counseling sessions I'd done in university and during my internship, the cognitive-behavioral tricks and mindfulness and lifestyle they'd advised, all my own research—they usually worked to give me good control in social situations...until an unexpected environment or an asshole like Dead Eyes triggered my PTSD and shot things all to hell.

I was heading toward a full-blown panic attack and shook my head hard against it.

No!

Breathe!

I sucked in a deep breath. Another. I focused on how the March drizzling rain pattered off the stagnant water of the Drumheller Fountain, where the actual fountain never seemed to be on.

Dead Eyes.

No! Focus on the pretty woman who dropped in on my class. What was that all about?

And breathe.

Again.

Better. Good distraction, the woman. I'd talked to few women socially since coming back to the West Coast. In fact, Jude Spiegelman, my roomie from Illini, meaning the University of Illinois Urbana-Champaign, sometimes called UIUC, had been calling me about this repeatedly for the last month. He was worried about me. He knew he was the only real friend I had in the world right now, outside of my big sister. There just weren't many people who could handle the deep level of my mental dysfunction. Just Jude. And my big sister.

Without them...

"Professor?"

I jerked around to see Mikael standing in the cold rain about six feet away. He was a big youth, over six feet and built like a football running back. Square jawed. Fierce eyes. But now he was carefully keeping his social distance and holding up his hands like he was trying to calm a skittish animal.

That would be me.

"Mikael?" I said. "You got the room locked up?"

"Shawna locking up. You doin' okay?"

I cleared my throat, running a hand back over my wet hair, struggling and failing to meet Mikael's eyes. This was simple social anxiety—fear over what this impressive young man thought of me. "I'm...fine."

"You know we here for you, right? All o' us. You just gotta reach out."

I nodded, still not meeting his eyes, fighting the swelling of tears in my own because, despite bringing myself back under control with thoughts of my best friend and sister, and despite my ability to teach and comfort and reassure anxious clients, my subconscious simply *did not believe at a fundamental level* that it was safe to reach out to others for help. Not when my memory held onto such clear moments of human evil and the pain it brought.

"Yes. Yes, thank you, Mikael," I said. "I appreciate that, but I'm fine. And I need to go now. Thank you."

I oriented myself, turned left, and without once meeting Mikael's eyes, began threading my way between buildings to get back to my office in Guthrie Hall.

Much later, I'd wonder if I had reached out to Mikael then, maybe just managed to go for coffee with a few of my students, would it have short-circuited my reactivated guilt-fear loop and changed what was to come?

Or were the next steps of my journey so preordained that I couldn't have changed course if I'd tried?

What do they call that?

Payback.

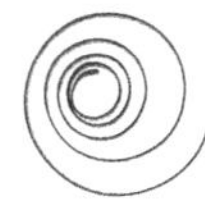

I dallied on the way to my campus office, lost in a mental turmoil of self-doubt and memories. Mikael, my other students, they couldn't know what I had gone through before I'd reached their age. The awful choices I'd made the day they cut up Kenny and the days that followed. How I'd failed him.

I was soaked to the bone by the time I arrived at Guthrie Hall and took the stairs up to the third floor.

My door was unlocked when I arrived. Odd. I rarely forgot to lock it.

I got even more of a shock when I stepped in and found someone waiting for me. The mystery woman from the lecture hall. Even half-turned from me, sitting in the oatmeal-cloth seat I kept in front of my desk, I could see her olive skin, brown eyes, high cheekbones, proud nose, and wide, full lips. Persian heritage? Israeli? She stood up and smiled, and again I got the synesthesia-like experience of smelling fresh air and floral perfume just from her appearance. Like she *should* smell wonderful because she looked that way.

But she wasn't wearing a mask. I wasn't wearing a mask. This was so wrong.

I was too discombobulated to get farther than that. Neither of us offered to shake hands, of course. I just slicked back my wet hair and goggled at her, my mouth hanging open.

Finally I got hold of myself and flushed with acute embarrassment. Clutching my soaked leather satchel to my side, I half stumbled around her and my desk until I reached the safety of my chair and sat.

"I'm..." I began. Then I realized I was still clutching my satchel, so hard now that my knuckles were turning pale. "Um... excuse me."

I carefully put down my satchel and pulled my laptop out of it. Still relatively dry, thank goodness. I grabbed a towel I kept in my lower drawer for just such Seattle weather emergencies. I wiped the laptop dry with careful deliberation to give myself time before looking at her again. Finally, I set the laptop on my desk and sat, as did my guest. I didn't keep a separate computer here. I just lugged my laptop with me everywhere I went—to class, to this campus office, to my counseling office, to my rented apartment and its oh-so-comfortable bed.

I looked up to find my female guest watching me and blushed to think she might somehow know I was picturing my bed, then seeing her.

"Um, I'm sorry. I shouldn't stare, and..." I pulled my office mask out from the right-hand drawer and pulled it over my mouth and nose, but I didn't take my eyes off her as I did. Her hair, I noticed, was not only gloriously thick, but curly brown with auburn highlights, and in this rainy weather, a bit of a frizzy mess. I unconsciously ran my laptop towel over my own slicked-back hair, my face, my neck, before I noticed what I was doing and dropped the towel back into my open lower desk drawer.

The woman's hair was parted in the middle but bounced thickly around her shoulders, one side pulled back behind her ear. I didn't dare scan down to see what her body looked like, even though I was aching to.

I had a flash of Dead Eyes staring at me, Kenny screaming, then Jude laughing and telling me to chill, to stay in the moment. Be here now.

My guest gave a half smile and pulled the hanging side of hair back behind her other ear. "I hope you don't mind," she said, pointing to her mouth and licking her lips. "I was in one of the early vaccine trials, and I still get tested monthly. Lots of antibodies. No discernable viral load despite a confirmed exposure two weeks ago. I usually wear a mask inside and in crowds outside to reassure people who don't know. I can put one back on if..."

"No, no, no, please," I said and took off my mask. I'd had my first dose last week. Then, "Do you know me somehow?"

"We've never met," she said at last, and I felt myself thrill to the sound of her voice. That self-assurance again. It reminded me of my sister, Kansas, and of my mother. And she was wearing virtually no makeup, I realized. A touch of eyeliner? Some blush? Not that she needed anything. When she smiled, there was just a hint of wrinkling around the eyes and that uncovered, generous mouth that shouted, *I'm alive!*

"I know that. I'd remember," I said about having never met before. "Eidetic memory."

"Good to know. But you're probably wondering why I was at your lecture and why a staffer let me into your office to meet you."

"Yes. *Yes.*"

"Well, Professor Traine—"

"Jackson."

"Jackson. My name is Doctor Lena Cortland. I teach physics and do research at Berkley. My specialty is elementary particles and fields."

She'd given me her title, which meant *Respect me*, and both her first and last name. Out of courtesy because I'd offered my own first name? Or was it an invitation to choose how I'd address her? A test?

My normal bubble of social anxiety began to rise again. I was usually able to suppress it in one-on-one meetings when the roles were clear, like in my psychology practice, but this beautiful woman's full name and title threw me. How to address her? A challenge. I felt my face grow red and my hands started to sweat.

She seemed to understand and said quickly, "Call me Lena, please. And I'll call you Jackson. Just two colleagues, okay?"

The rush of relief made my eyes water as I looked at her and she did me the honor of accepting that without looking away. She simply nodded and continued.

"I'm here in Seattle because one of the tech companies here offered to sponsor some research I'm doing and insisted it be done here."

"Which company?"

She smiled. "It's not Expedia, Big Fish, Zillow, Remitly, ExtraHop, or Getty Images."

"Ah." I stared at her blankly. "Is that supposed to tell me something?"

Still the smile. "Do you know the names of *any* big tech companies here?"

"Um...Microsoft."

"And...?"

I frowned. It was an area I rarely paid attention to, but I'd obviously read about it somewhere because an answer popped out. "Amazon."

"Two for two." She laughed. "Now, fair's fair. Do you want to ask me what famous psychologists or psychiatrists live around here?"

"I don't know who the best are, but if you want the most famous..."

"The point is I only know of one."

"Who? Marsha Linehan?"

She laughed again. "I have no idea who that is."

"Then who... Oh."

"Jackson Traine."

"I'm not exactly famous."

"Give it time."

During this exchange, I had managed to subtly (I thought) sneak a glance at her body as she laughed and shifted in her chair. The simple cream blouse and gray slacks she wore didn't reveal much but promised enough that I forced myself not to look again in case I got caught staring. The shame I could probably live with, but I'd die if I gave this woman any reason to regret coming here.

"I looked you up," Lena continued, apparently oblivious to my struggles, "because I came across your paper on clients you've worked with who seemed to believe they've lived past lives. Other lives."

"Past life regression," I said. "Back in Chicago. My first year fully licensed. I was answering the paper by Dr. Gabriel Andrade that weighed the therapeutic benefits of how hypnosis is usually used to make people believe this fantasy against the downsides of doing so."

"What downsides?"

"Lack of informed consent for starters, since the patient is consenting to undergo a procedure that purports to do something there's no solid evidence for—traveling in his or her mind to a supposed past life."

"But—"

"And even more troubling, not informing the patient of the potential risks, such as forming false memories that become part of his or her psyche and may impact not only their life but the lives of others."

Lena frowned. "Like people who falsely remember child abuse."

"Yes. There seem to be rare cases of a person forgetting childhood abuse and remembering it later, but most abused children don't forget, even if they don't understand or share what happened. But you still get some therapists, hypnotists, or well-meaning laypeople who think they can help bring back 'repressed' memories and end up helping their patients 'remember' things that never happened."

"You don't believe in repressed memories?"

"Like I said, *rare* cases. On the other hand, there's loads of evidence showing how we can create false memories in people. Elizabeth Loftus made her career on it. You don't have to look far to see that the human brain has immense abilities to believe in things that aren't there or never were. Sometimes such beliefs can comfort people and give them hope. Other times, like when whole communities are torn apart by children being persuaded to recount tales of their preschool providers performing sexual acts on them as part of a satanic ritual, not so much."

I looked down. The real abuse in the 1980s and 90s "Satanic Panic" cases had been by the so-called specialists brought in to question the children. Even mentioning it caused an automatic roiling in my gut because of course this kind of craziness never went away. Witness Pizzagate and QAnon.

Lena obviously saw that and waited a few moments in respect before asking, "So how did you guard against that with the past life regressions you did?"

I swallowed a sour taste and fingered the wood of my desktop. "I had some success with hypnosis when I first started my practice. I helped people stop smoking, lose weight, and find better ways to deal with their anxiety."

"Even their social anxiety?"

I grimaced, assuming she'd figured out my own struggles. She was uncomfortably observant. "I had three different prospective patients approach me about past life regression therapy, meaning hypnosis that would help them believe they were remembering an earlier life they'd lived. I agreed to do so with each of them as long as they agreed we would both treat it as an exercise of imagination, a way to explore who they would have *liked* to have been, and how that imagined life might help them understand who they are now. And who they might become."

"Were they struggling with gender dysphoria?" Lena suggested.

"You've been doing your research. One was trying to get over her childhood sexual abuse. One was struggling with having multiple people in his life die within an eighteen-month period."

"So what happened?"

I looked at her. Really looked at her. And I understood she was asking me not to have me tell her what happened. She'd obviously read my paper in which I described the experience. Which meant she was what? Trying to understand why I'd done it really? How it had affected me?

"I never did so-called past life regressions after those three," I said and let the sorrow and disappointment and anger at my own folly register on my face. I'd *known* the dangers of what I'd done. And even with the warnings I'd given and the agreements

I'd extracted from my patients, I had, in my judgement, made two of their lives worse for the experience.

"It hurt you."

"It hurts me to hurt other people. Yes."

"And to fail, even when you did your best."

I tilted my head, looked deep into her eyes, and suddenly had a flash of fear. Did she somehow know about Kenny? Was that what this was really about? She was secretly tied to Dead Eyes and whatever the Demon Monks had become. She was luring me into talking with her beauty and...and her incredible mind. It was no coincidence she and Dead Eyes showed up the same day.

My face went rigid, and I was suddenly glad of the desk between us, though this room was far too small for me to feel safe.

"What are you doing here?" I asked.

I saw her eyes cloud over in confusion at the change in me. She blushed with the kind of sudden embarrassment you get when you see someone has turned against you, that you've made some grave error. "I told you," she said. "I'm interested in your experience with past life regression patients."

"Why?"

She started to speak and stopped, too flustered to be acting, clearly not some kind of hit woman, maybe only exactly what she'd said she was. Which meant *my* reaction right now was just my PTSD paranoia, something I regularly told my anxious clients to guard against.

I turned from her to collect myself. When I turned back, she'd pulled a business card and pen from her purse and was writing something on the back of the card.

"Look," she said contritely, "as much as I'd love to just tell you everything right here, it's too big a thing for that. I also have a meeting I have to get to. But I've written the address where I'm doing my work on the back of my card. Plus a security code. Don't lose it. Show it to the guard at the gate, and use the code to get into the building. Please come. Let me show you what I'm doing. It will explain everything."

She reached over my desk to deliver it.

I was amazed that with all the pain and paranoia she'd stirred up in me, I still wanted desperately to apologize. To give us a chance. I felt the warmth of her fingers as she held on a moment before letting the card go.

But you're not allowed to be attracted to women, Jackson.

Jude says I am! My therapists…

They're wrong! Kenny's dead. What about him? You have no right.

Survivor's guilt. It's just survivor's guilt.

I held up the card. "When?" I asked. Shorthand for when should I visit the address she'd just given me.

"Tomorrow," she said, understanding perfectly. "Anytime between six a.m. and ten p.m. would be good."

Then she stood and walked to the door.

I jumped up to open it for her, but she was out and walking down the hall before I could reach her.

Watching her go, I marveled at how upset I was that I hadn't gotten close enough to see if she smelled as lovely as I imagined. Which only added to my wonder of how strongly she affected me. Yes, she had the confident intellect of my mom and sister, with a beauty completely different and worlds above either of theirs. And a sense of humor. And she seemed to see my anxiety and not hold it against me. She even seemed…attracted to me. The hair preening. The smiles. The moment with the card.

Given my general inability to nurture any romantic relationship before now and the general emotional dysregulation caused by Dead Eyes' appearance, there was no way this was going anywhere.

But I still whispered an apology to my dead brother, Kenny, and began Googling how early I'd have to start to get to Lena's workplace by 6:00 a.m.

2

Jump back

THE DAY'S EVENTS AND a ferocious nightmare about Kenny woke me up in the middle of the night with my heart racing. I was up for hours before I finally slept again and didn't wake up until nine. That killed the six a.m. plan. I had back-to-back clients at ten, eleven, twelve, and one. No time for yoga or my usual run through Interlaken Park or even a short one through the smaller, closer Volunteer Park.

I made the mistake of playing a YouTube news clip as I pounded back a quick breakfast of porridge with fruit, nuts, and yoghurt. It was more follow-up on the January 6 insurrection at the Capitol. More footage of the right-wing Trump supporters smashing flagpoles into Capitol police officers, using pepper spray on them, breaking things, chanting about hanging the vice president.

Their faces reminded me too much of Cutter's. And Dead Eyes'. And Flat Hand's. The Demon Monks might have been motivated by money and power, the Trumpists by lies and ethno-nationalism, but the delight they all took in violence, breaking the rules... There was a commonality between the gangsters and the so-called patriots of January 6.

I shut the news clip off in disgust, showered, and drove my sky blue Chevy Bolt the eight minutes it took to reach the office space I'd rented near the bottom of Washington Park. Five months ago, when UW had recruited me from Chicago to teach a two-times-a-week course for the winter quarter, I'd flown out here immediately to find a place where I could also relocate my counseling practice. And this place near the bottom of Washington Park had seemed to be in a sweet spot between the rich neighborhoods of East Roy and those on the Lake Washington waterfront but also close enough to downtown and the university that anyone in need there could easily get to me.

The evidence so far said I'd been right.

After a gradual startup, helped by social media networking and generous word of mouth from former colleagues and clients, I now had as big a client load as I wanted to carry. I'd even had to hire a part-time psychometrist to handle testing and administrative duties.

I found it all invigorating, I reflected, as I walked past the elevator and climbed the single flight of marble stairs in the padded hush of the building. Especially my clients.

I pulled on my mask as I entered the even-more-hushed reception area of my office, all wood panels and broadloom. I nodded to my psychometrist, Megan, and led in my first client, a woman who'd really been coming out of her shell in the last few sessions.

Because the sessions were all about the *client*—I was just the catalyst, the listener, the guide, the coach—my anxieties rarely flickered here. The wonder of being able to help people as I wish I'd been helped so long ago swept me into a state of flow that took me through this client and the three who followed her.

After I showed my last client out at two o'clock, I scanned and filed my notes for the day's sessions, typed in additional comments, then reviewed with Megan the personality and career-aptitude tests she'd administered and scored the day before.

I was out of flow now, so the mental chatter started again, hopeful this time.

Now? Now? Can we go now?

Not yet. Food.

Keeping my mask on, I jogged down the stairs and splashed across the street to the amazing Asian-themed salad takeout there. Defying the tough business climate of the pandemic, it had opened up almost concurrently with my own practice and was flourishing. It seemed like a sign that I, too, was in the right place at the right time to flourish. I'd escape my ever-recurring guilt and fear of judgement and actually find happiness. I'd train myself to interact normally with people other than clients in a natural, spontaneous, open, and loving way.

I'd become whole.

It hadn't happened yet, even with my adjunct professorship giving me regular social exposure practice. But I would keep trying. Focus on the now. I was in the shop.

I selected two types of fresh tuna for my proteins and asked Izumi and his wife, Hiroko, to add brown rice, sliced cucumber, chopped kale, imitation crab, avocado, julienned green onion, tomato, grated seaweed, and the takeout's special sauce, medium spicy. The smells of umami and vinegar, the salty crunch of the seaweed, and the anticipation of the burst of tuna and rich comfort of the avocado had my mouth watering as I pulled out my wallet to pay.

And out popped Lena Cortland's business card.

"Ahm," I grunted involuntarily as I caught it and stared at it, my body suddenly consumed with an entirely different hunger.

Which didn't negate the first.

I paid for my amazing poke bowl, stepped outside, and dug in with my chopsticks, watching cars, pedestrians, and bikers pass me, avoiding everyone's eyes. The cloud cover overhead suddenly broke and sun spilled down the street, making the rain-slick pavement glint and glitter like it was embedded with thousands of diamonds.

Another sign—the good food, the sunshine, the card of a beautiful woman popping out of my wallet. My life was turning a magical corner.

I could feel it.

I changed into an aqua green sweater that my older sister had once told me flattered my skin tone and brought out my eye color and drove east, crossing the Evergreen Point Bridge. I worried a bit when the address I'd keyed into my GPS took me out past Redmond, heading into the twisty roads of the mountains. Not a lot of electric charging stations in those hills. It would also be a really easy place to kidnap me if Lena really was associated with the Demon Monks after all.

Except the more I'd turned the Demon Monks angle over in my mind, the less sense it had made. Dead Eyes had looked wrecked, doing his own odd thing, while Lena was 100 percent a scientist. The probability of her being a gangster wasn't zero but pretty close to it.

Any niggling doubts I'd had were laid to rest when I reached Lena's business park address and an ATS Security guard who was definitely not a Demon Monks kind of hire looked at my card, then let me through the gate. The sun hadn't completely set. The days were getting longer.

I rolled past a warehouse and three nondescript concrete buildings with small windows before I stopped in front of Building #4.

Pulling out Lena's business card again, I double-checked the address on the back, pulled on my mask, and left the car to walk to the building's blank, metal front door. I keyed in the entry number, entered on the buzz, and walked to the only visible door, an elevator.

Inside it, I had to enter the code again, and the elevator began rumbling *down*. And down. And down. Clunked to a stop.

The door opened with a ding.

I stepped out into what, even through my mask, smelled like an antiseptically cleaned basement. But it had a thirty-foot ceiling over a swimming-pool-sized room, with walls covered in pipes and cables and vents and metal rigging. Even more disconcerting was I'd entered onto a gray metal walkway that was a third of the way up the wall I'd entered through. A bright red set of rails with a DO NOT CROSS sign guarded me from spilling down ten feet into the concrete pit directly ahead. Down there, covering most of the floor, were dozens of interconnected child-sized white metal pods, backed by more pipes and gauges and wires, as well as an open area that held an overturned plastic bucket and mop and a chest-high rolling tool chest.

And running in a big rounded square around the room's circumference, like some kind of mad scientist's small-animal race track, was a silver ring of interlocked metal cages. They looked five feet tall and deep and were strung together with curling red-coated electrical cable on bolted-down cylinders. Inside them, taking up maybe the lower third of the space, ran a glassy-smooth metal pipe.

Foot-thick concrete walls ran around the outside of this track and rose up to the level of the metal walkway where I stood.

Most eerie, though, was the silence. Apart from a faint hum that I assumed came from one or more of the bright fluorescent light ballasts on the ceiling, there was not a whisper or appearance of another life form. I was it.

I took off my mask and stuffed it into my pocket.

As I did, a clang made me jump. I looked to where it had sounded and some wildly curly auburn hair came crawling out from under a set of pipes near the far wall—Lena, now dressed in form-fitting blue coveralls, her hair pulled back in a thick ponytail, her face smudged. She saw me, smiled, and waved.

"You made it!" she said.

"I did. Where am I?" I replied.

"You haven't seen pictures of something like this?"

"Maybe in a movie?"

"Hunh."

Lena walked the crescent wrench she was carrying back to the rolling tool chest, pulled out a drawer, and tossed in the wrench. She rattled the door closed and turned back to me.

"Come on down here," she called and pointed to some stairs to the right of the door that I'd missed.

I reached for my mask, then remembered I didn't need it around her and just boldly went for the stairs and descended. It felt like I was entering the boiler room of some futuristic battleship. A vaguely burnt-plastic smell greeted me down at floor level. From here, the ring that ran around the circumference of the space looked like it could shoot some kind of current around and around it until it powered up and shot its destructive force out of...where?

"The long gray boxes over there," Lena said, apparently reading my mind and pointing. "It's called a beam stop. It's where the electron stream is siphoned off after most of its energy has been retrieved."

She stepped over beside a chest-high box with a lot of switches and screens. "But this is where it all starts. This is where we power everything up and inject the electron streams." She pointed to the nearest child-sized pod. "Most of those puppies power the electromagnets, which work with some other stuff to separate, condense, and recombine beams to keep them all on track as they go around and around. Then that set of gray linked boxes, the main lynac cryomodule, accelerates the beams and later strips them of their energies to syphon them off into the beam stop. That was Cornell's innovation."

"For...what purpose?" I asked.

"Well!" She raised her eyebrows dramatically. So fine and clean, her eyebrows. "Traditionally, particle accelerators basically speed up particles to near the speed of light, then smash them into each other or some kind of target to create different kinds of subatomic particles. We study those and learn about how the universe works. Also useful for materials science, cancer research, that kind of thing."

I heard the excitement in her voice. "That's not what you're doing with this one, is it?"

"No." Her eyes sparkled. "Here we're creating controllable closed timelike curves. Like a black hole that creates a fold in space-time." She waited for me to catch up. Finally gave in. "We're sending photons back in time to collide with themselves."

"Back in time..."

"Like some Australian physicists proved was mathematically possible five years ago."

"Time travel. But...a photon. That's just a piece of light, right? It can only go so fast."

Lena waved her hands and stepped close to me, putting her hands on my chest. The warmth and intimacy of it made it hard to hear anything but my heart as she went on excitedly. "Except we found something new. There seems to be a simpler kind of time travel that exists when a wave becomes a near-perfect replica of its earlier form in every quantum. It seems to create a superattraction through the energy of spacetime, with like drawn to like. We started manipulating the exact quanta of photons and saw them vanish. And as we started developing our ability to do these manipulations, we started measuring individual photons at release. Right here where we flicked a switch to turn it all on"— she pointed to the box beside her with all the switches—"we measured a near-instantaneous flicker between release and acceleration in which the photon subtly changed its total quanta signature to the ones we'd later create."

I frowned. "Is that, like, something quantum mechanics predicts?"

Her hands went to my face now. Her hands were hot. Her face was flushed. "No! That's why we're testing and retesting! This is... a whole new paradigm in physics. It might prove string theory, maybe embedded universe theory. And suggests that maybe all those patients of yours? The ones with past lives...?"

There was a scuffling sound behind us, and we both turned at once toward the elevator door.

It dinged open and a man in a sand-colored camo jacket sprinted out, looked, saw us, and tore down the stairs like a rabid dog with an eerily blank face.

Dead Eyes.

I instinctively jerked back just as it became clear that Dead Eyes wasn't going for me at all. In fact, his shoulder slammed me out the way as his hands grabbed Lena's right arm and yanked her back against him.

Dead Eyes' left arm snaked under her arm around her chest. His right hand was up against her throat with a short, gleaming knife. Shorter than Cutter's knife had been that long-ago afternoon. This one was maybe one and a half inches. Still deadly.

I felt faint. The violence. Life attacking. My nightmares in the flesh. It was happening all over again.

"Stop it!" I yelled, shifting from foot to foot, wishing I sounded stronger than a pathetic seal.

"Just don't move, man," Dead Eyes said and sniffed. "In fact, sit down. Right there. Like a good little hipster."

My face flushed at the wildly inaccurate characterization as I sat, shamed by my hopelessness, my lack of manliness. Except the insanity of it was almost too much, pushing to the edge of panic, then past it to where there was only... *Fuck it all. He'll cut her throat if I just sit here.*

I can't. Just. Sit here.

"SIT BACK DOWN, MOTHERFUCKER!" Dead Eyes yelled as I climbed back to my feet and his knife drew blood so that Lena cried out, too.

My eyes found Lena's and saw her terror. I couldn't even feel my own legs and wondered if I'd pissed myself, but I made myself growl at Dead Eyes, "What do you want?"

"Fuck it. Okay. Good," he said, sniffing and grinning. "You and her, you're both coming with me."

"Where and why?"

He barked a laugh at me. "Not your fucking business, dipshit!"

"It is if you want our cooperation." It sounded fake even to my ears, so I spoke louder, almost shouting. "Otherwise, what? You stab her? Then me? Then drag us both up the stairs to the elevator one at a time? That's not a good plan!"

Dead Eyes frowned, shaking his head, his energy making his arm around Lena tighten and his knife hand shake. My eyes never left him, but my peripheral vision saw Lena's eyes shift from terror to determination. Despite Dead Eyes' arms around her chest and throat, her left arm was free. She reached it back behind her, waving her fingers around. For what?

Her fingers brushed the chest-high box with all the screens and switches. They start up the accelerator, she'd said. A distraction. Yes! Anything!

Dead Eyes bared his teeth and spoke with a frightening intensity. "Okay. Okay. Here's what happens, you piece of shit. You do what I say, or I slit your *Moo*slim girlfriend's throat. Yah! Then I cut off your fucking nose and drag just *you* up the stairs. So put your fucking hands on top of your head before I count to three, or—"

Lena grunted and twisted. Her left hand hit the switch. A loud clanging hammered down on us from overhead. Then it got lost under the thrumming whine that rose around us like a giant electric monster had just woken up. The metal boxes that circled the room hummed and lit up with a growing rush of lights until it seemed an electric sun god was rushing around the ring— *THRUMMM!*—trying to break out but condemned only to fly so fast in circles that only a god at its level could even see the movement.

Dead Eyes looked around him crazily, his knife jerking away from Lena's neck, his grip shifting on her torso.

I leapt at him.

I managed to grab his knife hand and drove him backward, away from Lena, until we both thumped hard against a set of man-tall metal boxes that were bolted to the floor.

Lena was running for the rolling toolbox, but I shouted at her, "No! Get out! Get help!"

She froze, unsure what to do.

Dead Eyes took advantage of my distraction to rip his knife hand free and swipe at me, gashing my right shoulder as I stumbled sideways toward the humming ring of metal boxes. I smelled the blood from my shoulder but felt nothing through my rush of adrenaline.

I kept my feet as Dead Eyes advanced on me, waving his knife, his dilated, flat eyes focused now like they were seeing me stabbed over and over and bleeding out on the floor. Oops, sorry, he'd tell his boss. The prof didn't make it.

He leapt at me with his knife out, and I jumped backward, tripping and falling hard, with my hands behind me, against the thrumming cage of the electric sun god. My hands convulsed into talons against the steel as I felt an overwhelming force rip through me, battering my mind, my chest, my belly and groin, my jerking legs.

Death. Death. From the moment I walked in here, I was ....

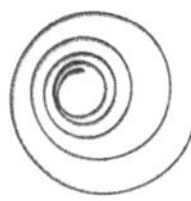

I stood on the gray metal catwalk, momentarily disoriented.

"Come on down here," said Lena's voice.

I looked past the red metal guardrail with DO NOT CROSS painted on it and saw her. She was in her dark blue jumper, with her curly auburn hair pulled back in a ponytail, that smudge across her cheek, no blood on her neck. I looked to my own right shoulder. No gash. No blood.

Lena was pointing to the stairs to the right of the door. They led down from the catwalk.

"Well?" she said.

In a daze, I slowly walked to the stairs, gripped the red handrail hard, and descended to the concrete floor below. *Like the boiler room of a futuristic battleship. And the ring around them…*

I looked at that metal ring now. Silent. Just cold metal. No electric sun god thrumming inside it.

Lena had been returning her crescent wrench to the rolling toolbox. Now she walked back toward me and waved her arms around to indicate the metal ring with all the wires that ran around the room. "You know what this all is?" asked Lena.

"Particle accelerator," I mumbled.

She raised her eyebrows. "Very good. For a boy who doesn't know his Seattle tech companies, I'm impressed."

"Modelled after the one in Cornell."

"Wait. How did you know that? Are you secretly a physics nerd?"

"And that panel to your left. That's where you start it up and shoot photons into the ring."

"Okay. I'm impressed. Yes."

"Which would normally be to study cancer and stuff, but you're studying time travel."

Lena frowned now. I didn't like her frowns. But I also didn't like having no clue what the hell was happening to me. Was I dreaming? Had whatever happened when I hit the accelerator knocked me into some kind of coma that had me recreating my last memories?

"What time is it?" I asked. "And the date."

Increasingly agitated, Lena pulled out her phone and glanced at it. "Five twenty. March third. Why?"

"I think I'm dreaming. I think it's probably more like seven o'clock, and I'm in Redmond Urgent Care. Or maybe I've been transferred to UW Medical already. I'm in a coma and dreaming."

"You're not dreaming," Lena said angrily. "I asked you to come and see a *highly secret* project that I've been working on with a team totally zip-lipped with NDAs, and you just walked in knowing all about it. How?"

"Exactly," I said. "It's not possible. Therefore, I'm not here. When confronted with an impossible scenario, head trauma is the most plausible explanation."

Lena stalked up to me and gripped me by the arms. "Listen to me, Doctor Jackson Traine. This is not an hallucination. You are not in a coma. You are here with me at my invitation. How you suddenly have knowledge of what we're doing here, I don't know. But this is real."

"Prove it."

She furrowed her brow at me, then stepped up close, grabbed me on either side of my face, and pulled my lips down to hers. The kiss was warm, soft, but urgent. Desperate almost.

When she pulled back and looked at me, I realized my breathing had accelerated, and my body seemed flooded with more warm blood than I'd known I possessed. My lips were tingling. My hands were tingling. My groin was responding so fast it was embarrassing.

For what seemed like minutes we just stood together like that, staring into each other's eyes, then I breathed, "That's…"

"Nice? Real?"

"Unexpected. I know you're vaccinated and all, but…why?"

"Fastest way to wake someone up."

"You've tried it before?"

Now it was her turn to color. Her cheeks actually became a dusky rose, and her eyes blinked furiously as she moved her hands from my face, down to my arms, but still not stepping back. "Not...like that. No."

"Good. I guess."

"Very good."

"Okay."

"You?"

"What? Oh, the kiss? You're asking me if I've ever... Not like that. Certainly not in a very long time. Years. But..."

"Good," she said and smiled.

We were still standing toe to toe, almost groin to groin, except that I was a few inches taller. Which made me realize just how tall Lena was. She had to be at least five-nine, since I was just under six feet. And so warm. I could feel her body heat through her blue overalls. I could feel the light pressure of her breasts on my chest.

I shook myself and took a step back, instantly regretting the loss of contact but knowing I had to clear my head. "It doesn't change the impossibility of what's happening here."

"Which is what?" Lena said, matching my seriousness. "You know about something you couldn't possibly know about."

I shook my head. "That's not it. It's how I know. I've done this before."

"I thought you just said you hadn't. At least not like this."

"Not the kiss. That was new. Delightful. But...entering this place. Seeing you appear from behind there somewhere and invite me down to tell me all about your research and what you're doing here, what you think you've discovered."

Lena was looking at me very strangely, and I found myself wondering again whether I was in a coma. Because this was exactly the type of sad, social anxiety dream I'd have in a coma—meet a beautiful woman, say stupid things to her, and have her realize I'm clearly demented or stupid, someone she made a huge mistake being nice to.

And again Lena apparently read my fear like I was an open book, which was terrifying. Except her response wasn't to laugh at me about it. It was to put a warm hand on my arm and rub it up and down in comfort.

"Okay," she said calmly. "Some kind of déjà vu is happening. We'll figure it out together."

I again felt a rush of gratitude, but just as quickly my mind jumped forward to what else had happened, and I jerked back from her, looking up at the door where he'd entered. "Someone else came in!" I blurted.

"What do you mean? There's security on the front door and security on the elevator. You had to punch in the code I gave you. Remember?"

"How long were we talking last time? Never mind. You invited me in, asked me questions, explained your theories. Showed me stuff. Pointed it out, so..." I looked about the room wildly, recreating it clearly in my mind. Knowing *exactly* how it had gone down now that I accepted it had. Because my memory was like that. Me and my sister and brother. Kenny had always laughed at how easy it was to pass tests in school as long as you read the material or listened in class. The answers were always right there.

And the answers to this test were right here for me as well. The facts, at least. What had happened. What I'd experienced. But putting them together in a way that made any real sense was...

There was a scuffling sound and dinging from the elevator door, and I turned to see exactly what I expected to see.

Dead Eyes. Wearing the same wrinkled, tan battle jacket he'd come at us in the last time.

He leapt down the stairs and ran at Lena.

Against every normal instinct I possessed, I stepped in front of her and swung a fist wildly at Dead Eyes, who took it on his raised right forearm with a look of surprise but didn't slow down. His barreling body hit me and drove me back against the same bolted-down, tall, metal box I'd driven him into the last time. My head snapped back, hit metal, and I went gray for a moment.

When I came fully back to consciousness, Dead Eyes had his one arm around Lena's body and the second up around her neck. Knife out. "Back the fuck up and sit down, hipster!" he barked at me.

Receiving the same strange insult again made me want to laugh. It was like some crazy joke time loop. And maybe it was that very craziness that short-circuited all the normal fear I should have felt, because I had no inclination to back up or sit down. None. I danced back and forth in front of him and Lena, noting that she was too far from whatever buttons she'd pressed last time to turn on the particle accelerator.

Which meant this was all up to me. I had to tackle Dead Eyes without having him stab her. Because Dead Eyes didn't *want* to stab her, did he? The last time, he'd talked about bringing both Lena and me to see someone. So if I just rushed in now...

"Don't even think about it, fuckface," Dead Eyes said, pulling the knife right up to Lena's skin, pressing it in so tight a ribbon of blood formed along the edge and Lena cried out.

That should have brought me back to normal, too, but my adrenaline was raging in me. If I'd just grabbed Kenny and run years ago! If I'd just leapt at Dead Eyes the first time he showed up! No more hesitations! No backing down! My body was a go. My mind was a go. *I* was a go.

I roared and leapt.

And as I did, time seemed to slow, because I saw everything in hypercrisp detail.

My body arced toward Dead Eyes and Lena.

Dead Eyes spun away from me, carrying Lena with him, and dragged the knife across her throat as he went.

Lena's eyes went wide as her blood ribboned out into the air.

I hit the floor, wishing, almost like my gut was sucking the world into it, that I had one more chance to—

3

Gotta be a way

I STOOD ON THE gray walkway with the red guardrail in front of me, DO NOT CROSS painted on it in bright yellow. My face mask covered my mouth and nose, and I felt disoriented, sweaty, my head swimming, my stomach churning.

I tugged off my mask in the silence and breathed in the smell of some kind of antiseptic cleaning solution. Then I heard a clanging sound, and Lena emerged from behind a set of pipes near the far wall. She walked, a smudge of dirt on her forehead but otherwise beautiful and unharmed, past the rows of child-sized pods she'd told me powered the particle accelerator's electromagnets and stopped near the control box.

Her thick, curly hair that turned frizzy in the rain was pulled back behind her head in a thick ponytail, and she was looking up at me with her beautiful brown eyes and half-smiling mouth.

"You made it!" she said.

I nodded my head, fully clear again. Fully present.

Without waiting to be asked, I hurried down the stairs to the concrete floor and walked over to her. I wanted to take her in my arms but knew that wasn't appropriate. She didn't know. In this time stream, if that's what it was, she hadn't kissed me yet or faced death with me. Maybe we'd recreate the kiss sometime, but I was perfectly happy to avoid the facing death part of our experience.

Committed to it, in fact.

I couldn't be sure I wasn't in some kind of strange, looping, coma dream, but I was pretty sure that if I didn't treat this as real, the outcomes were just going to keep getting worse.

"Jackson?" Lena said, obviously reading my momentary indecision.

"You're right," I said quickly.

"About?"

"Particles that are in almost perfect synchrony with their earlier states feeling a superattraction to those earlier states. They can travel to those earlier states."

"Wait. What?"

The look that shot across Lena's face now was a kind of terror, flipping to confusion, then revelation and an even deeper kind of fear that rode on a crazy, bubbling excitement. I was amazed I could read it so quickly. Except that I'd been going through the same kind of wild emotional journey over my last two trips. She was just smarter than me. She applied logic to the impossible and came up with the miraculous.

"You," she said. "You're not some kind of foreign spy who's been tracking our research?"

I shook my head.

"No. And you didn't meet some colleague of mine who drunkenly spilled the beans?"

Another shake.

"Which means you did it. Because I was going to tell you all of that today, and you already know it. You've been here before."

"Yes."

"What happened?" She saw the look on my face. "What happened here, Jackson?"

I pursed my lips. "You turned on the particle accelerator. I... interacted with it."

"And what? Other than maybe electrocuting you, there's nothing that—"

I held up my hands. "You know what? We'll discuss it later. We need to leave. Now. There's a man in the building, or who *will* be in the building shortly, who somehow has the codes to come down here, and he does. And he's dangerous and wants to kidnap us. It doesn't work out well."

She looked into my eyes, saw the darkness, and nodded. "Okay. Let me just collect a few things and we'll go."

There was a ding as the elevator door opened and Dead Eyes lurched out, way ahead of schedule and now brandishing a pistol.

Shit.

"Hello, crazy science geeks," he drawled through his patchy beard. "It's collection time."

His hair was as greasy as his clothes were filthy and slept-in, I noted. Like he slept on the street. Like a homeless person? Mentally disturbed? No. His sniffing. The dilated pupils. Drug addict.

"You're early," I said, waving Lena to back away from me.

"Sitting on top of the elevator and listening, hipster. And I don't know how you knew about me, but I guess you can tell that to the shot callers. They just loooove squeezing answers out of pretentious assholes like you. Stop right there, sweetie. I'm taking both of you."

"We'll spit on you!" I called up. "We've both got COVID."

"Fuck off. She's on a vaccine trial, and I've been following you. No symptoms. Now get up here. Both of you."

I knew how *that* turned out, so no. "Where are we going?" I stalled. "To see whom?"

"You don't know? Not so smart after all." Dead Eyes aimed the pistol at us, and his eyes took on that seeing-us-dead look. "Come on up *now*, or I start shooting."

My bravado slipped away, and I was about to walk when Lena suddenly stepped to my side, leaned in close, and furtively pressed the crescent wrench she'd been holding into my hands.

Right. She hadn't had time to put it away this round. "I'll distract him at the top," she whispered.

I slipped the wrench into my back pocket but whispered, "Don't mess with him. Just...do what he says."

She gave me a disappointed look, and I felt about two feet tall. Or maybe four years old, standing in front of my father, trying to explain why I'd wet the bed. And I suddenly wondered, *Did my social anxiety start that far back? Was I* always *afraid?*

Then Lena marched ahead of me to the stairs so I had to hurry to catch up. Near the top of the stairs, I was horrified to see Lena had lowered the front zipper on her overalls so it was nearly at her breastbone. She couldn't honestly be thinking...

She was. As we reached the gray walkway, she turned to Dead Eyes and put herself between him and me. "You know," she said in a husky voice. "I could show you what the accelerator does. There's a reason Professor Traine 'interacted' with it."

"Give me a break," Dead Eyes said. But his eyes still flicked down to her cleavage.

When they did, she grabbed for his gun arm, shoving it to the side so that I could have a shot at him. And against the screaming orders of every emotional brain cell I had in my head, I whipped out the crescent wrench and swung it at Dead Eyes' head.

It barely clipped him but was enough to stagger him backward against the wall, dragging Lena against him as she wrestled for the gun. Then Dead Eyes' free hand had Lena by the hair the same way he'd held Kenny all those years ago. But not to hold her head still. With a roar, he twisted his body and thunked her head against the concrete wall.

She went instantly limp and slid to the floor.

"No!" I yelled and leapt to grab her, tripping over Dead Eyes and hitting the metal walkway with my knuckles that were still curled around the wrench. I felt something snap in my hand and wrist.

But before that pain could register, my peripherals saw Dead Eyes whipping the pistol at my head.

I jerked away, and it clipped me no worse than I'd just clipped him with the wrench.

I scrambled up to my feet, and *then* the pain of my broken right fingers and wrist hit me like a series of crackling bombs. I howled and my vision started fogging red. But I wasn't blacking out. I was going over the top with a fight-or-flight response that was clearly set to *fight*.

"Asshole!" I shouted. I shook my head to clear my vision and squared off with Dead Eyes, who was also back on his feet.

"Yeah?" Dead Eyes ran his left hand over his head wound and swore when he felt the blood. "Fuck you!" He turned and shot Lena. Once. Twice. She never even twitched. Might have been dead already.

I roared and leapt at Dead Eyes as he aimed at my chest and fired...

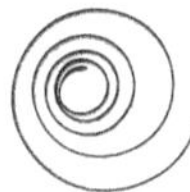

This time, I was in the elevator, going down. Wearing a mask.

I stumbled a little as I pulled it off and stuffed it in my pants pocket. My legs had gone all funny and I worried I was going to collapse. My chest hurt. My head felt like it was splitting open with pain. But my fingers and wrists, I noted, were fine. I reached my fingers to my chest, to the back of my head. No blood. So why did I feel like I was going to pass out?

I leaned back against the wall of the elevator and slapped it a few times with both hands, gritting my teeth to force blood back into my brain. I took a series of deep breaths. *Get it together!*

I looked up and found the line of the roof hatch. Dead Eyes had said he'd been on top of the elevator. Could I take him out now? Run the elevator up to the roof and trap him there? Except the code I'd entered only took me down. And even if I tried something, couldn't Dead Eyes just force his way down into the elevator? He'd knock me out or cripple me, then go after Lena.

Not to mention the fact I was having trouble just standing up and breathing normally.

Think! If I could just... If I had any actual control over these crazy jump backs in time...

But I didn't. No control. No guarantee they'd even happen the next time I or Lena was about to die.

Damn it!

The elevator dinged softly and the door slid open.

I forced myself away from the wall and walked shakily out of the elevator. By the time I was standing on the catwalk, something seemed to have fit itself together inside me and I felt... fine. Scared. My heartbeat was rising. My stomach was in knots. But these were familiar physical symptoms of fear, not leftovers from the jump. Manageable.

I forced myself to breathe and listen to the elevator. It had closed behind me, but there was no sound indicating it was moving again. Of course, since there was no one calling it from above. Meaning it would just sit there with Dead Eyes on top. Listening. Waiting. I should have pressed the buttons or something to send it back up.

Too late for that. Move.

Without waiting for Lena to come out from under the pipes near the far wall, I quickly and quietly descended the steps and walked toward where I knew she was.

She obviously heard me coming, because she started ducking out from under the pipes. Her eyes grew wide as she stood up to find me right there, index finger held up to my lips. I stifled my usual discomfort at getting so close to a relative stranger as I leaned forward to whisper in her ear, "There's a man with a gun and knife who rode down on top of the elevator. I don't know how he got there, but he'll be coming in any minute to take us hostage. It probably has something to do with your time travel research. And yes, I know all about it. Long story, but I've lived this ten or twelve minutes of time three times so far, and each time he's killed one or both of us. Is there another way out?"

I pulled back and looked into Lena's eyes, willing her to see that I wasn't crazy. I saw shock, doubt, and fear run across her features, then an odd flash of wonder, followed by a cold determination that she was going to trust me. At least until we were somewhere safe that we could talk.

"Loading doors over that way," she whispered, pointing toward the gray linked boxes she'd called the main lynac cryomodule a few time jumps back. "It's how they brought all this equipment in."

"Let's go. Fast and quiet."

She nodded and, still gripping her crescent wrench, she led me between the rows of child-sized electromagnet controllers, ducking pipes and cables as we went. I bit my lips and almost reached out to stop Lena as we reached the section of particle accelerator beside the lynac cryomodule and she hauled herself bodily up onto the same type of connected, wire-covered metal cages that had electrocuted me at the other end of the room. Of course, the particle accelerator was turned off now. No electric sun monster running through it. But still...

Lena looked back down at me. "Come on!" she hissed. Then she turned to hop off the other side and stumbled, caught herself but whacked the side of the steel boxes with her boots so they thrummed like a metal drum.

A scuffle and ding from back at the elevator told me that Dead Eyes had heard it. Or maybe he'd just figured Lena and I had been too quiet.

I hauled myself up and over the steel boxes as fast as I could, hearing Dead Eyes' shout as he jumped down from the catwalk on the far side.

"He's seen us," I hissed. "Go. *Go*."

Lena nodded and ran the remaining twenty feet to the set of gray metal double doors that had been virtually invisible from the entry area. I was hot on her heels.

At the door, Lena keyed a number code into the box on the wall and a thunking sound said the lock was sprung. Lena grabbed the handle of the left door, pulled, and a rush of cold, dank air rushed over the two of us. Lights clicked on beyond the door, showing a wide, twelve-foot-high tunnel.

A loud bang exploded chips of concrete off the wall over our heads. Dead Eyes!

"Go on!" Lena said and pushed me through the door. I looked back in time to see her whack a red, palm-sized button below the number pad, which set off a siren and a whir of red strobing lights from around the room.

Lena swung through the door, and it closed with what sounded like a solid thunk of bolts locking it tight. It was followed by a set of muffled gun shots and thuds on the doors themselves.

"He won't get through that with a pistol," Lena said. Her face was flushed, and she was breathing hard as she looked at me, heart likely thudding as hard as my own.

Now there was a dull thudding sound from the other side of the door, like Dead Eyes was pounding with his foot or kicking with his boot. And muffled yelling. I pressed my ear up to the metal door to hear.

"Come on, we've got to go," Lena said, tugging on the sleeve of my sweater.

But I ignored her for a few more seconds until I was sure I'd understood what Dead Eyes was yelling over and over at the door.

"...the five buildings," Lena was saying. "There's a sloped garage at one end but I think an elevator before then. And the park's security should be showing up soon. I need to get to a place where my cell phone will work so they know they're facing a shooter. We have to *go*."

"Yes," I said as I pushed away from the door, my knees suddenly weak.

She must have seen something on my face, because she paused for just a second. Then she grabbed my arm more forcefully and started walking so I had to jump to match her pace. She started talking again, too, telling me what I was going to say when we met security, how I was to explain my presence, how I would tell them I'd heard the sound of someone on top of the elevator, and that's why I'd convinced her to run with me out the rear service tunnel.

But despite my earlier intense attraction to Lena and my relief that on my fourth try at this situation I'd gotten us both out alive, I could barely process her words now as we hurried along the corridor.

Because the words playing over and over in my head were the muffled ones Dead Eyes had shouted through the door at me, maybe ones he should have led with on any of his four collection attempts:

It's your brother! He wants to see you!

4

Who is Dead Eyes?

BECAUSE MY SENSORY PROCESSING worked at extraordinary levels whether I was fully focused on the input or not, I somehow brought forward all of Lena's admonitions about how to deal with the business park security officers, and they bought the story. I even managed to meet the eyes of the security chief who interviewed us. Speaking in the near dark with my mouth and nose covered by a mask helped. I was gratified they were wearing theirs, too.

Now, twenty-five minutes on, I still sat beside Lena on a flat-topped electrical box out front of Building #2, where we'd come up from the service tunnel. It had grown dark and was cold enough outside that security had brought two blankets for us to wrap around ourselves while they did their interview.

The ATS Security team hadn't caught Dead Eyes by the time Lena and I were fully debriefed, though. By the time the extra guys they'd called in had gotten down to the particle accelerator room, Dead Eyes had vanished. He'd probably managed to pry open the elevator doors and climb back out the top and up the shaft. ATS was searching the building and grounds, but it was dark now, and it would have been pretty easy for a single man to disappear into the shadows, then the surrounding countryside.

They did retrieve and hand over Lena's purse and street clothes before they went back to their cars to write their reports.

"We'll send you a copy of our report for your bosses," the chief ATS officer said, flipping his own spiral notebook closed. "And I'll personally call the Redmond PD and have them follow up with you. We'll leave two guys here overnight, just in case. Send one back home with each of you."

Lena nodded at all this sagely, but my head was thrumming with a kind of inarticulate rage. I needed these guys to apprehend Dead Eyes so I could question him. I'd just had the strangest day of my life—meeting a woman who checked every box for the perfect mate; getting stabbed, pistol-whipped, and shot at; and, oh yeah, learning I could somehow time travel in a stupid way— but it all paled beside the fact Kenny might be alive.

Or not. Because Dead Eyes could have just been lying to mess with me. What did they call that? Trolling. Perfect. The monster under the bridge who wants to eat you. Who'll say anything to make you face him.

Kenny alive?

After my parents had come home to find Kenny gone and me wearing hospital bandages and taking pain pills, I'd said I'd looked for him but just gotten beaten up. Never found him. So they'd called the cops. Nothing. They'd called Kansas. No luck from her either.

Then, two years later, in 2005, in the major gang war between the Demon Monks and a Seattle street gang called BAM, when dead bodies were reported almost daily, we figured we'd finally hear something. Anything.

We never did.

Eventually we stopped waiting and assumed Kenny was one of the lifestyle's John Doe bodies, found in some shooting or overdose, maybe in another country, maybe never found at all. I was in the second half of my undergrad in the University of Illinois by that time, consumed by guilt and fear and taking courses in abnormal psychology, addiction, and learning, trying to find a way out of my own messed-up head.

As the ATS Security guy who'd interviewed me and Lena now walked back to his car that was parked in front of Building #4 with its top lights still flashing orange, my head went from thrumming to a pounding headache. I tugged off my mask and took long, deep breaths. I wasn't coping with this well.

Moments later, the interviewing officer had his car at the business park gates, where he joined up with the other two flashing cars parked there. They talked inaudibly, and one of the two gate cars started up and drove back toward us to replace the interviewing officer's car in front of Building #4. One guy got out and entered the building. One stayed inside the car. The other two cars drove away.

I ground my teeth. "Does your boss actually pay these guys? Or are you the boss? Do you report to anyone?"

"A little testy, are we?" said Lena.

"I've been slashed, electrocuted, body slammed, broken my wrist and fingers, pistol-whipped, shot at, and seen you... Never mind."

"Seen me what?"

"I said never mind! I haven't eaten since lunch. Low blood sugar."

"Me too. Let me take you out to dinner. I have lots of questions."

I took a deep breath and forced myself to look Lena full in the face. Her eyes caught me again, made me want to tell her about Kenny, about this strange, jerky time traveling, about how she'd kissed me, and how I'd seen Dead Eyes kill her twice.

But it was just too much. Too much for tonight. I was likely to fall apart if I got started, and I knew that was not a good look for a psychologist, a professor, or even just a man who wanted a woman to actually like and respect him. Maybe even kiss him again sometime.

"Tomorrow," I said. "I'm not in great shape right now, and I think I'd be better off eating alone."

Lena looked hurt. She visibly shrank back into herself but then straightened and tried to shrug it off with a smile. "Okay. What time? And where? Your university office?"

"I teach in the morning, then have clients. Let me call you late afternoon."

"Sure." She gave me a game smile again, and it tore my heart out. I was failing her, too. Like I'd failed too many people in my life. Well, like I'd failed Kenny, and my sister, and my early patients, and the pathetically few women I'd tried to date, the colleagues who'd tried to be my friends. Being able to spontaneously jump back in time *did not make that better!*

"Okay," I said. "You'll stick with these security guys?"

She nodded. "They're supposed to send a guy back with you, too."

"They only left one car. And I just can't… Sorry, but I have to go." I took off my blanket, handed it to her, then walked to my car, got in, started it up, and drove off without looking back.

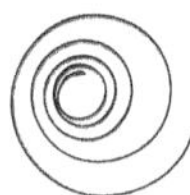

That night, after locking all the doors and windows of my apartment and putting a hammer on the nightstand beside my bed, I pulled out the Bankers Box I kept in the back of my closet and sat with my back to the wall, the box on the floor between my outspread legs.

This was my Kenny box, filled with letters and postcards and photographs of Kenny, with his lanky body and long, bony face. I fingered a bunch of the threadbare Boy Scout badges he'd earned and shown me to convince me to join the Scouts as soon as I turned ten. We'd studied for the communication badge together, learning Morse code for it before we discovered it wasn't required anymore. Kenny didn't care. He loved the idea that we now had a secret language others couldn't follow. *You and me against the world,* he'd say, *like that Paul Williams song.*

It was just like that.

I laid the badges out in a neat line on my lap and pulled up the baseball Kenny had signed for me when he was a senior in high school, the blue ink mostly faded but the smell and feel of the scuffed leather just like it had been back then.

"It's the actual one I hit, Jacky. Twenty-eighth home run this season. School record."

"Thanks, Kenny!"

"Call me Kentucky now. I've earned it."

I turned the baseball's smooth and rough edges over in my hands. Twenty-eight home runs. That was probably the last good thing Kenny ever did in high school. He was already running with the Demon Monks by that time. They'd hooked Kenny on heroin and crack. He'd pretty much stopped attending classes. He was kicked off the baseball team a week later and dropped out of school.

And a couple months after that was the first time he called on me to come and pull him out of a bad place. A rival gang from Seattle proper had come south and smashed Kenny's kneecaps, taken his wallet and drugs, and left him in a Dumpster behind the Fortune Casino.

Our big sister, Kansas, was already away at Vassar, studying foreign languages. The Traine parents were, as usual, out of state at one of their national building center franchises. So I, Jackson Traine, fourteen years old and not yet in possession of even an intermediate driver's license, "borrowed" our dad's black Chevrolet Corvette ZR1—his midlife-crisis car according to our mother—and roared into downtown Renton. I parked behind the casino, left the engine running, and physically grunted Kenny's bony, six-foot-two-inch frame out of the trash and into the passenger seat of the Corvette.

Nearly blacking out with pain, Kenny had directed me to the Valley Medical Center that was only a short drive from our house. He'd told me to dump him at the front door and drive away so I wouldn't be caught driving without a license. I'd pulled up to the front door, then balked.

"I can't!"

"No, you can, buddy. I know you can."

Then he'd opened the passenger door and spilled out of it, somehow managing to kick it closed behind him so hard that my right foot stomped on the gas pedal in surprise and I almost crashed as I drove away.

That was only the first of a lot of calls for help. Not the last one involving a hospital.

"Oh, man," I sobbed, stuffing the baseball and the Boy Scout badges back into the box and closing it, lifting it up onto my lap and not wanting to let it go.

Of course, I knew by heart and photographic memory every last item, newspaper article, letter, postcard, and scrawled note that was in that box. And some unrecorded calls and conversations that were not. I could flip through them in my mind, going through each painful one—Kenny's deteriorating physical state, his confession he was doing some dangerous drug deals for the Demon Monks, and the shootout with the same rival gang that had cracked his kneecaps three years earlier.

When he got out of the hospital, he was tried for narcotics possession and given early parole on the condition he undergo a state-sponsored rehab program.

The rehab stint was the first of three. And I was always there to drive Kenny in, visit him, and drive him home again.

Until Kenny told me the last time not to pick him up because he was already out and back with the Demon Monks. But I didn't listen to that, did I? I had to drive from place to place until I finally found him with a bunch of other Demon Monks in an old auto repair garage he'd pointed out to me one time as a gang-owned place to strip down stolen cars.

And, well, we all know how that all went down.

By the time the Seattle PD were busting all the Demon Monks and BAM gang members and parading them through the courthouse like zoo animals, I'd already run from Renton to study in Chicago. Like my sister and parents, I assumed Kenny was dead. If I'd stayed in Renton, I was pretty sure I would have died, too. From guilt.

And now?

It's your brother! He wants to see you!

True or not true? Dead Eyes had referenced "shot callers," which was gang lingo, or used to be, for people like Cutter who gave orders. So Dead Eyes was likely still part of some kind of street gang. Was Kenny there too? Or was it just Dead Eyes remembering how I'd once tried to save Kenny and using it against me?

How was I supposed to check? Let myself get kidnapped?

Yeah, no.

I swung the Kenny box off my lap, turned onto my knees, and shoved it back into my closet.

Then I just sat on the floor awhile, trying to think through the insanity. Forget the time jumps, even the stuff with Dead Eyes made no sense. If Kenny had heard I was back in town and sent Dead Eyes to collect me, why hadn't he taken me yesterday after class? And why go after Lena?

Or had Lena been the real target, maybe to blackmail the people who'd set her up in that laboratory? Maybe Dead Eyes had been following her, saw me, remembered me, and reported it to Kenny, who really was alive and much higher up in the ranks of whatever gang they were with now, and Kenny had ordered him to abduct me as well. A two-for-one special.

Except why would Kenny, if he was still alive, have done that after all this time? On a whim? To bring me into the gang? Not believable.

"*¡Dios mío!*" I muttered in frustration, throwing up my hands in a way that would have brought tears of pride to the eyes of the

Mexican nanny who'd pretty much raised Kansas, Kenny, and I until Kansas left for university and things slowly turned to shit.

Yeah, *¡Dios mío!* My God. I wanted to lay it all at the feet of my traveling business tycoon parents and their absentee parenting. Except that would have made me even more pathetic in my own eyes than I already was. And psychoanalysis or family systems explanations all fell apart anyway once time travel and thugs with guns got involved.

Hugging myself until I thought I had my despairing emotions under control, I stood up, went to the computer I had set up in my den/yoga room, and did a search for the closest Seattle police department.

Great. They were closed to any and all public visits. I vaguely recalled that had started months ago. Another casualty of COVID. Maybe also fallout from the Black Lives Matter debacle?

I called anyway.

The next morning, after a quick yoga sequence and a run around Interlaken Park but still a good three hours before I had to drive up to UW to start my course review with my students, I opened my laptop and checked my email. There, sent early this morning, was the Zoom link the police night clerk had promised I'd get.

I clicked on the link, and in a moment, the face of a boyish-looking white cop came up on my screen. The image included a group of desks and police in the background and jumped around as the young officer adjusted his computer's webcam to include a long-haired black man with glasses and a white-speckled beard. The black man sat in a chair near the officer at his desk.

Both wore masks. Good sign.

And I myself wasn't melting down with anxiety as I looked at them on the screen. Yet.

Out of habit, I set a third-party screen recorder running on my laptop so I'd be able to review the call with other people, like Lena, if need be. I was also tempted to put up one of the mildly subversive backgrounds I had at the ready, but decided against it. The Seattle PD were barely past their nightmare 2020, what with COVID, then the demonstrations after George Floyd's murder causing them to abandon their East Precinct for a month to protestors, homeless squatters, artists, and assorted activists.

The taken-over precinct and surrounding area had been named the Capitol Hill Autonomous Zone (Chaz), later the Capitol Hill Organized Protest (CHOP). It had been a fascinating study in crowd psychology and shifting forms of authority while it lasted. And the Seattle PD was still facing some massive changes in the years to come, with the city listening to voters and cutting funding as they tried to negotiate new models of policing.

But what I needed right now was good old, simple help identifying a bad guy and protecting me and Lena from a known threat.

After I identified myself to the officer and repeated the background of my case, the young man nodded with the best gravity he could muster and introduced himself as Patrol Officer Miller, handling this before he actually went out on patrol. "I have with me here Ziggy Cheester, a forensic sketch artist. Very skilled."

"Thank you, Bryan," the older black man said with a musical island accent that made it Bri-*ahn*. Then he turned to face what I assumed was my face on the monitor. "Now you talk to me, Mr. Professah, and I'm gonna sketch out your bad boy."

I liked him immediately.

After about twenty minutes, I thought Ziggy had captured a good likeness of Dead Eyes and called young Officer Bryan Miller back from where he'd gone to talk to a female the next desk over. When Miller came back and saw the picture, he squinted hard at it, laughed, and said, "You know who this looks like? Hey, Bo! Is Gillespie back out in the field?"

A gruff answer came back from somewhere out of the webcam's line of vision.

Miller looked at me onscreen, which meant he was looking down a little bit, but was obviously feeling friendly. "Just hold on a sec."

Miller took the sketch out of Ziggy's hand, who shrugged at me and started cleaning his nails.

A few moments later, Miller returned, and his friendliness had been replaced with a pale, neutral expression. "I'm sorry, sir," he said into the webcam. "We ran the picture through our facial recognition program and got no matches. We'll put the picture on file in case something else comes up."

I tapped my fingers on my desktop, a small, attention-grabbing gesture that could sometimes disrupt blocking behaviors by clients. It had the effect now of making Miller's eyes twitch right and down, which, in the collective circumstances, told me the man was lying.

"What about personal protection?" I asked.

"Unfortunately, we don't have the manpower to stake out your home and office, sir. For Ms. Cortland, any protection would be up to the Redmond Police. Have you talked with them yet?"

"No. I get the feeling their budget might have been slashed, too."

The corner of Miller's mouth twitched, and the slightest hint of his earlier warmth returned. "Best I can suggest is to take personal precautions. And call us if you see someone's following you or trying to break in."

I paused a long minute, giving the young officer time to say anything else he might want to slip out. But the kid had been corrected. Might even be under the eye of "Bo" this very moment. So I finally said, "Thank you, Officer. I'll do that," and I cut the Zoom connection. Then I stopped the screen recorder and sat and thought.

Could this be like that Scorsese movie where a gangster infiltrates the police force? Because the guy who'd come after me and Lena was definitely the same Dead Eyes who'd been in with the Demon Monks back in 2003.

I turned back to the keyboard and Googled "Officer Gillespie detective Seattle police." It brought up a story about a retired, dead Bob Gillespie, a polygraph specialist Gillespie, some Breonna Taylor protestor named Gillespie, and then spread out to other jurisdictions and countries. But on page five of the search results, through some quirk of the Google algorithm, I found a reference to war hero James William Gillespie getting some kind of medal back in 2008. With a picture that sure looked like Dead Eyes. And he'd been wearing some kind of military camo jacket when I'd seen him. Maybe it had been a real one?

So…what? Dead Eyes/James Gillespie had left the Demon Monks to join the Army, left the Army to become a cop, then worked himself up to be a detective, only to go undercover with maybe the same gang he'd been with before the Army?

That was pretty stone-cold. The cops couldn't have known he'd been a criminal before. So he'd lied to their faces. The real question was whether he was somehow trying to make amends working as a cop or was just playing them. Or had he gotten drawn back into the drugs and lifestyle? Very Scorsese.

I picked up my cell phone and called my sister.

I got routed to a mailbox I was sure was monitored by numerous supervisors and analysts when any keywords were said. Kansas Traine had always told her family she'd gotten a job translating for low-level government agencies like the Department of Agriculture, the Peace Corps, and the Bureau of Indian Affairs, but Kenny and I knew she was way too smart for that. Beyond genius. Kenny had been sure Kansas was recruited by the CIA. But after Kansas had come to see me accept my doctoral degree, I'd joked about that and Kansas had commented tartly that the CIA was filled with inbred backstabbers who dreamt of being James Bond. Not where people went when they wanted *real* intelligence. There had also been the fact Kansas had known everything about my degree, my advisors, and about every person I'd ever emailed or chatted with online in any fashion. She was clearly in deep enough to find whatever she really wanted to find. About anyone. Which made her NSA, helping America collect and collate signals intelligence and human intelligence from all over the world.

"Hey, sis," I said brightly into her voice mail. "It's your baby bro here. Just wanted to ask you some questions about how we're going to celebrate Mom and Dad's fiftieth. Give me a shout back when you get the chance."

Ten minutes later, she called me back from what I assumed was a secure line, given the intense way she said, "Like our parents would notice. What are you really calling about?"

"A name. Gillespie. I think he's a former war hero who's now a Seattle Police officer. Probably a detective. Maybe fired recently. Maybe undercover with a street gang. First name might be James William."

"Why?"

"He's trying to kidnap me and another professor I've been spending some time with."

"Who?"

"The professor? Lena Cortland. She teaches down in Berkley. She's up here doing some research and we met. It's...got potential."

"What do you know about her?"

"Nothing, really. But there's something else. Might be bullshit, but Gillespie claimed Kenny wanted to see me."

There was a long silence on the phone. Not unusual in conversations with Kansas. I waited. She finally said, "I'll call you back on this phone in an hour if I find anything. Don't call me like this again. It's not okay."

"Then how *do* I call you, Kansas? You gave up your cell phone. You're not on social media."

There was a long pause. "Assuming I'm still in my job in June, I'll schedule some social time with you and Mom and Dad, okay? Or with you, at least. Who knows where they'll be."

"That sounds good. Thanks, Kansas. I miss you, you know. More than I let on."

Another long pause, then, "I miss you, too, Jacky. And Kenny."

The click when she hung up felt like an arrow to my heart. Hearing both the loss and the love and reassurance in her voice touched off my own feelings of loss again. I felt the intense, childlike need for someone who would just give me answers and tell me everything would be okay. Kansas might have been the only person in the world I would trust to tell me that.

When she called me back in an hour, that didn't happen.

5

Collateral target

"JACKY, STOP LOOKING."

Kansas' words on the phone sent a chill down my spine and made my fingers tingle. "What do you mean?"

"Until I can find some more stuff, stop looking into Gillespie. Don't throw Kenny's name around anywhere. Don't go to the police, the FBI, any government agencies. Just hire a bodyguard. Put an alarm system on your apartment and your office if you don't have ones there already. Buy a gun."

I assumed she was joking about the last one. My psychology office did have a security package, so that was good. My apartment building, on the other hand, was old, so its only security was its front doors and locks for each apartment. Anyone could easily follow another resident in through the front door and up.

But if Dead Eyes wanted to get me, all he had to do was wait until I came out for a morning run. Or find me at the university, like he had already. He might even be there now in my campus office, waiting for me.

"Can you tell me why?" I said into my cell phone. "Gillespie's a cop, isn't he."

A pause. Kansas' heavy breathing. "Yes. First NYPD, then Seattle PD. But that's not the scary part. When I pulled his name up in military and police systems, I found all sorts of hidden tags and software mine alerts that were meant to tell people someone was looking."

"Does that mean you're in trouble?" My self-loathing over hurting another person who loved me revved into high gear.

"Chill, little brother. I don't go on personal fishing expeditions without precautions. I went in through an Eastern Europe subnet and actually disabled enough of the traps and locks to see Gillespie's file and a few of its links."

"Links to what?"

"More than just the undercover work he's doing. He's in with what used to be the Demon Monks, but you probably guessed that."

"I thought they'd been wiped out."

"Officially. Unofficially, the remains of the gang joined with BAM and somehow took it over. Engineered a disappearing act for most of its junior members."

"Why?"

"I think that's what Gillespie joined them to find out."

"Rejoined. He was a gang member back when Kenny was taken."

"Interesting. Anyway, the gang went dark around the time you were getting your master's, then started showing up linked to a right-wing domestic terrorist group."

She fell silent but didn't hang up.

"That's not the important part," I guessed.

"All the codes the new Demon Monks used for communications on social media—that's how they coordinate their meets and drug trade—they're American government. Probably CIA. I'm guessing the CIA's using the Monks for some kind of domestic op. Things go wrong, they disavow all knowledge."

"What does that have to do with me?"

"I'm guessing you're a collateral target. Gillespie was following Dr. Cortland. When she met up with you, he shared it with someone who'd find that interesting."

"Someone..." I knew what she was going to say.

"I don't know why or how he's involved yet, but Gillespie wasn't just trolling you. Kenny's alive."

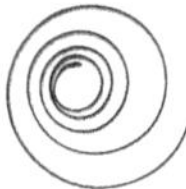

My emotions were swirling so hard I felt almost none of my usual social anxiety when I addressed my U-Dub students at the Thursday, eleven a.m. class. I was expecting Gillespie to run in with a gun at any moment and almost welcomed it. He'd take me to see Kenny, and I'd finally get some answers to whatever this was.

It meant I had no focus and no energy for the coursework review, and my students could tell. The ones who clearly valued their time with me were concerned and tried to subtly nudge me back on track.

It made me feel twice as guilty when I abruptly cut them off and did something unusual for me—I began scrawling notes on the room's whiteboards. I wrote out not only key study points but sketched things in hierarchies with red stars indicating what would definitely be on the exam, with exact page numbers and sections they needed to understand and memorize. When I'd filled four whiteboards, I went back to the first, erased it, and kept going.

As the students caught on, the room's whispers fell silent, replaced by the sound of students taking notes as fast as they could, either by hand or typing, and snapping photos of the boards, not daring to get up or move around in case they missed something.

When the clocks indicated the end of class, I called, "That's time!" and went back to the first board to start methodically erasing what I'd written.

I paused at the fourth board, giving the slower students time to take pictures or finish their notes, then I erased that board, too.

When the last student had left, I adjusted my mask and limped out of class like I'd just been fighting a war. I was halfway back to my office in Guthrie Hall when I remembered to look around myself in case Dead Eyes, aka Detective James William Gillespie, had just been waiting until I was alone before jumping me.

No one there. Gillespie was probably scoping out Lena's workplace right now. She was clearly the priority target. I was the bonus catch, like Kansas said. Likely the only person who wanted me kidnapped was my surprisingly alive brother.

But why?

WTF, Kenny?

And even as I asked it, some part of me knew. It was to save him. Whatever he was caught up in, he was *caught*, unable to get free. Because Kenny had, frankly, lost most of his ability to control his life around the time he turned fourteen and his bipolar disorder started taking over. Boy Scouts, baseball, and school had been only stopgap measures to fight it. Even by his junior year, he'd started experimenting with weed to control the mood swings. In senior year, he'd discovered various kinds of uppers and downers and became totally vulnerable to anyone who understood his weakness.

It could be Cutter and his crew were no longer controlling him, but I knew in my gut *someone* was.

They'd made him vanish, all traces of him gone so even Kansas hadn't been able to find him. They'd also shut him up or locked him up, or else he would have contacted me, at least. I was sure of it.

Something must have changed, though. Maybe he'd earned enough trust or importance that he'd finally slipped me a message through Dead Eyes. Not a clear message, but one that I, as his baby brother, the guy Kenny had earned a communications badge in Boy Scouts with, was supposed to get.

I'm alive. Save me.

The weight of it was suddenly like liquid metal filling my lungs. I stopped walking in front of the Chemistry Library on Okanagan Lane and swayed in the gray cold of the day, feeling it press down around me.

You wanted another chance to save him. Here it is.

I looked around me and decided to ditch putting in any office hours today. My exams were ready. My students were ready. It was time to massively switch my priorities.

Save Kenny.

I waited for the internal chatter about how I'd failed at it all the earlier times I'd tried, so of course I would fail again.

But instead, there was no chatter in my head. Just quiet. No, more than that. Beneath the crushing sense of doubt and responsibility, a tingle of excitement was growing. Because, unlike the last time I'd failed Kenny, when I'd been an emotionally weak teenager with limited financial and physical resources, I was now a doctor of psychology. Ridden with PTSD and social anxiety, yes, but also fortuitously given an almost godlike power to step back in time. If Lena could help me make this power repeatable and controllable...

I'd save Kenny.

Thereby save myself.

Maybe win Lena's love in the process?

Tapping into the excitement of it, I shrugged off the weight of the world and jogged to the campus Central Plaza Garage to collect my car.

En route home, I phoned Lena, but my call went to voice mail.

I started to hang up.

There was a click, and I heard her out-of-breath voice, like a clean drink of water or a burst of sunshine through the clouds. "Jackson! Don't hang up! Don't hang up, please. I missed your first call because we've been in the middle of a massive new test run, seeing if there was any change from the interaction you had yesterday with the accelerator. Are you there?"

I grinned at the Montlake Boulevard traffic I was weaving through and said into my hands-free, "I'm here. You find anything?"

"No. One of my team thought he saw a smoother energy conversion. The other three didn't."

"Four...men?"

She chuckled. "Much older than me, other than Salazar, who's a savant and sees other people as math equations. I had them take yesterday off so I'd be free when you came by. You want me to send them away again?"

I considered, remembering the kiss she'd given me but knew nothing about. Of course, her interest in me was now inextricably tied to my claim of time traveling, but I was sure that wasn't all that was between us. And if she was ready to send away the rest of her team so it was just us again in the lab...

Thoughts of the lab triggered a spurt of panic. *Dead Eyes!* I licked my suddenly dry lips and forced myself to stop pressing hard on the accelerator as I zoomed over the Montlake Cut and the Canal Waterside Trail, heading south. "No security issues?"

She must have heard the tension, because she came back with the calmest, most reassuring tone. "I got the Renton Police Department to provide a sketch artist, and they've broadcast an all-points for our attacker."

"Company security?"

"ATS has me covered here and where I'm staying, but their chief said I shouldn't let a threat of kidnap restrict my freedom in the city. He gave me a phone that's essentially a panic button and beacon. They said they can reach me or find me anywhere in the greater Seattle area in about twelve minutes."

Partly because of the residual fear the thought of Dead Eyes, aka Detective James Gillespie caused in me, I was tempted to attack that plan. The more I thought about Gillespie's behavior, though, the more I wondered if both I and Kansas were wrong. It was entirely possible that Gillespie was just a drug-addicted loose cannon. He'd seen Lena or read about her, gotten some crazy notion in his head, and stalked her. It had bombed, badly. That might be the end of it.

Or not! Stay left ahead.

Or Gillespie actually had been sent by the Demon Monks, but it was to just talk to Lena, issue an invitation. That also had bombed. Gillespie might just say he invited her and she declined?

If he tried again, there was always Lena's locator/panic button.

That wouldn't help.

"Don't send your team away," I said. "Let's go out for dinner tonight instead. You can ask me about you know what, and I'll tell you everything I know."

Wait. What?

"Yes." Her breathlessness was gone, but her excitement was still there.

"Also, other things I found out."

"Did you...travel unexpectedly?"

"No. Not things about me. At least not directly."

What are you doing?

"Okay. I'm on a very nice expense account. Can I swing by and take you out to the Canlis restaurant? It's on the west shore of Lake Union."

"That's a bit of a drive for you."

"I'm staying at my aunt's house in Bridle Trails. It's right near the highway. I looked up your counseling office. I'm assuming you live close to it. I'll make reservations and pick you up at six thirty. Upscale casual?"

"Okay." I gave her my address.

"Great! This is…epic. Gotta run."

She hung up on me.

I shook my head as I realized Montlake had become 24th Avenue East, and I was passing Interlaken Park on my right, Washington Park on my left. I was plunging through beauty here and going out with a beautiful, assertive, brilliant woman tonight.

You know it's for business, right? Science.

Sure. Important stuff.

Don't fool yourself.

But the beauty around me swept my anxiety demon and all the things I *should* have been thinking of out of my mind for just a moment. No PTSD, no time travel, no thoughts of Kenny or guilt or danger. Just…

On the spur of the moment, I speed-dialed Jude and continued my lucky streak when he answered on the second ring.

"Hey, dude," I blurted. "I've got a date tonight!"

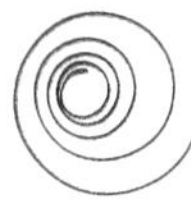

At 8:40 p.m., in between our second and third courses of food and wine, Lena and I sat almost side by side around the corner of our table, looking silently out the huge picture windows over the descending conifers, streets, and grassy hills to the romantically lit boats that rocked in their nighttime slips on Lake Union.

I should have been squirming with anxiety over what she thought of me by this time, but I wasn't. Because, frankly, it had felt almost like she *wasn't* thinking of me. At least, not as a man so much as a space-time unicorn. She'd started asking questions from the moment she'd picked me up in an old-style Buick to drive us here. Had me describe the four battles in the particle accelerator lab in excruciating detail—the disorientation and physical feelings that had come with each, the circumstances immediately before each time jump, what I was thinking, what I was feeling in each part of my body. She'd gasped and given sympathetic murmurs in all the right places, allowed me a few bites of my meal, sips of my wine, then asked more follow-up questions.

I'd also told her about Gillespie and almost told her about my brother and what my sister had warned me about, but I'd held back at the last minute, still not a hundred percent sure where we were going with this.

Until now.

Now, for a few brief moments, I could feel we were a man and woman. The lake's dark waters outside were colored by the white, yellow, and red reflections from the docks on the near and distant shores and by the moon that peeked through the broken cloud cover above.

I let myself fully take in Lena's floral and citrus perfume. Her warmth, her presence, filled all my senses both with delight and just the starting edges of the creeping terror my social anxiety demanded.

The terror was broken by our masked waitress clinking down a plate before me and explaining that the shape on the left side of this black stone crockery dish was a small piece of barely singed, dry aged ribeye steak. It did smell warm and spicy and was lightly ornamented with a small gratin of potato and fermented cabbage. Also, some kind of white sauce with what looked like chocolate pieces floating in it.

Lena's plate held a mild white fish called sea bream that was flavored with stewed onions, horseradish, and what I gathered was a kind of salty chicken sauce.

"The wine is a Sobroso cabernet," the waitress said as she placed the new half-full glasses before us. "From Portugal.

You'll find it's very fresh and balanced with good volume and a very fine, long finish."

Then she was gone, and all we had were these exquisite dishes, the wine, and each other.

As Lena silently sampled her sea bream and I, my ribeye, I finally let my gaze carefully rove over her off-the-shoulder, dark-turquoise velvet dress that plunged low in front and set off the glowing olive skin of her neck and bosom. She'd pulled back her thick curls on either side of her head with hammered gold combs that glittered like the lake water outside, and she'd worn just a touch more makeup than I'd seen before. It made her lips redder, her eyelids smokier.

My throat was so tight it was hard to swallow the piece of meat I'd been chewing.

I was glad Jude had told me to skip the "casual" part of the dress code and do my best suit and tie. Canlis, he'd read off his computer screen while we'd talked, was known for its romance. Lena had chosen it, he assured me, to send a signal.

Except that all her conversation up to now had been scientific. It had reduced my stress because all I'd had to do was relate what had happened. But now...now her manner finally matched the attraction she'd shown when she'd kissed me in that second aborted timeline in her lab.

It was both exciting and terrifying.

She leaned forward as she sampled her fish, her shoulder almost touching mine, the light floral scent of her—jasmine and citrus—holding me in its spell. I swore I could feel her body thrum beside mine, her breath filling *me*.

She put down her knife and fork. "What I still want to know..."

"No," I blurted and held up my hand. Swallowed. "I want to hear about you now."

I made myself look straight into her eyes. I felt completely exposed, showing my naked interest in her, making that demand, and my eyes watered in protest. Yet it exposed her, too. No more science to hide behind. At the lower edge of my vision, I saw her mouth tremble and her hands drop to her lap.

"I was a tomboy growing up," she said. "A late bloomer. But an only child of two parents who loved me to bits and told me I was the smartest, prettiest child in the world who could do anything I chose to do. So I chose math and chess club and skipped second grade and was mouthy enough in correcting teachers that I got into trouble a lot but was still the youngest valedictorian my high school had ever had. Is that enough?"

I shook my head and took a bite of her sea bream. I swallowed it and reengaged her gaze completely. It was easier now because she'd answered my request to shift to more personal ground without judgement. She'd even welcomed it, I thought. Like she'd been waiting for me. "Racism," I said. "Did you face any growing up? Or later? What's your ethnic background?"

"Well, that's direct."

"Too much?"

"Just...why?"

"I knew a couple Black kids in school who had it tough. Also, my Mexican nanny told me about some of the stuff she faced."

Lena nodded with mock seriousness. "Ah. I remind you of your nanny. "

I smiled. "No one's as sweet as my nanny. And you don't look Mexican."

A smile back. "Persian. My mother was a math genius in Tehran. Met my father while teaching in Harvard. She kept her name Ahmadi, but she encouraged me to use my father's last name. It made things easier."

"Easier but not easy."

"In my field, being a woman was the bigger challenge."

"Hm."

"What?"

I swallowed, calling on the skills I used with patients and my students to say, "Let me start again. Did you fall in love in high school?"

"Once. He was really good looking, really smart, and totally lacking in character."

"University?"

"UCLA undergrad. And yes, I fell in love there twice. Both disastrous again. I avoided men when I went to MIT."

"Did they avoid you?"

"No."

"So?"

"Okay. Another disaster there, too. Satisfied?"

"Totally. You have terrible taste in men. I'm really glad you're not interested in me, because what would that say about me?"

"You're right," she said, blinking for the first time. Once. Twice. Thrice. "I'm not interested in you. You're a science experiment. You can freaking travel through time."

"And that's it? Your entire interest?"

"Completely. What did you think?"

I looked in her eyes and, for just a second, couldn't tell if she was being serious and I'd read this wrong, but there was a sparkle there, almost a tear, that seemed to invite a risk, that was leaving it up to *me*, emotionally damaged, frightened me, to make the first move. So, with my entire heart in my throat and my whole body trembling, I said, "I think that I can hardly control myself sitting this close to you. One part of me is so frightened that it wants to leap up and run away. The rest of me, more and more of me every second, wants to take you in my arms right now to kiss you like the kiss you can't remember because *this* you has never done that."

The slightest of nods. "You mentioned that kiss. Was it a good one?"

I kept my eyes on hers. "The best. I think I've basically been hungering to share it with you again every second since it happened."

"Well, it would seem like a good time to do that."

"But I still have a lot to learn about you, so…"

"Oh shut up."

Suddenly Lena's hands were on either side of my face, her lips meeting mine as urgently as I remembered she'd done yesterday, but this time my arms slid around the bodice of her velvet dress so I could draw her body close to mine, feel the warmth and softness of her press into me.

At which point my elbow and shifting knee somehow caught the tablecloth and pulled it toward us so both of our wine glasses wobbled and mine tipped, going over in a clink and splash of red wine across white linen.

Lena and I separated with matching cries, and I quickly caught my rolling wine glass and started to mop the flood of wine with my napkin.

The waitress came running. The couples and groups at all the spread out tables around the dining room turned in their seats to look. I basically turned into a blushing tomato, again feeling like I had as a seven-year-old with nocturnal enuresis, told to stand silently in front of my parents while my older brother and sister watched and be dressed down for poor hygiene, self-discipline, grooming, and character.

Grown-up me started to hyperventilate. My heart rate accelerated. My anxiety demon was literally shouting at me inside my head. Over and over. It hadn't been this bad since—

"It's okay," Lena said beside me, her warm hand covering mine that was still trying to mop up the wine. "Breathe."

"I'm sorry. I'm so sorry." *Shut up, demon! It's not helping!*

"There is nothing to be sorry about." She turned to the waitress, who was trying to clear the dishes and the tablecloth. "Give us a minute, please."

The waitress nodded and retreated. Lena stared around the room at the other diners until, one by one, they turned back to their own meals.

"How do you do that?" I said, forcing my breathing to steady but still unable to raise my head and look at her. "Where do you find the strength?"

I caught a quick head shake in my peripheral vision and felt the squeeze of her hand. "You're the strong one. Whether it was the trauma of your brother or other things that trained you into this, I am so amazed at how you fight it every single day. And help others at the same time. *That* is strength. I was just lucky enough to be born into a family that told me I'm so perfect my poop doesn't stink. They still tell me that. It lets me breeze past the racism and sexism, but it also makes me unbearably entitled at times."

"I could see that," I said. My breathing was almost normal. My heartbeat had slowed.

A solid beat later and I was able to raise my eyes up to meet hers. They were wet and open. Waiting.

"Thank you," I said.

"No, thank you. That kiss... I can see why you were hungering for it. It's already started a similar feeling in me. Right here." She touched her chest. "And pretty quickly moving down...and down... to here." Her descending hand now rested lightly in her lap, palm down.

I licked my lips, looking at the mess on our table. "Do you want to skip the last two courses? Since it's on your expense account and all..."

She nodded and signaled the waitress.

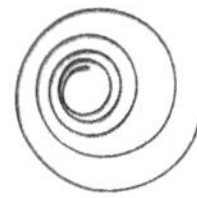

That night, after Lena helped me past another flare-up of my anxiety, we'd rumpled the Egyptian cotton of my bedsheets, exploring each other's bodies in a tangle of kisses, tastes, furious strokes, and crazed attempts to absorb each other into ourselves.

We rested briefly, then ran the process again in a more systematic fashion that let each of us truly study each other, appreciating each other's wants and doing our best to fulfill those desires even as we sated our own.

And after that ended with a pair of satisfying his-and-her explosions, we settled into long, gentle touches, bodies pressed close. We murmured memories of childhood, things we each laughed at, and shared tastes in movies and music. Again, I didn't share any specifics of what had happened with Kenny after he'd gotten tangled up with the Demon Monks. I didn't share that after he'd vanished, we'd thought him dead, and now that I'd found he wasn't, I was going to rescue him.

But as we approached 2:00 a.m., I did fearfully raise a more immediate concern. It had nothing to do with our mutual fascination with each other's bodies and minds and everything to do with closed timelike curves and how I'd somehow jumped through one three times yesterday.

"I have to figure out if it's repeatable. Maybe controllable."

Lena rolled to face me, and I almost lost my nerve. The ever-present city glow that streamed in from my balcony window made her face and naked body luminous. The eyes, now so dark yet familiar. Her right shoulder and arm framing her breasts. Her right hip. The trimmed, hairy center between her legs that was such a tiny sister to the wildly curling, dark mane up around her face.

"We can probably repeat it," she said huskily, and her fingers reached to encircle my penis that amazingly, despite its recent workout, bobbed its agreement.

I grinned. "No probably there. That's definite. But my *other* talent. Any ideas about that one?"

"Calling this a talent now?" She hadn't given up. Her hand was slowing pumping me up and down.

"Um...you're not going to talk seriously right now, are you?"

"No," she said, bending her head down to where her fingers were working. "My mouth's going to be occupied. But you go right ahead."

And a few seconds later, I couldn't remember even what I'd been about to say.

At 2:40 a.m., our third go-round, which had impossibly been more energetic and exciting than the first two and ruined the possibility of me ever even thinking about having sex with anyone else ever, ended with a short, intense orgasm for me and a long, rolling one for Lena that just seemed to go on and on so long that I almost wanted to get up and take some clinical notes for my records.

Then she finished, rolled off of me, and got caught up in some serious giggling that turned into tears and clinging to me.

And the weird thing was, I understood completely and clung to her as well.

We kissed. She closed her eyes. Moments later she was asleep, still wrapped in my arms.

I listened to her soft breathing and smiled. This was one set of hours I would never ever want to lose with a jump back in time. Ever.

But I still needed to learn whether I could make a time jump happen on demand. Because for all my rationalizing that got Lena into my bed, I had no doubt that Kenny or Gillespie or whoever was pulling our strings wasn't finished with Lena or both of us yet. I could almost sense them regrouping. I needed to be ready for them when they struck again.

As if on cue, Lena startled and woke up. Half woke up. Just enough to turn toward me.

"I know what caused your jumps," she breathed. "I think it's repeatable."

6

Nasty science

THE NEXT DAY, AT the crack of dawn, Lena was up and looking impossibly fresh. She said she always kept food and a change of clothes at the business park that housed the particle accelerator in its basement, so she was going to drive straight there to prepare for me. I should join her at the Building #4 entrance at one o'clock.

That worked. I went for a run, showered, changed into comfortable twill pants, belt, loafers, polo top, and gray cardigan and ate before seeing two clients in the morning and fielding an urgent Zoom meeting with one of my students, Mikael of all people, who had an exam-scheduling issue he needed to work out.

I was done by lunch, ate, then drove out to join Lena.

She greeted me wearing a pair of baggy green parachute pants and a form-fitting peach top with a V-neck that almost-but-not-quite reached down to her cleavage. It made it hard for me to think about anything but touching her, smelling her skin. But I suspected she could be dressed in the most shapeless of jumpsuits and I'd always feel like that now. I remembered precisely what her body felt and smelled and tasted like, every dusky curve of it.

I put that aside as best I could and was relieved when she led me up to the third floor, not down into the accelerator lab. En route, she explained that her research team knew where she was but were only to contact her in an emergency.

Then we arrived in what looked like a run-of-the-mill, white-walled medical clinic, recently constructed. Brand new desks hugged the walls, along with shelves of packaged medical supplies like syringes and swabs. Near them stood multiple plastic chairs that had either never been used or had been so carefully disinfected after their last use that they *looked* like they'd never been used. Thanks, COVID protocols.

There was also another woman in the room.

She was much shorter than Lena, with a very round, squashed, serious face that was much darker than Lena's. She wore her black hair up on top of her head in a tight bun. And she was dressed in full personal protection equipment, from her full surgical gown and blue gloves to the N95 mask and face shield.

"Jackson, this is Irene Gopal," Lena said. "She's an excellent medical technician and physician. Here to help run some equipment I requested."

"And to patch me up if things go sideways?"

It was a joke, and Lena smirked at me. Dr. Gopal's eyes did not even twitch. Her reaction set my social anxiety twitching a little, but surprisingly, I found the rest of the medical atmosphere relaxing. It reminded me of a summer job I'd had in my university years, working in a psychiatric unit. Somehow, working with patients with more serious mental issues than my own, who were cared for as real people, not freaks, and whom I was actually able to help in measurable ways, gave me a real sense of hope and empowerment. Those feelings fueled my determination through a lot of difficult times that followed in my studies.

They fueled my determination now. Medicine was a good thing. It applied reason to the craziness of the world. It boiled human craziness down into measurable biological processes.

Gopal made a small gesture to follow her and led me deeper into the room and around a corner, where she'd collected a number of carts and electronics. She seated me in a heavy, steel armchair with vinyl padding, considerably heavier than the stackables near the entry, though the back only came up as high as the top of my shoulders. Then she rolled over a chest-high cart with a large, dark video monitor taking up the top quarter of it. Various arms, baskets, and wires sprouted out below. The monitor was turned enough toward me that I could see my head reflected in it.

Still without making a sound—was she mute?—Dr. Gopal pulled from one of the cart's baskets a fancy electroencephalograph cap with twenty-plus fingertip-sized electrodes that were held together in a proper mesh arrangement by an elastic spandex fabric. I'd played with simpler EEG setups in both my job on that Chicago psych ward and in one of my neuropsych classes. This looked a tad more advanced.

Dr. Gopal gestured for me to remove my cardigan, which I did, letting it drop to the floor, which looked cleaner than any surface in my apartment. Then she fitted the EEG cap over my head, feeling and measuring my forehead, temple to temple, then adjusting the front row of little metal-disc contacts so they lined up properly. The contacts felt cold and hard on the bare areas of my forehead but not yet wet. Elsewhere on my head, the electrodes merely pressed down through my hair, which was very fine, but even so...

"You don't need to shave my head?" I asked.

"Would you like me to shave your head?" Dr. Gopal responded, her muffled voice like something I imagined a newly risen barber vampire would use. Not mute.

"Um, no? If you don't need to."

"I don't need to."

Then she pulled out a bottle of EEG gel and began injecting the clear liquid through what I presumed were holes in the top of each metal-disc contact. As she moved around my head to a different angle, the reflection I saw confirmed it. And as she moved, my nose registered the sweet, pungent smell like you got from nail polish. *It's the toluene in the polish*, a budding cosmetologist I'd dated briefly in Chicago had told me. *Really toxic. It can cause brain damage.*

But this was presumably *not* nail polish toluene. I hoped.

I felt a wetness flooding under the cap at each contact as well, the metal seeming to sink in harder through it. Not painful at all, but...there.

It was frankly all kind of mad scientist cool.

Lena, meanwhile, had brought over a number of other rolling metal carts she'd loaded with cameras and what looked like motion and decibel sensors. Also more computer monitors with arrays of switches and buttons beneath them.

And here I had thought I was just going to try to recreate my jumpback time travel and self-report on the experience. Which might be why psychological experiments were often accused of being very "soft" science.

"Are you going to explain any of this to me?" I called over to Lena where she had turned on a few monitors and was apparently checking the video feed or motion or sound detection.

"When you're done with Irene," she called back.

I frowned and looked at the short Indian doctor who'd just finished turning on the EEG monitor and checking it was working. She now turned it off and said in quiet, grave voice, "You must take off your shirt now."

I looked over at Lena but she was busy. Feeling suddenly self-conscious, I nonetheless unbuttoned my flannel, tugged it off, and dropped it beside my sweater on the floor. The chair's vinyl backing felt slick but not cold as I leaned back.

Dr. Gopal had brought over yet another rolling cart while I was doing this. More wires, bigger individual electrode pads, another monitor. An ECG machine?

Dr. Gopal confirmed this when she surveyed my blond, wispy chest hair and frowned.

"You need to shave it?" I asked, feeling absurdly proud I had enough hair there to cause a problem.

"Yes. I can do just the spots for the electrodes or shave it all."

"Lena?"

Not looking up from her work, she grinned and said, "Shave it all. It'll be sexy."

I took a deep breath. "You heard her." I sat back and breathed deeply as the woman pulled a small cordless razor from a tray on the ECG cart, turned it on so it sounded like a happy bumblebee, and ran it over my chest in vibrating, ticklish passes, being careful to circle my nipples and to whisk the cut hair to the side of the chair away from my where my shirt and cardigan lay.

"A very delicate touch," I told her when she was done.

She nodded and took out what looked like a small square of fine sandpaper and packaged alcohol swabs. She felt for my clavicle, intercostals, and below-rib locations, roughed up each target patch of skin, cleaned it with alcohol, and attached the sticky ECG electrodes. She tested the measurement, and I saw a familiar jumping line on one screen as well as a bunch of other readings I wasn't familiar with.

"Is that it?" I asked. This was only two measuring devices—head and heart—and already the number of wires and sensors were quickly moving from cool toward claustrophobic.

"One last thing," said Gopal through her mask, "to measure your stress and adrenal hormones."

"Which are probably climbing."

"Yes." Gopal held up what looked like a bulky mouth guard that had tubes, not wires, running out of its front. She signaled for me to open my mouth, and when I did, she put it in with quick precision. Then she attached the tubes into a second, round-topped piece of monitoring equipment on the same cart that held the ECG light show.

A few more flipped switches and Dr. Gopal called over to Lena, "We are ready!"

"Good!" Lena replied. "Thanks, Irene."

Lena flipped a few switches near her and pressed some buttons, and I could see bits of myself in all my freakish, wired-up glory on the monitors near her. I wasn't sure what Lena expected to record happening, but she was clearly trying to cover as many bases as possible.

Lena now picked up one of the stacking plastic chairs like those inside the room's front door and carried it over to me. As she did, my own crazy appearance made me appreciate Lena's casual magnificence once again. The way she moved, with her hips swaying like a jungle cat, her eyes sharp and focused on me. I flashed back yet again to our passion of the night before, and my peripherals caught Dr. Gopal running over to the ECG and stress hormone monitors.

Lena smiled and glanced down at my crotch. There was no need for any equipment to monitor that, I knew. It was visually telling her exactly what I was thinking.

"Okay, Jackson," she said, placing the plastic chair directly in front me, sitting on it, and looking down at her hands folded in her lap like she didn't want to look at her wired-up experimental monkey. "From the stories you told me about what happened two days ago downstairs, your time displacement events—"

"Just caw them jumps," I said around the awkward mouthpiece.

She looked up at me. "Fine. Your jumps. You said they happened at times of life-threatening stress."

"Yoah life, oh mine."

"Extreme threat, then. High stress. Your adrenaline would be high, your heart racing, fast breathing. Does that sound right?"

I closed my eyes to remember, but she slapped my knee.

"No, don't try to recreate it exactly because I think that's a second big part of why you jump."

I frowned at her.

"Not that I think recalling yesterday's circumstances would give you an exact enough recollection," Lena explained.

I frowned again, waiting for her to explain.

"Each time you jumped, it was backward in time by about ten minutes you said."

I nodded.

"And you say you've got an eidetic memory."

Another nod.

"Which means you can recall sensory inputs like sights, sounds, smells, and touches in almost perfect detail almost indefinitely. Now most people, when they want to remember something, concentrate and try to form associations with the input. But they lose the precision of it very quickly. They might recall words or numbers or sound or smells, but what they're really remembering is a *representation* of that input, which they managed to process into their longer-term memory."

I stared at her. I'd described to her how my memory worked. It was nothing like that.

"Right," she responded to my look. "*Your* memories aren't modified representations; they're the actual input as it was perceived at the time. Which can apparently, with the right stimulus and focus, create the same kind of superattraction across the time-space continuum for your *mind* that we've been exploring with photons. It's proof the collection of thoughts, sensations, memories, and emotions that comprise your mind might be created and supported by your body, but aren't tied to it. Or at least not to your body in a particular point in time."

"Why on'y ten mih'uts?"

"Don't know, but I'm guessing the perfection of your memory degrades slightly beyond that."

"An' no going for'ard."

"Right. We don't even know if there *is* a forward until it happens. But I think we can collect proof today that you can jump backward. Measuring your physiological responses will be part of it. The other part involves me telling you a story about my childhood. One you haven't heard before. One that I don't think anyone but my mother knows. And you've never met my mother, correct?"

I shook my head. "I hah'n't meh 'er."

"Good. So listen carefully. There *will* be a quiz later."

And she launched into a long, exhaustively described story about a trip to a pet store she'd taken with her mother when she was only six or seven. It went on and on and on, with her not looking at me, like the story wasn't even *for* me, exactly. So I eventually let one part of my mind listen and remember, while the foremost part of my mind just enjoyed the way Lena's lips moved as she talked. Her tongue. Her limpid brown eyes dancing down and to the side as she remembered. Her chest breathing. Her phenomenal legs and hips shifting on her chair.

At one point, far into the story, I wondered if the story had an end and finally understood that its length was as important as its content. Lena was going to make me jump at some point, somehow, and she wanted to make sure that when I did, I'd come back to a time when I was already wired up. Very clever. No, brilliant. Because *she* was brilliant. Unfortunately, she would realize at some point that I was nowhere near her intellectual equal and lose interest in me. But as long as I was useful to her research, that long at least...

She stopped her story and looked into my eyes. "You've figured out what I'm doing, haven't you?"

I nodded.

She looked at her watch. "Good." She looked to her left at Dr. Gopal. "Irene, do you have the baselines?"

The smaller woman nodded.

Lena turned back to me. "So do I have your consent to try to stimulate a jump by scaring the shit out of you?"

My mouth went dry. Of course I should have foreseen it would be something like this. And of course I had to consent. But it still took me a long beat before I nodded.

Lena visibly swallowed. Then she forcibly kicked back her chair and stood up. "Tie him down, Doctor," she ordered Gopal, and then she walked out of sight like she was leaving the room.

I wanted to smile around the mouth-filling saliva sensor in my mouth. It was all a joke. Lena pretending to leave. And the idea of this little Indian woman's restraints, doctor or no, was just...

Then I saw what Gopal was carrying. They looked like something out of the Middle Ages—heavy metal shackles, black and cold looking, each sprung open on one side.

"Put your hands on the armrests," Gopal said in her whispery voice of death.

I complied and watched in a kind of horrified fascination as her gloved hands snapped one of the shackles onto my right wrist and turned a screw on the side to tighten it. The other shackle dropped onto my other wrist, and she tightened that. Then she knelt down, pulled my left ankle to my left front chair leg and slapped a shackle around those two. She shackled my right ankle to the right front chair leg. Finally, deftly, a simple rope that looped through the back of my belt and around the back riser of the chair.

I couldn't help but test the belt restraint and each shackle and found them more immovable than I'd guessed. Gopal's smooth, precise touch had snugged each of them brutally tight.

While I was checking, the small woman had produced from somewhere a black metal pole that she now slid down into some welded metal rings on the back of my chair. The pole now ran from the floor up behind my head, like a kind of stiff demon tail. And while I studied that in the camera monitors, Gopal suddenly slapped a final, oversized shackle against my bare throat and snapped it closed and tight so that the back of my neck was cinched hard against the tall pole.

I almost spat out the saliva-monitoring device as I tried waggling my head and found it could only rotate slightly. Any off-axis movement caused immense pain and threatened to make me throw up in my mouth.

This was all silly playacting by Lena and Gopal, but it made my heart race. What would happen if I did throw up? With my head so bound, would I suffocate on my own sour vomit? And I couldn't move almost any part of my body. I couldn't *move.*

Lena strode back into my eyeline. She hadn't left.

What she had done, though, was become another person. Her face looked hard and cruel as she hitched up her parachute pants a little, pushed wires coming out of all the electrodes and mouth sensor to one side, and swung one leg over mine so she could sit on my lap, facing me.

Like Cutter did with Kenny that last time. But I didn't tell her that detail. How did she know?

My heart rate spiked higher, and I broke into a cold sweat even as she wriggled the warmth and weight of her forward on my lap, grinding on my quickly growing erection.

"You've made a mistake here, Jackson," she said. "You've assumed that I was attracted to you as a man, not as a curiosity. Because if I was attracted to you as a man, if I cared about you at all, then surely I would never let you come to any real harm in this experiment. Isn't that so? Don't bother answering. You're starting to drool." She turned to Dr. Gopal and said, "Tape his saliva sensor in place. I don't want it falling out."

Gopal nodded, and Lena leaned back fractionally to let the doctor wrap duct tape over my mouth and all the way around my head even as I was finally deciding I needed to spit it out. When the tape went around three more times, I couldn't have spat out the saliva sensor even if I'd wanted to.

Which meant I could only breathe through my nose. And if Lena decided to play with that...

A cruel smile lifted the corner of her mouth, and Lena reached her right hand up to pinch my nose closed.

I whipped my head to the side, surprising her and sucking in air through my nostrils with everything I had.

"Now, now, Professor. Don't shake your head at me. Help me hold his head, Irene."

Then Dr. Gopal's two gloved hands, stronger than they looked, and one of Lena's more substantial bare hands held my head turned uncomfortably to the side I'd chosen as Lena's other hand once again pinched my nose closed.

Panic roared in me now as I felt my lungs fight uselessly to suck air through closed passageways. My stomach sucked frantically in and out, and I tried to buck Lena off my lap as my chest started to scream and my heart pounded harder and harder in my ears.

"Our own version of waterboarding, Professor," Lena's voice said from somewhere. She'd stepped off my lap and stood beside me now, still holding my nose shut. "Don't pass out on me here."

Her hard slap and the release of her fingers brought me back from the gray zone, with life rushing in. Then she grabbed my nose and shut the airway again.

"Do you want to die?" she called out to me. "Do you want to *die?*"

Slipping into the gray again, that seemed like a valid question. But apparently my body didn't agree, because—

My mouth was open around the saliva sensor jammed inside. Cold air flowed in around it. And in through my nose. I could breathe! My head was swimming a little, trying to refocus, but…I was alive!

Lena was seated in the plastic chair directly in front of me, looking down at her hands in her lap.

"From the stories you told me about what happened two days ago downstairs," she said, "your time displacement—"

"An event!" Dr. Gopal called out in a surprisingly shrill voice.

Lena turned her face to Gopal, then jumped up from her chair to see closer. All the display monitors showed lines and numbers bouncing about like crazy.

Which I could see because I could turn my head. My whole body. I spat the saliva sensor out of my mouth and stood up, ripping off the EEG cap and the ECG electrodes one by one, then in clusters by yanking a group of wires hard. The sticky glue that had held them on ripped at my skin before letting go, leaving burning red marks and even blood on my lower left side electrode. The wetness of my hair and its nail polish smell sickened me.

"What are you doing?" Lena cried, turning to me.

I ignored her. I scrambled for my shirt and tugged it on, did up the buttons with shaking fingers. Then my sweater. I was hot, burning up, but I needed the comfort and protection of it. Something that said I had control, that what I'd just gone through hadn't happened. And the paper towels on the counter by the wall—I grabbed them and tried furiously wiping the EEG goop off my forehead and out of my hair.

"Jackson? Jackson, please," Lena was saying from a couple feet away, obviously scared to come closer.

Smart woman.

Clearly too smart for me.

And too fucking *evil*.

I couldn't see a trash can, so I threw the used paper towels on the floor.

"Jackson," Lena pleaded. "You jumped. I know you jumped. The changes in all the gauges, every measurement... It's like you were one person one second and then suddenly another person altogether. Or at least in a completely different state. Not the hormones. Adrenaline can't jump immediately that much. But the brain activity. The heart rate. It's... This is proof!"

"Of what?" I spat at her. "Inexplicable physiological changes. So what? I could have just had a psychotic break and you'd get the same thing. And that's pretty much what you just did to me."

"I did to you...?" Lena's eyes went wide. "Oh my god. I carried out the plan, didn't I? I discussed it with Irene, how to make you really believe you would die, but I didn't believe you'd ever *really* believe it. That I would make you. Oh my god, how far did I go?"

Lena's legs actually gave out under her, and she collapsed down onto the white tile floor, her shoulders jerking as her mouth dropped open and her eyes filled with tears.

Despite myself, despite my madly pounding chest and racing adrenaline, I felt the cold hatred against her that had welled up like a hard stone in my chest start to dissolve, like I had no. Goddamned. Character. At all. "Lena..." I said harshly.

She sniffed and didn't look up. "Just go, Jackson. I told you I was privileged. I didn't tell you I get major tunnel vision at times. Enough that I'll step over boundaries, do whatever I think I need to do if the end seems to justify the means. It's like...it's like if I'm chasing an actual secret of the universe, then that justifies anything I might do or any price I or anyone else has to pay for it. Do you understand? The ends justify the means. Like...like Hitler. Like the atom bomb. Like... Oh my god. I debated it back and forth with myself, understood rationally what I was doing, and I *still* decided that however far I went was justified. Do you understand what that says about me? That I was prepared to... That I *did* do something only a psychopath... Oh my God."

I took one step toward her. Then another. Then it seemed only right when I sat down beside her to comfort and heal her because that's what I did in my life. That's who I was. Even with someone who'd come this close to suffocating me in the name of science. Or maybe especially with someone like that, in some twisted abdication of my own right to exist because of all my own failings or survivor's guilt.

I took one of her trembling hands, but she still wouldn't look at me. Yet her breathing and trembling, her confusion and pain and need—they all put me into my best flow state, who I was meant to be.

"Your mom never let you have a dog," I said quietly.

"Wh—what?"

"That's the story you told me. How she took you shopping one day when you were six or seven. You started by looking at clothes, but then you wandered by a pet store and saw a bunch of puppies. She took you in and let you play with them, but she laughed when you asked if you could take one home. And even though a puppy was what you really wanted, you asked if maybe you could take home a cat instead. Or a bird. A hamster. Finally, a fish. Just one fish."

I knew Lena was staring at me now with her wide-open, red, swollen, wet eyes. As was Dr. Gopal, from a healthy distance. But I didn't look at either of them. My mind was on the little girl in the pet shop, and with the instinctive empathy that had led me into psychology, I was standing in that pet shop right beside her.

I squeezed the little girl's hand and felt Lena respond. Because of course she was still that little girl in the deep, primitive way that each person carried their child selves inside them. And in moments like this, those child selves were often the ones a therapist needed to speak to most.

"You knew in your heart that even though you'd never have a brother or sister to look after or share things with, that if you had a pet, a little puppy to take care of, that he would become your closest friend. That you would be able to share with him the burden of everything your mother and father expected you to be and do. That he would know you didn't want to *only* study in the summertime. You wanted to go to a summer camp that was just about swimming and playing."

Her hand was shaking in mine.

"You even came up with a name for your puppy. You were going to call him Goldie because that was the color of his fur. And when you shared this with your mother, she laughed at that, too. Then she told you that this trip into the pet store was meant to show you the things that people with inadequate direction in their lives used for emotional support. But that you were better than that. Stronger. She took your hand and walked you out of the store. And you never raised the idea of getting a pet ever again. You understood that while your mother and father loved you intensely, there were rules attached to that love. One was that you must always be strong. Another was that when they made up their minds about something, that was the end of it."

Lena's shaking stopped and became gentle sobbing.

Still holding her hand, I looked up to find Dr. Gopal looking very nervous. On her face, this meant a slight twitching of her heavy eyebrows, a tension in the way she stood.

"Dr. Gopal, Irene," I said calmly, in full counselor mode, "we won't be using any more medical equipment today. And we can tidy up here. You can go. Lena will call you if she needs you again. Thank you."

I kept staring at Gopal—incredibly difficult for me—until she finally gave a terse nod and hurried off toward the entry door. A moment later, it opened and closed, and I could feel the absence of her in the air.

After a few moments of Lena's quiet sobs, I drew her curled-over body into mine and let her sobs swell for a time before they finally subsided and the two of us simply breathed together.

"I would never have told you about my parents' conditional love," Lena finally murmured against my chest.

"Not in words. Not directly."

"And I would have been happy with a fish."

"No, you wouldn't."

"No. Fish are to eat."

That evoked a surprise chuckle in me, and I realized how tightly I was still clinging to my own sense of loss. Of what? Innocence? My schoolboy notion that Lena was perfect? Or that some birth families were?

After another moment, Lena said, "You realize that telling me a story I had *planned* to tell you either means you heard it in a future that never happened for me or you read my mind somehow."

"Those explanations sound equally implausible."

"But reading minds shouldn't make all your biological systems jump the way they did. Or tell you about a man that was *going* to jump out of the elevator to kidnap us."

"So Occam's razor lands on the side of time travel."

Lena pushed herself off of my chest and looked into my eyes. I made myself hold her gaze as she said, "You know it was never about whether I believed you."

"You're a scientist. It would be antithetical to your training not to doubt."

"Trust but verify?"

"And you'll never be able to see or experience it directly. Can you work with that?"

She snorted. "I'm a theoretical physicist." She sucked in her lips for a moment and dropped her gaze. "I'm so sorry."

"I know."

Still not raising her gaze. "And I understand if…if you can't forgive me for what I did, if we can't go back to being…friends. I don't know that I could if I were in your shoes."

I reached out, raised her chin, and held her gaze. "You forgive my weakness and I'll forgive your episode of batshit psychopathy. Deal?"

She nodded. "But you still have to learn to control your jumps."

"I have an idea about that."

7

10,000 seconds

BEFORE WE PUT AWAY the various measurement devices, including the cameras, I insisted Lena work with me to remove all recordings of the experiment I'd just gone through.

"No one is going to know about this," I said. "I'd wipe Irene Gopal's brain if I could."

Lena shook her head. "What did she see, really? Nothing she's going to share with anyone. Besides, this is the second time she's worked with me against her husband's strict forbiddance. And I'm sure this experiment freaked her out. She's probably already telling herself it never happened."

"Fine, then we just erase the records..."

"Couldn't we just..."

"...so that people or organizations with even fewer qualms than you had about maybe killing me have nothing to make them look my way."

Lena's face fell. "Right."

The video, audio, and movement recordings were easy because Lena had selected that equipment. A few beeps and clicks and the SDHC cards were empty. The medical stuff ended up being more challenging, but we figured it out together. Then we packed everything away or clattered it back to its usual storage area.

When that was finished, I brought out two plastic chairs and set them in the middle of the white tile floor, facing each other. I sat on one and waited for her to sit in the other.

"Your idea?" she asked tentatively.

"It builds off your theory of how the right stimulus forces my mind to recall exactly a former state, thereby creating a kind of superattraction between my essence now and my essence then."

"I said that?"

I blinked. "Oh, right. That came after the period I jumped back to. So no, you didn't say it. Not in this time stream. And actually, you said it a little different even in the time stream where you *did* say it. You talked about my mind being superattracted to an earlier version of itself. I'm changing it to my essence because whatever jumps back is actually dragging a very different conscious mind with it."

"So what jumps? Your soul?"

"That word usually suggests something metaphysical that exists without the need of a physical body to generate and sustain it. So no. It's just that whatever superattraction I'm creating, it has to be a part of myself that's rooted deeper than that, strong enough to suck itself back ten minutes yet still recall all the differences it had built into itself over those ten minutes."

"Your unconscious."

"Maybe. Along with that deep repeating loop of neural impulses that tell me who I am."

Lena was frowning at me, trying to follow, but obviously dubious. "Does any of this make a difference to what you do now?"

"It tells me that I need to focus on how to create the superattraction, I think. Not just the remembered perceptions of the earlier moment, but the whole being of who I was then. I think extreme threats to myself or critical people in my world somehow focused that in me. I just have to learn to do it without the threats."

"So...?"

I grimaced. "I'm waiting for the painful stuff with you to be far enough in the past that I don't jump back into the middle of it. We made it through. I don't want to risk screwing it up with a redo."

"We spent at least ten minutes just cleaning up."

"True. Okay."

I pulled my ankles up and pretzeled myself into a lotus position, *padmasana.*

Lena blinked and clapped. "Now that's something I didn't expect."

"Focusing now," I said, tuning her out and taking control of my breathing and letting my eyelids flutter, my vision go soft.

Breathe in....

I recalled exactly how I felt watching Lena erase the SDHC cards in the video recording equipment, what I smelled, what I heard, what I understood, who I was.

Breathe out....

I recalled my breathing, my body, the dull, closed-in air of the room, everything in my past that informed my understanding of what a "room" was, what "white" signified in my emotional lexicon, what possibilities existed in each split second of time, and the endless combinations of things that bounced around my brain just below my consciousness that told me what I believed about the nature of the universe.

Breathe in....

I advanced second by second, tracking every modality of my being and the world it was connected to. Over and over and over again, tracking the endless chains of perceptions, memories, and thoughts that had been with me that every instant, until...

I snapped my head up and looked at Lena. I was refreshed but intensely frustrated.

"I'm coming back to what's worked," Lena said. "There's something about the shock of near death. Or the adrenaline rush and thudding heartbeat and—what? Fear? Surprise? Try running around the room with the expectation and fear that it's going to happen."

So I unfolded my legs from my lotus position and stood, doubtful. Nonetheless, I shook myself out and began running. Which was awkward in this room because the room was L-shaped and filled with random equipment carts we'd put away and sharp cupboard corners and chairs and Lena.

"Faster!" she ordered me as I completed one circumference.

I picked up the pace.

I was slipping now at the corners, bouncing off walls and banging my hips and shins on carts and handles in the L-section, swearing as I almost tumbled. My heart thudded in my ears.

"Faster!"

And I plunged on, getting angry, getting scared when I nearly crashed at the far wall and slipped again as I passed Lena, feeling stupid and gangly and—

Bang! Something slammed to the floor.

I almost lost a step but kept going, aiming at the next corner, the next turn, and as I came out of the L, I saw Lena standing by a slammed-down metal tray, looking at me with a hint of the frustration that was roaring in me now. *Suck it up, buttercup!* I mouthed as I passed her.

I cut too close to the entry door as I passed it, and it caught my hip, throwing off my stride and making me skip and swear and sprint faster, boiling with rage and frustration, back toward the L, only to see Lena standing directly in my path with no time for me to—

"Boobies!" she yelled, jerking up her shirt.

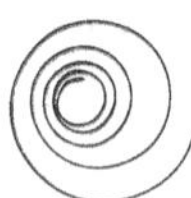

I stood beside the EEG cart, watching Lena's backside as she pushed one of the other carts into the L...and I almost fell down.

Lena heard my huff of breath and turned with concern. Then her eyes went wide, and she burst into a smile like I had never thought I'd see on her face again. "You did it?"

I nodded, fingering my chest where my heart was thumping oddly, as if confused about what it was supposed to do. As was my breath. And my vision. There was at least a five-to-ten-second adjustment period, I realized, as my mind, shocked into an old state and sucked back into the last time I was in that precise state, somehow struggled to update the old me with a memory of what had happened but now never would.

I held up a hand and explained what had happed to Lena, beat by beat, but then leaned over and grabbed my knees in frustration. "But you weren't going to die! So it's something other than just the threat of death..."

"I actually shouted 'Boobies'?" she asked, looking at me sideways like I was making that part up.

"Yes! Which means the jump could have been caused by adrenaline plus surprise or danger or weirdness or sexuality..."

She gave a tentative smile. "I guess we'll have to explore that?"

"Seriously, Lena..."

She sniffed and pulled herself upright like she was consciously putting away the memories of everything she'd recently learned about herself—how willfully she'd toss her humanity aside for knowledge, and maybe exactly where in her childhood that coldness came from—and focusing on the now, on what she and I were here to do. I admired that, even as I ached for the way it kept her from processing her trauma.

"I am serious," she said fiercely. "We try variations. Find what works. Did you ever read Malcolm Gladwell's maxim in *Outliers* about having to practice something for ten thousand hours to become an expert in it?"

I sighed. "He stole that from a friend of mine, K. Anders Ericsson. He died this year. Not COVID. He was seventy-two."

"Whoever said it, you've got to do it—put in the hours to figure it out and master it. It's not just a gift, Jackson. It's a secret of the universe unlocked."

"In ten thousand hours."

"Or we can start with ten thousand minutes."

"That's...like..."

"A solid week," Lena said, doing the math in her head instantly. "Unless we can figure the specific trigger or triggers in the next three hours, and we'll call it baby mastery in ten thousand seconds."

"Yeah. That sounds about my speed right now."

"But here's the problem," Lena said.

I quirked an eyebrow at her.

"I think we can probably rule out simple surprise. Otherwise, you would have been jumping back the first time you crashed against the doorknob or almost hit the equipment as you ran around the room. I'm also inclined to think it wasn't just thoughts of sex, weirdness, or even weird sex with me or you'd have jumped a few other times before now."

"Which leaves . . ."

"Me being hurt or you believing you're about to die. And we're not going either of those places."

"So what do we do?"

"This is a mind thing, and I'm a physicist. But you're a shrink. Why don't you give yourself a session on the couch and draw it out."

"I don't use a couch."

"Whatever, Jackson. Try. Out loud, please."

JACKSON: I'm feeling a bit nervous here, Doc. Exposed. Does she have to watch?

DR. TRAINE: She's a keen observer. But she doesn't judge. She only wants what's best for you. So do I. Can you believe that?

JACKSON: I have to hear her say it.

DR. CORTLAND: You have my word on it, Jackson. I won't judge. I only want what's best for you.

DR. TRAINE: Do you accept that?

JACKSON: Do I have a choice?

DR. TRAINE: Yes. We can stop this right now and ask her to leave.

JACKSON: No. No. I like her here. She has nice eyes and...

DR. TRAINE: What?

JACKSON: Nice boobies.

DR. CORTLAND: You're making this difficult.

JACKSON: I'm serious.

DR. TRAINE: I think he is. I think he's trying to actually understand what's been happening in his brain and why he's responded as he has. [Holding up a hand.] No humor here, Dr. Cortland. He and I are being serious. We need you to just listen.

[A nod from DR. CORTLAND.]

DR. TRAINE: Now, Jackson, I want you to think back through each time you've jumped back in time. And I want you to focus not on the physical circumstances around you or what physical things were going on in your body, but what you *felt* about them.

JACKSON: I don't understand.

DR. TRAINE: Each time you jumped back in time two days ago, what was consistent about the situation?

JACKSON: I was about to die, Lena was about to die, or Lena did die.

DR. TRAINE: And what did you feel about each situation? Anything in common?

JACKSON: That it sucked.

DR. TRAINE: And...

JACKSON: It was my fault.

DR. TRAINE: How was it your fault?

JACKSON: I was there. I should have been able to stop it, especially after my first jump back, but I couldn't. I failed.

DR. TRAINE: And today? You jumped back twice. Lena wasn't going to die either time.

JACKSON: But I was going to hit her. Or I did something to make her crazy.

DR. TRAINE: She stepped in front you the second time, and she was playacting the first.

JACKSON: It didn't... I didn't know. It was just... I don't want to go there.

DR. TRAINE: Go there.

JACKSON: I should have been able to jump back! Then it wouldn't have been... I'm a screwup. I can't do anything right. I let everyone down. *I always let everyone down!*

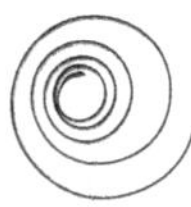

I couldn't continue with my role-playing because the overwhelming nature of my failure grabbed me as tightly as it had the day I went back to pick up Kenny and found he'd checked himself out a week early to rejoin the Demon Monks.

Not to mention the fiasco of my subsequent rescue attempt.

I hunched forward in my chair, breathing deeply and trying to contain my racing heart and the feeling all my blood was rushing out of my body, wishing I had an *actual* separate self, a Dr. Traine to put his comforting arm around me and explain that all of this was healthy. That you had to first identify your deep pathologies, your pathological guilt and self-loathing thought spirals. Then you had to accept them, understand them, learn to forgive yourself, and change the narrative.

I heard Lena scraping her plastic chair over beside mine and a second later felt her warmth as she put her arm around my hunched shoulders and burrowed her face down beside mine.

"It's not objectively true, you know." Her voice was soft; her breath, warm. "Your statement that you can't do anything right. I came to see you teach that day just to ask whether you thought any of your patients actually traveled to past lives. And instead, I got totally caught by *you*. Your intelligence, your ability to listen, your consideration for others. And a day later, the ways you almost overpowered a trained detective three times and outwitted him the fourth time around. And today, with me. I can't even—"

I jerked myself upright, aware Lena also had to straighten up quickly or be knocked over.

"That's it," I said, my blood racing in a good way now. "It's not the objective situation. It's the intense feeling I've failed again. That's what makes my psyche let go. It needs to escape so badly that it jumps my mental tape to an earlier state of being."

"Ten minutes."

"Roughly. I'm guessing something about the initial shock of the particle accelerator set the interval. The triggers of adrenaline or shock are callbacks to that first one. They remind my brain what to do."

Lena took one of my hands and squeezed it. "Is it something you can recreate?"

"The feeling of total failure? Easily. It's part and parcel of my particular social anxiety. The trick is finding a more reliable physical anchor to remind my brain what to do."

Lena stood and pulled me to my feet. "Continue now or wait until tomorrow?"

I flashed back to the dead-eyed face of undercover detective William Gillespie as he slit Lena's throat in one timeline, later slammed her head into concrete and shot her repeatedly in another. I'd mentally labeled him a drug-addicted loose cannon, but it was worse than that. Whatever had happened to him in his undercover assignment had obviously broken something inside him. Or unleashed it.

He was not going to simply give up after Lena and I had escaped him once.

Lena had her security guards when she was working here, but her meeting with the Redmond Police had been cursory and they hadn't even bothered following up with me. And I had no protection anywhere. *Hire a bodyguard,* Kansas had said. Easy for her to say. I had neither the money nor the inclination to do that, which made me an easy target.

Unless I could jump back in time on command.

"We do this now," I said and stood up, shaking myself out. "One thousand seconds to start, and we'll go from there."

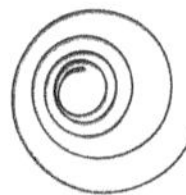

Lena and I worked together for another three hours, during which time I managed to jump back eight times.

And it was getting progressively easier.

We discovered that, as masochistic as it was, if Lena was cheering me on and picking me up at my lowest points, I could let myself intensely feel my failure, then apply a relatively mild physical jolt—a painful slap or pinch—as I told myself I'd fucked up and *had* to let go, and...pow!

A side effect we discovered as my control improved was that jumping back twice in a row, approximately twenty minutes, could give me nosebleeds and start to addle my sense of where I was. And jumping three times, with no break between jumps...

Well, here's what happened when I tried it, from Lena's perspective.

In her timeline, it was after only my second successful jump back after figuring out my trigger. We'd been at it for almost three hours, and I'd finally managed a jump back that hadn't needed the shock of us almost killing each other. It had called for a crazy, happy celebration.

That meant happy laughter, me hugging and kissing her, nuzzling her neck and laughing some more...

I suddenly started jerking about. I fell to the floor and screamed in pain, clutching my head. My heart stopped. My breathing stopped. Lena told me later that she'd snapped into doing CPR, like she'd been trained while considering medicine before giving in to her heritage and devoting herself to math and physics. "One hundred to a hundred and twenty compressions per minute to a depth of at least two inches. Call nine-one-one if you can. Use your Automatic External Defibrillator if you're not getting a response. I was going for the AED. Never had a chance to try that one on a live person before. But you came right back in about twenty pumps. *Then* I let myself get terrified."

She'd been almost ready to call the whole thing off until I gasped out what I'd done—back once, jump again, and again, no breaks, so I'd gone back at least half an hour in maybe ten or fifteen seconds.

"Did I say to do that?" she said when my heart and muscles had smoothed their function and I lay on my back on the floor with my head on Lena's lap, she looking down on me and stroking my red, still blood-mottled face.

"No. I just...figured it out," I murmured up at her, lost in her eyes and the warm, floral smell of her. "The trick of it. Dissociating. I got carried away."

"Your brain and body obviously need time to incorporate their extra minutes. You cram too many of them, too many different futures into them too quickly, and they can't cope."

"Sounds reasonable," I said. "Kiss me."

"Why?"

"I've earned it."

Lena smiled and did, bending down low over me so I could feel the warmth of her bosom against my cheek as our lips met and blended and I tasted the sweetness of her.

When she pulled back, I painfully rolled up to sitting, then to my knees, and finally, unsteadily, to my feet. "We're done for the day," I said.

Lena stood and looked at her watch. "Want to share an early dinner?"

"Early for you. I feel like I've run a marathon, and I've been at it at least eighty minutes longer than you."

"You jumped eight times? Did I...tell you more stories before some of those?"

I grinned. "Oh, yes. Come to my place and I'll let you know what they were."

Her face grew serious. "Can't. I have to talk to my team. We have a progress report due on Monday. I'll be writing it up all weekend."

"On photon time travel."

"The only kind I have hard data on."

"Or can ever tell people about."

"That too."

"You'll have security around you at all times?"

"They drive me home. They bring me here. They stake out the site and the building, keep a guard around my aunt's home while I'm there, check on me every couple of hours. I've got the panic button if I need to go somewhere else. My sponsor was pretty upset about the attack. And about me going out last night, frankly." She touched my face as if just now remembering that I didn't have the same protection detail. "What about you?"

I kissed her palm, then her mouth, and wondered if she'd go for a quick lovemaking session right here on the white tile floors. Except that my associations with this place were too fraught. And I selfishly didn't want our sex to ever be anything but wonderful.

So all I said was, "They had their chance all of yesterday and didn't take it. I'll be a lot harder to catch now."

"Good."

Besides, I thought, *I'm going after them first.*

8

Field testing

AS FAR AS I could tell, nobody followed me home.

I ate, had a second shower to clean off all the sweat I'd pumped out this afternoon, and dressed in fresh, dark, nondescript clothes. Then I put some lemon essential oil in my diffuser and walked around my apartment for a couple hours, working out what came next. I saw the arguments and list I was making in my mind, so I didn't have to write it down. I wouldn't forget.

First, my brave statement about going after *them* before they came for me or Lena—it was true but only part of the plan. After Kansas had confirmed Gillespie was associated with the Demon Monks and that Kenny was still alive, the likelihood that Kenny was involved in this had gone way up. So tracking down Gillespie or the Demon Monks, stupid scary as it was, might not only short-circuit their attacks but also lead me to Kenny. I'd get that second chance to save my brother.

No brainer.

But why not get outside help?

That consumed me for a while, bringing me to a halt to stare out my living room window over the rooftops and through treetops to the distant, darkening blue of Lake Washington as I ran through my options. Kansas had warned me away from the police and FBI because they both seemed somehow involved in this. I'd called Kansas again to see if she'd found anything more, but she wasn't getting back to me—maybe too busy preventing World War III or something. I could maybe hire a private investigator to look for Gillespie, but if I didn't give them all the cautions about the police and FBI and street gangs, they'd almost certainly trip alarms. If I *did* tell them, they'd either run the other way or ask for way more money than I could pay them.

Besides which, I had three things neither Kansas nor a PI had: 1) former direct contact with both Gillespie and other Demon Monks; 2) a mind that forgot nothing it absorbed; and 3) the ability to jump back in time to escape (almost) any situation I might run into.

That third ability also gave me a possible way around Kansas' admonition to not approach the police. Because if I approached them to get, say, Gillespie's contact info, then jumped back in time to before the approach, for *them* the approach would never have happened.

I get the info. They don't know I have it.

I nodded and resumed my pacing.

My next logical steps were to get Patrol Officer Bryan or some other cop from the Seattle PD East Precinct to tell me about Gillespie, use what I learned to find him, make him take me to Kenny. Or to the Demon Monks, who would tell me where Kenny was.

But before *any* of that, I needed to field-test my power to make sure I could do it outside the lab.

I'd do it tonight. I could jump into my Chevy Bolt and squeal down to Capitol Hill, which I knew held not only the Seattle PD East Precinct but also an endless array of nightclubs, ranging from gay and goth to swanky and techno. I would walk into a busy line-up at the door or simply enter. I'd introduce myself to the first interesting-looking person I saw, male or female, even if they were standing in a group. If they didn't all look at me at once, I'd make them. I'd shout. I'd sing. I'd do a dance and act the fool. Until they all looked at me. Judged me. Whispered about me. Laughed at...

Oh God, I could already feel my heart racing in panic. Ramping up the fear about a situation that screamed danger but wouldn't physically kill me.

Probably.

I forced myself to stop pacing and take deep breaths. Calm myself. And as I did, I remembered with a relief that ran through me with a rush of cold tingling, that this whole scenario couldn't work anyway. Because I'd read...when? Back in mid-November. On the fifteenth, the governor had reimplemented a shutdown of all indoor bar and restaurant service. And cases had gotten so much worse after Christmas that I was pretty sure it would be a while before indoor social events, especially those involving alcohol, became legal again.

Except...hm. I frowned. I remembered my students had talked about getting around this supposed "infringement" on their personal freedoms.

Who had?

Mikael, of course.

I pulled my phone out of my pocket and stared down at it. I kept all my students' numbers in there. Invited them to text me with questions and concerns.

I brought up Mikael's number and the text I'd sent him that very morning, right after our meeting after he'd had another thought that might help him wrap his head around the difference between anxiety conditions that grew out of identifiable traumas and ones with no clear, identifiable cause.

This was my use of texting—answering questions and passing on help. Being a teacher. A giver.

Making it work the other way was as foreign to me as simply hanging out with a group of other people and enjoying their company. Even asking for professional help was hard unless, as with Lena, I knew there was just as much in it for her as for me.

With me texting Mikael, it came down to this: I either needed to find a social group where I could socially terrify myself to field-test my power, or I was going to have to go out trolling Seattle's back alleys to confront the homeless and drug addicted and have them physically terrify me to the point I'd let go of this place in the time stream. The second option had a more permanent downside if I failed.

I texted:

Mikael. Prof Traine here. Got a second to chat? Question for you.

Sent.

I slipped my phone back into my pocket, my palms going sweaty, and it dinged before I'd released it. I pulled it up to read:

Sure.

So I called, and Mikael's deep, swaggering voice answered over the sound of some kind of pumping techno music on the other end. "Yo, Prof. 'Sup?"

A part of me wanted to go there, into the fascinating black speech patterns that seemed to dance along beside more mainstream American English like a pride of lions might bound along beside their slow-moving elephant cousins.

Except if I tried, I knew I'd sound foolish, so I stuck with, "You mentioned four Tuesdays back that the lockdowns of clubs and bars didn't bother you because you and your friends found ways around it. Were you referring to hosting parties in each other's homes, or were there hidden clubs, *are* there hidden clubs now, where a person can go and dance and drink and party in groups, masked or not?"

For a moment there was only thumping techno coming through the line, then the thumping line seemed to go through a huge slide down to a new line lower down. The "drop." Right. One of my younger patients back in Chicago had explained it was called dubstep, but it was on its way out.

As I thought it, the music turned way down, and Mikael's voice came through the phone more clearly. "Why you askin'?"

I took a deep breath and licked my lips. I'd never been good at lying. I'd become good at telling when *others* lied. It was part of my job as a therapist to hear the truth behind words people used to hide their truths because they'd learned that telling them caused too much pain. For me, my one lie was trying to pretend I was normal. Anything more caused pain inside me for too many reasons to count.

So now I kept my story true, if incomplete. "I'm exploring my ability to handle social interactions," I said slowly. "Something more than being a teacher, more than being a therapist. You're bright. You must have picked up on the ironic fact that I suffer from the thing I'm teaching all of you about."

I heard Mikael blow out through his lips. "No shit." Then, "How wile you wan' go?"

Another swallow. "Wild. Not fatal."

Mikael chuckled. "You wa' me wit you?"

"Just an address."

There was a rustling, then Mikael came back on the line and read out an address. In Capitol Hill. Not surprising.

"Thank you," I said with a heartfelt rush of feeling.

"Jus' be wit that ballin' my test."

"Long as I make it out alive."

I hung up, and my phone started ringing again. Lena. My thumb itched to answer it, but I knew if I talked to her, I wouldn't want to stop. Or I'd tell her what I was planning, and she'd talk me out of it.

Neither of those worked. I had to do this.

I let it go to voice mail.

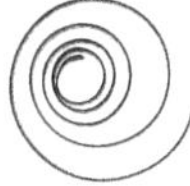

Twenty minutes later, I had parked my car in a lot on East Pike and hurried with my mask on to the address Mikael had given me. When I reached it, I felt a moment of doubt. I couldn't hear any music, and the building looked as dark and dead as an accounting shop where *no* one ever burned the midnight oil.

The security intercom beside the door lit up when I touched the screen, though. It displayed a numbered list of various doctors and associated health professionals. When I scrolled down to the number I'd been given, I chuckled. It purported to be for a speech therapist.

I pressed the entry com button and was asked for a password.

I guessed. "I want to speak easy."

"C'mon in, turn right, go downstairs to the white metal door. Knock three times."

The intercom disconnected, but a second later, the door buzzed open. I entered and sprinted through the directions to reach a door I could hear and feel the music through. Time was ticking. My heart was already racing, both from the run and the dread of what was to come.

I tugged off my mask and knocked.

Rap. Rap. Rap.

The door opened. The thumping dance music spilled out with a rush of hot colognes and soaps and body odor. And a very thick-necked, thick-chested, thick-armed Hispanic man with a shaved head and chinstrap beard looked me up and down like he wasn't seeing me so much as he was looking for weapons.

"Sixty bucks," he growled over the thumping. "Drinks are extra."

"I...uh...pay you?"

The doorman gestured with his chin to a small table just inside. Behind it sat a heavily tattooed young woman with big rainbow-colored hair, who was playing some kind of game on her phone. I stepped past the doorman and up to the rainbow girl.

I was momentarily frozen in my tracks because I could now see into the room. After almost twelve months of careful social distancing and mask wearing, it felt like I'd entered another world. The place was jammed. The room might have been as big as thirty by eighty feet, but the ceiling was only eight or nine feet. Colored laser lights shot out over the sea of bouncing, jerking, swaying bodies, but there wouldn't even have been enough room to hang a disco ball from the ceiling. The music had no voices, just electronica with a heavy beat. Somewhere in the back there had to be a place for drinks. Maybe a bathroom or two.

"Hey!" The Kool-Aid woman.

She wasn't looking at me, just reminding me to pay. I tugged out my wallet and pulled out three twenties. Handed them over. She took the bills without raising her eyes.

"I like the art!" I said, pointing to her tattooed arms and thinking, *Look at me look at me look at me.*

She finally glanced up. "Coats," she said and jabbed a thumb to her right, where I saw coats and boots of all kinds just stacked on the floor, there in the shadows. No coat check. Honor system apparently. It's what you did.

So I shrugged off my peacoat and threw it on top of the nearest pile. Then I turned and walked into the dancing crowd like I knew what I was doing.

And they let me pass. Just danced a bit to the side. Ignored me.

Was this the "Seattle freeze" my students complained about if they'd moved in from somewhere else? It was like being in a crush of people yet being all alone. I felt both elated at my ability to be here and worried that the entire point of my trip, to terrify myself into jumping back in time, was a bust.

Until I let myself really *look* at the dancers I was shuffling between. At their sweaty, unmasked faces, some of them obviously high on drugs, some drunk, some just...

A cute twenty-something girl with cornrowed blonde hair and a dress so thin it was hardly there caught my gaze and smiled at me.

I froze and broke out in a sweat.

She licked her lips and made her body undulate, then squatted down so deep I could see she wore no underwear.

Someone bumped me and grabbed my right arm. The bearded guy, twenties, sweaty, and very drunk, called into my ear, "You're bougie as fuck!"

"What?"

The cornrow girl bumped up close. "He's just thirsty. Hey, you crying?"

"Allergies."

"You need a drink," the bearded guy said, still hanging on to me, weaving. "Pansy-pop."

"How *old* are you?" said cornrows. Then she turned around and shouted gleefully over the music, "Hey, everbody! Grampa alert! Gram-pa!"

"I'm...I'm not..." I stammered, finding it hard to breathe. Hard to move. Trapped. Heart pounding in my ears.

Others were turning toward me now. Not all in their twenties. Hell no. Some looked like they were still teenagers. And they looked at me in horror, like I was a perversion, an abomination, out of place.

Out of place.

I can't breathe.

Save me.

Save—

I was on East Pike, looking at the building with the address Mikael had...

Wait.

The world spun a little, and I clutched my chest through the thick wool of my peacoat. My peacoat that I was wearing. Because I hadn't yet buzzed my way into the building. Hadn't gone downstairs, found the white metal door and knocked on it. Hadn't seen the thick-bodied doorman and the tattooed rainbow woman, the pile of coats, the dancers, the cornrowed woman wearing almost nothing...

I looked up at the overcast Seattle sky, the low cloud ceiling glowing with all the streetlights even though the nightlife that would have once made it dance was locked away.

Or inside this building, downstairs, behind a white door.

And I suddenly realized I hadn't pinched myself. I hadn't suffered any pain. I'd just been caught in the deep fear of my social anxiety, near paralysis, sure I was about to suffer a fate far worse than death, and my self-preservation instinct had kicked in with its new skill like it was just something I could do now.

But I hadn't *chosen* it. I hadn't controlled it in any way.

That wasn't a field test; it was an embarrassment.

Swallowing dryly, I stepped up to the security intercom system, found the number of the "speech pathologist," and pressed the button.

I managed three more tries. The last one left me on my hands and knees and puking on the sidewalk.

They went like this.

My second and third tests were decent. I never got to hurry up a jump by focusing on my failure because the anxiety, the sheer social terror, that the place evoked in me was apparently enough to make my essence need to leave. But each time, I managed to delay and delay it, *then* slap my leg and do a jump.

On my fourth try, though, I got cocky and decided to confront the near-naked cornrows girl on her egocentric behavior. Which, ironically, excited her so much she dragged me to the impromptu bar, plied me with shots, then jammed her tongue down my mouth and her hand down my pants. Then she pulled my now alcohol-impaired self into the middle of the dance floor and made me lie down while she pulled down her panties, crouched over me, and peed on my face.

It cut through my drunk enough to make me time jump involuntarily. But only back to where the cornrows girl was plying me with shots.

Which made me desperately pinch myself to jump a second time to avoid what was to come.

But that only got me outside the downstairs entry to the party, and I had to stagger back along the hall and up the stairs and out, feeling like I was having a heart attack, before I let myself collapse to my hands and knees and puke on the sidewalk.

So expertly done, I told myself, still on my hands and knees, staring at the sour contents of my stomach dribbling away along the sidewalk because it had begun to rain. *Such elegant control.*

Finally, worried some cop would come by and arrest me for public drunkenness, I painfully pushed myself up to my feet and limped back to the parking garage where I'd left my car.

I stank. Not from the urine, which had never coated this timeline's body, but from my vomit and sweat and self-loathing. My entire body trembled as I unlocked my car and sat inside. Closed the door. I breathed shakily and took a minute to wipe my nose and face, slick back my wet hair. My mind was filled with the horror of what I'd just put myself through, probably setting back my self-prescribed anxiety therapy by at least a year or two.

Feeling like a child in need of reassurance, I pulled out my phone and pulled up Lena's voice mail that I hadn't listened to earlier. It told me she knew someone who could arrange extra security for both of us.

I smiled at the thought but didn't call her back.

Yes, don't, chuckled my anxiety demon. *She doesn't want you anyway.*

No, that wasn't it. It was that I'd proven I might not have as much control over my jumpbacks in the real world as in the lab with Lena, but I had some. I also, apparently, had a pretty reliable reaction to intense emotional distress. I'd jump when it counted. When I had to.

I didn't need security.

And tomorrow the real hunt began.

9

Tracking old demons

THE NEXT MORNING, I woke up with a brutal headache, made worse by the morning sun, but it settled with a couple Tylenol, breakfast, and a cup of coffee.

I noticed Lena had texted me a few times early this morning, and I sent a quick greeting back that didn't say much. Then I dialed the Seattle PD East Precinct and was told that Patrol Officer Bryan Miller was in fact on today but not in the office. He was on patrol. Was there an emergency?

"There's no way to contact him directly?" I asked.

"You can leave a message with me, and I'll pass it on to him."

I wasn't going to do that. I respected Kansas' instincts on this and didn't want anyone to log the call and pass my name on to anyone who might connect me with trying to locate their rogue undercover cop, Gillespie. At the very least, Gillespie's cop friends might tell him someone was looking and I'd no longer have the element of surprise.

"Never mind," I said and hung up.

I wasn't giving up on Patrol Officer Miller as my quickest route to Gillespie and, through him, to Kenny, but I'd just had another thought, probably one that every real detective would have had at the top of their list.

I pulled on a pair of running shoes, grabbed my light, navy down jacket, and headed for my car.

Ten minutes later, I was on the I-5, driving south. Driving back to King County, to Renton, to my childhood, at least all of it that I could remember, since I sure as hell didn't remember the first month of my life in Jackson, Mississippi, or the next three years in Pennsylvania before my itchy-footed parents finally settled in Renton and made it the headquarters for the home renovation business they'd franchised and been growing year by year, state by state.

Renton. Or more correctly, a suburb of Renton called Cascade-Fairwood. I had long ago concluded my father had chosen the area because it was literally blocks from a lake surrounded by forest. The fact that Lake Youngs was a reservoir and fenced off from the public didn't seem to affect his assessment. And the house they bought and did minor renovations on over the years was nothing special. Twenty-five hundred square feet of board-and-batten glory. It had been big enough for Kansas, Kentucky, and I to each have our own rooms, with one left over for the nanny, Carmelita, who raised us all from the time we were in diapers.

But over the time I went from Carriage Crest Elementary to Northwood Middle School and finally on to Lindbergh High, Traine Renovations grew from five struggling franchises into seventy-two successful ones, each one paying hefty, ongoing fees to Andy and Anita Traine, who ensured their continued success by holding regular regional conferences and training sessions that kept Andy and Anita traveling more than three hundred days per year.

I was pretty sure they were rich by the time I hit grade six, but little changed in our house except the firing of our nanny because Kansas had turned sixteen, obtained her driving license, and was presumed old enough to care for her two younger siblings when Andy and Anita were not home. And once Kansas left home at eighteen, of course Kenny was supposed to take up the slack.

Yeah. That had worked out well.

Reaching the bottom of Seattle, I turned off on the 405 and decided to take it all the way to Renton-Maple Valley Road rather than the 167 south to 43rd, mostly because I didn't want to drive past the Valley Medical Center down there. Too many memories.

So I drove down to the old family house from the north, past the golf course, past the Fairwood Mall with its McDonald's and pizza and the Safeway where I'd learned how to shop for a week's worth of meals at a time for me and Kenny.

When I finally wound my way onto the tree-lined 183rd Street, it was still early enough that the morning sun was cutting through the leafless poplars and thick firs as I drove, making even the power and telephone lines take on a bucolic glow. Then the memories and feelings associated with this place came flooding back—laughter, pain, loneliness. My chest squeezed tighter as I drove, until I had to slow and pull over for a moment to collect myself.

The street looked untouched by time. Some of the houses might have been renovated, but there were still no cars parked along the roads because everyone here had expansive driveways. There was a community mailbox ahead, but those had gone in before I had left seventeen years ago.

Seventeen years. Almost half my life.

The air smelled the same—the wet rot of fallen leaves and logs, a wood fireplace burning somewhere. I could have been six years old, walking to school with my big brother, kicking stones and telling him jokes I'd heard. Or, later, I could have been riding my ten-speed to Northwood, my stuffed backpack cinched tight as I pumped hard to make it before the bell. Or just walking and talking with Kansas, her so-much-wiser voice explaining to me why Kenny just got crazy mad sometimes and had to run away.

I squinted up the road to where I knew the old house waited and spoke quietly. "You should have been here, Mom. And Dad.

You know what kind of attachment issues you caused in us three? No guarantees it would have saved Kenny, but it might have saved me. Taken from my shoulders the responsibility of saving him all the time."

That anger toward our parents was why I hadn't told them I'd moved back to King County, barely thirty minutes away from here in good traffic.

Of course, even if I'd told them, I probably wouldn't have seen them any more than in my Chicago days. Or when I'd been living in their house.

It was odd to have parents who never gave you up but were also never really there.

Which was why they wouldn't be home today, either, I thought as I restarted the car and pulled back onto the road for the last two blocks.

They weren't. But there was a cheap Ford two-door in the driveway that I guessed belonged to whomever it was they'd hired to look after the place while they were gone.

Or it could be Kenny's car.

I drove in and parked behind it, shut off the engine, and got out. I pulled on my mask, then went to the door and knocked, bracing myself for what I would do if Kenny answered. I'd have to grab the doorframe to make sure I didn't collapse. Maybe to make sure I didn't punch the guy. Or blubber all over him.

But when the door opened with a whoosh that let the overheated inside air rush out around me in a cloud of sickeningly rose-scented air, the person who stood there was an old, Hispanic woman who looked vaguely familiar.

"*¿Sí?*" she said, looking up at me from her dark, round, dumpling figure and dumpling face.

I was amazed that I felt no rush of shame or fear of judgement at all. Which made me wonder if she was so nonthreatening, so... But no, that wasn't the feeling. It was more that I wanted to...hug her?

And it suddenly clicked.

"Carmelita?"

The old woman squinted up at me suspiciously. "*Sí*. What is you wanting?"

"Oh my god. I mean, my goodness. I can't believe my parents even knew where to find you."

Now the woman's squint became ferocious. "You no Kentucky... Jacky?"

I pulled down my mask, and she studied my face from corner to corner. Then suddenly her squeezed-up face burst into a wide smile of happiness that sent a warm rush of comfort and safety through me that had been so forgotten I almost couldn't recognize it.

And suddenly my childhood nanny's arms were wrapped around my lower torso, squeezing me hard through my jacket. Her dumpling cheek with all its surround of gray hair was pressing into my lower chest, sending up an aromatic wave of cinnamon and spice that brought back every memory I had of waking up to her making pancakes with bananas and maple syrup for her three charges.

I squeezed her back for a moment, then tried to release her, but she didn't let go, so I gave her another squeeze. On my third try, she finally released me and looked up with a face that was flushed red, covered with tears, and smiling happily.

"You come home! You mommy daddy not say!"

I pulled my mask back up. "Yeah, well that's probably because my mom and dad don't know. They think I'm still out in Chicago."

"Chicago. Yes! They say!"

"And I don't want them to know I'm back in Seattle, okay? Not yet."

"Secret. Shh."

"Exactly. But there's something I need to ask you. Since you've obviously started looking after the house for my mom and dad…"

"Long time, yes."

"Right. During all that time, has Kenny ever come by?"

Carmelita drew back a step and looked at me sideways, her face suddenly grave. "He…ghost?"

I shook my head. "Not Kenny's ghost, no. So I'm assuming you haven't seen him. Has anyone come here looking for him?"

The old woman shook her head, now looking confused and a little scared.

"It's okay. Really. I mean, that's good. You know he hung around some bad people."

She nodded.

"Right. And I just wanted to make sure none of them ever came around to bother you or my parents. If they haven't before now, I'm sure they never will."

Carmelita looked doubtful, and I mentally kicked myself for planting a seed of needless fear in her mind. If it *was* needless.

I bent down and kissed her on her forehead. "I just need to check for some stuff in his room and mine, okay? I'll be just a minute."

She nodded and I stepped around her and hurried to the stairs and up to the second floor. A couple minutes later, I'd gone through both my old room and Kenny's. I was unsurprised that they looked exactly as they had when I'd left to go to university. They'd been tidied up and dusted regularly—mine still had posters of Jesse Owens, Carl Lewis, and my first celebrity crush, later-disgraced Olympic track star Marion Jones—but were otherwise unchanged. Kansas' room was equally dead and sterile. Like either our parents kept hoping their children would come home to visit, even their dead child, or they just never got around to repurposing the rooms because they were so rarely home.

Unbelievable. And unbelievably sad.

When I clumped back downstairs again, I found Carmelita sitting on the living room couch in a state of intense distress. I sat beside her and held her tiny, soft hands in mine.

"You know this isn't our home anymore—not mine, not Kansas', not Kenny's. I think it pretty much stopped being a real home the day you were sent away."

Carmelita nodded, and her eyes started streaming with tears. "I back now."

I nodded. "Yes. You are. But I'm afraid it's too late. Some things can never be reclaimed or made new again."

"That not true!" the old lady said and squeezed my hands with a sudden intensity that belied her age. "Never too late! Never!"

As she said it and squeezed my hands, her old eyes found mine and held my gaze with a fierceness I'd forgotten. It was the gaze she'd used when she'd told Kansas she was a beautiful fairy princess. When she'd told me the kids who laughed at me when I spoke up in class were just jealous. When she'd told Kenny he was smart enough to be the president of the United States.

It made her zero for three, but I still found myself wanting to believe. And in one sense, I obviously did, didn't I? Maybe that was what I'd really been looking for when I came back here. It was a starting point from which I was going to bring Kenny back to life. Maybe reclaim my own life in the process.

Never too late.

"Okay, Nanny. Okay." I squeezed her hands again. Then I leaned down close to her ear and murmured to her the childhood Mexican hush-a-bye song that I still remembered her singing to me and Kenny on nights when a storm raged outside or, for Kenny, in his always-too-active mind. It wasn't the refrain of "Arrorró mi niño" that I murmured but the verse that had always haunted me on lonely nights:

Este niño lindo
se quiere dormir
y el pícaro sueño
no quiere venir,

which translated roughly into:

This cute boy,
he wants sleep
and bad dreams
don't want him.

I pulled back and smiled at Carmelita through my mask. Then I turned and left the house to go and catch some bad dreams on purpose.

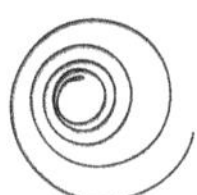

When Kenny had first started running with the Demon Monks in his senior year in high school, he told me he'd met them first at the Fairwood Mall. Kenny had been going through what I'd later come to understand was one of his manic episodes. He'd skipped school but lost his car keys, so he'd decided to run home. He got distracted on his three-mile run by a fight going on outside the Fairwood Mall's convenience store—two guys with knives and a pretty girl with a ripped shirt and black eye.

Kenny had jumped into the middle of it, managed to wrestle away the knife of one guy and shout and argue the other guy into giving up his knife. The guy who gave up his knife freely was the Demon Monk boyfriend of the girl with the black eye. Together, he and Kenny kicked the ass of the other guy, who'd *given* the girl the black eye, and then Kenny and his new friend and the girl had jumped into the new friend's car and roared off to the Gene Coulon Beach Park. There they'd hidden in some trees, and the guy and girl had shown Kenny how to shoot heroin into his veins.

I drove by the mall now after leaving my childhood home and checked out the convenience store. It looked cleaner than I remembered. No evidence of gang activity.

I drove on.

I went northwest into Renton proper to start going through every place I'd ever fished Kenny out of trouble and every place Kenny had told me about that were Demon Monk hangouts. There'd been an old flophouse here (gone), a video arcade there (now an alternative medicine store), a hardware store basement (still standing but only used for storage), and the Lucky Casino (same as always but no one inside I recognized).

It wasn't until I drove west all the way to Tukwila, dropping into more casinos as I went, that I spotted a Demon Monks goon Kenny used to run with.

He was in the Big Wheel Casino on the banks of the Duwamish River. I'd just come through a COVID temperature check, taken off my jacket, and wandered with the jacket over my arm to the gaming tables when I saw him.

I remembered the guy being huge, with a bald head, thick neck, and a chest that threatened to bust out of his tee-shirt when he rolled his shoulders back in a primitive alpha male display. He was the goon who'd flat handed me when I'd tried to run past him to get to Kenny that last day. He'd grabbed me by the collar of my sweatshirt, twisted it, and walked me over to watch Cutter carve up my big brother.

Flat Hand was still bald and huge but now wore elastic-waist, polyester dress pants and a button-down gray shirt with sweat-stained armpits. His muscle had mostly turned to fat. The face was more wrinkled. It still sent little shots of fear adrenaline coursing through my body, though. He looked stupid and mean as he sat hunched over his place at a table, rapping his knuckles on the felt. *Hit me.* Card. *Hit me.* Card. *Hit me.* Bust. Chips gone. More chips placed.

I did a nervous self-check. Did I really want to get mixed up in a world of gangs and violence that I'd managed to get away from completely after Kenny vanished? And did I truly believe I'd be able to jump backward in time if things went wrong? It sounded preposterous as I said it to myself. Despite yesterday. Despite what had happened two days ago in the particle accelerator lab.

Except...

When I looked around the casino, taking in the lights everywhere, the muted dinging of the slot machines nearer the entrance, the clink of glasses, the comforting smell of cooked meats and fat from the restaurant portion, the vaguely rank smell of bodies all around me who'd lost track of time, their bank accounts, and any semblance of normal life and its responsibilities, I knew it was all permanently *in* me the way that every place, every time I walked through was in me. I could jump back here if the fear got great enough.

Which it would.

And ultimately, I didn't really have a choice. My unwillingness to sacrifice myself to save Kenny when Cutter had offered that all those years ago had pretty much cratered my emotional life in the years following. Despite all my academic and professional success. I think my PTSD and social anxiety might, at some level, have just been guilt.

Yet here I was, years later, given a second chance to save Kenny *and* a special power to see it through, and I was just going to back off out of fear?

Like I said, there was no real choice here.

I took a deep breath and walked forward to stand directly behind the bald thug's right shoulder. Close. At first the man ignored me, playing and losing another two hands. But finally he turned his large body slightly toward me.

"You want something?" he grunted.

"Yeah. Take a break from losing and talk to me." I wished it hadn't come out sounding so squeaky, but my mouth was as dry as baked mud. No tears in my eyes, though, because I didn't care what this guy thought of me or whether he judged me. My fear was for my physical body, and it was already as intense as when I'd faced Gillespie, but it was not *social anxiety fear* I realized. It made me once again aware how crazy the social anxiety part of my PTSD was, how all the personal threat signals got so mixed up in my brain that drunk millennials laughing at me felt as dangerous as a thug who still looked like he could snap me like a twig. Ironically, physical fear was easier because I didn't care what I looked or acted like so long as I survived.

Now that thug swung all the way around in his chair so that I had to take a step back. Even gone to fat, he still looked like an enforcer. Easily my height and probably twice the weight.

He looked me up and down. His face, unmasked of course, showed no recognition. "Take your mask off, doofus."

I licked my lips and pulled my mask down. Waited.

"Yeah, I don't know you."

He was about to turn back to the table when I said, "You still with the Monks? Or did they let you go when they joined BAM?"

The guy turned back and was off his chair fast, shoving me backward so that I stumbled against the back of a player at a nearby table, causing an uproar as chips were knocked over. The thug came after me, but before he reached me, a huge, young security guy was at the thug's left arm, talking to him low and direct.

I saw the thug's face twitch, but then he nodded and started walking for a side exit door. He stopped halfway out and motioned for me to follow.

Already feeling enough adrenaline pumping through me to make my head light, I did. This was expected. Part of the plan. I hadn't expected anyone associated with the Demon Monks to just *give* me information.

A moment later, the two of us stepped outside into an empty walkway. We were out of sight of everyone, I noticed.

The thug turned to me with a red face. He looked like a bull as his nostrils flared and pumped hot steam into the cold March air. "You got one minute before I pound your fucking face. Talk!"

"Tell me about Kenny Traine."

"You're no fucking cop."

"You don't know me?"

He squinted at me. "I'm fucking retired."

With a concussion or two, I guessed, my confidence growing. "Okay, then just give me how to talk to someone high up in the Monks. A shot caller. I need an address, phone number, name."

He suddenly yelled and shoved me back against the wall, rattling me and making me suddenly scared *I* would get a concussion as he held me and yelled at me, and then I wouldn't be able to jump back out of this to save anyone. All because of this...this...Neanderthal who was holding me like he'd held me all those years ago while his boss beat up Kenny, carved up Kenny's face!

I roared so loud in his face that he let me go and stepped back a second.

It wasn't enough.

I launched myself off the wall with my fists and arms like battering rams, slammed them into the fat man's chest, and staggered him backward. "Give me a name, you fat pile of puke!"

Flat Hand recovered his balance and looked at me. His sluglike lips curled up in a smile that said happy but not in a good way. "And here I was having a bad day." His meaty hands came up, squeezing into fists.

He lunged and I sidestepped him, swinging a solid roundhouse punch into the man's head as he went by. I was no fighter, but I was a good fifteen years and a hundred pounds lighter. And rage was burning me up now, making me feel fast, strong, and invulnerable.

It lasted all of five seconds as Flat Hand's next lunge was just to grab my jacket. With his weight, he yanked me off balance and slammed me to the pavement. Then a hard-soled shoe connected with my ribs. Again. And again. Then I might have desperately wanted to use the felt-failure trigger technique I'd learned with Lena, except the son of a bitch was finally spitting and yelling stuff I needed to know. I couldn't consciously process it because I was curling up like a crayfish to protect my belly. Which meant he started kicking my back.

I felt something crack, and now every gasp of air lanced pain through me even in between the kicks. I had to get up, roll away and get up! Find a way to jump back. But the second I tried, the thug was on top of me, driving a meaty fist into my gut, spittle flying into my face as he yelled, "*Time to die, fucker!*"

His big hands connected around my neck and squeezed.

I couldn't breathe! I was going to suffocate! No! Dissociate *now—*

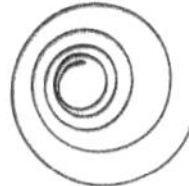

I weaved just a bit on my feet, integrating my mind with this time's body.

I stood in the middle of the casino tables area, my navy jacket slung over my bent left arm. Ahead and just to the left was a blackjack table being physically dominated by the fat, bald thug in his polyester pants and sweat-stained gray button-down. I took in the smells of cooked meat and fat, rank sweat, the muted ding of slot machines, conversations, Flat Hand saying, "Hit me," and rapping the felt of the blackjack table.

I went over in my head what had happened before I'd jumped back here, and this time I could ignore the pain of being kicked to death so I could focus on what my ears took in while that was happening.

"Shot callers Daddo! Dixon! Dougie Buckets at the Palace! Eat you alive they ever saw you!"

Then it had been mostly profanity up to, *"Time to die, fucker!"*

Even just focusing on the aural part of the memory, the fear I'd felt, again coming close to death, flooded through me, and I almost choked. This was *not* healthy. Not just the pain and the fear but the repeated trauma. Was I supposed to get used to this now? I never had as a teenager. It, plus the guilt of failing to save Kenny, had scarred me for life. Was it going to be any different now just because I could jump back in time and pretend it had never happened?

I leaned over, dropped my jacket to the floor, and grabbed my knees for support.

The motion drew a male casino employee over. He wasn't the burly bouncer who'd handled the bald guy in the future that would now never be, but he still had the kind of professional presence that told you immediately not to mess with him.

"Are you all right, sir? Can I get you something? Did you get your temperature scanned when you came in?"

I picked my jacket up off the floor, straightened, and looked at the eyes above the man's mask. And maybe because I was still emotionally exhausted and traumatized by what I'd just been though, I felt no need to cringe or hide. I just shook my head and took a deep breath. "I got scanned. It's not COVID. Just some emotional fatigue."

"Do you need..."

"I'm fine actually. I think I'll be going now."

I turned and left.

Daddo. Dixon. Dougie Buckets at the Palace...

Not a lot to go on.

I banged my hand against the driver's wheel as I drove away, wondering if I should have tried another round with the fat, bald guy. At least I knew his moves now.

But I had a gut feeling that I wouldn't get a lot more out of him. He seemed too cagey to trick and too tough to talk under duress. Assuming there was any way I could put him under duress short of picking up a gun or Taser somewhere and planting it outside that side door…

Nah.

At least I had one name with kind of a location.

I pulled off into a golf course parking lot and found a place at the far end, away from other cars. Then I pulled out my phone and did some looking. "Dougie Buckets" turned up nothing. Not a surprise. "The Palace" near "Seattle" turned up about thirty places, ranging from a dog grooming shop to restaurants to an historic hotel, a childcare place, a rug dealer.

I sighed and started with the restaurants. Hit the contact phone number, waited, then, "Hi, I'm looking for Dougie?…Yeah. Dougie Buckets…Oh, sorry. Wrong place." Dialed the next place.

It took me about twenty minutes to go through most of the list, and I was almost thinking of going back to the bald thug in the casino when a guy I asked about Dougie Buckets said, "Sure. He's here. Gimme a second…"

I hung up, my pulse suddenly racing. Holy shit, it had worked.

I looked at the name and address of the place I'd called. It was a gun store. Which made sense because, hey, if your street gang was going to own any legit business…

It was located in South Park, nestled into a block of commercial buildings between a Boeing lab and the South Park Marina. Way north of what the Demon Monks used to call their territory. Maybe part of what they took over when they joined and absorbed BAM.

I punched the address into my car's GPS and pulled out of the golf course parking lot, heading north.

The windows of the Gun Palace were boarded over, but a sign by the door said they were open, so I pulled on my mask and walked in.

The long box interior was lit by two banks of humming fluorescents on the ceiling that cast the wall displays of guns I saw as I entered with a yellow, uncertain light. It looked like hunting rifles and assault weapons mostly, held horizontally on pegs, presumably so you could get a sense of how badass you'd look as you held them out in front you, advancing on your prey. The handguns and ammo, I guessed, were stowed in the lit-up display counters that ran around the far side and right corner of the room.

I turned to my left and saw that this wall, running right across where the windows once let in sun, was covered with hunting and flak jackets. And a pair of yellowing American flags, pinned so they were at full extension.

A Latino man stepped out of the back room wearing a green flak jacket and matching baseball cap. He had a bushy brown handlebar mustache that made him look impatient without him saying a word.

He stared hard at me.

And while I spent most days of my adult life feeling like I was being judged for not fitting in, this was one case where I *knew* I didn't, couldn't, never would. It meant, like with Gillespie, I didn't have to worry about earning this goon's approval with my honesty and good character. I could therefore say and do whatever was necessary to get what I needed.

"I'm looking for someone," I said, feigning interest in the ball caps being displayed under glass like the pistols. "Dougie

Buckets."

I felt the man's stare grow even harder, and he spoke with a strong accent. "What you want with Dougie, hey?"

"It's what he wants with me. He sent someone to get me. Now I'm here."

"Who're you?"

My impatience overcame my aversion to eye contact. I raised my head, and a sarcastic greeting my nanny used to use for men she thought were being too forward popped into my head. "*Mira güey*,"—roughly, *Hey, dude*—"I'm not here for you. Tell Dougie there's someone out here he wants to talk to, or I'll just leave now."

I held the tough guy's gaze until my own eyes started to water from not blinking, but the man turned just before it became obvious, and walked through a door into a back room.

I let out a short gasp. It's what I'd *hoped* would happen, the tough guy breaking. Because the bald guy had referred to Dougie as a "shot caller," meaning someone higher up in the gang. You didn't want to piss off a shot caller if there was a chance I was someone important.

But being right just meant I was really stepping into the hornet's nest now. If Dougie Buckets was high up in the gang and part of the order to kidnap me, he wasn't going to let me just walk out of here. And deep in my heart, I still didn't trust my ability to jump back through time yet. I'd gotten the power suddenly. I might lose it just as suddenly.

I glanced at my watch, noted the time, estimated how many minutes I'd been inside already, and began wandering around the shop, checking out the handguns and the cheesy "American Patriot" hats and mugs. Some non-firepower weapons, too-- brass knuckles, something that looked like a polished wood nightstick, Japanese throwing stars...

What was taking so long? Should I just leave now?

Another chill of doubt about my time travel gift ran through me. This time, not only about whether I still had it but whether I really wanted to go through the kinds of things that were necessary to make it work.

Maybe instead I should slide over one of these counters, grab an automatic rifle off the wall, find some ammunition for it, figure out how to load it in. Then if Dougie came out with a bunch of guys to beat me down, I'd be in a better position to "negotiate" without *having* to jump backward in time to survive.

Yeah, 'cause that's why I'd run from all this gang stuff seventeen years ago. To train in gun-fu like John Wick. To become...*Action Jackson*.

The thought made me crack up. Good luck with that, Professor Traine.

An inner door slammed somewhere, and I heard voices arguing. I glanced at my watch. It had been almost five minutes since the Latino tough guy had gone to get Dougie.

Now the door he'd left through opened and a welterweight guy with hair so fiery orange it looked dyed came prowling out of the back room. He was followed by the original tough Latino and another one who could have been his brother. Both had the same heavy mustache.

The welterweight redhead walked to the near end of the counter, opened the counter's latched gate, and all three men walked out, the welterweight directly in front of me. He looked me up and down. He walked a circle around me, checking me out like I was some show animal on display, and finished up in front of me again, in my personal space looking up just a little to get right in my face.

I opened my mouth to speak, and the man shook his head.

"So who the fuck are you?" he said. It came out all grotty and smelling of alcohol.

"Are you Dougie Buckets?"

"Gimme your hand."

"You with the Monks? You know Kenny Traine?"

There was a clicking sound, and I felt something cold and metal pressed up against the side of my head. I half turned to look that way and saw one of the Latino toughs had put a gun to me.

The red-haired welterweight said, "Gimme your fucking hand."

I lifted my right hand and the man took it with both of his. His fingers were rough and blunt as they suddenly shifted to spread out my thumb and pinched the fleshy area between thumb and palm so hard that pain shot all the way up to my neck and I cried out.

"Now you fucking answer my fucking questions, or I'm gonna cause you so much fucking pain you'll wish you were dead."

My head was down again, staring at the concrete floor, trying to get my bearings. "Let go of my hand," I said.

"Who the fuck you from? You too white to be Crips or Boyz or Islanders," said the welterweight and pinched so much pain through my hand that I thought I was going to pass out.

And that couldn't happen. If I passed out and too much time passed, I couldn't jump back far enough to make things right.

Which is why I shocked myself by gritting my teeth and growling through them, "Let go of my fucking hand."

A beat. Another one. Then the welterweight let go of my hand.

I staggered a little, shook my hand, and tried to conjure up the intense sense of failure I'd used with Lena to trigger my jump. I had to jump. I wasn't going to get anything from these guys because they were as simple-minded as Flat Hand had been and I had no leverage here. I'd made a mistake. I had to reset. Find the failure. C'mon. Deep dive into that soul-shredding darkness, then pinch or slap yourself, and...

I...couldn't.

My "field test" hadn't needed it. Flat Hand hadn't given me the chance. Now, my lazy, ego-protecting sense of self was simply refusing to go there again. Holy shit.

Come on!

No no no no.

"Okay, tough guy," the welterweight said. "You got two seconds."

Fuck you, said a voice inside me that might have been my anxiety demon or my sadly rational, this-is-the-only-way-now-if-you-want-to-survive-and-find-Kenny voice.

I looked down at the welterweight and gave him my best sneer. "If you don't know who I am," I said, "then you're not the shot caller I'm looking for. You're just a punk."

The welterweight's cheeks and forehead grew as red as his hair. "You…" He looked past me. "Hit him."

A fist slammed into my lower back, lancing pain through me and lancing ice through my legs.

"Again."

Another fist. More pain. Something wet in my mouth. Vomit? Blood? All of my earlier bravado fled, and my mental state shot straight to terror.

"Again!"

Dissociate. Now! Let go. Let—"Ahh!" Something cracked inside me. I was—

"Who're you?" said the Latino thug behind the counter.

I staggered a bit and blinked. Disorientation, but …no physical pain.

Reorient.

Settle in.

Forget the pain and terror. Forget it. This was where I was, when I was. And I surprisingly knew what I had to do next.

"I asked you—"

"I heard you, *mira güey*. But I don't answer to you. You tell Dougie there's someone out here he wants to talk to, or I just leave and you can explain to him later."

Again the moment of indecision, then the thug exited through a door to the back room. Which I heard click closed. But there was no sound of a lock being thrown. The guy had the confidence of a thug who saw me as some kind of nonfighting civilian. It would have been a reasonable assessment...if I hadn't seen already where that would get me. *Where that got me.*

Forget it. Focus. Save Kenny.

Assuming a process like last time, I had five minutes before the reheaded welterweight emerged with his thugs. I vaulted over the countertop and went straight for the brass knuckles and the billy club I'd seen earlier. I put brass knuckles on both hands and stuffed the club down the back of my pants. I didn't know how to use guns, but my hand hovered over a pistol anyway. Maybe just to threaten with?

No. That would only encourage them to shoot me. I'd stick with the less-immediately-threatening knuckles and clubs that I at least knew how to use. More or less.

I checked my watch. *Go. Now.*

Taking a deep breath, I grabbed the doorknob the thug had exited through, turned it, and slipped through the door.

A short hallway. Door to the left had voices, scraping chairs, and the sound of cutlery. I smelled fried chicken. Door to the right, no sound.

I chose the door to the right.

My heart leapt when the dark shapes inside suggested an office. I flicked on the lights. Sure enough—a filing cabinet, battered metal desk with a computer monitor and printer, and a couple old wood-and-cracked-vinyl armchairs. Very last century. On the wall by the desk were a couple maps. One was a map of the world. One was a blow-up of the Seattle metropolitan area—Seattle, Tacoma, Bellevue—but it had a red circle around a spot in northeast Redmond, which I guessed was Lena's particle accelerator lab, and other red circles and black and blue lines drawn here and there all over Seattle itself, Renton, Tukwila, all the way down to Tacoma, even some out on Vashon Island in Puget Sound.

There were inscriptions, too, hard to read, but I knew my mind would remember the shapes. I'd figure them out later. I tried to consciously see everything there was to see there.

Then I turned to the map of the world. It had few markings, and most of those contained question marks, like whoever was doing the marking was exploring some idea more than recording something.

Done, I turned to the filing cabinet and computer, knowing I was pushing my luck. But if the map had circled Lena's location, there might be something in the filing cabinet, or more likely the computer, that explained why.

I hurried over to the filing cabinet and tugged on the top drawer. Against all other signs of the gang's sloppy overconfidence I'd met so far, the drawer was locked. So were the other drawers. And the desk drawers. What? Was Dougie paranoid?

I found the computer box under the desk and hit the power button. An Intel machine. Slow. Seriously slow. Then the Windows screen popped up, and the opening sound with it made me just about jump out of my skin.

Shit!

I froze. Heard nothing through the door. Not even the arguing voices I recalled in the old future I'd jumped back from. Damn it. They might be out in the main store now, wondering where I'd gone. Any moment they'd be back here.

Heart pounding so hard I feared I'd pass out or jump back in time spontaneously, I pushed the space bar and enter key and escape key, willing the desktop to pop up. But of course it didn't. It just popped up Dougie's username and demanded a password.

Of course. Which would be what? P-a-l-a-c-e, I typed carefully so that my brass knuckles didn't bump the keys. Nope. D-e-m-o-n-[space]-M-o-n-k-s. Nope. B-A-M. How about Buckets? B-U-C-K—

The door banged open, and I jumped back from the desk so that my back slammed against the locked filing cabinet.

In the door stood the redheaded welterweight who'd had me beaten in the other timeline. Behind him stood the two thugs who'd been with him that time.

"Hey there, whoever you are," said the welterweight, stepping up to me. "See you found some knuckles."

My breath was high and fast in my chest. I felt like I was going to pee my pants.

The welterweight reached behind his back and whipped out a pistol that he pressed to my forehead. "Want to know why they call me Dougie *Buckets?*"

"I really don't," I said, dropping and driving a brass-knuckled fist into his groin as I mentally yelled, *Dissoc—*

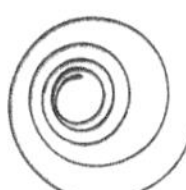

I was standing, a little dazed, inside the gun shop. The brown-handlebar-mustached Latino in his green flak jacket and matching baseball cap was staring at me silently.

Once I had full control over my body, I forced myself to look into the eyes of the man and asked, "Have I...um...said anything to you yet?"

The man pulled back his bushy upper lip. "You just did, *mamón.* You want something?"

"You know what? I don't think I do. Thanks anyway."

I retreated out of the store.

No one followed me, but as I walked back to the car, I started worrying. While I hadn't spotted them, there were certainly cameras in that gun store. Maybe even out here in the parking lot. Which meant they had me on video. So if someone who *did* recognize me reviewed that video, or if, for some reason, the police saw it, what would that mean?

Was it enough to warrant another jump back so I never went into the store at all? Or far enough that I never drove into this parking lot at all?

I just had to find some way to terrorize myself, hurt myself, and jump back into a me whose guts would suddenly start churning, head pounding, heart squeezing. All while I drove on the highway.

No thank you. Not this time. Not for such a slim possible downside.

Besides, I had what was likely my final destination.

I jumped in my car and drove off.

10

Tell me not to go

FORTY MINUTES LATER, I was procrastinating, going for a last meal and final phone call.

It was in a freestanding sandwich restaurant I'd never visited before. Not surprising since Seattle had thousands of these small food joints, and this one was in a part of town I rarely visited.

The area was SODO, or South of the Dome, meaning the mostly industrial land south of the Kingdome, home of the Seattle Mariners baseball team until it was demolished in 2000 after being replaced in 1999 by what was now called the T-Mobile Park, which was funded by both private money and state bonds, and soon after, construction added a neighboring multiuse stadium now called the Lumen Field, which was home to the Seattle Seahawks, a *football* team.

To even follow that set of shifting names and corporate sponsors, you had to either be a sports nut or have read about it sometime and just, like, never forget stuff.

I wasn't a sports nut.

Wasn't a sandwich aficionado either, but I'd read about this place. Paseo SODO. It boasted of having "The best sandwich in Seattle." I figured that was arguably true if you liked juicy shavings of Caribbean flavored pork shoulder smothered in caramelized onions, garlic aioli sauce, pickled jalapeños, and fresh cilantro and romaine lettuce served inside a fresh-sliced and toasted baguette.

A bit messy. Had me licking and wiping my fingers repeatedly as I ate. But not a bad last meal for someone planning a suicide mission.

Breathe. Chew. Savor. Drink.

And when I was done and left with only my glass of beer to finish, I finally pulled out my phone. I hadn't spoken to Lena today. I hadn't called her this morning because I hadn't known how any of this was going to go down and didn't want to alarm her. But now that I *did* know what I was going to do and was beginning to appreciate just how bad this could get, I needed her to know…

What? That I cared for her? That she'd changed my life? I'd only known her for five days. Of course, I had saved her life in that time, shared a world-shifting discovery with her, slept with her, then had her try to kill me…and train me.

And now she was preparing her research report, and I was chasing down criminals from my past to find Kenny. Who might be a criminal like them.

Without knowing what I wanted to say, I wiped the Cuban spiciness from my lips one more time and found myself dialing Lena's number. She picked up on the second ring. "Are you alright?" she said.

"Hello to you, too. Why would you ask that?"

"I don't know. Something about how you didn't come over here to see me last night or this morning."

"You asked me not to. You said you'd be working the whole time against a deadline."

"And you didn't need me enough to ignore it?"

I fell silent, suddenly unsure whether I wanted to laugh or cry about that.

"Jackson? *Are* you alright?"

She could read me even over a phone line, just from my voice. How was she the physicist and I the psychologist? Or was it only me she could read in this way?

"Jackson?"

"Some things I never told you," I said in a rush. "My brother Kenny vanished when I was eighteen, and we all thought he died in a gang war. But when Gillespie came after us in your lab, he yelled through that door at me that Kenny is alive. My sister thinks he's right. So I went out looking for gang members today. The ones I think Gillespie's mixed up with. And my brother."

Now it was Lena's turn to be silent.

"I found a guy I recognized, got names from him, and jumped back to before he ever saw me. The names led me to more gang members, which got me an address that might be the new gang clubhouse. I'm close to the clubhouse now."

I could hear her breathing get deeper on the phone like she was bearing down or trying to calm herself. This time I waited her out. When she spoke again, she had control of her voice, but I could hear something very unstable just underneath.

"One of those guys I went out with before MIT?" she said at last. "He joined the Army and became a Ranger. He's done some crazy stuff and knows a lot of guys just as crazy as he is. They all live in or near Seattle. Let me call them. If they're not on deployment right now..."

"This is a guy you still keep in touch with?" I was surprised to feel a nasty tingle of jealousy creep up my spine.

"I do. As a friend."

"I thought you said your college romances were disasters."

"Not someone I'd want to marry or sleep with now. A *friend*. Let me call him."

I considered it. It made sense on the surface—step back, give this to some real action heroes. Except Army Rangers weren't cops, and I didn't even know what I was going to find yet. "I love that you want to help. Maybe if I find something concrete and can't get the police interested."

"Jackson..." I could almost hear Lena chewing on her lips. When she spoke again, the unsteadiness under her voice was rising. "What about your sister?"

"I told you. She said don't ask questions. And don't call her again. I did anyway, and she didn't answer."

"But..."

"You know what? I think I called just so you'd ask me not to go..."

"Please don't go."

"...because I'm scared. But if there's anyone who has a get-out-of-danger card, it's me. You know that. I proved it a bunch of times last night and again today. So I think what I now need is just to hear you say you believe in me."

Silence.

"Lena?"

"I...don't want to fall for someone who's going to get themselves killed."

My heart curled up inside me. "Another disastrous relationship."

Silence. Which meant yes.

"Okay, then. Good luck with your report." I hung up.

When my phone rang a moment later, I swiped red for *don't answer* and turned it to silent.

11

Into the belly of the beast

THE PLACE I'D CALLED a "clubhouse" was actually just another spot circled in red on the map I'd seen in Dougie Buckets' office. But it had also had a date on it. Today's date. So maybe not a clubhouse but almost certainly a place where something gang related was going to happen. Maybe a heist, a drug shipment, something big enough for Dougie Buckets to know about.

Whatever it was, I was betting important gang members were going to be there. So I had to be there.

I drove my blue Chevy Bolt north up a quiet Occidental Avenue to the cross street I'd seen and kept going up that block, glancing to my right to take in what I was now calling in my mind "Ground Zero." It was a concrete-walled, boarded-up shop of some kind. Its north end was connected to a storage depot with old furniture outlet signs now covered with graffiti. The north end of *that* was connected to a long warehouse with now-shut truck loading bays. White smoke still puffed out a couple pipes that jutted from the storage depot section's roof.

The three connected buildings looked dingy and sad as I drove slowly past, but together they took up the entire east side of the block. Lots of room to assemble an army of gang warriors with trucks with bombs in there if you wanted—for the domestic terrorism with white nationalists Kansas had speculated about. Except the Demon Monks had always been multi-racial and seemed more about money than ideology.

So...a place to traffic drugs or other contraband? Human trafficking?

I turned left at the end of the block and saw I was only a couple blocks from the BNSF railway lines that served the Pier 30 docks and international shipping waters. That fit the smuggling theory.

Circling the block to do the Occidental Avenue run again, I noticed there were a few railway lines on the other side of Ground Zero as well. So maybe you loaded trucks out of the Occidental Avenue side of Ground Zero and freight cars out its rear.

I parked by the curb the next block up from Ground Zero's north end, climbed out, and walked behind the building where the freight cars ran.

This rear strip was mostly gravel, with scrub grass lining the empty train tracks to my left, Ground Zero to my right. No people. The sight and sound of city traffic mostly blocked. Easy to forget you were just a couple miles from downtown. On top of all that, the sky had turned overcast, and a steady northerly was blowing the briny smell of ocean up this corridor as I crunched along.

I studied this side of the warehouse building as I walked. It had truck loading bays every fifteen feet or so, all the roll-up metal bay doors shut tight, about four and a half feet above ground level. This would let a transport truck back up to them and have its loading door level with the floor of the bay door. Warehouse workers could then just roll pallets, boxes, etc. directly into the back of the truck.

But to accommodate people entering and leaving the bay doors on foot, a long, concrete platform ran along the back of the warehouse at the level of the bottom of the bay doors like a buffer between backed up trucks and the doors themselves.

Covering that buffer, supported by sturdy metal poles, was an equally wide strip of metal awning that would have protected goods and people from the rain when warehouse workers were loading goods into trucks.

The metal awning also let whoever ran the warehouse leave a bunch of cardboard boxes and two squat dumpsters outside a black-painted man door and not worry about the rain. (This *was* Seattle, after all, where the rain, it raineth'd every day.)

Stairs ran from ground level up to the platform at regular intervals, including right to the black door beside the dumpsters.

What the whole setup showed me was a way an agile person like myself might climb the steps to the concrete landing by the dumpsters, then the poles to the top of the awning, then jump to the one short section of second floor that had actual windows showing and enter the building.

Why break in here?

The parked cars. Not only was this the one stretch with dumpsters, it was the one place with cars. A collection of twenty-eight new-looking Audis, BMWs, American muscle cars, and even a Tesla were parked messily near the stairs to the black door.

They looked clean, like they hadn't been here long.

I looked around to see if I was being watched, then scooted to the steps and up. Tried the door. Locked. No surprise. I saw there was an entry keypad. That would have saved handing out keys or some flunky coming to unlock the door for each new arrival.

But you had to know the code. I didn't. So my criminal life was about to begin with a cat-burglar-type break and enter.

Before swinging my way up one of the poles to climb onto the metal awning, though, I did jog down the entire length of the platform, trying every door I could find, just in case. They were all locked.

So I came back to the black-painted door and looked at my watch. 2:03. If I came back to this point in time, all would be good, right? What could possibly go wrong?

Stop stalling. Go!

A quick hop onto the stair railing, steadied by an awning support pole, a jump, grab, and heave, and I was onto the metal awning. Surprisingly solid. I hurried, as light-footed as I could, to the wall below one of the windows and reached up to check it. It was not only open, but one that slid up from the bottom with no screen. No sound from inside.

I was about to jump and pull myself up through the window when I became aware of a growing cacophony of motorcycle engines that sounded like they had turned east off Occidental Avenue and were slowing to turn down this back corridor behind Ground Zero.

Oh shit. Go!

I grabbed the sill and jumped, hauling myself up and through in almost one motion, except the shaking of the window frame slid the window itself down into my lower back and trapped my butt outside.

The rumbling of motorcycles was suddenly deafening.

I rolled sideways, pushed the window up, then jerked my lower half through so I fell fully into the room, dragging the side curtain down with me as I did.

I rolled up to my feet and ducked to the remaining side curtain to peek out. A set of eleven motorcycles—big Harleys, a couple that looked like they had Vs or wing designs—had just driven into the packed-dirt-and-gravel road where I'd been just a minute ago, and parked with the twenty-eight sedans and muscle cars already there.

Rival gang? A Hells Angels affiliate? Either way, getting back to where I was at 2:03 wasn't looking safe anymore. Figure that out later. At least none of them were shouting and pointing to the window where some dude's feet had been sticking out.

Go!

I did a quick survey of the room I'd spilled into. There was a wooden chair, an open box filled with Bubble Wrap, a couple empty beer cans, a well-thumbed-through *Modern Homesteader*

Magazine (for the gangster who wants to get away from it all?), and an old metal-frame double bed with a rumpled, but not dusty, bedspread and pillow. What was it for? Sleeping in between gang business? A place to take female groupies that felt like a cheap motel? Or to stash me and Lena after they kidnapped us?

No. It wouldn't have held us, as I'd just proven. *Move on.*

I went to the closed door, heard nothing on the other side, opened it, and slipped out.

The hall went left and right. Five rooms lay to the right and four to the left. Directly across from me looked like a common area with couches and a TV. To the right of it lay a kitchen and what I guessed was a bathroom. To the left of the common area were stairs leading down.

A booming came from the floor below me. Presumably one of the motorcyclists banging on the black metal door to be let in. Then a loud, squeaking hinge and a tromp of boots and male voices talking as they entered downstairs. No one going up. Yet. If they did, it would be for the washroom. I couldn't be standing in the open like this.

Go!

I ran as lightly as I could to room one and in, closed the door behind me. It was another bedroom, but this one had a suitcase of clothes. I listened at the door and still heard no one coming upstairs, so I swung quickly out the door and into room two and closed that door behind me. A bed, clothes, and stacks of boxes filled with bagged comic books, action figures, and early pulp fiction originals. Like the occupant had knocked over a collectible store and was trying to figure out what to do with it all.

Thumping boots outside confirmed my fears one of the bikers had climbed the stairs. A moment later, I heard sounds of explosive intestinal relief, a toilet flushing, door slamming, boots tromping down the stairs.

I started to sweat. This was too close. Too gross. If I got caught now and couldn't jump back for some reason, I was so screwed.

Or dead.

Don't think about it. Go!

Rooms three through ten all had beds and assorted personal items. I guessed that if the head capo or shot caller or big boss in this gang slept here, it was in room four, nearest the kitchen. And it had the biggest bed.

Or maybe the only gang members who stayed here were ones who had no homes of their own. Or ones being disciplined or held prisoner. Who the hell knew? Stop analyzing! I'd finally heard the last of the bikers leave downstairs. I could quietly follow them to their meeting.

Go!

No.

I looked at my watch first.

2:10. I was past my time to jump back out safely before the bikers arrived, but I hadn't been seen yet. Which meant, theoretically, I could jump back to *this* point later, then sneak back out and still no one would ever know I'd been here.

Or you could just leave now.

I stood at the edge of running, trying to figure if there was anything I was going to realistically learn if I went down and managed to follow the assembling criminals. I'd *thought* I was only going to have to elude or deal with a handful of top gang shot callers, but now it seemed like I'd landed in the middle of some kind of gang summit.

Go or stay.

Be a man or a nothing.

Go back to Lena, and have her send in her Rangers.

For what? To do what? I don't even know what's going on downstairs!

It was my frustration with myself that finally broke my stasis and got me moving. Counting each fast-passing minute in my head—but moving.

Downstairs, the poorly lit entry hall was empty. I quickly checked the door that had been locked from the outside and found it was locked from inside, too. An internal, keypad deadbolt. No way in or out without the code.

Well, that was…claustrophobic.

I turned back to the entry hall. Actually halls. As my eyes fully adjusted to the gloom, I realized the hall that held the entry door and bottom of the stairs had a cross hall made of unpainted drywall just past the stairs and a second cross hall beyond that.

It all smelled endlessly of the dusty glue smell of newly framed-in drywall. Dusty walls. Dusty floor.

It was like the Demon Monks had built a rat warren inside this building, maybe to gradually turn it into a giant clubhouse or maybe just to mess with the heads of folks who came visiting. During my teen years, I had certainly had the impression the Demon Monks were smart but always on the edge of blowing everything up. It wasn't hard to imagine them bringing that craziness into BAM, taking them over, and making crazy the way the amalgamated gang did everything now.

Which now left me a mouse in a dark maze, avoiding a bunch of rats with sharp claws and teeth who wanted to tear me apart.

Thumping on the entry door made me jump in my shoes, and I spun in fright. Late arrivals. More banging, then voices, probably calling on their phones to be let in. They obviously didn't have the entry code. Which meant gang members would be coming down one of these halls to let them in. Which one? I knelt down and walked on my hands and knees, squinting to see if there were signs in the dust on the floor showing which way all the bikers had gone. And there were. The dust past the first intersection looked mostly undisturbed.

My head jerked up again at more banging from the door, then swiveled toward the answering yell from down the hall where the bikers had gone. Approaching. Coming to answer the door.

Gotta move. Now or never.

Go!

Heart racing, I ran as light-footed as I could for the far intersection and turned left.

Three times while I was exploring, finding blacked-out rooms and dead-end hallways, I heard cursing and banging from other hallways. The first was the sound of the gang member leading the latecomers to the meeting, and I tried to figure out which way the sounds were going.

As I attempted to parallel those sounds and kept hitting dead ends, I also twice heard the sound of loud talkers close by, probably lost on their way back to use the washroom. One of them I nearly ran into. I heard a British-accented "Cucking ballcock!" approaching from around the next corner. I jumped backward to pull myself into an empty room and closed the door behind me just in time to hear the man's heavy boots clomp by.

The randomness of people moving around made it suicide to just go back to the start and try to pick out the heaviest scuff marks on my hands and knees. Those marks would also likely be all confused now. And if I took a wrong turn, I'd bump into a bearded Hells Angel or Nazi. Jump back to the wrong place and they'd grab me while I was reorienting.

Easy-peasy in and out, I'd thought. *No one can grab me if I can just jump back through time,* I'd thought.

Great. Just great.

Go!

After repeated heart-in-throat backtracking and taking new corridors, I finally heard noises that sounded like a crowd. I slowed and crept forward on the balls of my running shoes, softly blowing my nose into my jacket sleeve and fighting the urge to sneeze from all the dust I'd been breathing in.

And suddenly, over the smell of dank cement and drywall, I smelled other things. Coffee. And... baked bread? Cheese?

I peeked carefully through a half-open door at the end of the hall. Couldn't see enough. So I slipped quietly through it and slid left into a shadowed semi-alcove behind a stack of empty wooden pallets. From there, I could awkwardly study the destination all these gangsters had come to.

The room was a gritty warehouse pod, unevenly lit by long rows of high bay fluorescents hanging from a twenty-foot, metal-girded ceiling that looked well covered by rust. The wall I was on had endless stacks of closed boxes and plastic-wrapped pallets on stackable shelf bins as well as a couple stacked shipping containers at the far south end. Maybe it was stuff left behind by whomever was driven from this building when the Demon Monks moved in. Maybe it was illegal contraband waiting for trucks or railcars to take it out for distribution.

The wall opposite was likely west, the Occidental Avenue side. I saw three closed bay doors.

The main action was going on in the middle of the broad, concrete floor.

Lit from above, the Demon Monks looked like they were holding a low-rent business seminar for not just their members but for representatives from at least six or seven other gangs as well. The sixty-plus folding chairs that filled the center space were divided into sections that held groups of gangsters mostly segregated by race—Black, Hispanic, East Asian, South Asian, Pacific Islander, and all-white with the bikers, some of whom were still collecting coffee and sweets from the food tables near the north side of the room where they'd come in. Almost at an angle where they could see into my shadowed corner.

Facing all the chairs was a presentation table on which sat a lit screen that had to be a projection model. It looked at least five feet high and eight feet wide.

Except there was no screen ripple and no projector that I could see. Not to mention the screen looked like it had a base of two flat, broad, silver feet on either side holding it up. And the cords coming out from underneath ran over to a knee-high, silver box on a table that two men hunched over in deep conversation.

Then one man stepped back and left the other with the keyboard and mouse controls. I didn't recognize the man on the keyboard, but the one who stepped back and turned to face the room with a wide, unpleasant smile—him, I knew.

Cutter.

The skinny guy with bad teeth who'd cut up Kenny's face over a decade ago. He no longer had his raggedy mustache, and his hair was only shoulder length now, not tied but still brushed back, probably to hide a bald spot.

Cutter.

Before I could get past the way the sight of him stopped my heart, he turned to lean into the chest of a tall, blond gangster wearing a sports jacket. Cutter muttered something to him. Like Hitler to an Aryan standard-bearer. They were working on some kind of domestic terror plot, Kansas had said. That would have made sense, almost, if it was only the bikers they were meeting with. But the Demon Monks were multiracial, and the bikers were the only ones who looked like white supremacy types.

No. Kansas' intelligence was wrong on this one. There was something else going on.

And I was sure it was all coming out of Cutter. I'd lay bets he was *the* shot caller on this one. Because I could still feel the evil power he carried with him. That power, a kind of greedy sadism, rolled off him in the way he talked to his underlings and looked at his audience, the way he flicked his long, skinny fingers and vainly used them to push back his greasy hair. Couldn't *they* feel it? How could they just sit there? Was I the only one who saw the uncaring danger of him? Or were all these people somehow *looking* for the crazy nihilism Cutter exuded?

And he cut up Kenny.

He took Kenny away.

Made us believe he was dead.

Destroyed my life.

It all threatened to short-circuit my brain the same way Dead Eyes, aka Detective James William Gillespie, had when he'd gone after me and Lena. I had to grab the rough wood of the stacked pallets to make myself stay put. Squeezed the wood until my knuckles went white.

I consequently hardly heard what Cutter was saying, hardly processed the map being shown on the giant TV screen. Because I was hearing Kenny's screams in my head as Cutter dragged the tip of his knife through Kenny's flesh. Seeing my big brother's snotty tears and the look of cold glee on Cutter's face.

Then the picture on the TV screen shifted as a new window opened and was made full screen. Zoom? Skype? Something.

Kenny's face appeared.

12

Brother, Brother

KENNY'S FACE ON THAT oversized TV screen looked so much older than it should, maybe fifty, not thirty-seven. His hair was graying. His face, quite apart from the ragged pink-and-white scars of the D on his right cheek and M on his left, was wrinkled and drawn. The eyes had a haunted cast as he looked out over the room. I now saw the webcam sitting on top of the monitor.

"Is this everyone?" his voice said, the amplified croak booming out of the television speakers.

"Area leaders from us and the other main gangs," said Cutter, "street coordinators, officers, board members, advisors, and one of our co-leaders. Me."

"You and Dixon?" Kenny's giant face on the TV seemed to look directly at Cutter.

Cutter shifted back and forth on his feet. "The Dix is out. Demoted. Juarez is working his lieutenants right now. Negotiating with South Park and the Crew. Like we're doing here. Like you wanted. A *Pax Criminalis*." He leered at the camera like he was seeking approval for his edgy brilliance. But even from where I sat in the back, I saw, or maybe heard in his voice, something very different going on at the same time.

Some of Cutter's broader audience seemed to sense it too. There was a tightening of the tension. A few of the sharper faces, who'd probably never trusted Cutter to begin with, were looking around the room now. Maybe wondering if there were shooters hiding in the shadows or feds surrounding the building. One of the Demon Monks near the back looked toward where I hid and stared a long time, like he could see me through the wood slats.

I held my breath, thinking furiously at him, *You see nothing but wooden pallets.*

Whether he never saw me or my Jedi mind trick worked, he finally looked away. I started to edge back toward the door. *I certainly didn't trust Cutter, and I'd already pushed my luck hard enough here.*

"Who are the leather-hat cluster near the back?" Kenny's face on the screen asked. "And the man near the door?"

"Wha-fuh?" Cutter turned and, like most of the room, stared at me.

Again I froze. And it was like Kenny had given an order for everyone to turn and pin me with their stares all at once. My body felt pierced in every private place, social anxiety taking hold for a second in this insane situation where I'd never have guessed it could. Almost simultaneously, I felt a rush of panicky, white-hot rage, against myself as much as anyone. Rage that I'd thought Kenny had to be trapped against his will. Rage against my naïve assumption he'd never *choose* to be one of the bad guys.

I found myself two steps toward the TV screen and shouting, "Then why'd you come after me, Kenny? You asshole! *You should have just stayed dead!*"

Kenny blinked hard once, twice, like it took my voice for him to recognize me. Or maybe the webcam on the screen just didn't have the resolution to see back this far.

"Jacky?" Kenny's face whispered through the speakers. It came out like a sour wind blowing through the leaves. Totally surprised. Like he hadn't expected to see me here, or anywhere. But if he'd asked Gillespie to kidnap me... Or had I been right earlier when I'd figured that had been just *Gillespie's* decision?

What the hell?

"What do you want with the scientist?" I shouted, trying to get *something* out of this encounter as I willed everyone else in the room to just stay where they were for just a moment more. Just one more...

"Cutter, I have something important to tell you," Kenny said softly.

Cutter ignored him and stabbed a finger in my direction. "Grab him!"

I turned and ran.

I booted it down the hall I'd entered by but forgot to reverse my turns in my memory and went the wrong way at the T, only figuring it out when I met a dead end with a door that opened into yet another room of unfinished drywall, office sized but with no lights yet, just a wired-in electrical box in the ceiling. *Damn it!*

I ducked inside, pulled the door closed after me. No lock. I threw myself flat-backed against the wall the door was on so in case someone checked this direction, they'd look in quickly and not see me.

My heart pounded. My breath sucked in and out raggedly as much from fear as from my run.

The sound of other runners sounded outside but far away. They'd assumed I'd turned right, going back the way I *should* have gone.

Good.

Breathe.

Then one set of pounding feet came my way. My heartbeat and sucking breaths picked up again.

The door flung open, flooding the small room with light. The guy looking in was a shaved-headed brute in a tee-shirt and dirty jeans who was short but obviously pumped iron. Full-sleeve tats on his right arm said he could take pain. Maybe liked it.

In a split second, I decided I was going to be seen, so I leapt at the thick little gangster, grabbing one wrist and pulling it hard as

I went by. And even though the guy probably outweighed me by thirty or forty pounds, my speed and motion overcame that and pulled the man in, twisting him as he came.

The gangster fell and I, who'd ended up bouncing against the nearest wall when I'd let go, recovered first and ran out the door.

Only to see two other gang members, who'd obviously heard or seen the commotion, barrel down the hall toward me like they wanted to rip me apart.

Oh shit. I wasn't Daredevil or Bruce Lee. I was going to die.

Dissociate. I pinched myself hard, almost crying as I grunted, "Dissociate *now*."

The runner leapt at me...

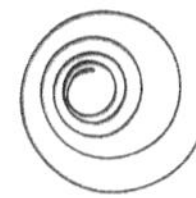

I stood in a dim hallway, a little dizzy.

"Cucking ballcock!"

Whuh?

Then I was fully in my body and mind from ten minutes earlier, and of course it had to be *this* point in time.

The guy who clomped around the corner was about my height but seemed bigger, from his long hair and brutally crooked nose to his full-leather biker's garb, his jacket undone to show a dirty, gray tee-shirt with some kind of faded gear logo.

"Oy!" he shouted in my face, like a transplant from a British pub. "What you skulkin' about for?" He whipped out a knife from somewhere because it probably helped him think.

I jumped backward and my head hit the wall, stunning me. Then my left shoulder near where it met my chest exploded in pain as the biker's knife plunged in and then out with a sucking sound, spattering the left side of my face with blood.

"You ain't supposed to be here. I can smell it. Right?" the ballcock said and grinned.

Dissocia—

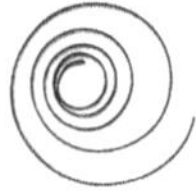

On my knees. Why was I on my knees? Where was I?

It was harder to focus. Why was it so hard?

Two jumps in a row, right. Had to bear down. Concentrate. Dark hallway. Dusty floor. Sounds of feet coming down a hall somewhere? Which where?

Come on. Get it together. Stand up. Orient. Shoulder's fine. Not stabbed.

Okay.

It finally snapped in when another familiar face came stomping out of the hallway I'd just been kneeling in front of. Yes. I'd been checking the dust for footprints I knew now. Because I'd heard latecomers to the party banging on the door. Then someone coming to let them in. And look, here he was.

He wasn't a gangster I recognized. He was an Asian kid, early twenties with a blunt haircut and a pockmarked face that said he'd had bad acne as a teen. Not super buff, but sharp-eyed as he looked at me, sizing me up.

A look of recognition hit his face. "I saw your photo, yo. Holy shit. You're the professor. Chuba was s'posed to bring you in Wednesday. What happened? How'd you get away like that?"

Chuba? I shrugged. "Just smarter than him, I guess."

"Why you here now?"

"Invited."

"Yeah, by who?"

I was about to say Kenny, but something about the whole setup back there made me doubt Kenny had any role in the day-to-day business of the Monks. "Cutter."

Pockmark looked doubtful. "An' he gave you the door code?"

"Yup."

Thumping resumed on the entry door behind me. They must have been able to hear the talking.

"So why ain't you let in latecomers?" said Pockmark.

"I wasn't told to play doorman."

"Cool." A flicker of a thought crossed Pockmark's face. "So do it now."

"Your job, man."

Pockmark looked me up and down. "You know, you be pretty scuffed up. Like you fell. Or maybe you just broke in. Don't know the code."

"You too lazy to do your job, dude?"

Pockmark reached into a back holster and came up with a gun. "You too stupid to do what you told?"

I raised my hand halfway. "Come on..." *Oh shit oh shit oh shit.*

Pockmark raised the gun to point at my center of mass and took a couple steps back. Not as stupid as he looked. Probably wouldn't be alive this long in a gang if he was. "Open the door or I gonna shoot your leg or your dick, then drag you to see Cutter, *dude.*"

I shrugged and turned toward the door, my face burning, my heart thudding in my ears. But when I pinched my leg hard and commanded myself to dissociate from this reality, nothing happened. Like I wasn't quite scared enough.

Well, shit, Jacky! Just how much do you need?

I slow-walked to the door and stared at the number pad, stalling, heart hammering, wondering if maybe the most-used numbers had telltale wear marks. As it was, the lighting in the entry was so bad I could barely make out the numbers at all.

"You got a flashlight?" I said and started to turn around.

"Fake!" screamed Pockmark, and he pistol-whipped the back of my head.

I stumbled against the wall and sank down, my vision swimming. *Don't go dark. Come on. Don't go dark!*

The shadowy figure of Pockmark was jamming buttons on the door pad and talking on his cell phone at the same time. "We caught the professor," he said. The door unclicked. Pockmark swung it inward past my legs, and a set of five more leather-clad bikers tromped in, stepping over me and turning back.

"Pick him up," Pockmark told them. "Trespasser. Cop. Something. We carry him to Cutter."

And amidst a bunch of swearing and grunting, I was hoisted up over two of the bikers' shoulders like a side of beef or rolled carpet, my arms dangling painfully down and my spine and shoulders waggling like they were going to snap.

In a sudden desperation, I heaved and kicked and managed to clock the guy carrying my legs with a kick to the head.

Then I was on the floor and boots were kicking my body and head, splitting my lip in pain. My eye took a direct hit and my mind screamed, in an almost orgasmic shot of pain, *Dissociate!*

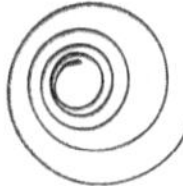

I was standing on top of a stair railing, holding the pole that tied it to the metal awning above.

Wha—?

Outside the warehouse. Trying to climb up to the windows?

I couldn't breathe. Choking.

Heart skipping.

Head pounding.

Couldn't control my muscles.

Right. Third jump without...enough... Too. Much. Stuff. *Help.*

I lost my grip as my legs failed, and I tumbled down onto the stairway.

Can't move. Can't breathe.

There was a rumbling sound from somewhere. Familiar. Coming closer. Rumbling? Motorcycles?

Oh God. They can't find me...like this.

Oh God. Move.

Head spinning, gasping for breath, I pulled myself up one step. Two. I was on the concrete loading platform. The black door was ahead of me. They'd all be coming here. *Here.* I couldn't be *here.* Looking left, I saw the squat, heavy metal dumpsters and piles of cardboard. If I could...

I got my knees under me. Pushed up with my hands. Fell back. *Move!*

The rumble of motorcycles had turned right off Occidental Avenue. Any moment now they'd be at the turn into this back gravel road. They'd drive up to here and park. Come up the steps and see me. Wouldn't know who I was, but they'd grab me.

Crawl!

Like I was a gut-shot soldier, I began crawling for my life. A foot. Two feet. Four. I reached the bottom of the first dumpster and pulled myself up against it. The motorcycles sounded like they'd turned into the gravel road that ran to where I was. But when I looked, the pole and stairs and some other boxes on the raised loading platform blocked my view of the approach. Which meant they couldn't see me either. For one moment more.

With my last strength, I gritted my teeth to clear my head, shoved up the lid of the chest-high dumpster, jammed my right foot against an outside bottom protrusion, and launched myself up and in, scraping my head and back and legs as I tumbled onto a pile of smelly bags and boxes, the lid clunking closed above me.

I let out one brief cry of pain as the roar of arriving motorbikes drowned it out, then I bit it down hard. Tried to think.

My head was swimming, and I was afraid I was going to pass out even though my chest was squeezing in pain and my muscles were still jerking like they couldn't figure out who I *was.*

If I just slipped away here, I feared, I might never wake up.

So with my last, last, last strength, I managed to fumble out my phone and, with twitching fingers, texted Lena:

> **S Manning, first rt east off Occidental Av S onto gravel rd btwn warehouse and train tracks. Where warehouse has 2 stories, motorbikes, see green dumpster top of steps. Im inside need medical. CAUTION violent gangs in warehouse. Mbe 45 min before they exit. If ur that slow, will be dead anyway.**

I hit SEND and closed my eyes. My chest squeezed tight.

13

Somehow they know

I WOKE UP IN a hospital bed and yawned. My throat felt scratchy and horrible. My left arm itched when I moved it, and I saw I was hooked up to an IV. Of course. Fluids. The ability to pump in meds. I could hear someone else in the room with me, groaning, but privacy curtains were pulled around my bed, so I couldn't see if it was a man or woman. Just as well, since I was in a hospital gown myself and had probably had all types of health workers buzzing around my exposed body trying to figure out what was wrong with me.

Which right now was nothing at all, other than my scratchy throat. My mind had fully reintegrated in my body. It was an exhausted mind, though. It kept wanting to feel where I'd been stabbed and pistol-whipped and kicked in the ribs and groin, like an amputee victim reaching for a missing leg. I could see it getting difficult to separate what had happened in what timeline. Might add an interesting new psychiatric condition to my existing PTSD and social anxiety. I could call it Dissociative Timestream Disorder and loan it out to past life regression patients who couldn't give up the fantasy that their other lives were real.

I heard footsteps, and Lena's hand pulled back my curtain. She looked scientific and professional in her sky blue button-down blouse and navy slacks with a gray-and-white wool coat over top and her thick curls pulled back in a tight ponytail. Her face above her navy mask looked paler and more pinched than I remembered, but she seemed unsurprised by my condition.

"It's four oh five," she said quietly, pulling off her mask. "I saw your text at two fifteen and called nine-one-one. The Seattle Fire Department sent a Medic One unit, who fished you out of the dumpster at two forty and brought you here to the emergency room at Harborview Medical. They jump-started your heart en route then intubated you because you still weren't breathing properly. Yes, that's why your throat's scratchy. Swabbed you for COVID, too, if your nose hurts. I arrived here at three o'clock and consulted with the emerge doctor who set you up here. I explained your situation was a still-being-investigated neurological issue you've experienced once before that would likely resolve on its own once the heart and breathing issues resolved. He seemed doubtful."

"Not surprised," I said, and the gravel in my voice made me massage my throat again.

"Three jumps?"

I nodded like it was nothing, but she read me too well. Looking around to make sure the privacy curtain around us was fully closed, she walked to the chair by my bed, drew it up closer to my head, and lowered her voice to make our conversation just between us.

"It was bad."

"Stabs, kicks, punches, pistol-whipped, and I saw my brother."

She looked down for a minute with pursed lips, making me remember our last conversation, piling on the guilt. When she looked up, she said, "Successful mission then?"

"I deserved that."

"You did." A long pause. "But seriously, he was in the warehouse?"

"Remotely. On a giant TV screen. Talking live to the room of gangsters like he was their overlord."

She looked searchingly into my eyes, probably trying to figure out how I felt about what I'd discovered. Disappointed? Angry? Suicidal? The truth was, the more I went over what had happened, how Kenny had looked, what he'd actually said and done, the more I questioned whether he was really as in charge as he'd seemed. Which meant...

"I don't know what I feel about it yet. Is that what you're looking for?"

She sat frowning at me, clearly reluctant to say something.

"What?"

After a moment, she whispered, "I asked the nine-one-one operator to warn the medics there might be a motorcycle gang parked there that you were hiding from. They said there were no motorcycles or vehicles parked near the two-story section of the warehouse. If you hadn't given the two-story bit and the color of the dumpster, they wouldn't have been able to find you."

"That makes no..."

Lena held up her hand. "It gets worse. I'd called my ex, the Ranger guy, right after nine-one-one, and he was there about ten minutes behind them, talking with me on the phone, scoping out what you'd gotten yourself into. He said no bikes, no cars. He crawled in through an open window on the second floor and found evidence some people had been there recently, but when he explored both upstairs and downstairs, the place was dark and empty."

"No," I hissed. "What about chairs, food tables, cables, an internet hookup?"

"Scuffed floors, pallets of what might be illicit cargo in the one room where he turned on the lights. He didn't mention anything about chairs, food, or electronics. Definitely no people, though."

I let my head fall back on the bed, calculating. "Thirty-seven minutes. From full-on gang summit to complete clear out? Why? In this time stream I never even went in."

"They saw you climb into the dumpster?"

"They would have alerted the scuzz buckets inside, who would have recognized me, hauled me in, maybe revived me, maybe not."

"Or someone inside saw you before you went for the dumpster?"

"And what? Got so freaked out they packed up everything and ran? I mean, I know I'm terrifying, but..."

Lena looked down. "These jumps, they've been hard on you. Emotionally. Have you...been taking any medication?"

I snorted and pressed my head back into my pillow.

"Have you?"

I met her eyes. "You know why I went into psychology, not psychiatry?"

"You didn't want to do a medical degree?"

"I saw both a psychologist and a psychiatrist after Kenny vanished. One told me the sort of things I'd have to face and how I might overcome them. The other mostly prescribed pills. To a kid whose brother had been taken over by heroin and crack."

Lena's face colored. "The pills might have helped."

"Maybe. Heroin and crack and booze might have too, in their own way. They're not my way. I'm not suffering a serotonin deficiency or imbalanced hormones. And I'm not a normal human who creates false memories. The real ones are so exact in my mind they're like an endless series of sights and sounds, feelings, smells, tastes, all burned into my hippocampus in layers on layers of immediately retrievable organic experience that I've had to learn how to *ignore* and still sometimes can't. You want proof? You want me to tell you more of the stories you told me about yourself that you haven't told me in *this* timeline? Word by word? I can probably imitate the exact intonations if you want."

Now her face was actually so blotchy with embarrassment, matching mine, red with frustration, that I started feeling guilty again.

She said, "I do want to hear those stories at some point so I know what you know about me. But not now. I believe you, Jackson. And I want to hear all that happened. All of it this time. Especially about your brother. But not here, okay?"

I nodded, breathing hard, coming down from the angry panic of describing the mental hell I'd been fighting so hard to manage in my life for years before I'd discovered this time travel trick that demanded I absorb trauma after trauma to make it work.

"Let me see if I can get you released," she said. "And I think maybe you should phone your sister again, and keep calling until she answers."

Checked out, bill settled with the help of my U-Dub contract, and nose-and-mouth masks firmly in place, Lena and I left together, and she drove me back to Occidental Avenue so I could retrieve my car.

After promising to meet up with her again in the Redmond medical office space where we'd explored my power yesterday, I drove off to find some sushi takeout. I ate it on the dark drive out to northeast of Redmond. At the building that had the particle accelerator in the basement and medical offices a few floors up, Lena buzzed me in.

Up in the white-walled space, I was surprised to find waiting for me not only Lena, with her glorious hair pulled back into a tight, businesslike bun, but four mask-wearing, buff men in dark-green cargo pants, boots, bomber jackets, and matching ball caps with tiny gold stitching over their brims that said Lead the Way.

My social anxiety flared up as they all stared at me, and I had trouble meeting their eyes. But then the reason for their presence here clicked in for me and, combined with what I'd just been through and my deepening appreciation of what it was doing to me, anger overtook anxiety. I raised my eyes and studied these new people with a defiance that probably made me look like a toddler. I didn't care.

The way the man closest to Lena grinned at me from behind his mask told me he was her ex. He had baby-smooth, plump skin and bright blue eyes that gleamed with the kind of self-satisfaction I figured Lena might go for. It would have taken someone with real *cojones* in high school or college to make a play for the smartest, prettiest girl in the class.

But Lena surprised me by pointing to the guy furthest from her, a lanky, shadow-eyed guy who looked like a standing moray eel. "This is Alvin Westor," she said, "my college crush, who checked out the warehouse. The others are Kai Nishikawa, Kajika Bighouse, and Ryan Renn. They served together in the Rangers seventy-fifth in Iraq and Afghanistan. All retired. They formed a security company called—"

"Lead the Way?" I said.

Lena blinked. Ryan pointed to his hat, and she got it. "I asked them here so you could tell them what you saw and quiz them on what they did."

"Because?"

Again she looked flustered. Like I was questioning the obvious. It made me reflect that for all the intensity with which I and Lena had connected, I still knew little about her emotional history beyond her stories of choosing poor romantic partners and never having a pet. But I could gather from the fact she was running a team of older scientists, and the way she'd run me through my paces when she wanted to investigate my power, that she was used to calling the shots and surrounding herself with people who did her bidding.

That was not something I'd signed up for, and I was pretty sure everything about my body language now was telling her this.

It was also telling the Lead the Way team. The Japanese guy, Nishikawa, shortest one in the foursome, looked sideways at Alvin with an inscrutable expression that still screamed *What are we doing here?* The thickly built Native guy, aptly named Bighouse, stared up at the ceiling like he was in his own private world. While smiley Ryan Renn just kept grinning away inside his mask, looking back and forth between me and Lena, sucking in the conflict.

"When you texted me," Lena began slowly, unconsciously touching where the hair was pulled back tightly over her ears, "I knew it could easily take me forty minutes to reach you, which meant you could be dead before I got there. So I called nine-one-one. But if you'd actually found the people who were after *both* of us, I also wanted to know who they were and if they were going to follow you to the hospital."

I folded my arms and stared at her.

"The police aren't doing anything," she pleaded. "And you're not trained..."

"Thanks for the vote of confidence."

Baby-face Renn held out his hands, palms up. "Hey, dude. People hire us to do dangerous shit so they don't have to end up in the hospital or dead. That's all."

"Were you all there?" I asked him. "Did you all check out the warehouse?"

Renn shot a sideways look at the eel, the ex, Alvin, who shook his head. "I was the only one in when Lena called. I did the recon, told Lena what I'd found, and she asked me to bring the team to meet you."

"To tell me you found nothing," I said.

"Not nothing," he said. His voice was dry and edgy. "There were beds and knickknacks upstairs. Nothing personal. Nothing in the fridge. There were footprints in the dust like a bunch of people had walked the halls recently. But it could have been construction guys. All the fresh drywall. No lights on anywhere. It was deserted."

"Surveillance cameras?"

"No. And no wires for them."

"Did you question any of the store owners on Occidental? Did trucks carry stuff out?"

"No. Were you in the warehouse? You texted there were gangs inside. Did you actually go in and see them there?"

My gaze shot to Lena. She'd shown Alvin the text! I looked back at Alvin. "I went in. I saw. I heard. There were tables, chairs, food, coffee, and at least sixty people from different gangs, most notably from the Demon Monks and BAM. That's what I saw and heard directly. Out back, where I lay in the dumpster, there were twenty-eight parked sedans and eleven motorcycles. Would you like me to give you the makes and models?"

"Do something for me," Alvin said in his dry voice that made it as more of an order or threat than a request. "Turn around so you can't see us."

I frowned but complied.

"Now tell us all our names and what each of us is wearing."

Ah. Okay. I paused a second to see them in my mind and proceeded to describe the group in precise detail, starting with the way Alvin stood, how his boots and shoelaces, belt and zipper, and even the brim of his cap were more worn than those of his teammates, which might indicate the age of them or, more likely, some nervous habits in the way Alvin dressed and wore his clothes. Also that the shoulder holster in which he wore his gun obviously chafed him because of his slouch, since he had unconsciously adjusted it twice since I had entered the room.

By the time I got through Renn and his faux-friendly smiles, which only half worked when he was masked, I had given them the full Sherlock Holmes with my own psychologizing twist, noting in particular what I'd already surmised of the power dynamics and personal habits of each one of them and the team in general.

It took almost twenty minutes.

When I turned back around, all four team members were looking at me with stares of intense concentration. Lena, by contrast, had wrapped her arms defensively around herself and wouldn't meet my eyes.

Of course. In my power play to get some respect from these total strangers, I'd probably scared her into permanent self-consciousness, because she now understood that what I told her about my memory didn't apply just to myself. It meant I saw and remembered and judged everything she said, wore, and did as well, whether I wanted to or not.

Welcome to my world of feeling judged all the time.

"You *were* inside the warehouse," said Alvin. "You *did* see the gangs there and the vehicles out front."

"Yes," I said.

"You want to tell us how you managed that, got out without a scratch on you, but still had a heart attack in the dumpster outside?"

"No."

"Did they see you?"

I had to think hard about how to answer that. "Only if they saw me outside after I came out."

"You're sure of that?"

Was I? Because a niggling thought had occurred to me, just an outside, insanely improbable possibility that I wasn't sure there was any way to check. Still... "Ninety-eight percent sure."

I saw Lena's head pop up and look at me in surprise. I caught her gaze briefly, wishing we were alone so I could tell her what had just occurred to me.

Alvin had caught it. He didn't miss much. "Okay. There's stuff going on that you don't want to share. We get that. Part of the world we run in. But if it's going to impact our ability to protect you, we'll need to know."

"Pardon?"

Alvin raised an eyebrow at Lena, then turned back to me. "Lena's hired us. Mostly to check up on the security she already has and to take over protecting the two of you."

"I don't have the kind of money that takes," I said, blushing. I hadn't told my high-flying sister this, nor Lena, but part of the way I ran my business was to take on only the number of clients that I could serve well, teach at the university, and have a balanced life that let me work on my mental issues. I had enough to live comfortably in an expensive city, not enough to hire full-time security to babysit me.

Alvin nodded like this was not only normal but expected. "Our clients are usually CEOs, visiting foreign emissaries, movie stars, that kind of thing. But Lena's one of our stockholders. She put in money when we first started up. For her, we cut our rates."

"That's still not..."

"It's basically pro bono. You know what that means?"

"For the public good."

Alvin looked at the other team members and gave his version of a smile. It was like the edge of his lips moved up a few centimeters against their will. "Is that what that means? I just thought it meant free."

I cleared my throat. "The problem is that I don't want you or anyone else following me around, staking out my house or workplace, whatever it is you do."

Lena's mouth dropped open. "You're still planning to go after Kenny."

I looked at her, annoyed at that moment how easily she could read me. "I've gone over everything I saw. I don't know if it's the Demon Monks who have him, or someone else, but he's a captive and being forced to play a role."

"You're sure of that?" Lena pressed.

"Enough that I have to save him. I owe him. You don't know."

I could tell Lena felt the pain and the obsessive need under that statement and was dying to get me alone and pry the whole story out of me. I just didn't know if that was the maybe-girlfriend in her or the scientist.

Alvin cut in, curious. "So you want to rescue someone from a bunch of mobsters all by yourself?"

"My brother. And...it's not your concern."

Alvin looked down, and I was surprised to see what I was pretty sure was genuine respect on his face. "What about we just leave Kai with you?" he said. "He's a doctor, specialized in emergency medicine. Handy if you were going to have another heart attack or whatever."

I seriously considered it, then shook my head.

Alvin waved the team around him and wandered them back out of earshot so they could talk. While they did, I walked over to Lena, finally. She was still standing with her arms clutched around her, frowning and intense. I put my hands on her arms.

"You didn't tell them about..." I began.

"What you can do? Of course not. I'd never do that without your permission."

"But you understand why I can't have someone hanging around me all the time?"

"No."

"I'm going to be trying things, going places, that anyone who can't do what I do would be crazy to do."

"Which means they're crazy for you to do, too."

I looked at her and realized that just maybe what I was seeing on her face was more the maybe-girlfriend than scientist, after all. She looked scared. For me. The only people I ever really remembered worrying about me were Kansas and Kenny. Kenny's worry had been ironic, given that he was the one who always brought danger into our lives. Kansas' worry, meanwhile, had been and still was that I'd get sucked into Kenny's troubles. I'd felt the love my siblings gave; I just wasn't sure how their worry helped.

Was Lena's any better?

"Hey." I waited until she met my eyes. "Another reason it's got to be just me is I don't know what I'm going to find with Kenny, which means I don't know what I'm going to have to do to get him out. I can't have someone who might get in the way of whatever that is."

"That's not reassuring me, Jackson!" Lena said, and suddenly her intense demeanor cracked, and she had to wipe away a tear. "Oh, damn. Look what you're making me do!"

"I'm sorry." I swiped at a tear she'd missed. "Not my intention. Really. Look, how about I offer a compromise..."

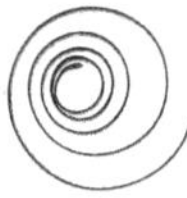

Twenty minutes later, Lena and I escorted the Lead the Way Security team out of the building to their extended-cab truck with the understanding, mutually agreed to, that beyond fortifying Lena's security, they would be on call for me on a rapid response basis for the next couple weeks. After that, they'd reevaluate.

If nothing else, I had reasoned with Lena, being able to call on Dr. Kai Nishikawa when I jumped too many times and overstressed my body-mind connection meant 9-1-1 could stay out of my affairs, and my university insurance company would be endlessly grateful.

"You did notice something about your last jumps?" Lena said as we walked back to Building #4.

"What? Besides ending up on a pile of garbage."

"You told me in the hospital that you actually jumped back to standing on top of the stair railing, right? You managed to climb down, crawl to the dumpster, open it, climb in, and use your phone before you finally blacked out. You remember how long you stayed conscious the first time you triple jumped?"

I frowned. I'd been doing a lot of jumping back in the last few days. But three, one right after the other? The only one I was sure had been like that was that first one in the medical lab here... yesterday? Had that been only yesterday? My days had gotten so much longer since I'd started living the most intense parts over and over.

"You remember?" Lena pressed. We'd reached the building, and she buzzed us in.

"I clutched my chest and passed out."

"Bang. Just like that. Your heart stopped. Your breathing stopped. This time you managed to climb down, crawl, climb in, phone. How long did that take?"

"A couple minutes?"

We entered the elevator, and Lena used her card again to make it rise. "That's better. How about the jumps, getting into them? More controllable?"

I remembered how getting mocked in a speakeasy had triggered one, while getting terrorized with a knife in the warehouse hadn't. There it had taken getting stabbed. "A bit uneven," I said.

"Hm."

I'd wanted to say *frighteningly* uneven, but that would also take admitting that after I'd left the lab, I hadn't once been able to use what I'd discovered there with her—consciously focusing on my failure as a trigger to jump. It was somehow more terrifying to intentionally go down that emotional hole all alone than to push others to hit me with some kind of pain so horrifying it made my mind jump ship.

Even then, I didn't really trust it would work. Everything about this jump back power seemed inconsistent and unreliable. Hardly what you wanted to be betting your life on.

But sometimes you just had to act even when you didn't feel like you had all the answers or, frankly, when you were terrified that you did not. If I had avoided all the times I was afraid to do something, mostly because it involved interacting with other people, I'd never had gotten my doctorate, started my psychology practice, become a university professor, met Lena, slept with Lena, won (amazingly) her affection...

Going after gangsters seemed easy in comparison. Especially when the prize was getting back my brother and my life.

The elevator arrived, and we stepped back into the medical office space that was becoming all too familiar. Lena said, "I've got some ice tea in the fridge here. Or pop or water. Can I get you one while you call your sister?"

"Ice tea."

Then she walked to the fridge around the corner of the office space like she knew I needed a moment to collect myself. Or privacy for the call.

I pulled over a plastic chair, straddled it, and called Kansas. Checking my watch, I saw it was almost eight o'clock. It felt like midnight, which it almost was on the East Coast where I presumed Kansas was working these days.

I also assumed all of her calls to the only number I had for her got routed to her, and she'd somehow see them even if she was asleep, assuming she slept, and would decide whether to answer them.

This time she answered on the fourth ring after a short burst of static.

"What?" she said.

"Secure line?"

"Transferred it when I saw you calling *again*."

"I saw Kenny."

"Where?"

"On a big-screen TV. He was talking to a roomful of gangsters —Demon Monks, BAM, some motorcycle gang—like he was in control of all of them somehow. He's aged a lot. Looks like shit. He recognized my voice when I called out to him."

There was a pause. "How are you not dead?"

"Are you alone?"

"I'm alone. It's a secure line. I don't need to take notes. You know that."

"Yeah. Okay." I looked up to find Lena had walked back into my section of the room and quietly sat down, watching me. Listening. I nodded, then spoke to Kansas. "I need your brains and maybe your resources, so I'm going to tell you something only me and the scientist I'm dating know. It's going to sound crazy or like I'm pulling your leg, but it's true and I'm not pulling your leg. Do you believe me?"

"I believe you're going to tell me something that *you* believe is true."

"Fair enough. So this is the full story of what happened the day before I called you on Thursday..."

I told her everything, from the three jumps backward in time in the particle accelerator lab to my experiments with Lena here in the medical office space, with Dr. Irene Gopal attending to the first jump.

Kansas stopped me there. "Irene Gopal. Does she live in Redmond? In Seattle?"

I turned to Lena, who gave me Gopal's address. I repeated it into the phone.

"I assume that's Dr. Lena Cortland in the room with you? The scientist you're dating?"

"Yes."

"I checked her out. Impressive CV. Something hinky with the money funding her current project. Has she told you where it comes from?"

"Not directly. I'm assuming the company with the smile logo."

There was a pause. "She might think that. It might even be true and the hinky comes from some kind of tax dodge. I'll look into it further. Regardless, you'd better know it's not just whoever Gillespie is working for that wants her. The US military is watching her research closely. I've found chatter that suggests Russia and China are, too. So if she reports anything at all about you…"

"She won't."

"Or even if she doesn't, you being with her in whatever way you are puts you in their crosshairs, too. Just so you know. You'd be safer to walk away."

"I'm not going to do that."

"Of course you're not. You didn't walk away from Kenny either, and look what that got you."

"Can I finish my story?"

"Does it get worse?"

"I end up in a summit of gangs, shouting at Kenny."

"Yes, it does. Go ahead."

So I told it all, ignoring Lena's gasps, blanched face, and the way her hand grabbed mine at various points in the story. Kansas only interrupted twice—first to get the names of the physician who saw me at Harborview Medical and any nurses or other personnel I interacted with there, and later to get the names of the guys of Lead the Way Security.

When I had finished, Kansas said, "Is that all?"

"All but the questions I have for you."

"Which would be?"

"Is Kenny working for the government?"

There was a long pause, and I could picture my sister's face like she was sitting right in front of me. Like Kenny, she'd always taken more after our dad's features than our mom's. It meant her face was very pale, long, and bony. With makeup, Kansas would have an exotic kind of beauty. But she never wore makeup. She wore blue-light filtering glasses to protect her eyesight from the hours she spent, even before she left home, staring at one or more computer screens. She kept her brown hair short so she didn't have to fuss with it. And when she was concentrating hard, or considering whether to lie, she would become dead quiet with a gaze so fixed a casual passerby might take her to be a mannequin or wax statue.

Kansas was that quiet now.

When she spoke at last, her voice was uncharacteristically subdued. "I don't have any concrete evidence for or against that, which makes me believe he is. It may not be by choice."

"And is it possible," I pressed, ignoring her vocal mood, "that the government has some kind of device, maybe attached to him or to his workstation, that would register if a timeline got changed?"

"You mean something that warned them before their gang summit was fully underway that someone was messing with the future?"

"There's no other way they could have cleared that room and that warehouse of their presence in the time they had. They would barely have gotten Kenny's face on their TV screen when the firefighter medical unit arrived."

Kansas gave a long sigh like I hadn't heard in maybe fifteen years. "Jacky, Jacky, Jacky. You're missing the more obvious conclusion here."

"About what?"

"Your time travel, such as it is."

"Such as it is? You've already told me the world's power players are in knots just monitoring Lena's potential to jump a photon back in time, and my time travel is second rate?"

"I didn't say that."

"You implied it."

"Fair enough. I never thought there'd be the kind of limits on it you seem to have."

"You never thought..."

"C'mon, Jacky. You think you're the only one?"

She hung up on me.

14

The other self

I STARED AT MY cell phone in disbelief, both because I couldn't believe my sister had just hung up on me and because of what she'd implied before she did.

"C'mon, Jackie. You think you're the only one?"

Like an epic mic drop.

Kansas had always been an elliptical communicator, rarely directly answering a question if she could avoid it. Her preferred mode of communication was dropping all the information that a person with perfect recall and proficient reasoning skills needed to arrive at the conclusions which Kansas had reached even before the question had been asked.

It had made her incredibly irritating as a big sister who pretended to help me with my math and science in my early years. I could just imagine how frustrated her bosses must be with the reports she gave them, making them work to figure out what it was she'd pulled from the flood of signals intel I assumed she lived and breathed daily.

"Who's monitoring my research?"

I looked up to see Lena looking at me from her own plastic chair with a stricken look on her face. From the question she'd just asked, I guessed the stricken look had been caused by my careless comment back to Kansas after Kansas had said Lena's research was being monitored by—I thought back to what I'd said—"the world's power players." I hadn't said foreign nations, so maybe she'd think it was the other big tech companies?

"Is it Britain? Russia? India? China?"

"Um, she mentioned Russia and China. And our own military."

"Everyone I work with on this has signed NDAs. I was assured no one would get the results until I had something I was ready to share."

"Which is what you've been working on this weekend, right?"

She looked into my eyes. And in the still understanding that passed between us, it was like the separate oceans inside each of us were suddenly one. No waves. No rush of anything. Just…one.

"You're not going to deliver," I guessed.

She shook her head slowly. "I've already outlined the basics that we found. I was going to get into the outlier results and the superattraction theory next, but I think now maybe I won't."

"What about the others on the project?"

"Dr. Salazar knows what I'm shooting for but will just assume I'm being careful. The others believe we're more concerned with refining the acceleration process."

"So you're never going to deliver?"

"I'd like to talk that over with you. Tonight. At your place, as long as you let my security guys put a car outside the building."

I smiled. "Fair enough. Let's go to my place, eat some food, and 'talk.'"

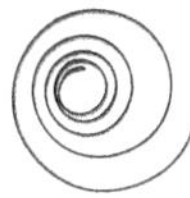

It didn't occur to me until after Lena and I, a car from ATS Security, and an SUV with Kajika Bighouse all convoyed back to my apartment building that Lena may have chosen my place partly so Bighouse could check out how easy it would be to break in there.

I shrugged it off. I could handle some security stiffs guarding me and Lena tonight. Because once again, for all I knew, this could be my and Lena's last time together. I had mentally figured out my next logical step to locate my brother, and it didn't guarantee a happy ending. I had been lucky in my gang summit escape. There was no guarantee my luck would hold.

Up in my third-floor apartment, the view over the rooftops and half of Seattle to see Lake Washington was still bright and clear. I took Lena's plaid, wool coat and hung it up, then clicked on the gas fireplace for some heat and headed into my galley kitchen to start dinner.

It was hard, as I started pulling out salad ingredients and a package of chicken breasts from the fridge, not to run through in my mind the steps I would take tomorrow. Even the early, non-life-threatening ones made my stomach roil over how they could, likely would, go down. It made me almost put down the dinner ingredients and have a prophylactic breakdown. I didn't, though, for the simple reason that I'd tried walking away from my Kenny failure once, and it almost killed me. I wouldn't walk away again.

"Chicken breast and salad okay?" I called to Lena.

I saw her wandering around my place, touching my books, my couch back, my hung photos of my parents, me, Kansas, and Kenny. And it occurred to me that Lena had never really had a chance to take any of this in on her first trip here. That night we'd been so focused on exploring each other that we could have been in a Motel 6 out by the airport and never noticed. And watching her move now, her breasts straining the buttons on her blouse, her hips making her plain, navy slacks far sexier than they had any right to be, I was rapidly getting back into that exploratory mindset.

"Perfect," she said over her shoulder. "It's a pretty place."

She stopped to stand at my living room window, looking out over the glittering lights of the city and the blurred reflections of those on the dark lake they encircled. I put the chicken I'd pulled out to one side for a moment, washed my hands, and wandered over to share the view with her. And touch her. Drink in her presence.

"'A lake is the landscape's most beautiful and expressive feature,'" I quoted. "'It is earth's eye; looking into which the beholder measures the depth of his own nature.'"

Lena turned to me and smiled. "Who said that?"

"Henry David Thoreau. When I first read him, I thought maybe I'd found a great social anxiety compatriot. He went into the woods for two years to commune with bean sprouts and weaving. But it turned out he loved visitors. He had more of them at his little one-room cabin than he'd ever had in the city."

"You don't like visitors?"

I ducked my head, instinctively withdrawing slightly. "No. I love people. They fascinate me. I'm just...scared of them, their dark sides, the parts that can unexpectedly rear up and tear you apart."

Lena nodded. "Like I did."

"I've been thinking about that. About what you did in the lab when you tried to scare me into a jump back by almost suffocating me. And I was finally able to *feel* the fundamental difference between someone who gets so caught up in a noble purpose that they can't see the harm they're doing and someone who wants to cause harm."

"Blindness versus cruelty?"

"Something like that. I've been guilty of blindness with my patients. I clearly see what's causing their distress and get so excited that I jump in too soon and make it worse."

"And how do you avoid that?"

"By listening, understanding, and somehow embracing all that a patient is, all their weakness, all their beliefs and needs. That single act helps people more than anything else in therapy."

"Even people who really need to change their beliefs or behaviors or both?"

"Especially them. Because they can't change until you're down in the foxhole with them, seeing what they see, feeling what they feel."

"Because no one else has wanted to do that."

"No one else who simultaneously can hold onto healthier beliefs and behaviors and gently lead the way out of the foxhole."

"I'm amazed you've never gotten lost."

I laughed. "Right? Feels like I'm always this close to losing it. It's why I regularly need nature. Forests. Lakes. They help me find myself again. At least enough to keep going."

"What about me?"

I looked at her, surprised. "What about you?"

I saw she was blushing as she asked, "Now that you know I didn't want to cause you harm, do you think you'll ever find some peace in me?"

A wave of something like gratitude swept through me, and I recalled the moment when I'd looked at her in the medical office maybe just forty-five minutes ago when I felt my thinking and feeling had merged with hers so completely. And even before that, she'd been the reason I'd been able to use my sense of failure as a trigger in our first experiments—I'd had her to come back to, to hold me up and reaffirm my worth just by being there with me.

Was that the sort of peace she meant? Was that like what I usually found in nature, the balm that helped me rediscover myself?

"I...don't know," I said. Though, what I really wanted to say was that she couldn't expect me to rely on her sticking with me given how quickly I was killing myself with my time travel jumps.

Yet here she was, smiling at me so brightly it lit up her whole face. "That's a good start," she said.

She tugged out the band that held her hair back in a tight ponytail and shook her head. Her great mound of curls tumbled down around her shoulders like a forest bursting free of its restraints. Even in her simple blouse and slacks, she was transformed into an Earth goddess. She took my breath away.

"Beautiful," I blurted.

"Even better. So you wanna get frisky?"

"Dinner?"

"Later. I've got some things you can nibble on first."

I started with the lips on her face.

Later, in the bedroom, then the shower, then the bedroom again, Lena became such a wondrous blur of cheeks and hair, breasts and nipples, slick labia, legs, toes, fingers, and always her eyes, watching me and reading me and wanting me, never judging, but applauding, laughing *with* me, falling into me as I fell into her so that when I entered her, it was like we were completing a design that nature had kept promising with its sweet flowers and trees, fresh lakes, and smooth stones.

For me, it was like digging my toes into the silty dirt of a river bed or rolling in freshly fallen snow.

Connection.

Pure.

Electric.

And in the powerful joy it created that I knew had to end...

Absolutely terrifying.

Our kitchen trip (for food) and pillow talk afterwards was not about love and connection but about what Kansas had said and how it promised to change everything, including Lena's research and how she was going to manage it. Which meant our talk really *was* about love and connection because, to me, sharing fears and speculations with Lena felt like I was sharing them with my oddly separated other self.

Falling too fast, Jacky.

Not falling. Being.

When we were done wondering if Kansas actually knew of other time travelers (Kenny?) or was just guessing, I was delighted to find that my body was up for one more joining with my beautiful, curly-haired, brilliant, funny, gleaming-skinned, direct other self named Lena.

After that final joining, our bodies tapped out and we slept like the dead, half curled around each other through much of the night.

In the morning, of course, I woke to see this dusky vision of beauty in my bed, and my fear returned. I tried to be cool when she woke up. I made her a breakfast of eggs over easy with bacon and coffee and a couple slices of cantaloupe.

But when she suggested we spend the day together, I demurred, saying I had to double-check the questions I was giving my students on their upcoming final exam. And she had to finish her report, shortened as it was, for her corporate bosses.

Lena looked a little puzzled and sad but agreed that was probably a good idea.

She donned her wool coat and went to the door with her hair pulled back in a loose ponytail but then turned and gave me such a lingering, tongue-filled kiss as she went that I almost changed my mind about...everything.

I could pull her back inside, make love to her, tell her all the things about Kenny that I'd still held back, and offer my entire heart to her to do with as she wished. We'd bring Lead the Way Security in to protect us both since Lena would now be living with me. We'd count on those ex-Rangers to catch whoever came calling, maybe helping the police get enough information and evidence to go after whoever sent them. Maybe they'd even find Kenny for me and save him if he was trapped or help the police arrest him if he'd actually gone bad. End it that way, but *end* it.

While Lena and I would just be two professors, one a therapist, one a theoretical physicist, shacking up and taking their relationship to the next level where *nothing else crazy or violent ever happened again.*

"Call me later today?" Lena murmured as we broke out of that sexy kiss.

"Yes," was all I said.

And she was out my door to go to where she'd parked on the street.

Follow her? Call her back?

Maybe if I'd been 100 percent sure we'd make it, that she was my future and worth sacrificing Kenny for and my chance at redemption. I wasn't there yet. I felt we were definitely *heading* that way if I lived long enough, but I'd known her just five days. It felt like more, like months, given our connection, all the life-changing stuff. But five days versus thirty-five years that were roughly half chasing after Kenny and half believing I'd failed him.

So, simple choice. I wanted Lena, but I had stuff to take care of first.

And if Kenny's a criminal?

He was being controlled.

You lied to Lena about that. You don't know.

I still get him out!

Whatever had happened to him, I loved him, I owed him, and I'd failed him. He was my phantom limb that I kept chasing down a deep mental rabbit hole. So whether he was a victim or guilty as sin, I wasn't doing it just for him. I needed to get us *both* out.

I walked to my landline phone. I took a deep breath, thought of Lena and of Kansas' admonitions about playing it safe, and dialed the Seattle PD East Precinct again to see if I could talk my way into speaking with Patrol Officer Bryan Miller. I was told Miller was out on patrol, but if I left my name and a message...

I declined and hung up, annoyed but not surprised. I'd already decided last night that I'd probably have to go directly to the East Precinct, find Miller or another officer who could get me to Gillespie, who could get me to Kenny, or to Cutter, who'd get me to Kenny.

Whatever it took.

Gillespie knew what I looked like and what I drove, though, and if I reached him today, I wanted the element of surprise. To that end, I'd ordered a Zipcar online this morning before Lena had woken up—a gray Honda Civic. I just had to walk a few blocks down to East Mercer Street to pick it up.

I also figured Gillespie and the police I planned to question to find him might not want to help me, so I'd selected clothing for myself that would do double duty—disguise my identity and protect me from serious injury.

I went to change into my beatdown gear.

15

Hiding behind the blue wall

AFTER THE CASUAL CRAZINESS, violence, and lovemaking of Saturday night, it felt like I was driving through the streets of a different planet when I navigated the gray Civic around the blocks that circled the Seattle Police Department's East Precinct on Capitol Hill.

Everyone I saw walking the streets was wearing a mask.

Almost like we'd finally woken up to the fact that half a million Americans (so far) had died from COVID-related causes, mostly massive organ failure or suffocation.

Of course, none of the gangsters I'd seen yesterday had worn masks. Then again, they also dealt the kind of drugs that had killed another 81,000 people last year. And probably directly shot and killed a bunch more.

No jump backs. No returns.

I parked in a small lot on East Pine Street and set out with my black mask up over my mouth and nose, and my beatdown gear —black running shoes, an athletic groin protector, my thickest jeans, three bulky sweaters covered by a zipped-up old brown-leather bomber jacket, a leather and fleece lumberjack hat with the ears tied down under my chin, and impact protection winter work gloves.

I figured I looked like a lost Canadian hockey fan. A little much for Seattle but an effective disguise. And if I ended up using the tire iron I'd stuck in the back waistband of my jeans, the personal protection aspect of it was going to come in handy.

So, feeling like an overstuffed scarecrow, I lumbered my way south a block, then to 12th Avenue and north on the sidewalk opposite the Seattle Police Department's East Precinct. Looking past the steady drone of traffic, I took in the tall two stories of flat concrete and glass. The blue metal around the windows and doors and dividing the first from the second floor was a nice touch. It was like steel bars, keeping the public out.

Cowards.

On the south end, there was a police cruiser entry with a roll-up metal door, a metal delivery door, and an unmarked blue metal side door. At the north corner was the entrance meant for the public, except it now looked closed and abandoned, which fit the message I'd gotten on the internet and on the phone.

I checked my watch and crossed the street to the public entrance.

My mission here was simple. Get inside the precinct and find Detective Gillespie's partner or one of his other friends and make them tell me how to reach the man.

I didn't want to use violence, but...whatever it took.

Standing in the building indentation that housed the double public entry doors, my first penetration attempt was simple. I rang the buzzer, then banged on the doors. Persistently. I saw no one inside the front reception area but was sure they had a camera on me somewhere.

I checked my watch again, planning to give myself five minutes before moving on to full vandal mode.

I got a response in two when the metal box on the wall beside the door squawked at me. "The precinct is closed to the public. If you have an emergency, please call nine-one-one."

"I need to talk to—" I stopped as the buzzing of the connection ended, and it was clear no one was listening.

Screw that.

My heart started beating faster as I contemplated the symbolism of the precinct's lockdown, their refusal to talk directly to the public, to people who needed their help, about one of their own detectives gone rogue. This was the blue wall. This was power that stomped out in riot gear and face shields to beat down mobs, then retreated into their concrete castle.

But they weren't invulnerable. They'd already given up this castle once, back in June, when George Floyd protesters had come out in numbers and force enough to make them fight an all-out war or retreat.

Versus now, when one very stupid, scared-but-determined psychologist drew the tire iron out from his backside and swung it like a major league batter against the glass door.

The tire iron whacked back so hard it almost flew out of my gloved hands, but it only got me swearing and swinging harder, this time ready for the snap back. Again. And again. And again. Until I knocked a chip out of the window that bounced off my lumberjack hat.

I hit it again, and the chip became a little crack.

I roared and kicked the door with my foot, which did nothing. So I went back to whacking with the tire iron until my hands felt battered and on fire.

Four minutes.

"Come on!" I yelled and swung the tire iron hard into the glass again, aiming at the small crack. How the hell had the insurrectionists broken those windows at the Capitol in January? And was I being as lawless as them? Only in *this* timeline, I rationalized. "Come *on!*" I swung again.

I staggered back a bit, breathing hard. I was pouring sweat off me into the frosty morning air. Looking around, I saw a couple of southbound cars had pulled over and were filming me with their phones. A crowd of pedestrians on the far side of the street had gathered to watch and point. Wondering if maybe they should join in?

Unrecognizable at a distance, I didn't care. Also, the plan had always been to jump back before all of this so no windows were broken and no one would have me on camera.

Assuming I managed to jump back.

I turned and began whacking the tire iron into the glass again, over and over, the sound so mesmerizing that I didn't hear the running tromp of boots until they were right behind me. I turned just in time to have two thick-muscled guys in their twenties, in Seattle PD uniforms, grab me by the arms and rip away my tire iron. I was slammed up against the concrete wall face first and so hard it felt like my right cheek had splintered.

"On the ground! On the ground!" they yelled at me like the ear flaps of my hat might mean I couldn't hear them.

They kicked my legs behind the knee joint, both my legs collapsed, and I hit the concrete knee first. Then my hip. Face. Pain blossomed everywhere, and I could taste my blood, hot and salty. Choking me. So much for my beatdown protection.

They grabbed my wrists and pulled them up behind me so that my shoulders felt stabbed with pikes. Cuffs on. Tight. Wrists felt like they were cracking. Like my fingers were breaking. I'd never be able to type again.

Then they had me up on my feet, half marching me, half carrying, through the now-open door I'd been trying to smash. When I twisted, trying to see their faces, they rammed a baton so hard through my leather jacket and sweater it was like I was naked.

I tried to speak through bloody lips. "Just... Just..."

"Shut up!"

"I just..."

A fist slammed against my face as they marched, enough to make my vision jump and start swimming.

Of course. Because now we were inside, out of sight of the public. They could do whatever they wanted to me. Slam me into walls and kick me to death. Or kneel on my neck. Or hit me in the balls.

Boots squeaked me over tile floors as my blood dripped down my front. I could see it in flashes. They were beasts and not taking me up anywhere for processing. They were taking me down into a basement, a dungeon, to be tortured and killed. I was never getting out of here. I'd hurt their home. Hurt their Sunday morning. They wouldn't let me speak. I'd get nothing from them but pain. I'd failed.

Dissociate.

Give up your hold on this timeline.

Let go. Let go.

Nothing.

Then really use your failure here. All the people you've—

"No," I mumbled and went for one last hit of pain instead. "Fucking pigs!"

A boot smashed into the back of my left leg, making my knee explode in—

I took two steps across the street before I realized where I was and stepped back onto the corner across the street from the police precinct. I backed up against the solid wall under a dark metal sign that said The Packard Building and stared at where I'd gone then jumped back from.

The precinct's front glass door was once again pristine, its police inside, enjoying their Sunday morning or out on their patrols. Among those inside were the two beasts who'd come out, but would now never come out, never beat my face and brain and knees and legs, never split my lips and leave me traumatized and scared of police officers for the rest of my life...

My eyes flooded with tears, so I had to duck my head and pretend to be getting something out of them. I felt my face, my knees, my legs. All sound, but my mind remembered. In my mind I could still feel the pain that had been inflicted there.

For just a second I wanted to turn around and run back to my place, call on security like I'd considered doing this morning when Lena had kissed me.

Except that didn't get me to Kenny, did it? That just kept me plunging into that rabbit hole deeper and deeper. Come on.

Whatever it takes.

It was time to pull up my big boy pants and keep going.

A series of deep breaths confirmed my body was as whole and uninjured as it had been when I'd left my apartment this morning. But I was already sweating through my shirt and useless extra sweaters and hat.

Grumbling at the cowardice that had made me dress like a stuffed sausage to begin with, I walked back to my rented car and dumped my sweaters, hat, and tire iron, reemerging with just my gloves, leather jacket, and athletic cup to protect me from the boys in blue.

Because, unlike them, I was essentially invulnerable. I mean, I could die if I was shot in the head without warning. For just about anything short of that, though, I could keep hitting reset, as long as I gave myself time to fully integrate after each jump back. I might also damage my mind if things got too tough, but could I really mess it up much worse than it was already?

It was time for precinct penetration attempt number two.

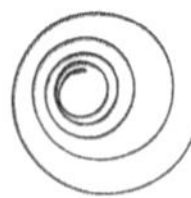

Attempt number two was as fruitless as number one, though more edifying.

I managed to rush after some officers going in through the unmarked blue side entry door. Convinced one of them to drag me up to talk to "Bo," a beefy, red-faced cop who was the partner of Gillespie. Bo pretended to listen long enough to bore the others, then took me down a back stairwell. There he punched me and choked me enough to convince me I'd never see daylight again, so my mind jumped back.

I had to do a triple because, with all my talking and walking and Bo stringing me along before trying to kill me, I'd been in the precinct with cops for over half an hour. My third jump only got me back to the corridor, approaching the main precinct room. My chest locked and I clutched it as I staggered, grunting with pain, my head swimming. This was too familiar, damn it! I collapsed on the floor, barking, "Heart attack!" and started convulsing.

I was too gone to see it but gathered later that the two officers escorting me called for assistance, and a medical staff appeared to carry me to a small treatment room with a bed.

An hour later, my body and mind integrated, and my symptoms seemed to magically disappear. I persuaded the doctor on call that it had actually been just a panic attack. I shared my credentials and a lie about being an expert witness, then asked, as one medical professional to another, if he could just let me quietly leave out a back way without needing a fuss or follow-up.

To my amazement, he'd not only done that but with such a warm bedside manner that I hoped I could meet the man later in a nicer setting. Dr. Emile Bresden.

I'd remember him.

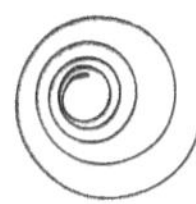

I didn't try attempt number three until almost noon.

After a great deal of thought, I'd decided to get rid of the athletic groin protector. I'd bought it for my brief flirtation with martial arts, but I'd cheaped out. It was good protection but not a custom fit and it chafed like hell.

Better to just face the chance of getting kicked down there and have my body jump back from the pain. My testicles would be fine once I jumped back to before they were kicked.

My second decision was to find a way to sneak into the building that didn't involve getting caught so I could sneakily search for answers, maybe without even needing to jump back.

To that end, I walked slowly around the East Pike side of the building. A few doors, all locked. I turned into the narrow alley behind the station. There was one door and some small windows about twenty feet up. Great.

I saw there were wall pipes on this back wall that I figured I could reach if I overturned one of the rolling trash bins back here. I could climb up to that row of small windows and try them. Or maybe climb all the way up to the roof.

Buuuut the roof had to be almost forty feet up. Over concrete. Doable? Maybe. But wall climbing had never been my sport. And if I fell and knocked myself out, I could wake up well past any chance of jumping back to before the fall. I'd be left with a broken arm or leg and maybe a fractured skull, a brain injury.

I turned in disgust and walked out of the alley.

As I stood on the sidewalk, considering my options, good fortune intervened.

"Mr. Professah!" a voice called to me from across the street.

When I looked up, I saw the older Jamaican sketch artist who'd drawn Gillespie from my description. His long hair and beard were as notable in real life as over the Zoom call. Ziggy Cheester. No mask. He was waving at me like I was an old friend.

I waited for a break in the traffic, pulled on my mask, and jaywalked quickly across the street. When I stopped in front of Cheester, I realized the man was holding a can of paint and some brushes in his left hand. Something about him was so relaxing that I could just stand here and look at him without flinching or having my insides curl up. Amazing.

Cheester smiled and indicated the colorful wall mural behind him. It had all kinds of crazy on it. Cheester seemed to be adding a stylized cow riding a fiery SUV.

"Nice," I said.

"Oh yes, mon. Got a studio inside. Patrol Officer Bry-*ahn* hid there in the summer riots, like he wants to check my work. He ask if I know how to draw faces. Make some money. Forensic sketch artist, woo!"

"Officer Bryan Miller, right," I said carefully. "You have a direct number where I can reach him?"

Cheester started adding red lines around the cow's nostrils. "No, but he comes by most days around one. Share de lunch. Shoot de breeze."

"Can I...wait here with you?"

Cheester paused in his nostril painting and smiled again. "Fo' sure."

As Cheester had predicted, a squad car pulled up alongside where Cheester was still working at five to one and Miller climbed out, pulling on his mask.

He saw me standing near where Cheester was currently adding sparkles to the flying SUV and frowned. I pulled off my mask to display my whole face. The young cop squinted, then nodded and smiled so widely under his own mask that his eyes crinkled.

"You're the guy who got attacked by someone who looks like...one of our guys."

I nodded and pulled my mask back on. "Your guy, James William Gillespie. Not 'looks like,' though. It was definitely him."

Miller suddenly looked nervously back at his squad car, like maybe he should skip this lunchtime break with Cheester.

But Cheester had managed to wrap up his last strokes and turned on Miller before the young cop could escape. "Hey hey, Bri-*anh*. Got your favorite onion and garlic focaccia with chicken breast, lettuce, pickles, mayonnaise, and just a touch of jerk sauce, my brother. I got warm spiced cider like Christmastime! You and Professor Jackson here, you join me now!"

Then Cheester opened the door to his studio, which was apparently inside the very building he was painting, and waved both Miller and me inside. I held out a hand inviting Miller to go first and, reluctantly, he did.

Inside was what looked like a busy printing shop, with endless scratching on art boards, tapping on computer keys, and the *thwip-thwip-humm* of large-scale printing machines that looked designed to punch out specialized labels. I thought I could smell the glue as well as the bite of acetone. Ink?

Most of the staff were wearing masks, and I realized that Cheester had donned one as he'd entered, smiling wide enough behind it at the printing staff inside that they could see it in his eyes and all waved.

The man was a marvel of social goodwill. There was a lot I could learn from him.

I was still glad, though, that they were all looking at him, not me.

Cheester led Miller and me past the machines to a space at the back that was only separated from all the printing commotion by a freestanding wall that stretched only some ten feet up toward the open-girder ceiling maybe double that high. Braced poles also held up cut plastic sheeting "doors" that Cheester pushed through, and we followed.

"Keeps de riffraff out and de spatter paint in!" Cheester laughed, waving at the doors and at the six-foot-tall canvases in bright comic book colors that he had lining the space in various states of completion. And there were indeed many splatters of colorful paint on the floor and walls.

Miller had pulled a chair up to a table where Cheester had laid out their lunch, and I pulled up a chair beside him, followed quickly by Cheester, who poured each of us a large ceramic mug of warm cider smelling of cinnamon and nutmeg.

As he did, Miller looked at me and pointed to his own mask. "Got my second dose last week. You okay with...?"

I nodded. "I've had my first," I said, and we took our masks off together.

"COVID not welcome heah!" Cheester declared and took a seat at the table. "First we eat, *then*, Professor, you ask your questions."

Given the mouth-watering spread, I had no trouble with that. Especially since a well-fed young cop was going to be much more forthcoming than a hungry, cold, nervous one.

It was easier than I could have hoped because Miller had clearly been stewing over the shutdown order he'd been given on Gillespie since it had happened. I had read him right. Bryan Miller was a good kid and still new enough in the police force to believe the police were supposed to be the good guys. The enormity of that loosened me up, too, more than I would have believed possible. It even had me honestly telling Miller just how scared Lena and I had been by Gillespie and how I now really needed Miller's help.

The moment the words were out of my mouth, my hands began to sweat and a cold chill prickled the back of my neck. Had I really done that? Laid my feelings out baldly and asked for help? Like I'd done with Mikael but this time with an almost complete stranger? I couldn't breathe as I waited for Miller's scornful rejection.

But amazingly, Miller took my disclosure of fear and request for help as not only normal but expected. A compliment, almost. The young cop frowned, nodded his head, and reached a decision.

"I asked around, quietly," he confided. "Way back before he joined the army, then came back and became a cop, Gillespie apparently knew some guys in the Demon Monks. So when he made detective out in New York, someone he knew back here who'd also become a police officer figured Gillespie could use his connections to get in with the gang, undercover, and help bust them."

He looked at me as if to ask if he was saying too much. I nodded for him to go on.

"Long story short," he said, "Gillespie moved back here and did that. Used to report in regularly. Then it got less and less. Captain apparently tried to pull him out twice, and Gillespie talked him out of it. Said there's this bigger fish he's trying to connect to BAM and the other gangs. Now he's like a ghost. I'm not sure he's even on the city payroll anymore."

"He say how he knew guys in the Demon Monks?"

"I don't know. Why?"

I paused and forced myself to keep this honesty thing rolling. "I saw him with them when I was in high school. My brother got tied up with them, and I was trying to get him out. Gillespie was an active member. Younger, but it was him."

Miller frowned and looked down. "Which meant he would have lied when he applied to be a police officer. That should get him fired. Would you be—?"

I shook my head. "Don't even think it, Bryan. Someone I trust is pretty sure the gangs are doing some kind of dance with the CIA and Gillespie's involved. No one's allowed to look at his files."

The young patrol cop's eyes had gone wide. "No shit."

"I probably shouldn't have told you, but you need to know why you can't go poking at this thing any more than you have."

"But you're going to."

"He's directly threatening me and my friend, so yeah. I think it's because of the scientific work she's doing. And no cops are going to step in to protect us. We've hired private security. But they're not going to be enough."

"So what do you think you can do?"

I stared at my empty plate, stabbing at the stray crumbs of focaccia bread with my finger and bringing them to my mouth in a bid to cover my total lack of a real plan.

"He's gwan negotiate," Ziggy Cheester said smoothly, looking at both of us like he could see into the future somehow.

And maybe Cheester could, I thought, as I recalled what Kansas had said. *You think you're the only one?* Because weren't scrying, foresight, fortune-telling, prediction all forms of time travel? Except with them, the mind's eye jumped forward then back again versus my mind jumping just one direction—back ten minutes.

A week ago, I would have ridiculed the notion of seeing into the future. That was a week ago.

"You're right, Ziggy. I'm going to negotiate. Because there are things I know that Detective Gillespie does not. And that he *wants* to know. So"—I turned back to Officer Miller—"any idea where I can find our rogue undercover cop?"

16

A blown cover

AS I DROVE SOUTH on Martin Luther King Jr. Way, I was still marveling over the conversation I'd had with Cheester and Patrol Officer Miller. Not just because of what I'd revealed and learned in return but because of how accepted I'd been. All because of the easy connection I'd formed with the two men, an instant friendship born of honesty and shared need. As a psychologist, I understood the principle intellectually, but as a man still ruled by the fears and trauma of my teens, it was a revelation that I could actually be a part of something so uncomplicated.

Also, the dirt I'd gotten on Gillespie had been exactly what I needed.

Gillespie's usual base of operations was Southend. Miller had described it as a fuzzy-boundaried area on the southeast side of Seattle, west of Seward Park and just north of South Othello. It was there that BAM and the Demon Monks ran most of their drug and protection rackets.

(I had wanted to ask Miller if he knew why they'd hold a gang meeting over in SODO, on the west side, but decided not to. Maybe it had been some kind of neutral ground? Maybe the Demon Monks and BAM wanted to extend their operations to the docks and shipping traffic? It had been so long since I'd tried to think like a gang member to understand Kenny, doing it now made my brain hurt.)

The important thing was that Gillespie had long had a letter drop at the Othello Park Church of Worship for use when he dropped off the radar for an extended period. Miller had heard Bo say that Gillespie went to church to stay sane when the shit with the Demon Monks and BAM got too crazy. It kept him from losing himself.

But my memory of Gillespie's eyes from Wednesday, and from seventeen years ago, said some part of the man had always been lost. Still, if I could find him at church, he'd probably be less likely to kill me outright. Maybe he'd even just tell me where to find Kenny and promise to leave me and Lena alone.

A church. Miracles. Could happen.

It was 10:05 a.m., Sunday morning, prime time for most Christian churchgoers, though not Seventh Day Adventists nor Muslims nor Jews. This was mostly just stored trivia to me. My parents weren't religious. I hadn't actually entered a church or mosque or synagogue before I'd explored one of each with Kenny when I was fourteen. I'd found the field trips a fascinating study in human need. Kenny had thought that was hilarious. It made me wonder, suddenly, whether Lena followed any religious practice. It couldn't be too restrictive given the way she'd been with me, but if—

My phone's GPS spoke: "Take the next left at...South Othello Street."

When I reached the Othello Park Church, I had to park on the side street because the church's parking lot was jammed. The King County COVID guidelines only allowed 25 percent capacity or two hundred people in a church service, whichever was less. There was no way all these cars were only taking up 25 percent of the small, barnlike church.

Foolish people.

Then again, maybe the rest of this particular community didn't care. On this side of the concrete apartment buildings that surrounded the Othello light-rail station, most of the houses looked as ramshackle as the church. They were mostly older-looking bungalows and two-stories with frozen brown lawns, dirt or concrete, sparse tree cover, and cracked sidewalks and fences.

I pulled on my mask, got out of the Civic and locked it, zipped up my leather jacket against the cold, and walked to the front door of the church. My nose wrinkled at a pungent, acrid smell that seemed to surround me as I walked. Maybe from my own body. My fear glands were probably pumping out *Go back!* warning signals.

I couldn't hear singing from inside. That much was good.

I sighed, pulled one of the double doors, and slipped inside.

As my eyes adjusted to the gloom of the back of the church—there was no separate vestibule—the black minister up front suddenly called out, "Amen!" and the packed-together congregation all lifted their heads with a collective gasp of breath.

I jerked back with a rush of adrenaline, prepared to flee, but as I stumbled back against the door I'd pulled closed behind me, my forebrain processed that no one had turned to look at me. Even the minister up front seemed unaware I was here.

Just crazy timing.

I held onto the back wall a moment to steady myself and make sure my fight-or-flight reflex didn't trigger a jump back in time.

Okay.

"Do you want to take a seat?" whispered a voice to my right.

I almost jumped again but managed to contain myself. It was a well-groomed Asian man. He motioned me to the back left of the church where there was a short row of still-empty stacking chairs. They were the same type, I noted now, that provided seating for the rest of these two-hundred-plus worshipers.

"Thank you," I said, not meeting the man's eyes, and hurried left.

But I didn't take a chair. Instead, I pressed myself to the far left wall and scanned the congregation row by row, starting from the back. My eyes had adjusted to the ancient tungsten overhead lighting that hung from the exposed wooden rafters and was pleased to see it was bright enough to make out most people's identifying features.

Quite the mix. Maybe 30 percent Black, 30 percent East and South Asian, 20 percent Mexican, 20 percent white like me. Street gangs often formed along ethnic lines, but the Demon Monks never had. It would make sense if they were now headquartered somewhere near here, in a neighborhood as diverse as this.

Of course, to find Gillespie, I was mostly looking for the long, straggly hair and beard, which I'd see before Gillespie's skin color or gray, dead eyes.

Halfway through. Nothing.

Row by row by row. A little harder to clearly determine features in the front half of the church. Nearing the front ten rows...

But something in the back of my mind told me to go back a few rows to scan again. Like my eyes had seen something close.

"...the message from Deuter-*on*-omy!" the minister up front thundered. "Chapter eighteen, verse nine."

That row? No.

Next row?

"'When you enter the land the Lord your God is giving you, do not learn to imitate the detestable ways of the nations there!' You know what this means. It means the *violence* and *drugs* and the *immorality* of the nonbelievers around you. They are not your people! They are *not—your—ways!*"

In the row ahead of the one I was rescanning, a head jerked to one side like the listener had been slapped. The long hair had been pulled back in a ponytail, the beard was combed, the shirt was clean, but it was Gillespie.

As I watched, my heart sped up. Gillespie obviously mumbled something to the people beside him and stood. He picked his way past the seated and half-standing of his row until he got clear, then hurried toward the back of the church.

I quickly took a seat and turned my face away as Gillespie reached the back of the church and pushed his way out.

I jumped up and caught the door before it swung completely closed. I slipped out after my quarry and squinted my eyes hard in the morning sunlight to see where he'd gone.

There.

Gillespie was already striding through the parking lot and north up the street where I had parked. Which meant he hadn't driven here. Which meant he probably lived close or had taken transit. Either way, the thing now was to follow him.

Confront him?

Not yet. Just follow.

Then run, Professor. He's getting away.

I ran.

North a block. East four blocks. I caught up to Gillespie at a fast-food joint on Rainier Avenue South. I didn't think I'd been seen. Not from any skill on my part but because Gillespie had been stomping along with his hands jammed into his pocket and his hairy head bent forward like he was an addled crazy man. Definitely losing it.

My mind skipped back to the minute Gillespie had stood up in church and caught the tail end of what the preacher had been saying. About not taking part in the immorality of the people around you. Right. Maybe it had pricked something in the undercover cop's tentative grasp on which side he was on.

A few more turns and Gillespie used a key to enter a decrepit rooming house just east of Rainier, behind a taco joint.

Stymied, I wandered along the rooming house side street a ways before deciding it would be too easy for Gillespie to slip out of the house again and disappear. And then what? So I did as much of a circle around the house as I could and actually caught sight of Gillespie in an upstairs window. He looked like he was getting undressed. Changing clothes?

I looked around. I guessed this was a stakeout, then. I'd seen the movies. Though my stakeout would have no car to eat and drink in, no partner to gab with, no bottle in which to relieve myself. Instead, I found a rock by some trees almost opposite the rooming house, sat down, and pretended to be taking in the sunny day. That might be something you'd do after an early church service by yourself, right? Loosen the tie, do up your coat against the wind, turn your face to the late winter sun?

I casually watched the rooming house and waited.

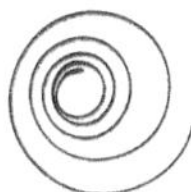

Some forty-five minutes later, right when I was thinking I'd have to move on or freeze to death, the rooming house door opened and Gillespie slipped out.

He now wore his more familiar filthy, tan battle jacket, layered tee-shirts, and ripped jeans. His disguise? His real self? Even his shoes looked worn out. His hair was no longer pulled back but hung in a tangled mop around his head as his face twitched back and forth, clearly not registering me. His mouth seemed to twitch inside his beard, the tongue snaking out and in quickly. One of Gillespie's hands jerked up to rub at his nose and face like it was crawling with invisible bugs.

Then he was off, striding with a determined gait back toward Rainier Avenue.

I jumped up and yelped at the stiffness that had settled in during my surveillance. I shook it out and took off after Gillespie, forcing myself to hang back as he reached Rainier. There he patted his hair, tugged down his shirts, and sniffed the air like a dog, probably tracking the smell of meat and tortillas from the taco place.

Then he was off again, me following.

Cracked sidewalks, car repair lots, cheap restaurants, low-rise apartment buildings, shuttered cannabis stores, bus stops, and telephone poles. People along here kept their heads down. I figured nobody even saw me as I tailed Gillespie.

About five long blocks down, just as he passed a motel sign in the shape of a giant horseshoe, Gillespie suddenly swerved right to cross all four lanes of Rainier. On the other side, he stumbled up a shallowly rising, treed street that ran between a broken-down industrial supply store on the right and a fenced, vacant lot on the left that was overgrown with spiky bushes.

I gauged the traffic, then crossed the road after him.

By the time I'd crossed and caught my breath, Gillespie was a block up this side road and turning left through some trees.

Shit!

I ran to catch him, forcing myself to ignore how suspect I must look sprinting up a quasi-residential street midday in a leather jacket. Or not, given the neighborhood.

I reached where Gillespie had turned in and followed.

It was a dirt path that followed another chain-link fence to what looked like some kind of institutional building. It was set in about twenty feet from the greenbelt I stopped in, only one story high with a shallow, sloped roof, gray-siding walls, and evenly spaced windows that ran far off to the right. There was a door along there that was covered by a metal grate and looked locked. A secure seniors residence maybe? A psychiatric facility?

The dirt path swerved left to continue on between the building's left wall and the shrubs growing along the bordering chain-link fence.

There was Gillespie.

He'd cleared most of the space between the forest I was in and the building but had stopped as three men came out from the path by the side of the building. They didn't look like health care workers or orderlies. One of them, a pasty-faced, tall, blond man, had his hands in his dark-gray sports jacket pockets like he was gripping a gun. I remembered him. The Aryan standard-bearer at Ground Zero. Cutter had leaned in to speak to him in front of the assembled gangs...who maybe never assembled in this timeline?

The other two men, both shorter, darker, and stockier, looked like twins who were used to beating and biting people to death. Not quite as big as the brute from the Tukwila casino, but they probably didn't have to be if they were a tag team. They felt familiar, like I'd seem them in too many mafia movies.

"Hey-hey," Gillespie said as he saw them. He jerked his arms open wide in the universal signal for *I'm not armed.*

"Whyn't you get a fucking car?" said one of the shorter thugs.

"And come in the fucking front way," said his twin.

"What? Like an em-ploy-ee?" Gillespie said. "Don't think so."

"You look like a fucking rubbie," said the first twin.

"Fucking stink," agreed the second.

Gillespie jerked his gaze to the tall blond. "You think so? You agree with these two whiny Guido bitches?"

"Where have you been?" The blond spoke with some kind of Nordic accent, stepping close to Gillespie so he looked like a disapproving father. His hands were still in his pockets.

"Church," Gillespie said. He coughed, sniffled, and wiped his nose with his dirty sleeve.

"Your church finished over an hour ago."

"I had to change."

"You got a message. You had to check in with your cop buddies."

Gillespie's chin hit his chest, and his head pulled back and looked up at the blond with exaggerated disbelief. "What the fu

—"

His question was cut off as the blond man smoothly moved the muzzle of his pistol from inside his pocket to between the open flaps of Gillespie's army jacket and into the triple layer of tee-shirts protecting Gillespie's heart. He pulled the trigger.

I remember reading that a gun silencer, also known as a suppressor, only cuts the sound of a gunshot by thirty to forty decibels by slowing the release of the propellant gasses. The bang of the release plus the crack of the bullet breaking the sound barrier can still hit 130–150 decibels, louder than your average police siren.

Turns out that if you fire directly into a multi-tee-shirted body, even without a suppressor, the sound you get is more like a loud thud. Actually, a thud-thud because the blond shot Gillespie twice.

Gillespie dropped to his knees, then fell over, his mouth working, then spitting up blood for a few seconds before he stilled.

I was on my own knees by that time, digging my fingers into the dirt and twigs, struggling to keep myself from puking even as I fought hard to keep my breaths slow, even, and *quiet*.

It didn't work. The flashback to Gillespie shooting me, to him kicking me as a teen, other gangsters kicking me as an adult, stabbing me, the cops smashing my face into the wall, punching my kidneys all shoved at me, ran like electric nightmares through my veins, making me want to scream, to run, to . . .

I retched so loudly I felt any birds in the area would have taken to the skies in terror.

The blond man lifted his head from where he'd been studying Gillespie's face and scanned the trees where I hid. He gestured to the short, dark twins. "Go kill whoever that is."

Tweedle Dark and Tweedle Darker both drew out knives and sprinted toward me.

I fumbled back from my mess of vomit in terror, slipped, and crashed backward through the branches away from Tweedle Dark, only to feel Tweedle Darker grab me from behind, his thick little arm around my face. Suffocating me! Holding my nose and mouth like—

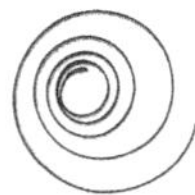

I stumbled to a stop on a sidewalk. A four-lane street to my right. Rainier. Why was I at Rainier? Who was I? When?

I blinked, shook my head, and grounded myself again. I saw Gillespie, in his slouchy army jacket and torn jeans, approaching a motel sign in the shape of a giant horseshoe.

He was about to cross the street!

"Gillespie!" I yelled over the roar of traffic.

His head jerked around, blinking furiously, looking tweaked and scared. Then the flash of fear passed as he saw me and identified me, and his eyes took on the cold deadness I was used to. He looked around like I might have brought backup, clearly concluded I had not, and came stalking back toward me.

He didn't pull a gun or knife as he came. Maybe he was under an order to not carry any weapons to that gang building. Which was why he'd held up his arms when the others had intercepted him there. But when he reached me, his dead eyes kept darting all over the place, definitely in withdrawal from something. Likely opioids, given his restless state. But there was something else there, too. Something about seeing *me*, specifically. Like guilt over how he'd gone after me? Concern that I'd tracked him down? Seeing an opportunity to kidnap me now to fulfill his earlier Demon Monks assignment?

He rubbed his nose. "What do you want, douchebag?"

"If you go to that place across the street, up that smaller street, through the trees, you die."

"What?"

"You heard me. They're waiting for you. Blond guy and two shorter thugs—Tweedle Dark and Tweedle Darker."

Gillespie frowned hard. His right hand grabbed at his beard and tugged it while his usually dead eyes sparked into a kind of self-preserving spark of curiosity. "How do you know that?"

"Heard them talking about you yesterday," I lied. "At the gang summit in the SODO factory."

"That was called off."

"Uh, yeah, but I'd found out about it and went, looking for my brother," I riffed. For someone who'd always been a terrible liar, it sounded convincing enough. Certainly better than the truth would have. "I heard some people talking."

"The Finn and the two Italians."

I shrugged, hoping that Gillespie hadn't been with them all day yesterday. "Could be. They didn't flash immigration papers."

"Why do they want to kill me?"

"They said you're an undercover cop. They said you exchange notes or something with your handlers at a church near Othello Station. One of them wanted to kill you the minute you left the church."

"The Finn."

"The blond guy. Yeah."

"Fuck."

"Are you really a cop? Is that why you told me my brother was alive? And why you haven't come after us again?" I let myself sound hopeful, not mentioning how I knew Gillespie had been perfectly ready to kill both me and Lena when he came for us. Because, in the time frame we were in now, all that nastiness never happened. He'd shot at us once, of course, but he could always argue he'd just been trying to get our attention.

Gillespie's eyes went dead again. I was beginning to understand it was his way of hiding what he thought or felt. But there were other tells. He kept staring at me even as his body, in withdrawal from whatever drug he was hooked on, kept wanting to dance away. It reminded me so much of Kenny in the early days I felt a filthy kind of *sympathy* for the man.

I also could read clearly that he wanted to know what I knew. Needed to know. Everything. To give himself bargaining power with the Demon Monks, maybe. Or to tell if it was time to pull the plug on this undercover operation and go back to being a real cop.

"You're a doctor, right?" he said finally.

"Of…psychology. Yes."

"Can you write prescriptions?"

I shook my head. "You'd need a psychiatrist for that."

"Fuck."

"Better in withdrawal than dead."

He shot me a withering look, then started walking back the way we'd both come. Stopped and look back at me. "You want to know what's going on or not?"

I nodded and hurried after him.

17

Betrayed

GILLESPIE'S RENTED ROOM WAS sparse and cheap but surprisingly clean. On one side of the room was his single bed, dresser, and a battered-looking laptop that was probably his sole communication and entertainment. On the opposite wall, he had a hot plate and a small fridge, with his cooking gear, plates, mugs, utensils, and food neatly stored in stacked plastic milk crates with cardboard-box inserts.

While he walked in and searched through a stash of boxes on the floor in the corner—searching for pharmaceuticals that just weren't there, I guessed—I stood just inside the door. He turned, saw me, and waved at me to sit down on the room's only chair, a rickety wooden thing that looked reclaimed from the side of the road on garbage day.

I sat.

"I would have thought you ate all your meals with the other Demon Monks," I said, indicating his makeshift kitchen.

"We grew up," he mumbled. But my question got him focused on his little kitchen. He jammed his hands in his pockets and shuffled over there. He filled a kettle with water from the spigot on a large, half-filled, clear plastic, square container of water that lay on its side near the hot plate. Then he put the kettle on the hot plate and turned the plate on. "For tea," he said. Then, "Why're you really here? How'd you track me down?"

"The church. I'm trying to find my brother."

"Right. Right." He seemed to lose his focus for a moment. "You know why I became a cop?"

"You want me to guess?"

"I got into the investigative corps when I was in the Army. Turns out I was good at thinking like a criminal. And I learned what it was like fighting for the good guys."

"Is that what you're doing now?"

He squinted at me. "Yeah."

"But you got hooked on some of what the bad guys are selling."

"Yeah. My bad. Something else I learned in the Army."

"Does Bo know?"

Another squint and his eyes went extra dead now. "Who's Bo?"

"Detective who beat me up when I went looking for how to find you."

Gillespie nodded. Again. Then his dead expression seemed to crack. Splinter. Break into a million little pieces. He chuckled, sniffed, and swiped at his eyes. "Still got my back. Even after..."

I quoted the passage that had gotten Gillespie to leave church this morning. "'When you enter the land the Lord your God is giving you, do not learn to imitate the detestable ways of the nations there.'"

"Deu-tor-*on*-omy!" Gillespie called back at me in a passable imitation of the Othello Park Church preacher. Then he grinned weakly, his eyes still wet.

"Yeah."

"Fucking hell of a thing."

"Especially since the Demon Monks must have seemed like home."

"Lot of the same crew," Gillespie confirmed, sounding happy he actually had someone nonthreatening to talk with. "Cutter. Big Mike. Spiegler. Gainesy. The Finn. The Italian twins. Lots of new kids, though. New goals. New allies. You want some tea?"

"Sure. Please."

He was back where the kettle had started bubbling and whistling. He pulled out two ceramic mugs, filled each with boiling water, and started going through one of the sideways stacked crates that had food supplies. Came out with a small box of tea bags. "Earl Grey!" he announced, putting a bag in each cup. Without asking, he poured in milk and stirred in heaping tablespoons of sugar for each cup.

I grimaced. I guessed he wanted to completely kill the bitter citrus of the bergamot orange peel, but all that sugar wasn't going to help Gillespie's jittery withdrawal.

He brought the two cups over, and I had a sudden flash of suspicion. Despite the fact I'd just saved his life and he'd opened up to me, like Cheester and Miller had, with his story of aspirations and weakness, he *had* tried to kill both me and Lena in a different timeline. It was in him. I'd seen the calculation in his eyes earlier. If he poisoned me now or just put me to sleep…

Gillespie saw my hesitation and got it instantly. He put the two cups down on top of an overturned milk crate near me, then stepped back, weaving a little. "Take whichever one you want."

I examined them, saw no difference, and chose the one on the left.

Gillespie picked up the one on the right and took a decent sip, even though I could see the steam coming off it. "Hot," he said.

I set mine down on the floor by my leg to let it cool a bit as he pulled back the milk crate, sat on it, and softly sang a tune I didn't recognize. Earlier-generation rock. Disco maybe. Something about living in a world of fools who were bringing him down—he sipped his tea—and him wishing they'd just let him be.

My eyes roamed around the room. Was this an act Gillespie put on, this place? Or was he, in his truest of hearts, more comfortable as a street person than a cop?

Finally, when Gillespie's tea was half gone, I started sipping my own, surprised the sweetness didn't bother me as much as I'd thought it would. The heat was good. This apartment was cold.

"Was my brother still there when you went back?" I asked innocently, as a test.

Gillespie nodded. "Still working with the Monks but not part of them."

"Meaning?"

"I don't know. He and Cutter had made some kind of arrangement before I got back into the Monks, undercover. Would have been about two years ago. They talk on the phone and Skype. Sometimes Cutter asks for things. Sometimes Kenny gives orders. Really weird."

"Orders about what?"

"Deliveries to be made. People to introduce to other people. Alliances the Monks need to make. Like Kenny's building an army. Maybe to take on Hells Angels? Cutter's on board but careful because he's got investments now. Crazy, right?"

"You know who Kenny's working for?"

Gillespie shook his head. "Could be the government. Maybe Russian mob. All I know is he knows too much and has access to way too much shit—weapons, buyers, dirty cops and politicians..."

"How does Lena Cortland figure into that? Who asked you to kidnap her? Was that Cutter or Kenny?"

Gillespie looked at me sideways. "The physics babe? That was me. Cutter sent me for you. I saw you two together and thought she might be leverage."

"What?" I frowned and put down my tea. "Me? Why did Cutter want me? How'd he even know where I was?"

He shrugged. "One of our techies. Not hard with all your social media shit. Jesus. I did *not* see you becoming a shrink. Or a professor."

"But why? What does Cutter want me for?"

"He never said. But if I had to guess, whatever arrangement he's got with Kenny? I'm thinking you're his way to change it."

I felt all the blood drain out of my face. It explained why Kenny had sounded so shocked to see me at that meeting that now never was. And his move to pull focus hadn't been a dismissal; it had been to draw Cutter's attention, to give me time to escape.

"Finish your tea," Gillespie said. "Gotta wash up." He glugged the rest of his down.

I followed suit and handed him my cup, feeling at a loss. I was more confused now than when I'd come in. If Gillespie was right and Cutter had never targeted Lena, she was safe and it was only *me* who was in danger. Unless Gillespie had told Cutter about me, and now Cutter wanted Lena, too. As leverage over me, in the same way he was going to use me as leverage over Kenny? Did that make sense? I wasn't sure anymore. I felt very muzzy headed. I needed Gillespie's help planning my next move. Had to ask him directly for it. That was the lesson that Mikael, Lena, her Ranger buddies, Ziggy Cheester, and Patrol Officer Bryan Miller had all taught me. Expose your need and just ask.

"Hey, Detective..." I began, trying to figure out how to start.

"Yeah." He had taken the cups to the counter and was wiping them with a cloth.

"You gotta call your precinct, right?"

He dropped his head a little. "I don't know. It seems a shame I gotta pull the plug when I'm this close to finding out what's going down."

"Better than...murdered."

"I know, but I think if I brought you in like I was supposed to do, maybe they wouldn't feel the need."

"Ha," I managed. This wasn't going the way it was supposed to.

Gillespie seemed to agree. He looked really sad when he said, "I'm sorry, Professor Jackson. You know, I gave you a choice. If you'd picked the other cup, then it would have been a sign."

"Fer whah?" *Uh-oh.* Now my tongue felt thick.

"To call it quits. Help you escape. You actually tried to save my life, and I appreciate it. But this chance... My fuck up Tuesday's why they turned on me. They assembled a whole new team that took Dr. Cortland this morning on the road between your apartment and her workplace. But they *didn't get you.* Ha! So if I deliver you, I'm golden."

No, not Lena. I tried to shake my head. It was so muzzy I almost fell off my chair.

Then I did fall off my chair.

I tried looking at my watch but couldn't read it before my eyes closed.

18

Some things can't be undone

I CAME TO, BLINK by blink, over the course of several minutes, my stomach rolling over and over, until I finally understood that I was in a small, bare room. No windows? The floor under my cheek was cold concrete, cracked and crumbled. Smelled dank. Old. The walls were dirty...wallboard? Painted wood? I wouldn't be able to tell until I got up and went to one. Touched it.

That might be awhile.

I groaned and rolled onto my back, making my head swim. The ceiling's single bulb, behind a wire mesh, stung my eyes until I shut them. This wasn't the disorientation of my essence settling into a younger version of itself. This had a distinctly chemical feel and taste to it.

Gillespie had drugged me, obviously. The tea. He'd let me choose which cup.

Shit.

And Lena had been taken.

That made me roll to my side and puke, then roll away from it with my eyes still shut, breathing heavily. More guilt in my basket. First I'd failed Kenny. Now... What was I? Some kind of walking quicksand? Get too close to me and you're sucked in?

It made my revelations about trust and asking people for help nothing but bullshit. Look what happened when I trusted people. Look what happened when they trusted me. Next time, maybe everyone should first ask who was *worthy* of trust.

If there was a next time.

Oh, grow up! Don't give in to despair. You made it to the Demon Monks' HQ, didn't you?

Maybe?

Turning my face away from the ceiling, I squinted my eyes open. It would have been nice to know how long I'd been out, but a quick, fumbling check told me that, just like my wallet, keys, and phone, my watch was gone. In any case, it was a sure bet I'd been out longer than ten minutes, so there was no jumping back. There was no brain record there to jump *to*. Whatever Gillespie had hit me with didn't even leave dreams.

An approaching sound from outside the room made me push myself up enough to slide back against the wall opposite the door. I sat up with my back against the wall, noting that my leather coat was gone, too. Some gangster must have figured it fit him better than me. Probably right.

There was the scratching sound of a key in the lock of the door. A thunk. The door scraped open.

Two gangsters stood in the doorway—the Finn in the dark-gray sports jacket he always wore and one of the Italian twins, the one I'd labeled Tweedle Darker because he had more stubble on his swarthy, pumpkin-shaped face. Tweedle Darker wore a long-sleeved, wrinkled purple jersey that looked like his attempt to dress up. Where was his brother?

At least the Finn didn't have his right hand in his pocket to hold a gun, nor the bump of a gun in either of those pockets. Good, I guessed. If they were here to beat me or kill me, at least it wouldn't be a quick shot I didn't see coming. And Lena—was she still alive?

"You're awake," said the Finn. "Get up."

"For what?"

Tweedle Darker started toward me with clear intent to hurt, but the Finn held him back and said, "There is someone who wants to see you."

Kenny! Even if he's not in the building, if I can communicate with him...

Fighting to keep my excitement off my face, I struggled up to my feet. Wobbly. "Just a sec."

"Do you need help?"

"A second!" I snapped. I wasn't taking any more "help" from killers. I'd learned that much now.

My legs and stomach and head steadied. I nodded and walked unsteadily to the two men. The Finn stepped back into the hallway to wait for me, but Tweedle Darker actually swelled his short, burly chest at me as I passed him. I smelled a sour hate that was barely covered by a cloyingly sweet body spray. Axe maybe? It smelled different on different people, I remembered someone saying. I noted how Tweedle Darker's right hand reflexively lifted to the rear of his right hip. Knife or gun there? The bottom of his jersey hid whatever it was. But he and his twin had used knives to come after me in the timeline where Gillespie bit it, so it was probably a knife.

Then I was once again in a rat warren corridor that gave me nasty flashbacks to the warehouse on Occidental Avenue. Ground Zero. Yeah, I'd been a bit premature with the naming of that place. Any bombs that blew up there had somehow been sucked away when I'd jumped back out of it. *This* place, on the other hand, had trapped me good. I had no way to jump out. So my plan was what? Fight? Not my skill set. I could throw yoga at them. Maybe psychologize them to sleep?

But even as a growing awareness of my situation sped up my breathing and heart rate, a stubborn self-preservation instinct made me focus hard with a double mind. One part of me paid extra attention to my surroundings as we walked down the long corridor outside my cell, the Finn leading and Tweedle Darker following me. This part of my brain noted everything from the regular space of ceiling lights and doors to dust and chemical smells, turnoffs to other hallways, cracks in the concrete floor. I saw two indents in the hallway where the doors were recessed into the wall for some reason. Hiding places! I saw a dimly lit emergency exit sign at the far end of the corridor we were in, which presumably pointed to a way outside. And though I still had a stumbling, draggy gait—Gillespie's drug had really zapped me—this first part of my mind also noted how my body *had* felt in my cell and now *did* feel, so I'd have strong references to jump back to either time, if it came to that.

That's why the second part of my mind was counting. *One, one thousand. Two, one thousand. Three, one thousand...* Talk to Kenny. Save Lena. Save myself. But Lena before me because she should never have been here. She'd done nothing wrong. Nothing.

At just under a minute, now in another long corridor that felt like we were backtracking, there was a buzzing sound from the Finn, in front of me, and he held up a hand for our little convoy to stop. Then that hand reached down into his right inside breast pocket to pull out a cell phone. He listened, then half turned to his right and swung the phone out almost like he was offering it to me.

But what *I* focused on, trying desperately not to look in that direction, was how his sports jacket bulged open to reveal the shoulder holster he wore that carried a large black pistol under his left arm. Muzzle tilted down. No security strap that would interfere with an easy draw. Almost grabbing distance if I jumped.

"It's bad reception here, but I think it's about your brother," the Finn said.

I blinked, then realized that was directed to Tweedle Darker behind me.

The squarely built thug stepped forward around my right side and grabbed the phone from the Finn. Stuck it against his ear.

As he listened, I realized all this intense focus and forced standing was making my knees wobble. I worried I might fall over. I almost wanted to. If I fell the right way, I could grab the

Finn's gun. And…and…what? If it had a safety or something, I'd be aiming and clicking the trigger uselessly and Tweedle Darker would finally have a good excuse to stab me. Then my body would either freak and jump backward in time or I'd just be dragged onward to wherever I was going anyway.

Where I *wanted* to go.

To talk to Kenny.

Even if it was to Cutter first, I was sure I'd end up talking to Kenny. Because that's what Gillespie had said Cutter wanted me for, right? To use against my brother? He'd have to at least show me to my brother.

It meant escaping now, before I had the chance to see Kenny, would have been pointless.

But I *could* have.

"Yeah," Tweedle Darker grunted into the phone, then stabbed the disconnect button and shoved the phone back into the Finn's hands. He turned and looked at me like I was a little puppy he wanted to beat, stab, and strangle.

But he just walked back behind me. His cloyingly sweet body smell now had an acrid undertone.

We resumed our walk.

A minute, forty-two…

We'd made two turns, a right and a left. Nearly identical hallways. Nearly. But there were little marks. I was feeling pretty clear now but feigned foggy exhaustion every now and then to make sure my brain picked out all the salient details. Though I'd seen no windows or stairs, I'd pretty much concluded we were underground. It was in the concrete flooring, the concrete walls we walked along on some stretches, the dank smell in the air, the chill, the oppressive *silence* that pressed in around us. Unless they'd taken me way out into the woods somewhere, there would otherwise be at least the rumble of traffic occasionally. There wasn't. Just the intermittent sputtering of a bad light ballast and the thrum of air circulating. I smelled gas and cooked food.

We were in a basement.

Probably under the closed-down seniors residence or health facility Gillespie had led me to before he'd gotten shot and made me jump back.

Two minutes, fifty-two. Two minutes, fifty-three...

Okay. I could picture my location. That helped. Whether it was true or not, I was going to cling to it.

Right about the time I'd reached that conclusion, I heard the buzz of people ahead and the Finn opened the door where our corridor dead-ended.

Three minutes. Three minutes, one...

It wasn't a big space the Finn led me into. Maybe thirty by thirty feet, and it felt smaller because the ceiling was no higher in here than the hallways had been, under eight feet. The walls were white and clean, though, with all kinds of fluorescent light banks strung along the ceiling and extra cables running beside them that must have been needed for the other lights and active computers that whirred and beeped around most of the room's perimeter. One stacked set of four monitors showed surveillance video on two that cycled through scenes of what I assumed was the above-ground building's exterior. On the other two monitors was cycling surveillance video of the basement hallways and various doors and rooms, one room being empty with what looked like vomit on the floor. Its door stood open.

They'd seen everything. Watched me wake up. Watched me stumble my way here.

I ran through my memory of our walk here and now picked out what those little knobs were above various doors. Did they cover every passage we'd walked through? No? I ran our walk in my mind again. Still no. When we'd turned and walked crossways to the passage that ended at this room, there were no cameras. At least not that I'd been able to see.

Noted.

Was Lena in here somewhere in a room like I'd been in? Was she in that surveillance cycle? Was she even still alive?

The scrape of a chair brought my attention back to the inventory of *this* room.

It looked like and had the low-volume buzz, clatter, and body-and-coffee smell of a scam call center. Three of the walls were lined with crowded computer cubbies—I quickly counted twenty-three—that each had operators, mostly pierced and tattooed, white, yellow, and brown, intense Gen Z kids too young to grow real beards. A few females mixed in. They wore headsets they were listening or talking into. Coffee cups, pens clicking and scribbling in notebooks, bound directories, and cell phones all crowded the monitors. Taped-together printouts hung on pins on some of the walls over the desks.

A galley kitchen took up one corner of the free wall, with a table and metal slat chairs near it. Also chairs, couches, stacks of brightly colored Nerf toys and magazines. And boxes with what looked like stolen wallets. Hooks and shelves holding almost as many pistols and rifles as the Gun Palace. *Place any weapons here before proceeding to your desk.*

Opposite the kitchen, taking up part of the wall to my right, was a big whiteboard with lists scrawled on it in different colors —money targets, stock ratios, buzz words that hinted at some kind of pump-and-dump scheme, and the names of banks for what I think was a totally different white-collar scheme going on.

Beside the whiteboard stood a huge thin-screen TV with a webcam on top that might have been the same one I'd seen in the aborted gang gathering at Ground Zero.

Three minutes, fourteen...

The gangsters on their feet supervising, talking with one another, were all millennials like me or older. Definitely tougher. Almost directly in front of the thin-screen TV were five guys that felt like the nexus of the space, even before the guy who'd been partly hidden from me when I entered now turned to look dead at me.

Cutter.

The counting and reasoning parts of my brain shut down, and my amygdala took over.

Danger.

He looked worse than he had at the now-never-happened gang summit. His hair was greasy and twisted, his eyes sunken and bloodshot, a shark among all the young minnows using technology to reach out and screw the world.

It didn't matter if he had the style of a stock trader himself or if he was so skinny you could see his ribs against the rayon of his button-down red shirt. He ate stock traders for breakfast. With steak sauce.

"It's the baby brother," he said now, with the hint of a smile, like it was supposed to be a joke. Except his voice was so flat that even though the whole room had obviously heard it and paused all their conversation and fingers tapping keys to stop, turn, and look, no one dared laugh.

I said nothing. I could hardly breathe. I knew it was PTSD flashbacks but couldn't stop it. *Cutting. Flesh. Slowly. Kenny screaming.*

Cutter looked around the room. "Get back to work."

When all his computer crew were back to listening and mumbling into their headsets, he ambled across the room to me, stopping close enough that he could probably smell the stink of my fear. He'd certainly be able to see my sweaty forehead and the way my whole body trembled.

Danger. Freeze. Hide. I wasn't sure I was going to be able to stay standing.

"I thought I told you way back when to never ever come looking for us," he said, and one corner of his thin lips curled up. "But I'm glad you did." He, thankfully, turned back toward the cluster of gangsters he'd been talking with when I came in. Gillespie wasn't one of them, I noted, breathing hard. I hadn't seen him anywhere in the room.

But Cutter wasn't talking to those guys. He was talking to the buzz-cut computer jockey beyond them, sitting at a terminal to the left of the big flat-screen. "Call him up," Cutter said. Then to the Finn, "Bring this pissant over by Gainesy, and make him face the screen."

The computer jockey by the flat-screen said, "Called him. He's not answering."

"He'll answer," Cutter said as the Finn grabbed me by my right arm and frog-marched me to my prime viewing position.

I didn't have to ask who Cutter wanted onscreen. I knew. I wanted him, too. *Breathe.*

Cutter stepped now between me and the screen. His presence, for being a short, scrawny man, was amazing. In a chilling, hope-destroying way. He gave me a big, feral smile now that showed me he'd had work done on his teeth, including a couple gold caps and sharpened incisors. With all the gum recession, it made his teeth look huge. Sharklike.

"What you're going to ask your big brother," he said, "is who he's working for and where they're based. Real simple."

I swallowed dryly. "Y-you don't know?"

His bony hand slapped my face so hard it made me spin sideways a little bit and stumble. Cutter spat at me. "I say you could talk to me, shitface?"

I got my balance back and stepped back to where I'd been, standing directly in front of him, looking down at him. And I managed a smile, despite my racing heart and fear adrenaline, because I'd seen something.

Another bony slap, but this time I let my head travel without my body following.

"What you find so funny, fuckhead?" Cutter said at me.

A clock, I thought back. On the right wall, just beside the door I'd entered through, there was a digital clock. I hadn't seen it coming in, but Cutter's slap had literally spun me straight toward it. It told me it was 6:06. Whether that was a.m. or p.m., I didn't know and didn't care. I had a countdown marker now. Whatever was coming, I knew how long I could let it go and still jump back to a place where maybe I could change things.

Yes, I was surrounded by sadistic goons and their lackeys in an underground maze with no way to make it like I'd never come here, but—I swallowed hard—at least if they tried to kill me now or cut off my fingers or brought out Lena and hurt her, there was *something* I could do. Get another chance. As long as I kept track of the time.

Cutter was about to slap me again, but the buzz-cut computer jockey shouted, "Got him! He's connecting! Starting a trace, but... you know."

I flashed to Kansas saying, *I went in through an Eastern European subnet...* Ways to hide.

Then, just like that, I was standing just four feet from Kenny's giant face with its horrible D scar on one cheek and M on the other.

He blinked back at me from the TV screen. "Jacky?"

Cutter nodded beside me. "That's right. Got your baby brother here. He has something to ask you, don't you, *Jacky?*"

"Um..." I said, honestly having trouble, for all my amazing Traine memory ability, to recall what I was supposed to ask. But of course it came back to me. "Who are you working for?"

There was a pause, then Kenny looked down and said, "I can't answer that."

I was actually shocked. Then wondered why I was. Gillespie had made it sound like this relationship between Kenny and Cutter had been going on for some time now. So if Cutter still didn't know who Kenny was working for, the game being played here was complicated. And all of a sudden, I wondered if risking so much to get in here just to talk to this enigma who could be anywhere in the world was...stupid?

And Lena? Gillespie had said he'd wanted her to use as leverage. Against me, presumably. But there was no guarantee that was Cutter's plan with her. She might not be in this building at all. She might be dead. I needed to know.

I opened my mouth to ask and Cutter slapped it.

"Okay," he said and made a hand motion. The man who stepped out from the wall and nodded was the young Asian guy with pockmarks who'd shown up at the end of my Ground Zero fiasco, challenging me to open the door, then pistol-whipping me when I couldn't. Cutter's kind of guy—not a computer nerd but smart and violent.

Pockmark slipped out the room's second door.

Cutter turned with deliberate casualness toward the TV screen and said, "Simpler question for you, Runner."

Runner? Kenny's gang name, obviously? Because what? He'd once run drugs for them? He'd run away from fights?

There was a clunking sound as the metal door Pockmark had vanished out of swung all the way open and hit the hinge-side wall. Pockmark came walking in backward, dragging what looked like a bloody corpse behind him. When he got close enough to drop the corpse beside Cutter, I saw who it was and my stomach turned over.

Detective James William Gillespie, a once hopeful and moral, but ultimately sad and addicted soul. He'd held up Kenny's throat to be cut, later gone to war and saved people, become a cop, tried to redeem himself, and gotten as trapped by narcotics as Kenny had been. As Kenny maybe still was.

It could almost be Kenny on the floor, his hairy throat cut and a bullet through his forehead. I wondered which had come first and felt tears welling in my eyes.

Cutter grabbed the head of Gillespie's corpse and raised it up to knee height. "This one of yours?" he asked Kenny.

"Why would he be one of mine?" Kenny said.

"He's a cop," Cutter spat and threw the head down.

"Ah. Interesting."

The expression and the dispassionate way he'd said it was so unlike everything about the Kenny I'd known that for just a moment I wondered if this was somehow a ringer, some special agent the CIA had made up to look like Kenny because the real Kenny was...what? Brain fried? Comatose?

It frankly looked like this simulacrum of Kenny was both of these things.

Except something in the way his eyes twitched at me, like he was trying to warn me of something, was so like the Kenny I remembered that I wanted to cry out to him.

And I knew what he was trying to tell me without having to read his mind. That I was leverage, like Gillespie had guessed earlier. Yeah. It meant that as long as Kenny was watching, this could get really bad. So why didn't he just cut the connection?

"Ching, take out this garbage," Cutter said, gesturing to Gillespie's corpse. "And someone bring me a chair."

Pockmark, aka Ching—his real name?—ducked in again, grabbed the body, and dragged it away while one of the thugs supervising the computer kids grabbed a metal-slat kitchen chair and ran to us with it. Clacked it down a hand's reach from me and Cutter.

Cutter turned to me. "Sit."

I looked around me at the staring faces. It felt like all my blood was rushing out of my body.

"This isn't wise, Cutter," said Kenny from the TV screen.

My knees felt like they were going to give out, so I sat in the chair. "Is Lena...?"

"Shh," Cutter said and slapped his bony hand over my mouth. "Cosmo," he said.

The cloyingly sweet smell of Tweedle Darker, Cosmo, whom I'd lost track of once Kenny had come onscreen, enveloped me from behind and one his rough, powerful hands suddenly grabbed my right wrist, yanking it back behind me and slapping something cold and hard around it that got tight with a ripping sound. At least Cutter's hand came away so I could gasp out my shock.

I started turning to see but Cosmo had already grabbed my left arm and yanked it back so hard my shoulder felt dislocated.

The cold clamp went around that wrist, too. Ratcheted tight.

Handcuffs.

Restraints.

Shit!

Like Dr. Irene Gopal all over again.

I tried moving my hands, but the cuffs' chain not only held my hands together, it was obviously wrapped around one of the back chair slats between my hands as well. Short of breaking the slat, breaking the chain, or breaking all the bones in my hand like I'd seen someone do in a movie, I wasn't getting free of this chair.

"Now, I don't know," Cutter said to Kenny's face, "whether you really care for your brother. I guess we'll find that out."

Then Cutter spun on his left foot and drove one bony fist hard into my gut, throwing his whole body behind it so much I could have kissed the top of his head as he drove it in. And even though he weighed probably less than one forty, it felt like my stomach got shoved up to my throat as my center exploded in pain.

I spewed a bit of sour liquid, coughed, sniffed, and took deep breaths to hide my overwhelming desire to cry. How did heroes do this? How did they take horrible abuse and just suck it up with nothing but a staunch grunt?

I did hold onto enough of myself to turn my head and note the time. 6:12. So 6:21 was the magic number. No, better 6:17. If I jumped by then, I'd go back to before the cuffs were on, and I could maybe talk my way out of—

The thought was literally knocked out of my head as a blast of pain exploded my right temple, throwing my head sideways.

Gunshot? No. I'd be dead. Not the crack of a gun butt either. I remembered that.

I raised my head to see he-I-now-knew-as-Cosmo flexing his right hand. Red knuckles. That had been a *punch?*

"What about it, Runner?" Cutter was saying. "You know it's only going to get worse from here."

I looked at Kenny and mouthed, *Save me.* He stared back with a sad look in his eyes, but that was all.

Cutter called out, "K-bite! You got anything yet?"

The buzz-cut computer jockey shook his head, focused on his computer screen, fingers flying over his keyboard.

"Keep on it!" Cutter said, then nodded at Cosmo, who dove his dark, blunt hand down to my scrotum, trying to get good grip through my jeans. I was fighting him, though, so he finally just spread my legs apart and gave me a pile driver punch to the area.

I yelled in pain, curling down, only to have another Cosmo uppercut slam into my nose with a grinding pop as my nose broke and blood exploded down over my lips.

Then the temple again.

The left cheek.

The right.

"Any feeling in there yet, Runner?"

"I've told you I can't. But there will be consequences for this."

"Consequences?" Cutter said. "Fucking consequences? I want to see you try. We got twice the firepower we had when you pulled that shit last fall. Five times the men. And it'll be public this time. Every channel. The entire fucking internet. You be the fucking CIA, the Cosa Nostra, yakuza, or the Russians—unless you nuke the whole fucking city, we gonna take you down! Feel me?"

"Are you officially declaring war on someone you don't even know?"

"I'm saying tell us the fuck who you are!"

"Maybe I should sign out now and—"

"Sign out and I kill him!"

There was a long pause while the two men stared at each other. Cutter was older. He'd been at least twenty-five when he'd carved up Kenny's face, which would make him early forties now. But Kenny's eyes looked so much older. Sadder.

Kenny did not sign out. Or look at me.

Cutter waved another hand at Tweedle Darker, and the beating continued.

Groin strike.

Knee strike.

Neck.

Kidney.

Left cheek.

Right orbital socket.

There was more, but I almost couldn't feel them. The pain was running together like my moans. And I couldn't see anymore. Everything was red. I was going to pass out. And if I passed out long enough, if I couldn't jump to before it, when I woke up, all of this mess would be permanent. *Oh God, dissociate. Let this go.* But I was too unfocused. I needed something clear and terrifying. So, like I'd done with the cops back at the East Precinct, I made myself raise my bloody face. I found the vague outline of Cutter's skinny form and said, "S-skinny little cockroach fuckhead."

I saw the glint of Cutter's knife stab at my—

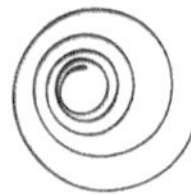

I swayed a bit as I stared down at Gillespie's face, drained and white, a scorched black-and-red hole in the middle of his forehead just big enough to stick a finger into.

"He's a cop," said Cutter, who was holding Gillespie's head up by its hair. He threw it down.

"Ah. Interesting," said Kenny's big head on the screen.

On the TV screen. Oh, right. This room was in the basement of the Demon Monks' headquarters. Probably. Gillespie was dead. Cutter was about to say...

"Ching, take out this garbage. And someone bring—"

"He's going to torture me now," I interrupted, speaking directly to Kenny. Out of the corner of my eye, I saw Ching startle. Interrupting his boss? How dare I? "He'll have Cosmo here handcuff me to a chair so the two of them can punch me in the stomach, groin, head, face. To make you talk. But you won't talk, will you?"

"No," Kenny said.

"Fuck you," Cutter said. "We'll see about that. Bring me a fucking chair! Now!"

And away we went.

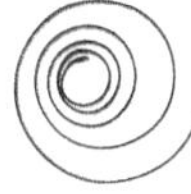

The timing of the second beating was so freakishly similar that I ended up jumping back to within ten seconds of my first jump back in this room. Pockmark/Ching was just dragging Gillespie out of the room, looking at me oddly, and the chair was coming over. I stayed muzzy-headed long enough that they had me seated with Cosmo handcuffing my hands behind my back by the time I was fully in my body. In this time stream.

Knowing what was coming, I asked myself why I'd waited so long the second time before jumping back.

And remembered.

It was that the more Kenny had just sat there and watched me get beaten, the more frustrated I'd become. I'd just about died for him once, and now he wouldn't even reveal who he was working for when my life and probably Lena's were on the line? Like it was going to make a difference if he said, "CIA," even if it was a lie?

"Just tell them, Kenny," I snapped at him now. "What have you got to lose? Seriously."

"I can't."

"You mean you won't!"

He just stared at me, seemingly unruffled but his tension coming out in his fingers, steepled up under his chin almost like a prayer, trembling. Tapping together.

Cutter went for the gut punch, but this time, as he drove his body in with it, I whipped my head down and cracked my skull into his as he connected.

Explosion of pain in my gut.

Explosion of pain in my forehead.

Felt like my skull had cracked open. *Ba-doom! Ba-doom!* And Cutter was screaming at the top of his lungs. Through my blinking, bloody vision, I could see him staggering around, clutching his head.

Then Cosmo connected with my temple, and I lost consciousness for a few moments.

When I came to, I startled and then startled again in terror as I feared I'd missed my ten-minute window. Except that Cutter was still staggering around, clutching his head, so it couldn't have been too long. I blinked and saw the time. 6:13. I'd been out less than a minute.

"He's awake," Cosmo said to Cutter.

Cutter turned and spat out blood. "Beat him *down*."

So Cosmo did. Worse than the first two times, though not life-threatening, just distracting enough that it took me a while to get terrified I'd miss my time. And the terror made me—

Handcuffs being slapped on my yanked-back wrists.

"Kenny," I said dizzily at the screen. "This is gonna hurt a lot."

"I can't tell them," he said quietly, but something in the way he said it, the emphasis on *them*, made me jerk my head up and stare into his eyes. There was something there. And in his fingers, steepled and tapping together under his chin. What? *What did—*

Cutter drove his fist deep into my gut, and we were off....

My next jump back, they were bringing over the kitchen chair. Clattered it down a hand's reach from me and Cutter.

"Sit," Cutter said.

And then Kenny says...

But he didn't speak. His hands were already steepled under his chin this time. Tapping together. Waiting.

Cutter jabbed his thumb into my side. "I said sit, dipshit."

I sat.

I looked more closely at Kenny, into his eyes, and could have sworn he looked older and more tortured than he had in previous versions of this.

"Cosmo," Cutter ordered, and Cosmo's sickening sweet smell surrounded me as the Italian thug dragged back my wrists, handcuffed me, stepped back.

Cutter went straight for the gut punch.

I bent in two, grunting, "Asshole."

Kenny had changed. Cutter's words and timing had changed. I had changed.

And then, shit, the beating changed as Cosmo seemed determined to tear me apart.

It went on and on and on until I was crying and yelling and *had* to jump but couldn't. Maybe distracted by the buzz-cut computer jockey, K-bite, calling out he almost had a trace! To *what?* Agh! My power wasn't *working!* I was stuck!

Then...

I was on my feet as Ching dragged Gillespie's body in, but for a second my mind simultaneously held onto being in the chair eight minutes later, racked with pain. I let out a crazy yell and dropped to the floor.

"Fuck, Runner," said Cutter above me. "Got a pussy for a brother."

Gillespie's corpse was dropped down beside me on the floor with its face directly in front of mine. I startled, fully back in my earlier, unhurt body now, and jumped to my feet, looking around to see if I could run. Ching was staring at me with a look of outright fear on his face, like he remembered me from Ground Zero? Except no, because I'd jumped back to a timeline where meeting him never happened. So was it just from seeing my photo? But why the fear?

Then Cosmo was beside me. He grabbed me by my right wrist and twisted it, dragging it behind my body, slammed on one of the handcuffs. Before I truly registered this radical change in the program, he grabbed my left wrist and dragged it back, slammed on the other cuff. Then he kicked me in the back of my knees so I crumpled down to the ground.

Cutter was holding up Gillespie's head by its hair and shaking the throat-slit, bullet-shot thing back and forth as he shouted at Kenny's face on the TV screen. "You see this cop, Runner? Your baby bro's gonna look twice as bad when we're done with him." Cutter threw Gillespie's head down. "Get this thing out of here. And where's my fucking chair!"

Then the chair appeared, and I was dragged onto it, breathing hard. Kenny hadn't said a thing. Just sat with his damn fingers tapping together, watching me with haunted eyes.

Probably because I was *not* holding it together anymore. I'd only been kicked in the back of my knees, but I could hardly see because my tear ducts were pumping out rivers. My nose was running snot. I was a pathetic, mewling mess. And I didn't care. I was already into the reality of what was going to happen to me *again*, but probably worse, given the way Cosmo grunted as he refastened my cuff chain so it wrapped around the slats and held me to the chair, and the way Cutter was spinning his knife in front of my face, saying, "All ready to go?"

My world was falling in around me. Kenny wasn't talking. I had no way to get out of here. No way to save Lena. My "power," such as it was, felt like it was sputtering out of my control.

God, I was going to die. Which meant Lena was going to die. I was never going to even find out what had *happened* to Kenny. How could I go through this again?

"I can't," I said.

"What was that, dipshit?" said Cutter, spinning his knife to a halt so he held it right in front of my neck.

But I wasn't looking at him. My gaze was locked with Kenny's.

"I can't," I sobbed.

"No, you can, buddy," he said quietly. "I know you can."

And suddenly the lights in the room flickered, and every computer screen seemed to let out a whine. They popped. Died.

Except the TV screen holding Kenny's face. Kenny, still holding my gaze, his fingers still now but the corner of his right eye crinkling in that half wink he had. Just for me. Letting me know. What?

That he had some power here to help me? Power over the electric grid of this place maybe. But he'd said, *I know you can.* Which meant I had to do something, too. Something Kenny knew I could do.

You're not the only one.

I'd thought Kansas meant Kenny could jump in time like me. Maybe she had. Or maybe she just meant that he had a *similar* power. Like maybe his trap of a mind saw when little details changed each time I jumped, and he *knew* somehow what was happening. Maybe he'd known what I could do through this whole sordid torture sequence and couldn't understand why I hadn't used it to its full potential.

Which was what?

Jump far enough back that I could escape?

But I couldn't. Not without Lena.

Still...

"I know how he does it!" I shouted out, just in time to stop Cutter from pile driving my face in frustration and fear over Kenny's stunt.

Cutter stopped his punch and hopped backward like a startled bunny. He stared at me. Glared at Kenny, whose face now looked off into space. Cutter glared back at me. Pulled out his knife.

I knew this one was going to be bad because I had nothing. Not one creative idea in my head beyond the usual—provoke the monster, accept the pain and terror, and...

Wait.

As Cutter was swishing his knife around in front of him like it was his penis, Kenny had slowly and deliberately steepled his fingers underneath his chin and begun tapping.

Tap tap tap. Pause with fingers apart. *Tap tap-hold.* Pause. *Tap tap tap tap-hold.* Pause. Tap. Pause...

Oh God, how had I missed it?

Cutter stepped back to me and hovered his knife blade in front of my right eye.

Kenny tapped faster now. The sight of his fingers was half hidden by Cutter and his knife, but Kenny's fingers hit harder. I could *hear* them. All the dots and dashes. Our secret language, learned in the Boy Scouts but just used to be badasses at school.

"Well?" Cutter said and pressed the knife tip under my right eyeball. "Talk."

I knew what the last two letters of Kenny's command were before he finished them, and I knew all the way down in my nuts that he was right. That when you looked at the whole picture here, the possible and the not, this ordeal, this time could only end one way.

Okay, then.

19

Failing backward

... S

  .- A

  ...- V

  . E

  .-.. L

  . E

  -. N

  .- A

"I talk when you let Lena go," I said.

With a flick of his fingers, Cutter spun the knife in his hand so it was pointing down, and he plunged it into my right thigh.

I screamed out in pain.

Cutter yanked the knife up and held the dripping tip to my right eye again. "Any more fucking demands?"

"I g-guess you don't want to know shit," I said.

He spun the knife and drove it into my left thigh. Ground it around there until my scream satisfied him, then pulled it up and back to my eye.

My breath was high and gasping. My head was spinning. I was going to pass out. I needed to jump back. Now. Save my legs. I had to dissociate. Had to focus. Couldn't. Apparently my fear of dying wasn't real enough yet. Or maybe now that I'd given up on finding Kenny *today*, I was finally ready to "go all the way" for Lena. Sounded funny in my head, just not enough to laugh.

I was suffocating on Cosmo's sickly sweet cologne from behind me and Cutter's stink and my own fear and blood from in front. I think I bit my tongue. My mouth was full of blood.

"Now what are you gonna tell us?" Cutter purred.

"Just…show me she's…alive," I said, aware I was dribbling blood as I spoke. I tried to swallow it.

Fingers grabbed my hair. Cosmo's? But Cutter started laughing. "Shit, and here I was calling you a pussy a few minutes back. You got balls, little bro." He lifted his head and yelled. "Someone got her on camera?"

"Could be a recording," I burbled. "I need to *see* her."

Cutter looked at me for a long beat, then he said, "Okay, Cosmo, you walk him, or carry him if he can't walk, to take a little peek in at the brown bitch. Then straight back here, and you're gonna tell us everything, right, little bro? Or else maybe we cut her up in front of you."

"Yes," I said.

Seconds later, my hands were free of their cuffs and Cosmo was jerking me to my feet. I yelled in pain again as the weight made blood pump from my thigh wounds.

Jump back! Now! Heal your legs!

But I couldn't. Not only because I wasn't dying but because I couldn't risk it now. There was no guarantee, if I did, I'd ever get Cutter's agreement again that I could see Lena. And I didn't know if I had the courage to go through the torture it would take to try. Next time, Cutter might go for something worse.

As I stood, my wounded legs screaming they wanted to collapse under me, one of the kids who'd been on a computer, a runty Hispanic kid, ran up and wrapped both my wounds with some kind of tape.

I started to fall as he did it, but Cosmo caught and held me upright. When the kid finished, I could almost stand on my own, but I was scared to move. Cosmo finally wrapped one of my arms around his shorter, burlier shoulders and held it there so I could half stumble where he wanted me to go.

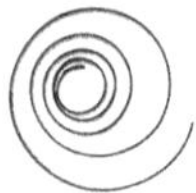

My mind was in three parts now, which was probably my limit, given the pain I was in.

One part was counting as we went out the same door they'd dragged Gillespie out of. *One, one thousand...two, one thousand... three, one thousand...*

One part, that I hardly had to pay attention to, was looking at everything I passed—*an open door there, a connecting hall, another emergency exit sign, a sign on the walls with arrows indicating north with numbers, no guards in the hallways themselves*—as I half stumbled, half just held onto the moving, sickly sweet smelling brick of a man holding me up. Down another hallway, turning left, west, heading for another corner room but almost the furthest corner from where they'd held me.

The last part of my mind, a critical part, was figuring my plan, what I was going to do. I couldn't fight or run with my legs barely functional, so once I knew where Lena was, I'd have to jump back at least to before Cutter stabbed me. As long as I made it back that far, a second jump would take me to my cell before the Finn and Cosmo came to get me. I'd be woozy from the double jump, but I could manage it. Bear down. Bring more awareness than I'd had back then. They wouldn't be expecting that. And then I could try some of the crazy escape ideas I'd had on my first (and so far only) trip out of that room.

But even if I escaped, I still had to get to Lena.

And if I made it to her, what then?

"Stop," Cosmo said.

"What?"

Given how rarely Cosmo talked, this was like the cement floor we walked on had spoken.

I turned my head to look at him as he propped me up against the corridor wall. It wasn't like I had healthy enough legs to resist. "What's the matter?"

"You. And your mouth."

"I didn't..."

"You told Chuba to look out for us, for me and my brother and the Finn."

I blinked. "Who?"

"The cop! The fucking undercover cop! *Brutto figlio di puttana bastardo!*"

Gillespie. Okay. But it still made no sense. How did Cosmo know that? He and his brother and the Finn hadn't gone after him in this timeline, had they?

"Don't look stupid. When he turned you over, he joked you'd warned him about us. And when we went to kill him like we fucking hadda, he was ready for it. *Cazzo di merda.* He shot Antony. Tried to shoot me before I took his gun and shot him in the head, then cut his throat."

I blinked at him, slowly putting it together, but the pain in my legs wasn't helping. "I need to sit down," I said and started sliding to the floor.

"*Cazzo.*" Cosmo scooped his hands under my armpits and lifted me back up, pinning me against the wall like a caught insect specimen. In that second, I remembered why Cosmo and his brother had always seemed uncomfortably familiar to me. I'd thought it was from watching mafia movies, but it wasn't. It was because as a child, I'd met a good childhood friend of my father's who'd scooped his hands under my armpits and lifted me to his dark face, sweet cologne, grizzled chin, and used that word on me. All the time.

"*Cazzo* means fuck," I murmured.

"You know what I want from you?"

"To tell you why the cop lied to you?"

"Antony died!" Cosmo roared, his spittle hitting my face. "That phone call in the tunnel when I was taking you out with the Finn. That was the hospital! He's fucking dead! *Che ti morisse la madre.*"

Then the squat man turned his face down to the side and wailed like a stuck pig, his face going red, his squeezed-closed eyes pumping out tears as he babbled some more in Italian. It made me wish I'd wanted to learn more languages as a child.

I waited for him to work through a grief I certainly understood, hoping it didn't lead to him shooting me. But then I felt a warmth spreading down my right leg. Whatever bandage the kid in the control room had wrapped around that leg, it was failing. I was losing a lot of blood. My head was already getting lighter. I was going to bleed out here in this nondescript basement hallway where Cosmo had decided it was far enough from everyone else that he could wail out his pain here, all alone. And I still didn't know where they were holding Lena.

At the risk of getting shot, I said, "What do you want from me, Cosmo?"

He opened his eyes, all bloodshot and teary, and his face was so contorted I wasn't sure if he was crying or preparing to rip my neck out with his teeth. "I want to kill you!"

"You think that will help?"

He worked his jaw around and shook me where he'd pinned me. "You didn't tell him?"

I shook my head.

"Then I want you to make it stop!"

"What, Cosmo? The pain?"

"Me seeing it in my head. The *mafankulo* shooting my brother! Over and over and over... You're a head doc, right? *Saputo.* Make it stop!"

Oh. If I hadn't been on the edge of passing out, I might have at least grimaced. This had to be the weirdest therapy setting I'd ever found myself in. But the pain, the ask, was a familiar kind.

Normally there'd be a whole history and we'd discuss a treatment plan, decide the best way forward. But for this, with me nearly ready to pass out, my options were limited. "Okay," I said. "Pay attention. When you see it in your head, what do you see? Exactly?"

"We tell him we know." Cosmo snuffles, unable to meet my eyes. "Suddenly he's got a gun in his hand. He fires point-blank into Antony's chest. Boom!"

"What does it smell like? What did you feel?"

"A burnt smell. Antony's bad breath blowing in my face. He stumbles into me and grabs my arm. But I hadda spin him around and shove him into Chuba. Who shot him *again!*"

"Before you grabbed his gun?"

"I hadda!"

"Cosmo, hold the worst part of that memory. Got it?"

"*Ai-eee!*"

"Where do you feel it in your body?"

"My fucking throat. I can't breathe!"

"Okay, look at my hand." I lifted my right hand up to his eye level, which was hard to maintain because of the pressure of his meaty hands as they held me against the wall.

But he looked at my raised hand, bewildered. "Wha—?"

"Just follow it with your eyes." I started moving it back and forth in a smooth plane before his eyes. "Keep your head still. Just your eyes."

I made the hand moves jerkier. Faster. Inducing the eye movements in Cosmo that I'd found most helped some of my PTSD clients reprocess their memories. It never worked on me, unfortunately, but I'd long ago come to accept that the relationship I, Kenny, and Kansas had with our memories was pretty unique.

And it *was* working with Cosmo. His breath had slowed. The tension in his face had eased. His dark, grizzled jaw had loosened and dropped.

I kept the movement going a full minute, then slowed it and finally lowered my hand. "How do you feel in your neck?"

"Good. I can fucking breathe."

"Okay. And the memory—still intense?"

"It's... *Dio cane!* It's, like, I almost don't see it. Like...there, but not biting, you know?" He looked into my eyes in awe. "What the fuck was that?"

"EMDR. It's a kind of baby hypnosis. It helps a lot of people with PTSD."

"No shit."

"You should really see someone for follow-up, though."

He snorted and pulled back a bit.

I slid in a heap to the floor, my thighs exploding in pain. At least it woke me up. "I need to see Lena, Dr. Cortland. I need to see her alive."

"Sure, Doc," said Cosmo, lifting me up and wrapping my left arm around his shoulder and his own right arm around my body under my arms so he could hold me like I was a weightless rag doll, even though I had a good foot in height on him. My feet dragged on the ground as he set off walking again.

And automatically, that part of my brain I'd told to pay special attention to directions continued to map the route, noticing markings on the wall, doors, the length of hallways, places where the lights were out or sputtering overhead...

But the other parts of my brain had completely shut down.

I'd lost all track of time.

I'd lost all sense of how I was going to rescue Lena and get out of here.

Maybe they'd come back to me, but right now the pain and lightheadedness were making it hard to even keep my eyes open. I wondered if my jump back sense was finely tuned enough to recognize that if I passed out from loss of blood, I might die here. I had trouble believing that. It felt too much like wanting to sleep...

Cosmo jerked me awake, and I raised my head just enough to see we were at the dead-end joining of two hallways. An outside corner then? No emergency exit signs nearby. And this door was very much like every other door we'd passed. Or maybe not. It looked like painted metal. Not all the other doors were metal.

And when my head fell back down again, I saw blood on the bottom of the door. Fresh? My stomach roiled. If that was Lena's blood... if she was inside, dying...

Why had I spent so much time dicking around trying to rescue a brother who wouldn't let me? Why hadn't I tried straightaway to escape the second I'd established Kenny wasn't going to tell me shit? I could have tried, jumped back, tried again, and again, and run and searched, over and over and over and...I would have been here *sooner*.

Holding my body tighter with his right arm, Cosmo let go of my hand around his shoulder and fished a key out of his left pocket which he stuck into the lock. From a really sparse key chain. Which meant, maybe, most of these doors shared the same key. Maybe all of them. Good to know.

Both my arms were dangling now, useless. As were my head, legs, and body. I was basically a barely conscious lump of meat.

But that bare consciousness paid close attention as the door Cosmo had unlocked swung open with a swish, rather than the floor-scraping my own cell door had done. And the sight of Lena lying on the mattress on the floor inside actually hit me like plunge into an icy lake, *demanding* I come back to alertness to feel *relief* that she was breathing, *fear* because she wasn't stirring in response to the door opening, and *rage* because blood stained her sky blue cotton blouse and cheeks. The band was gone from her hair, her navy slacks were torn at both knees, and she looked like a beaten wild thing. On top of all that, they'd left the overhead light on like they had in my cell, bright, harsh, and pitiless.

"Lena!" I said. "Wake up!"

She gave a groan and opened her eyes, squinting against the light. Then she saw me and tried to get up. Fell back down with a grunt of pain. "Jackson," she managed. "I just..."

"You ain't going anywhere, *zuia*," Cosmo said. "The doc here has seen you. Now he's got some talking to do."

And before Lena could get fully upright, Cosmo had pulled me out the door and kicked it closed behind us.

"I'll be back for you!" I called out.

Cosmo looked down at me, useless lump of pain that I was. "Yeah? How do you figure that, doc?"

Certainly not with my legs like this, bastardo, I swore silently. I closed my eyes. *Dissociate!*

Nothing happened.

Of course nothing happened. I wasn't dying. I was just going to pass out from blood loss. But Cosmo would then just drag me back to Cutter, who'd administer smelling salts or adrenaline or something, just enough to bring me back to consciousness so he could threaten to maim or kill me. And I'd give in or wouldn't. And then maybe I'd jump back to somewhere in this hallway. Maybe. Or I'd just die.

But I knew how to force a jump, didn't I? I'd learned it in Lena's lab. I was just too stupidly scared to *use* what I'd learned —the root emotional essence, the underlying trigger. Not fear of pain. Not fear of death. Not even fear of Lena's pain or death.

No, it was the overwhelming, soul-shattering sense of failure that underpinned every anxious, PTSD-ridden moment of my life. I'd used it so blithely in that jumping session with Lena because she'd been there with me, supporting me, somehow making it okay to be the utter wreck I knew I was.

But by myself? Acknowledging the horrible black hole of worthless, loathsome failure that was at the core of my being? That failed Kenny. That failed Kansas. That failed me, my parents, everyone...

To really go there, for even a second, made my heart squeeze into a twisted, thudding, hard lump. My breath caught in my throat. My blood rushed out of my extremities. And a great, dark shroud descended on me with the weight of a building, crushing me. Crush-ing-me.

Cosmo's voice: "Doc, you okay?"

Then...

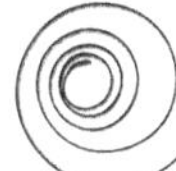

Where...?

Cosmo slammed me up against a wall. Right. I remembered this wall. I remembered what he was about to say. And if I was only back this far, I was even more of a fuckup than I thought.

Fail. Failure. Useless. Give up. And...

"Aaaahh!" *My right thigh! Pain! What the hell? Where the—?*

Cutter's bloody knife waved up in front of my eyes, but I could hardly see it. The double jump, the explosion of pain in my right thigh, had me so messed up that I didn't even know where I was or when or what was happening that—

Oh shit. Yes. I think I knew where...

"Any more fucking demands?" Cutter asked.

My mind raced and my head turned. The clock by the door said 6:12. *Shit!* If I—

Cutter grinned his ugly recessed gums at me, then plunged his knife down into my left thigh, and I screamed like a two-year-old, at the top of my lungs.

Shit. Shit. Shit. I'd just jumped back twice, and my stomach was roiling, my brain still fuzzy. If I managed a jump right now, I *might* be all the way back in my cell before the Finn and Cosmo walked in. But I'd collapse like I was having a heart attack or stroke—maybe it *would* be a heart attack or stroke—and they'd drag me to this room, and maybe I'd get resuscitated or maybe I'd die.

And this nightmare of torture would just start over.

But worse. Because I could only handle so much. The breakdown I'd had in front of Kenny the last time hadn't been fake. My mental purpose and clarity were nearly shot. It wouldn't be long before I started babbling about everything— Kenny, me, Kansas. Babbling and unable to jump.

I had to hang on. Thoroughly integrate into this body. Every minute I could think here, every muscle I could tense or flex...

"Now you got something to tell us?" Cutter said, holding his bloody knife in front of my face again.

I swallowed. Squeezed my eyes closed to fight the clamoring panic of the pain signals from my thighs. No! Screw the minutes. Focus on the seconds. Every extra second I hung on let my brain fully integrate, despite the screaming pain in my thighs! *Shit!*

My eyes sprung open. They'd be wet and bloodshot, but screw it.

"I need to at least see that she's alive," I said.

"Ha. You got balls after all, you little fucker. But the answer is no. Instead, though, I'm going to make you an honorary Demon Monk. Whadya say? Give you a second chance to do what you crapped out on the first time I met you. Take the place of your big bro."

Behind him on the TV screen, I heard Kenny—I'd almost forgotten he was there—say, "Don't do it, Cutter."

I almost laughed. I certainly knew now, intellectually at least, that Cutter's choice was fake and had been fake the first time, too. He'd never have given Kenny up back then. He wasn't even bothering to offer me anything for my choice now.

"Fuck you," I said.

Cutter ignored me and waved his knife at Cosmo, who appeared at my left shoulder. "Hold his head nice and still so I get the letters right."

Oh no.

Can't even get this simple delay tactic right.

What's that, loser? Louder!

CAN'T GET THIS RIGHT. CAN'T GET ANYTHING RIGHT. I'M GOING TO FAIL AGAIN. PASS OUT. LOSE LENA. BETRAY KENNY AND KANSAS.

LOSER! DEATH! FUCKUP! FAILU—

20

People die

I STUMBLED AND FELL to my hands and knees.

Cold, gritty floor. Where?

My heart squeezed hard in my chest. My head felt like my brain was swelling, about to explode. And I couldn't breathe. Couldn't see now. Couldn't...breathe.

Then my lungs opened and I sucked in air with a great, "Shuhhhh!"

I could see again.

The floor. A concrete floor. Wall close to my right side. Wall close to my left.

Something poked me from behind, rocking me forward so I almost collapsed completely. Instead, my stomach heaved and I vomited. But I couldn't crawl back from it, and the sour smell just blended into the awfulness that shot around my insides.

"Hey," said a rough voice behind me.

Ahead of me, a smoother, strangely accented voice: "What happened?"

"He fell."

"Yes. Get him up."

"He stinks."

"So do you. But if Cutter wanted to see you and you fell down, I would pick you up or drag you."

Cutter? Right. Even through the pounding in my skull and pain in my chest, a hundred tiny details told me exactly where we were in the hall. The door to the control room where everything went bad was literally steps away. So there would be almost no *time*, once again, to fully integrate myself into this time stream's body before everything started up again.

A cloud of sickly sweet, pungent air washed into the vomit smell as hands reached around my chest and lifted me...like a rag doll. Cosmo.

And of course the accented voice would be the Finn.

I looked up, squinting, and confirmed both conclusions. And my location.

Also, the fact that the pressure in my chest was easing, even with Cosmo holding me there while apparently trying to figure out whether he was supposed to let me find my feet or just carry me. And I was breathing.

I struggled weakly to bring my feet under me. I had to buy some time. Go for Cosmo's knife or the Finn's gun? Start stumbling away? Sing a song? Say something crazy? That minute I'd hung on between jumps two and three might be the only reason I was not dying right now. Or, like Lena had said, my various brains and bodies were learning to integrate more future histories faster without freaking out. Or it was both.

Whatever, there was no guarantee I could throw in a fourth jump without just dying. So I had to hold on a bit longer, damn it. Persuade this body that I *belonged* here with all that extra stuff in my trunk, then I could jump back one more—

The door that led into the control room yanked open, and Cutter stepped out. "What the fuck is taking so long? What did you do to him?"

"He fell down," Cosmo said.

"Fucker's faking it," Cutter said and marched right to me. He looked up into my blinking eyes, grinning that gum-receded smile, and *zwing!* His knife was in his hand again, right up in front of my eyes. "Are you faking it, little bro professor? You a pussy? You a little no-nuts who needs some educating?"

And suddenly my brain was jumping to all the punches and leers and grunts and knife stabs he'd given me, would give me, did give me in the future, that was now, that was jumbling together and screaming at me to jump away now.

I tried to swallow it back, tell myself I could live through this, *had* to for just a little bit longer. But my amygdala was screaming even louder now that it was too late. I'd failed. Like I always failed. That my whole life was a plunge into a black hole of—

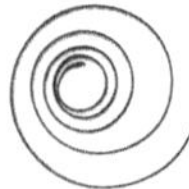

My eyes were blinking so fast that the small, bare room I was in—my initial holding cell!—was just a strobe effect around me.

I couldn't stop it.

Nor the seizing of my body. My knees jerked to my chest, then shot away so hard into an extreme back arch that my bones clicked and cracked.

No breath.

Arms jerked and whipped together, flew apart, and whacked the concrete floor under me.

Bum slammed down out of its arch. *Crack!*

No breath.

Body in a V, twisting. Knees hit the wall.

No breath.

Juttering now. Full body seizure trying to spit me out. This me.

No!

Breathe!

Mine!

Me!

Now!

Here!

BREATHE!!!

"SHUHHHHHH!" Air.

I gasped again and knew I was finally fully in my body. My heart was hammering so hard it felt like it wanted to leave this body I was fighting so hard to cling to. My head felt on fire, burning up. My body felt bruised and beaten all over, still jerking about, hitting the floor, but with smaller movements now.

Settling...

Come on...

Settling. Stopping.

Amazing.

Necessity, maybe the sheer will to survive, the extra seconds of pain I'd endured, my adapting abilities, a new clarity of purpose—they'd all given me the impossible and brought me through a fourth jump. Alive.

I was on my side on the concrete floor, drenched in a cold sweat and feeling like I'd seriously damaged my tailbone from when I'd slammed it into the floor. It throbbed in pain, something I read once would be called coccydynia, because the bone at the base of the spine was called the coccyx. Hopefully it was just a bruise, because my stomach was also rolling over and over, too.

That was serious. It was what I remembered was my body's state for just the first few minutes after I'd fully woken up from the drug Gillespie had given me. It meant there was no time before this that I could jump back to, only dreamless unconscious.

Shit.

It meant if I was going to pull off a risky escape, I only got a safety-net jump back if it took place at least ten minutes after my waking, which took me right to the door of the control room with Cutter stepping out.

Unacceptable.

Oh, listen to you.

Which meant ten minutes from now, I had to be somewhere other than there.

Action hero after all, are we?

Shut up.

I cautiously brought my knees up to my chest one at a time to see if I was ready for it. The moves hurt like hell at the base of my spine, but I didn't feel any shifting or grinding. Which I was going to take meant a bruise, not a fracture, so—

I heard the sound of footsteps pounding down the hall outside. Hopefully still just the Finn and Cosmo. But running now? Why? Alerted by my seizure?

I looked around the spare, square room for a camera, and my eyes finally slid over what looked like a little glass bubble sticking out from an upper corner to the left of the door.

I wanted to flip a finger at it but couldn't afford to change yet another element of this timeline, like having Cutter send extra people to help the Finn and Cosmo collect me. So I pretended to have seen nothing and acted dazedly surprised when the door of the room was thrown open and Cosmo came racing in with his too-sweet cologne, bristly chin, and short, heaving barrel chest. The Finn stood in the door, watching.

"You're awake," said the Finn. "Get up."

"For what?"

Cosmo lunged at me with a clear intent to hurt, but the Finn snapped, "Stop!" Then to me: "There is someone who wants to see you."

Kenny! The thought jumped into my mind unbidden. But this time, it wasn't followed by thoughts of rescuing him. It was to thank him for letting me go. For telling me in our secret language that this day, this time, right now, my focus could not be on our brotherhood. Right now, my focus had to be on how to save Lena and myself, and that started with my actions in the next three to five minutes.

Fighting to keep all of that off my face, I struggled up to my feet. Wobbly. "Just a sec."

"Do you need help?"

"A second!" I snapped, falling automatically into the rhythm I remembered from the last time I went through this time sequence. Cosmo wasn't placed exactly the same, but the Finn stepped back into the hallway ahead of me like he had the last time. And there was the same acrid tang of hate in Cosmo's sickly sweet scent. I knew where it came from now. I was counting on it.

And also counting the seconds again as I left the room. *One, one thousand. Two, one thousand. Three, one thousand...*

Again I was following the Finn, with Cosmo following me. And as I counted, I'm sure my brain registered many of the same details I'd noticed the first time, but none of them took any of my conscious attention this time except for the movement of Finn's sports jacket, specifically on the left side, where I could see in my memory exactly where the shoulder holster held his gun. I watched the way the swing of his left arm was ever so slightly different than the swing of his right, accommodating the bulk of his weapon. For all my playacting the wooziness I'd had the first time I'd walked this time sequence, my accelerated heart and sweat and seizures had completely cleared the effects of the drug Gillespie had given me, and my body was as taut as a pulled bow string.

"You're gonna die," Cosmo growled from behind me.

I almost stumbled, it was so unexpected, this breaking of what had happened before. Unnerving. It both showed how closely he was watching me and how things this time were not repeating the way I'd counted on.

Which is when I heard my mental count hit one minute and felt a cold sweat break out on my forehead. The phone call! The one telling Cosmo his shot brother had just died. It had come the first time at just under a minute! In the backtracking corridor we were in now! Maybe it was not going to come at all. Which meant he wouldn't step past me. And the Finn wouldn't turn my way with his right jacket pocket near my hand...

A buzzing sounded from the Finn, and he held up his hand for our little convoy to stop.

Why now? Why late?

Because my seizure was seen and they told them—

How?

—by walkie-talkie. Doesn't matter. It meant they ran to the room and arrived sooner.

So we left the room sooner.

So we got farther before the phone call.

And now we're back on track!

The Finn's raised right hand now reached down into his left inside jacket pocket to pull out a cell phone. As he listened, I did a quick head check and found luck was doubly with me for once. The last hallway camera had been positioned mostly to check out the approach to the room I'd been locked in. The next one, I saw in my mind, was in a hallway parallel to it that ran to the control room. But we were in a cross hall right now, a couple turns from that corridor. None of the surveillance screens could see us.

Finn nodded in response to what he'd heard on the phone, then half turned to his right and swung the phone out almost like he was offering it to me and said, "It's bad reception here, but I think it's about your brother." To Cosmo, of course, who was right behind me.

In proper sequence, Cosmo stepped forward to go around my right side for the phone, but this time he met my awkwardly shifting right leg and stumbled toward the Finn.

The Finn reached out to grab him, tying up both his hands.

I swooped down and under Cosmo's stumble to lunge for the gun in the Finn's holster...and missed!

The Finn had seen me coming and simply stepped back, letting Cosmo fall. Worse still, the falling Italian grabbed at me as he went down, and I was off-balance already, so I tumbled with him, adrenaline kicking in big-time.

It drove me to do something I'd never have thought of in my former life. But in those slowed-time moments of tumbling in the sweaty, sickly sweet weight of Cosmo's body, I twisted under Cosmo's falling body and opened my arms around him like I wanted to embrace him as we fell.

As we hit and rolled, my hands scrabbled for the knife sheath I knew was there, clipped to the back of Cosmo's waistband.

"What the fuck?" he grunted as we struggled on the ground.

Found it.

"Get the fuck off me, you faggot!"

We rolled apart but I sprung up behind him, holding the burly man by his throat and making him stay that way by jabbing the tip of his knife into his lower back when he tried to twist away.

Cosmo roared but stopped twisting. I felt blood from the back wound dripping back along the knife to the handle, making it slick. Or was that just my sweat?

The Finn, on the other side of Cosmo and now holding his square-muzzled black pistol, shook his head at me with a bemused chuckle. "What are you going to do now? Make threats until other people arrive? The phone is still on in my pocket."

My legs were half-buckled under me to take me down to Cosmo's height. I couldn't stand this way long. And my knees were exposed. In fact, we were close enough to the Finn that, if he was good, he could probably shoot me in the head. Only I suspect he had orders to bring me to Cutter in one piece, or I'd be dead already.

I brought my mouth right to Cosmo's slick, sweaty ear. "Walk to him," I murmured and poked him again with the knife tip to discourage resistance.

Cosmo walked.

The Finn backed up.

"Faster," I muttered.

"Listen, dickf—"

"Now!"

So Cosmo walked faster until we were almost trotting after the retreating, giggling Finn, like some kind of gangly carnival freak show creature.

"Keep going, my little *runkku*," said the Finn. "We're almost there."

And we were. To the uneven crack in the floor I remembered where either the concrete pour had been bad, or the ground had settled on this side of it. I'd almost tripped on it on my first walk down this hallway and noted exactly where it was relative to the nearby walls and doors, so I didn't even have to look down to hope that the backward-shuffling Finn would hit it right about... now.

His heel caught the crack, and I simultaneously shoved Cosmo's trotting body at him with all the force I could muster.

And only because my adrenaline was running me insane, I leapt after the two of them, stabbing Cosmo's knife at the lower arm of the Finn as he brought up his pistol toward me. Hit it!

He yelled out and the gun clattered. I rolled after it and grabbed it, still rolling as I made it to my feet.

It would have been very badass if I actually knew how to use a gun. A heavy gun. I looked at it wildly to see if there was some kind of safety switch I needed to flip. IOCK 45 AUSTRIA 9x19 on the barrel. A little thumb slide there that didn't seem to do anything. And what had happened to the knife?

Cosmo and the Finn were both back on their feet and ready to leap at me. Cosmo had the knife.

I swore under my breath, aimed at the Finn, and pulled the trigger hard.

Boom!

Shit! The sound and kickback made me almost drop the gun. Almost.

Baring my teeth at the two men, I saw that the Finn was staggering, blood spreading on his chest. Then he hit the wall and slid down it. His eyes stared at me in shock.

I couldn't hold his gaze, though, because Cosmo now held up his knife at me, sliding to my right. "Oh, you've done it now, *coglioni*," he said and followed up with more Italian.

I swung the pistol barrel toward him, tracking him, holding the gun now with both hands. Shakily. "Hey, Cosmo. You know what that phone call was going to say about your brother?"

"How'd you know my name?" he said, swishing the knife back and forth. We were barely four feet apart.

"I know your name, the name of your brother, Antony. I know how Detective Gillespie shot Antony, and you keep seeing that in your head over and over. Your brother's blood. The fact you could have saved him but went for Gillespie instead."

"I hadda!"

"And Antony's dead now."

"You're fulla shit."

"Check the phone in the Finn's pocket. He said it's still on. Ask them."

"So you can run."

"Maybe."

Except I'd been listening hard from the time I'd shot the Finn, and I hadn't heard the sound of running footsteps. Which said to me either the phone in his pocket was still on and the bad guys were creeping up on me because they thought I was dangerous —highly unlikely—or the call had disconnected before the shot, and the concrete twists and turns of these hallways had muffled the shot so they hadn't registered it in the control room.

Unable to help himself, Cosmo had gone to the Finn's now-still body and gone through his sports jacket pockets without bothering to shut the man's eyes. Cosmo came up with the phone and turned to me.

"It's shut off."

"Put his thumb on the reader," I said, moving closer. "Maybe you can redial."

"Yeah. That's smart," Cosmo said slowly. Then, faster than someone of his bulk should have been able to, he dropped the phone and sprung straight at me with his knife out.

With no thought but terrified self-preservation, I raised the pistol and shot him three times, the last shot hitting him in the face as he was dropping and the recoil was making my hand rise.

His blood and bone spattered my face as he thumped down against my torso and almost pulled me down with him.

I pushed his body off me and stepped to one side, staring down in mute horror at what I'd done.

Cosmo's body twitched twice, then was still, an almost formless heap of muscle and dark hair. On the other side of the corridor, the Finn lay equally still, eyes still open, staring, roughly rolled onto his back by Cosmo when he'd searched out his phone.

The phone.

I walked shakily over to the Finn's body and looked for it. Finally found it where it had fallen behind the Finn's shoulder when Cosmo dropped it. I stooped and picked it up, leaning down to rub my face back and forth a few times on the Finn's sports jacket to clean Cosmo's blood and bone fragments off my face.

I paused with my face pressed against the rough cloth and allowed myself one quick, choking sob before straightening up on my knees and grabbing the Finn's right hand to position his thumb on his phone's thumbprint reader.

One try. Two. Three. Roll it around. Four.

I'd just about given up when the phone unlocked, and I gave a breathy little cry. The phone had about 60 percent battery. I flipped quickly through the settings to see if I could keep it from timing out on me. Found an Always On and clicked it.

Could I call someone? Anyone? Not here. No bars. Zero cell service. Probably why it had disconnected in the Finn's pocket.

Finally I stood up. I looked at the two men I'd just shot dead and was amazed I wasn't puking over the insanity of it, or trying to jump back to make them not dead. But after all I'd been through this day, in all my timelines, I wasn't surprised that I just didn't have the energy or confidence that I could pull off anything better.

So just add this mental trauma to the growing pile. I was a killer.

However much I might suffer from this later, again, it was amazing how much an anxiety-ridden person could accomplish if they just bulled ahead anyway.

I had to go.

I briefly considered heading for the emergency exit sign I'd seen in the previous long corridor. If I got out, I could call the Lead the Way team and the police, let them rescue Lena.

Except I thought I could hear, finally, the sound of feet and voices approaching, probably coming to see why we were taking so long. And the long corridor had cameras. The approaching voices would find the bodies. The cameras would see me escaping. Knowing Cutter, he'd send someone to kill Lena before I even got the call out. Or maybe somehow vanish the whole operation like they'd done at Ground Zero.

Neither of those worked for me.

I had to get her out. ASAP.

It twigged the memory of being with Cosmo at her door as Cosmo keyed open the lock.

Keyed.

I jumped back to Cosmo's bloody body, held my breath like that would keep out the ripe smell of body spray and death, and furiously went through his pockets. Sure enough, a set of six keys. One of them, I was sure, fit the lock on Lena's door.

I stood, breathed, gagged at the smell, and put the keys into one front pocket of my jeans. The phone I carefully slid into the other. Then I looked around, reestablished where we were in the mental map I'd constructed from my memories of my walks here and to Lena's room, and licked my dry lips.

The question was whether I could get to Lena, free her, and get both of us out before Cutter and his men found us and restarted the nightmare I'd already gone through over and over. Or something worse.

Another race for survival.

Go.

21

Touching fingertips

I TRIED TO RUN quietly in the direction the Finn and Cosmo had been taking me but turned right at the corner and eventually left again when I reached the basement's outside perimeter.

What I'd concluded, based on incomplete data, was that the health facility or seniors residence above me had been constructed in a kind of hollow square, with a few crosshatched spokes connecting its sides, creating a series of secure inner courtyards.

Presumably, the foundations which formed the basement would follow the same design, though there seemed to be some illogical blocks that made you zigzag to get from point A to point B.

Nonetheless, if I avoided the central spokes, one of which held the control room, it stood to reason I could travel around the square perimeter until I reached the corner where Lena was held. Of course, once the gangsters found the bodies of the Finn and Cosmo, they'd fan out through the other corridors to find me. Cautiously, because they'd know I had a gun.

That meant I had to move fast, make it to Lena before they looked there—there was no reason in this timeline I'd know where she was—and escape with her up the emergency exit I'd seen when Cosmo had led me to her room.

I started running as quietly as I could, breathing through my nose, body low. Before the next corner, I stopped, inched up, and peeked around it. Clear. I ran again.

I was now a long way from any familiar corridors, effectively running blind, counting on a mental map that could be all wrong. At least the sound of footsteps hunting me were a memory. For now. That would change when they discovered the dead bodies.

My morning runs and general health worked for me now. Those plus the adrenaline made me feel like I was flying. I ignored the memories of beatings I'd taken in other timelines and just felt what *this* timeline's body felt—strong and powerful, a gun in my hand, my enemy's blood on my face. Weightless.

At the end of another long corridor, I hit a right angle, an outside corner, right about where I'd thought it would be. Lena! But when I stopped and checked the door in the dim corridor light, I saw no blood marks at the bottom of the door. Other subtle differences.

Shit! So much for being an alpha predator with a great sense of direction.

I wanted to take off running again but made myself stop and reassess. Pulling out the phone, I saw I now had one bar, off and on. I opened a map in a desperate hope it would show me the building I was in. When it finally came on, it showed I had the right building, but there was nothing deeper.

Then I swore at myself at not checking my cell reception as I'd run. It was time to call in the cavalry.

I dialed the first number of the Lead the Way Security group that popped into my head—Lena's former boyfriend, Alvin Westor, the cool and calculating upright moray eel who was supposed to have kept her safe when she left my apartment this morning. Or yesterday morning? I should have checked the time and date.

Before I could do that, Alvin answered with a crackly, "Who is this?"

"Jackson Traine," I almost shouted, then gave him the address of the aboveground facility, noting we were in the basement, I hadn't found Lena yet, and armed gang members were looking for us.

There was silence, little crackles, then Alvin's voice. "Repeat."

Which part? I gave my name and address. Repeated it three times. Said, "Copy."

More silence and crackles, then, "Got it. If—"

Silence. I pulled the phone from my ear to look at it. The one bar was flickering again, almost no signal. I chewed my lip and texted him the address and the facts of being in the basement with armed gangsters. Maybe that would send at some point when I hit an area with better connection.

Right now, I still had to find Lena.

I delicately pocketed the phone so I didn't accidentally shut it off and began loping down the next long corridor, looking for signs in each side corridor of anything I recognized.

Almost immediately, though, something felt wrong, like I was running with double vision and a horrible sense of déjà vu, the "before" walls just slightly to one side or the other as I ran. Something bad was about to happen. I was going to get caught.

I sped up and took the first left turn I came to, then a right so I was still running parallel to the outside wall. But the feeling I was reliving something I'd already done got worse, and the sense of danger intensified until I was sure my subconscious was hearing the sound of pursuers. Or all the trauma and adrenaline was finally getting to me, making me hallucinate, finally unable to separate out all the futures and pasts and...

Then it all made sense.

As I reached a T that said I'd gone as far as this corridor would go, I stopped before stepping into the cross hall, and the wall of that cross hall ahead of me set off a cascade of remembered pain and desperation.

It was the rippled concrete at the base of the wall coupled with a pattern of stains on the old painted drywall and the distant fizzing of a bad light ballast.

I had definitely been here before!

Yes! En route to Lena's room with Cosmo, being virtually carried by him because both my thighs had been stabbed and were leaking blood from their impromptu tape bandages.

This meant that Lena's room was only fifteen feet down this cross hall to the right.

But I knew, I *knew*, that if I just stepped around the corner to my right, I was going to get shot. I could see as plain as if it was happening that if I stepped around the corner with my gun up and saw...who? Yes, it would be the young Asian gangster I'd called Pockmark, who Cutter called Ching. He'd have what looked like a small submachine gun in his hands, held up and pointed at me. But then Kenny would finally get into the act remotely and make the lights flicker, make the green light that showed the status of the camera over the door of Lena's room blink out. And there'd be a sudden terror in Ching's eyes, and...

That was as far as my creative vision took me.

Guess my brain didn't want to fully imagine me getting shot.

But I was damn well going to take the warning of my subconscious seriously. I got a good double grip on the handle of what my brain had finally figured out was a Glock, with the G being a badly stylized box around the other letters, then I simultaneously stepped into the corridor and swung the Glock up to aim in the direction of whoever was guarding Lena's door.

There was no one there.

No one.

But...

I shook my head just to confirm I wasn't missing something, because I'd been so *sure*, but the emptiness of the corridor didn't change.

The one interesting thing was that the green light on the hall surveillance camera was not on, suggesting that maybe Kenny was helping out remotely after all. Of course, a blank surveillance screen might send people running this way as surely as one that showed my presence. Unless Kenny had blanked out *all* the surveillance screens.

Sure, I'd go with that.

Either way, the clock was ticking. I was *not* going to have to relive all the craziness I'd just gone through. No guarantees I'd kill Cosmo and the Finn next time. Or the time after that, *if* I lived long enough to jump back and redo my failures.

It would be nice, just this once, to actually succeed at something the first time.

As all this was buzzing through my brain, my fingers had pulled out the set of six keys Cosmo had been carrying in his pocket and begun trying them in the lock on Lena's door. I'd eliminated three right off because one was a transponder key that probably let Cosmo's car unlock the transmission, one was a tubular key like you'd use for a tough bicycle lock, and one was something I'd read was called an abloy key, which has no teeth and works only on impossible-to-pick disc tumbler locks like they use in every house in Finland. The Finn had probably recommended it to Cosmo for his home locks.

It left three keys. One wouldn't go into the lock at all. Both of the last two did but neither seemed to turn, however much I jiggled them.

"Hello?"

Oh God. It was Lena's voice from inside. Awake now. Apparently lucid. Which meant they must, in the future that would now never happen, not have drugged or beaten her until just before Cosmo took me to see her.

"Are you coming in?"

Trying to sound brave. I could see her in my mind so clearly that I wanted to weep over my helplessness, because if I couldn't get the damn door open, did I really want to raise her hopes only to dash them?

"Hello?"

"It's me," I said at last, unable to help myself.

There was a frantic rustling from inside, then it sounded like she was pressed right up to the metal door as she said, "Jackson? They took you, too? How did you escape?"

"Long—very long—story."

She processed that in silence, and I knew she understood and was probably imagining all the things that might have happened. I planned to never tell her all the things that actually had.

"We've got a problem," I said.

"Your keys aren't working."

"You could hear that."

"The big-chested Italian guy had trouble with it when he put me in here. A lot of pushing and pulling on the door."

"I could shoot out the lock," I joked tiredly.

"With a metal door? Will that work? And where did you get a gun?"

"Don't know. Don't know. And you don't want to know. Stand back and let me try the pushing and pulling."

And so I stuck the Glock into the back waistband of my jeans and commenced what felt like half an hour of pushing, pulling, twisting, grunting, cursing, repeat, try with Lena helping, double the frustration, repeat with the second key, and again...

"They're going to be here any minute now," I grunted after the last finger-destroying attempts. "Let me try shooting out the lock."

"And if that doesn't work?"

"Then you're stuck, and I'll have to jump back and find a different way in."

"How many jumps today?"

"Seven, nine, I don't know. I've lost count."

"You never lose count."

"I don't want to know."

She obviously heard the hopelessness that had crept into my voice, because she modulated her own climbing pitch down and murmured through the door, "Sit down with your back to the door."

I was too tired not to obey, only pulling the Glock out of my back waistband first.

Her voice followed me down and said, "There's a space under the door. It's small but big enough I can fit my fingers almost through."

"You want me to pass you the keys?"

"No. There's no keyhole on this side. I just want you to reach your own fingertips as far under your side of the door as you can."

I put the Glock on my lap and jammed my knuckles against the cement floor, then slid my fingertips back to find the door and inch their way in, just up to the second knuckle. "Far as they go," I said bitterly.

"I think I see them," her voice said at the bottom of the door, and I imagined her with her beautiful, curly dark hair crushed flat under her cheek as she strained to look. "I'm going to sit with my back against the door now and reach under to touch your fingers."

I frowned automatically over the fruitless nature of the action, but despite myself, I felt an excitement blossom in me to just feel the fingers of this one woman who truly understood me, mental shortcomings and all.

Then, the touch. It was a brush at first, against the fingers of my left hand, then the fingers returned to mine and stayed. A moment later, I felt a brush against my right fingers, too. It stayed. We both just sat like that for a moment as her presence filled me up. Just through the touch of her fingers and knowing she was reaching for me with her heart and will.

The phone in my pocket dinged and I laughed. Who'd that text be from? Cutter? The Finn's girlfriend? His wife?

"I gotta get that," I said and drew back my right hand. I shook out the squeezed fingers, reached into my pocket, and drew out the phone. The text message from Alvin said:

There in 5 minutes. Suggest nearest Emergency Exit. We'll find you.

The relief made my hands shake. "Alvin's on his way. I guess we should get you out of here to meet him."

With that, and a surprising return of energy, I stood, pocketed the phone, and tried the two keys in the door again. This time I focused on the one that felt like it had the most movement. And rather than my desperate brute-force shoving and pulling and twisting of before, I used gentle pressure and jiggling, back and forth until, amazingly, the lock turned with a snicking sound. I turned the knob and the door opened into the room.

Lena stood just clear of the door's swing and greeted me like we'd been apart for days, months, or years, not just since...

"Hey, how long have you been in here?" I asked.

"Since they grabbed me this morning."

"Okay. Good." I stepped forward and embraced her, thinking it through. I hadn't been knocked out that long by Gillespie's drug then. The first time I'd seen the clock in the Demon Monk control room, it had said 6:06, which I now knew meant 6:06 p.m. Lena had been here maybe eleven hours. I'd been here maybe seven, plus another two or three hours of relived time. Brutal hours, those.

I pulled back and looked Lena over carefully. No blood on her blouse or face. The knees of her navy slacks looked untorn. Which meant however she'd been beaten in the once-upon-a-time future when I'd come to see her with Cosmo, it hadn't yet happened. And it *would not* happen as long as I drew breath.

"You have that haunted look in your eyes again," Lena said. "This isn't your first time seeing me here, is it?"

I shook my head. "First time was just reconnaissance. You were in pretty bad shape. Not now, I take it?"

"Nope. I'm good. We run?"

"We run."

22

The lights go out

MAYBE IT WILL SOUND like cheating to gloss over the heart-pounding run, duck, and hide we did on the way back to the closest emergency exit sign I'd seen, which was actually near the beginning of the lost-future trip I took with Cosmo to Lena's room. Which meant near the gang control room.

But the terrifying run proved uneventful. We encountered no one. I was guessing Cutter wouldn't think I'd come all the way over to this side of the basement, and he'd sent all his searchers to scour the halls and doors on the other side of the basement.

We also got a helping hand when all the basement lights shut off.

Kenny, I assumed. Like in my déjà vu.

I brought us to a halt in the blackness, took Lena's right hand with my left, stuck the Glock revolver into the back waistband of my jeans, and led us in a fast, soundless walk, using my right hand to feel all the doors and corners as we went. I could see them in my mind's eye as clearly as I had when the lights had been on. A nice side benefit of perfect recall.

When we turned onto the corridor that had the emergency exit against the corner wall ahead, I saw that not all the lights in the basement were off after all. The emergency exit sign that was our target was glowing a soft, baleful red as we crept toward it.

Then everything went sideways.

Lena jerked me to a stop and pointed. I swore silently. Now, at twenty or thirty feet from the exit door, I could make out the gangster who stood just out of the light to the left of it, halfway around the corner. He'd probably been told to guard this unlikely exit but was scared to step too far away from the only light in his world right now.

To make things worse, I heard the sounds of gunfire and running feet from somewhere in these hallways. Alvin and Kai, Kajika Bighouse and Ryan Renn, I assumed, since I'd been too brain-punched to actually text or call the police. From the sounds, the Lead the Way guys had come in on the wrong side of the basement and were probably driving the bad guys toward us, making the guard at the door ahead of us start looking up and around.

Shit!

I reached back for my gun and brought it forward, raising it to aim with both hands, wondering if I could hit a target from this far off.

Lena's hand covered mine, and I could just make out her headshake in the tenuous spill from the exit light. She brought her mouth right up to my ear and spoke so quietly it was barely words at all. "He can't see us yet. Go along the far wall. Let me draw him out."

It sounded remarkably like the fatal play she'd tried in one of our attempts to escape Gillespie back in the particle accelerator lab. That had ended up with her head smashed into a concrete wall before she'd been shot dead. But before I could say no or grab her, she'd already hurried forward and walked loudly straight toward the gangster.

Another silent curse and I tried to blend into the left wall where I'd be out of the gangster's eyeline longer, stepping along quietly, trying to mostly keep up to Lena.

"Hey!" Lena called when she was less than ten feet from the thug guarding our escape hatch.

He stepped toward her into the emergency exit glow, and I saw a round-faced kid who really liked pumping his biceps and pecs and not much else. A junior gangster then, like Kenny had been, but not smart enough to do whatever computer crimes the other juniors had been doing in the central control room. Instead, he got to dress tough in black boots, black jeans, and a ratty tee-shirt. Trying to prove himself and getting shitty assignments like this in return.

It almost made me feel sorry for him until he pulled his gun and pointed it at Lena's face as he stepped forward.

No! All he had to do was delay us, that was all, and the bad guys being pushed this way would stumble onto us and make this so much worse.

Lena raised her hands. "Whoa. The lights went out, and I'm just trying to find someone who knows what's going on."

Smart. We didn't know whether this guy even knew that Lena was a hostage. Maybe he was also freaked, like me, by the approaching gunfire and pounding feet in the blackness so that—

Nope. His hands tightened on his gun. "You're supposed to be locked up."

Lena shrugged and moved closer to the wall on the guy's right, backing away from him a bit to entice him to follow her and keep her in his sights.

Okay. Okay. Good. Move. In a quiet rush, I was right behind the guy. He heard me, but I wrapped my arm around his neck even as he turned. I ground the muzzle of my Glock up to his cheek and swung the handle forward so he could confirm it was what he thought it was.

He froze.

"Hold out your gun, grip first, to the lady," I said, cold and fast. "And if you even think about doing something stupid like twisting or shouting, you lose the front half of your face."

It should have sounded phony. But maybe because I had already killed two people today, even I believed I'd do it.

The kid shakily tried to turn the gun around in the outstretched hand he held it with until I was pretty sure he was going to drop it and have it shoot into my or Lena's legs.

"Stop! Just let her take it."

He did and Lena did, turning from the kid with it to cover the lines of approaching darkness.

"Okay," I said, moving the muzzle of my Glock gun quickly from his cheek to the middle of his back. I could hear the sound of running footsteps getting closer. "Now you're going to *quietly* open that exit door for us and lead us up the stairs. And in case you think you can turn and knock the gun away somehow, remember this: I don't care about you. I will pull the trigger at the slightest provocation, and your spine will explode. Even if you avoid an agonizing death from organ damage and sepsis, you'll never walk again. Tell me you understand."

He seemed to have a lot of phlegm in his throat as he said, "Um...yeah. Yes."

"What's your name?"

"Jeff."

"Just Jeff?"

"Jeff Osterman."

"Okay, Jeff Osterman. Let's go."

The door looked rarely used and had a sticker on it saying an alarm would go off if it was opened. But once more, I blindly trusted that Kenny would have taken care of that. And when the door opened with a second hard shove on the push bar, there was no sound except the whoosh of basement air rushing into the stairwell.

We quickly piled into that concrete stairwell. It was lit with the same red emergency lighting as the sign outside and smelled of old, soaked-in urine and overcooked institutional food. A hellish heaven. Except... I held up my free hand to stop. With the emergency exit door clicked shut behind us, muffling the approaching chaos, we could now hear the muffled noises coming through the door at the *top* of the stairs, too. Shouting. Gunshots. It sounded like we'd be jumping from the frying pan into the fire.

I looked at Lena and she looked at me. "What do we do?" I said.

"Is there another door we could have gone out?" she asked.

I turned and tugged on the door handle. "We can't go back through this one. It's locked from this side."

"If we *could,*" she said, looking at me meaningfully, "is there another exit door?"

"Only where they'd have been hunting for me even before the fighting."

Lena's face fell. "Then we jam this door and wait. Maybe they'll think nobody went through it and Jeff just deserted his post."

"But—" Jeff began.

"Shut up, Jeff," I said and looked him over. "Take off your belt."

He didn't comply at once, and I jabbed the muzzle hard into his spine.

His hands started fumbling with his belt buckle. When he got it off, he held it to the side and I grabbed it. It was the buckle I was interested in—thick, steel, slightly curved, and patterned like a cowboy's big manhood display.

"If I give you this gun," I said to Lena, "will you be able to shoot Jeff dead if he so much as twitches?"

"I would fucking *love* to shoot him," she said with a gusto I was pretty sure was put on. It seemed to have the requisite effect on Jeff, though, so I let Lena shove the kid's gun into the back of her slacks like a badass, then take my Glock, keeping it pressed into the kid's lower spine.

I took the belt and jammed the buckle under the opening corner of the emergency exit door we'd just come through. Wrapping the leather part of the belt around it, I tried kicking it deeper into the crack. But I was wearing running shoes, which did nothing. The kid gangster wore hard-leather-soled boots. "Jeff! Give me one of your boots!"

With Lena's gun muzzle never losing contact with Jeff's back, the kid leaned over, tugged off a boot, and passed it to me.

I got down on my knees and used the bootheel to drive that buckle so deeply in under the door that it ground into the cement.

I fell backward as someone on the other side of the door suddenly tried to smash it inwards. Again, flashbacks—Gillespie pounding on that door we'd ducked through at the accelerator lab. But this time the door wasn't locked, just jammed up.

I looked at Lena, who was pressing her gun muzzle hard into Jeff's back. The kid's face was white, no doubt contemplating what spending the rest of his life as a paraplegic would be like.

None of us moved.

After a bunch more thuds and audible grunting and swearing that seemed to go on forever, someone said, "Some fire exit, hunh? Fucking piece of shit building."

It sounded like he was about to move on, but then another voice jumped in. "Or they actually went through this door and jammed it from the other side. Let me have a try."

Oh, shit. "We gotta move," I whispered.

Lena nodded and pushed Jeff toward the stairs, smoothly handing off the gun to me as the door behind us started booming again and Jeff started climbing.

At the top was a short concrete landing. To the left was a door that looked locked from this side. To the right was an emergency exit with a push bar opening, presumably exiting to outside the building.

"The gunfire's paused or moved on," Lena said.

She was right. An ugly scratching sound and burst of hallway noise from below said we were about to get some extra company in the stairwell.

"Let's go," I said, pushing Jeff to go through the door first.

23

Too many guns

JEFF OSTERMAN BURST OUT the door and immediately started running. I watched him, not firing but waiting to see if anyone else shot at him. No one did, so I slipped out the door after him, my Glock up and ready, scanning back and forth, half expecting to be shot or assaulted the minute I cleared the door.

It didn't happen.

What did happen was a slightly sick and confused feeling as I saw two dead bodies (gangsters?) on the strip of grass I stood on that ran east-west alongside a bland single-story wall of institutional concrete and windows.

To my left, toward what would be the building's west side, things looked like they opened up maybe forty yards away. I saw a distant curve of pavement and cars blurring over it, with the sound of sirens. Doors slamming. People shouting. Gunfire.

The cops had arrived.

Thirty yards to my right was the corner of what would be the back of the building where I'd followed Gillespie to and seen him shot before I jumped back and diverted and warned him...so he could get shot later.

I remembered Alvin had advised me to sit tight and he'd find me, but the fluidity of the fighting out here did not make that seem like a good choice. Especially with gangsters about to come up the stairs after us.

I waved Lena to come out after me, and she darted out with her pistol, the one Jeff had handed to her, raised like she actually knew how to use it. A story there that she hadn't told me, obviously.

The second the door clicked closed behind her, I said, "We head out the back, through the forest. Come on."

She nodded and we began to run.

We got two steps before a group of five men, four of whom I recognized from the now-never-happened gang meeting at Ground Zero, appeared at the corner we were running toward, saw us, trained their pistols on us, and advanced quickly.

I was calculating whether it was worth trying to shoot our way past them or for me to jump back, when the emergency exit door we'd come from banged open behind us and disgorged three more thugs with their guns up. The last of them was short and scrawny with greasy shoulder-length black hair, now falling wildly around his face, and was casually carrying a frigging assault rifle.

Cutter.

He waved at one of his two companions to cover the emergency exit door, then walked toward me and Lena.

Okay, the smart move here was to drop our guns and raise our hands, I thought. Especially since, despite everything I'd already been through today with Cutter in my discarded timelines, or because of it, I couldn't even meet the man's eyes. I felt my gun shake in my hand as I considered whether to aim it at him or any of the other six gangsters now circling us. It was like a heavy blanket of darkness pressed down on me now, making everything thick and hopeless.

But Lena showed absolutely no inclination to give up. She gripped her pistol tightly and moved its aim from one thug to the next, finishing on Cutter like she recognized him. Which meant he'd either been part of her kidnapping or had visited her afterward. Lena obviously hadn't been charmed.

And because she wasn't giving up, I obviously couldn't, even if I was almost blind with despair.

Cutter laughed. "You look like you're going to fall over, baby bro. Too much stress for you wittle tummy?"

I wanted to turn and snarl at him, but my body was too sluggish, my heart beating so hard and dark in my ears that I worried Cutter was right. I *was* going to fall over. And everything I'd gone through to get me and Lena out? It would all be for nothing. I couldn't just jump back to before the fire exit because it would probably be right about when I was supposed to grab Jeff, and I'd be so disoriented for a few beats that he'd probably just shoot Lena. If I double jumped, I'd just be feeling my way through in the pitch-black hallways with Lena or trying to open her door again, and I didn't have any better ideas about how to escape this many gangsters with guns coming after me.

Which meant this was it. Man up, Jacky boy. Feel the fear and do it anyway.

I turned my head to look Cutter in the eye and choked. Not from fear, though, but because Cutter stood between me and the front of the building. And from that direction, two policemen were advancing quickly with their service pistols drawn. One of them I recognized—young Patrol Officer Bryan Miller. Boy Scout. Honest Cop. Friend.

But maybe unrealistically hopeful when he called out, "Everybody drop your guns! Now!"

Cutter turned his back to us and looked at the advancing policemen. "We got two civilians here in a standoff. And more guns than you, shithead. You really wanna do this?"

I stepped shakily toward Cutter and pressed the muzzle of my Glock into the back of his neck. "I'm ready to go. You ready to go? Shithead."

Cutter shrugged and said to the men behind me, "Take the girl."

Lena screamed and fired once as they jumped her, making me whirl around and giving Cutter the opening to step to the side and deftly whack the Glock out of my hands with his rifle. The gun hit the grass, and Cutter kicked it away as another thug stepped up and put a gun in my back. One of the gangsters was holding his bloody shoulder where Lena must have shot him. The others had stripped Lena of her gun, and one held her tightly while another pointed a gun at her temple.

Cutter sneered at the police. "Your move, shitheads. You back away now and you live and they live. None of your concern. You shoot and you're gonna die. Five...four...three...two..."

He shot both policemen before the final count. *Bryan!* His partner dropped as Bryan staggered back, turned, and fell face-first to the dirt. I sickly hoped he'd done it to fall with his walkie-talkie usable under him.

"Okay, now—" Cutter began.

He was cut off when the emergency exit door banged open yet again and Alvin, Kai Nishikawa, and Ryan Renn shot out in an automatic spread, assault rifles up at their shoulders and trained on Cutter and company. I noted these Lead the Way guys had night vision goggles up on their foreheads like they'd known it would be a darkness scenario.

"Let the hostage go," Alvin said in his cool, dry voice.

"Or what?" Cutter said. "Big guns, little guns, they all—"

A *p-tak!* sounded, and the head of the man aiming his gun at Lena snapped forward with a spray of blood out the back.

The next second, the gangster holding his gun to my back jerked and dropped, a ragged bullet hole in his temple.

The third second, the neck of the man holding Lena ripped open as he spun her sideways to see what had gotten his buddy.

Seconds four through ten, Alvin, Kai, and Ryan shot a spray of back-and-forth gunfire that seemed to surround my head in an insane cyclone of sound and death. But it didn't touch me or the Lead the Way team at all as it dropped the remaining gangsters.

Except Cutter. The little weasel had thrown away his rifle, shot his hands into the air, and stepped away from the rest the moment the first two of his men had fallen. And the Lead the Way team had respected the surrender.

While Kai and Ryan ran into the killing ground to kick guns away from the fallen and check for signs of life—the first two shot were definitely gone but the others less definitively so— Alvin walked to me without ever lowering his rifle from where it was trained on Cutter's sneering face. He lowered his nontrigger hand to reach into the pocket of his flak jacket and came out with a couple zip ties.

"Cuff his hands behind his back," he ordered me.

Feeling like I was a shell-shocked ghost, I complied, tightening Cutter's zip tie cuffs maybe more than I should have, not out of malice but from a childlike fear that if this skinny little gang boss twisted loose somehow, he could still kill us all.

"Three living!" Dr. Kai called out from his examination of the fallen gangsters.

"Check the police officers," Alvin said. "Any aid starts there. Smiley, watch the perimeter."

As Ryan/Smiley stepped back to scan for any gangsters coming to assist, Kai nodded and jogged toward my fallen patrol officer friend on the ground. I thought I saw, hoped I saw, Miller's hand move and wished I could go to him, too. But I was finding it hard to move or focus. At least other police from the front of the building were now running toward us with their guns drawn. Miller would be looked after.

Near the back of the building, meanwhile, Kajika Bighouse walked somberly out from the trees, slinging the sniper rifle he'd used to take out the first three members of the men who'd been holding me and Lena.

I nodded at him, mentally floating further and further into a netherworld. Kajika nodded somberly back at me.

Then, somehow, Lena's arms were wrapped around my body, and her pounding heart and deep breaths against my own stopped my complete mental departure. I looked down into her tear-streaked face and nodded.

We didn't say anything. We didn't need to.

Finally, the cramping pain in my upper right abdomen intensified, and I looked down vaguely to see a small hole in my jeans down by my pelvis where blood was spreading. Weird. I'd been shot.

Maybe I could have jumped back then.

Maybe I didn't want to risk this almost-happy ending.

I slumped in Lena's arms and the world winked out.

24

Codas

THIS SECOND HOSPITAL TRIP in only two days was significantly harder than the first one.

To start with, my injuries were real and serious this time. By the time they got me into the Virginia Mason at Lena's insistence, my abdomen was bloating with peritonitis and internal bleeding. A CT scan got me into general surgery for an open laparotomy that required general anesthetic and hemodynamic stabilization with IV fluids and blood products. Turned out that the stray 9mm bullet that had entered my lower abdomen might not have had the shredding power of a .45 ACP, but it still tore through three loops of my small intestine before exiting my back.

Could have been a lot worse if it had hit my ureter or spine, but it still required the surgeon to manually examine the entire length of my small intestine, remove affected pieces with a splicing tool, then carefully line up the pieces left behind and use a zipper form of stapling to put them together. All topped off with lots of broad-spectrum antibiotics to deal with the fouling of the membrane that lined my abdominal cavity.

The surgery took five hours.

I was apparently touch and go at one point, as my body seemed to react like it had suffered other traumas, though there was no visible physical evidence of that.

The female surgeon with powerful forearms and tired eyes shared all of this with me shortly after I woke up and made her tell me about Officer Bryan Miller's condition (stable) and what happened to the surrendered leader of the Demon Monks, Cutter (she had no idea).

Summing up my own prognosis for recovery, she added that even though I'd likely return to full health over a few weeks, a number of patients with the sorts of operations I'd just had left the hospital feeling permanently damaged and unsure of their health or sexual function. I should be prepared.

I wasn't sure whether to break into tears or gales of laughter at that. I pictured myself putting a hand on her arm and croaking, "Doc, let me tell you about trauma…"

I didn't. I was too weak for that. I did manage to thank her for her amazing work and waited for Alvin and Lena to come back in, sequentially because of COVID regs, so they could update me on how everything had played out.

The key question of where I should go next to find Kenny, though, I couldn't ask them. Lena was still trying to process what I'd done, and Alvin, when he'd found Kenny never went physically near the Demon Monks, looked at me like I was vaguely brain damaged. My hunt for Kenny, in their minds, had run into a brick wall that offered no way forward.

Except that four days into my recovery, the way forward appeared in such clear, stark terms that I barked, "*Wow!*" loud enough to bring the nurses running.

The only question was who to share it with and how, and the answer to *that* depended on how all the other emotional codas to this messy adventure resolved.

Coda one: my emotional health

In days one and two after my surgery, Lena spent a lot of hours sitting in the chair by my bed, just holding my hand. I kept slipping into a mental review of all the horrors I'd gone through over the last week, and it was often only Lena's hand holding mine that kept me grounded to the current time stream. She assured me Cutter was in jail, awaiting trial, and the Demon Monks had once again taken an explosive hit. Maybe a fatal one. The detective who interviewed me on day two confirmed that.

Day three saw my mind wandering further into the other time streams I'd destroyed, not dwelling on the horrors but all the other elements there. I only came back when Lena squeezed my hand hard, worried about the distant look in my eyes.

"It's what Kenny had," I murmured the fifth or sixth time it happened.

"What?"

"The look in his eyes. Like he was wandering time streams…"

"You haven't talked about him, other than to say you saw him in the gang's control room."

"On a video link." And the memory of him saying he knew I could escape, then signaling me to give up on him and rescue Lena made me suddenly well up with tears again. I'd been doing that a lot lately. Like all the weakness brought on by my surgery, not to mention all the preceding trauma, had pricked my bubble of manly reserve and left me a labile, blubbering mess.

Lena squeezed my hand again, bringing me out of it until I truly saw her clearly for the first time that day. Maybe for the first time since my surgery. The beautiful clarity of her brow and deep hazel eyes had become knotted with worry. Over me? Yes, of course. And what had happened. What still might happen. So much fatigue there, too. Her world had been turned upside down.

I wiped my eyes and nose quickly with my hospital bedsheet and forced a smile. "I guess I'm a classic 'You never know what you're going to get.'"

She chuckled. It sounded pained.

Coda two: Lena's emotional health

To understand Lena's pain, I asked, "It's what? Wednesday? How are you doing? Did you submit your report? Have you gone back to your lab?"

"I submitted my report. They wanted me to keep going." She looked away from me.

"You're not going to?"

"Not for a while."

"Because…"

"I'm also looking to extend my sabbatical from Berkley. Depending on you."

"Me."

"Specifically the answers you give to a few questions I have." She released my hand and stood up from her bedside chair like the import of what she had to ask was jazzing her, like that electric god running around and around in the particle accelerator lab she was abandoning.

I took a sip of the apple juice that had come with my liquid breakfast. Put it down. "Ask away."

"You've said you don't want to tell me about all the things they did to you in that place. But what you've said so far suggests you were there a long time, a lot of repeating time streams, before you decided to rescue me. That was to rescue your brother?"

"To get information I could use to rescue him at some point. I learned from Gillespie before going in that Kenny was never there in person, but I still thought Cutter might know where he was. Turns out the whole reason Cutter kidnapped me was that he didn't. He wanted to use me to get Kenny to spill."

"Which he didn't do."

"Nope."

"When did you find out I'd been taken?"

"Late morning. From Detective Gillespie."

"Who's now dead."

"Yes. He told me after he'd already drugged me. I think he was dead before I woke up in my gang holding cell."

"Then they started torturing you to make Kenny talk?"

"Right."

"So...you knew I'd been taken, you knew your brother wasn't physically accessible, but you let yourself be tortured so you could talk to him?"

I studied her face to see if she was angry, but saw only a mask of scientific interest, which meant she was *really* angry. Or at least stressed. Taut. *Caution.* "So many years," I said carefully, "I thought Kenny was dead and it was my fault. When I found out he was alive, I wanted answers."

"Hunh." She began pacing. "Did you get them?"

"Some. Like the fact he has a weird power relationship with the gangs. He can exert some physical, long-distance control. Shut off their lights like he did during our escape. And I think he can tell when I've jumped back in time."

Lena changed course to go to the cracked-open door and shut it firmly. She'd wrangled me a private room, but it wasn't *that* private. I needed to watch what I said.

She strode back to my bed and stared down at me. "It was Alvin and his crew who shut off the light and alarms in the building, not your brother."

My mouth dropped open for a moment, then I nodded. "That makes sense. The timing of it."

"But you still think your brother has some kind of power? And that he can spot time traveling?"

"Yes."

"Do you know how?"

Coda three: mysteries of time and relationships

"I have an idea how," I said. Kenny's power involved layers of complicated crazy about multiple time travelers that only someone like Lena would truly be able to understand, but I wasn't sure I had the energy for it now. And something in Lena's pursed lips told me she had something else that had to be addressed first anyway.

"Okay, Jackson Traine," she said, "here's the equation. I care about you a surprising amount, enough that I'm considering a major change in my plans for the next six months to study you, help you, and be with you. But there are three conditions precedent."

"Which are?"

"One: you will share all your struggles and insights with me, not hide them away. Two: you let me bring Alvin and his team into our secret. And three: you let us train you in self-defense and in how to use your ability better."

I stared at her, reflexively wanting to object but kept quiet by the fiery challenge of her eyes, the jut of her chin. So instead, I asked, "Why?"

She took a breath. "To which condition?"

"All of them. Each of them."

"I need Alvin and the others in on this because they can't properly train or protect you if they don't know what they're dealing with."

"They already weren't able to protect you."

"Alvin didn't tell you what happened?"

I shook my head.

Lena grimaced. "Let's just say that whoever planned that attack..."

"Cutter, probably."

"...is a devious son of a bitch with no moral scruples whatsoever."

"You going to tell me what happened?"

"It's Alvin's story and you're avoiding my demands. What other condition don't you understand?"

I ran my hand over my face, feeling the bristles, knowing my hair was probably a mess but suspecting my externals mattered a lot less to Lena right now than my messed up internals. "Why do I have to share all my struggles and insights?"

"Because you're too used to doing things on your own." She poked an index finger at me. "You figure something out and go tearing after it, leaving the rest of us scrambling to catch up. It's one reason Lead the Way got taken by surprise. They'd left Big to watch your apartment building because he has the best eyes and ears. He almost missed your exit and freaked on the phone to Alvin. Then we were hit and Big came running. Too late."

"Okay. That would be sharing my insights and plans. Why my struggles?"

Lena stared at me. Then she walked to the bed, leaned her garden scent down over me, and kissed me on my lips in a way that, even if she'd been almost scowling at me up to this point, thrilled me with its possibilities.

She pulled back just enough that I could feel her warm breath as she said, "For a psychologist, you are incredibly stupid."

She straightened and left the room.

Coda four: loneliness

In my first fully conscious hours after my surgery Monday, even before being interviewed by the police, I had covered my last two classes by calling the UW dean and letting him know my situation. But only after I'd texted Mikael and Shawna and obtained their agreement to lead the last two classes in a review of all the material we'd covered.

The exam was all prepped, and I was determined, even if I was still pooping liquid, to be back at the university in a week to administer it.

I'd also had my psychometrist/office administrator, Megan, call all my clients for the week and either push their counseling sessions back or fill them in with some colleagues here whom I'd met over Zoom and had good feelings about.

I even gave Jude a call, keeping it light, letting him know I was still seeing Lena. He was overjoyed for me, caught me up on his latest. Signed off.

It all left me, on day three, after Lena walked out, all alone.

The safest way to be, right? Not depending on anyone. Not beholden to anyone. Not endlessly frightened of accidentally revealing the horrors of my teenage years, now the horror of my adult ones, but still secretly committed to finding my big brother and saving him from whatever he'd gotten caught up in.

Just...me, and now...an offer of more than that?

If I heard a client lay out a struggle like this, I'd listen so impatiently, knowing what they *should* choose to move toward health. I'd point out they've taken some baby steps of reaching out to others in friendship, and the huge step of finding a soul mate whom they hadn't manage to scare away yet, despite their best attempts.

They should follow up on all those things, especially the soul mate. But we all knew that shoulds weren't always coulds.

Especially when the things they suffered from ran deep. Then the traumas just kept piling up, and the very core of who they were now, who *I* was now, revolved around a crazy power to jump into the past, as long as I let myself be retraumatized over and over and over...

If I just gave up time traveling completely, I wondered, would Lena still want me?

Then I entered my fourth day post surgery.

Coda five: family secrets

I woke from a dream of Cutter and Cosmo punching, cutting, and battering me. It was so real I wasn't sure for a few moments if it was a dream or my mind was just slipping through my catalogued memory of my torture at their hands.

Thump. Crack. Slap! Grind. Slice.

While Kenny watched with his fingers steepled and tapping together. *Tap-hold tap-hold tap tap.* Spread fingers in a pause. *Tap tap tap tap.* And so on.

How many times had he needed to tell me to *Save Lena* before I'd finally...?

I stopped. I rewound the torture scene in my head and let it play again. I didn't just note Kenny was tapping for me; I watched *what* he was tapping. It did not spell out *Save Lena*. Not at all.

I scrambled to get Kansas on the phone.

When she finally found a way to make our phone call secure —I'd had Alvin bring me a new cell phone to replace my stolen one—she was uncharacteristically snappish.

"I told you to lie low and get a bodyguard!" she said before I'd told her anything at all about what I'd done or where I was. Probably nobody but me would have known that the stress in her voice reflected intense fear. I was guessing it was fear for me, caused when some trip wire she'd had on the news had given her the whole Demon Monks shoot-out and my involvement as a person of interest.

"And you told me," I said, "that you were going to find out who was holding Kenny and who was funding Lena. I never heard back."

"That is—"

"I wasn't going to sit around and wait for people to come for us," I barreled on. "Especially if one of them was Kenny. I *owed* it to him. I never told you..."

"I knew."

"What?" I almost dropped my cell phone onto the bed.

She sounded impatient as she said, "About how you went after Kenny in a chop shop. How the little psycho they called Cutter offered to have you take Kenny's place before he cut up Kenny's face. Then had you beaten to stay quiet. I didn't just search electronic chatter after Kenny disappeared. I hired human intelligence. My woman found one of the guys who was there with you, Kenny, Cutter, and the guy who became Detective Gillespie, now deceased."

I said nothing. Just breathed into the phone. I was reliving not the pain and terror of that time in the garage chop shop, but all the days, weeks, and months afterwards, when everyone questioned me about Kenny—Mom, Dad, the cops, Kansas—and I played dumb, my insides churning up a little more inside each time I lied.

And Kansas knew? She *knew?*

"All that time," I whispered, my voice breaking.

When Kansas, after a pause, cleared her throat and spoke, I was both shocked and ripped up inside over the *apology* in her voice. Kansas never apologized. "I...didn't want to embarrass you, Jacky."

I wiped my nose. "You know how alone I felt? How *burdened?*"

"It wasn't your fault."

My lability took over, and I couldn't speak for a while as my eyes flooded and I stuffed a bunch of my sheet into my mouth so I didn't sob out loud.

Kansas had the uncharacteristic grace to simply wait, saying nothing.

When my body had stopped shaking, I removed the sheet and said, "Kenny sent me a message by Morse code while Cutter and crew were torturing me. He repeated it over at least five different timelines, starting the next one where he'd left off the first. You get what that means?"

"Not unexpected," Kansas said. "I told you you weren't the only time traveler."

"You think he— Never mind. Can *you*...?"

There was a pause. "I don't believe so. What was Kenny's message?"

"He wanted me to find someone." I gave her the name. She didn't recognize it. I certainly hadn't.

"I'll find her," Kansas said.

"When?"

"Unless she's easy, not right away. The new administration is being tested the way they always do. The Chinese, Russians, North Koreans, naturally, but this time a lot of our allies are testing our grid too. Everyone wants to know if we're making the transition."

"But you'll tell me as soon as you find out?"

"Cross my heart, Jacky. And...um..."

"What?"

"You did really well for a civilian."

I sniffed. "Thank you."

"Now rest. Heal. Wait until I get back to you. Can you do that?"

"I can."

"I love you, little brother."

Another thing she'd never said before. I swallowed. "I love you, Kansas."

Her phone disconnected.

Finally: resolution

"I came," Lena said. "What do you want?"

She hadn't walked to my bed to sit down or physically greet me but stood in the middle of the private room. Her long gray-check coat over a bright blue blouse and matching bandana completely overshadowed the room's muted pastels and lack of style. She crossed her arms over her chest now like she was preparing to hold herself together should I now say something that would shatter her apart.

"Yes," I said.

"Yes to what?"

"To your preconditions. To sharing my problems, bringing in Alvin and his team, to training in self-defense and using my jump back ability."

Something was wrong. Her face, her arms gripping herself looked even tighter now.

"What is it?" I asked.

"I just found out that my mother, who refused to get vaccinated, was hospitalized with COVID two days ago without anyone telling me. She died last night. Do you understand what it is you're committing to?"

Aw shit. I looked down, studying my bare feet and pale, hairy legs sticking out from under my hospital gown. The room was hot enough that I'd long ago tossed the sheet and blanket to the side. "I'm so sorry, Lena."

She stomped her foot. "Don't be sorry. Answer my question. Do you understand what you're committing to with me?"

I raised my eyes to meet hers. "To being there with you. Supporting you. But also letting you into my struggles. Letting you support me."

"And *can you do that?*" She was barely holding it together.

"Okay, Lena," I said quietly. "Little speech coming, but it's important. Please, just let me get through it?"

She gave a shaky nod.

I cleared my throat. "Something I tell my clients who struggle with trauma, connections, and trusting other people, is that there are no guarantees in life. Loved ones die, leave you, betray you… But if you go through your life never connecting with others, not letting them connect with you, you're barely living. And if you're lucky enough to meet someone so special that just the thought of losing them makes you want to bury yourself in the earth and not make a sound, well, then the choice is even starker: Choke on dirt forever…or…fly."

Lena nodded. "You're afraid we'll crash."

I looked up at her. "I am."

"Me too. Terrified."

"I see that."

Lena sucked in her lips for a second, then said, "I want you to hold me right now. Badly. But there's one last thing. If things go wrong between us, if you do something that makes me mad or cry or run away, I don't want you jumping back ten minutes to change it. I don't want our time together to be cheapened by that."

I swallowed and blushed, ashamed I'd kept that as my last ace in the hole. But all I had to do was look at Lena now to understand why that was wrong. "I promise I won't do that. Whatever happens between us, we'll work it out as ordinary people."

"Smart people."

"Who care about one another."

That finally seemed to break her fear, and she walked around my bed to the side with the chair, swept my IV line to one side, and carefully lay down on the bed beside me. I wrapped my arms around her, kissed her once on her mouth, then on her cheek and forehead.

It felt like I was in an airplane that was taking off, the earth dropping away rapidly beneath us. I could see so much farther in every direction. Back there was my whole past life with its endless lightning strikes. Ahead, a future unfurling with blue skies and...fog banks, tornadoes, massive downdrafts that would try to suck me and Lena down and break us so thoroughly we would never rise again...

Kenny needed finding.

My power needed my pain.

I pulled Lena closer, and she responded almost like she was part of me, nuzzling into my chest and murmuring words more prescient than she could have known.

"Jackson Traine, it's going to be a hell of a ride."

Afterword

Thanks for sharing this sometimes-harrowing journey with Jackson Traine. I'm really excited for everything he has ahead of him as he discovers the true nature of his power and how that will reshape everything about his life and the lives of those around him.

If you enjoyed this beginning and would like help others get on board, please leave a review for *Jumpback* at your favorite online bookstore and anywhere else you talk about books.

Also by Terry Hayman

Novels

Chasing the Minotaur

Jessica Falls

Shelter

Bone Dance

Short Story Collections

Being Human: 5 heartfelt tales of fantasy and science fiction set on earth

Off-World: 5 tales of adventure set on other planets

Dark Paths: 5 short stories exploring the darker sides of human nature

Life Knots: 5 stories of ordinary people fighting their destinies

Messed Up: 5 stories of crime and consequences

Used by Magic: 5 stories of people caught up by powers unseen

Shorties: A collection of sublimely quick story punches to the head, heart, and gut

Vamp: 5 stories of bloodsuckers, romantic and otherwise

About the Author

Terry Hayman, former lawyer and son of a beloved psychologist, is the author of many novels and over a hundred short stories under various names. You can learn more about his work, subscribe to his newsletter, and download some free stories at www.terryhayman.com. (You can also get there by scanning the QR code below.)